Praise for #1 *New Yo[rk]*
Debbie

"As always, Macomber d... ...ng.g.g.
characters."

—*Publishers Weekly*

"Debbie Macomber is the queen of laughter and
love."

—Elizabeth Lowell

"When God created Eve, he must have asked Debbie
Macomber for advice because no one does female
characters any better than this author."

—*Bookbrowser Reviews*

"It's clear that Debbie Macomber cares deeply about
her fully realized characters and their family, friends
and loves, along with their hopes and dreams. She
also makes her readers care about them."

—*Bookreporter.com*

"Ms. Macomber provides the top in entertaining
relationship dramas."

—*Reader to Reader*

"Debbie Macomber's name on a book is a guarantee
of delightful, warmhearted romance."

—Jayne Ann Krentz

"I've never met a Macomber book I didn't love!"

—Linda Lael Miller

Debbie Macomber is a number one *New York Times* and *USA TODAY* bestselling author. Her books include *1225 Christmas Tree Lane, 1105 Yakima Street, A Turn in the Road, Hannah's List* and *Debbie Macomber's Christmas Cookbook,* as well as *Twenty Wishes, Summer on Blossom Street* and *Call Me Mrs. Miracle.* She has become a leading voice in women's fiction worldwide and her work has appeared on every major bestseller list, including those of the *New York Times, USA TODAY, Publishers Weekly* and *Entertainment Weekly.* She is a multiple award winner, and won the 2005 Quill Award for Best Romance. There are more than one hundred million copies of her books in print. Two of her MIRA Books Christmas titles have been made into Hallmark Channel Original Movies, and the Hallmark Channel has launched a series based on her bestselling Cedar Cove series. For more information on Debbie and her books, visit her website, debbiemacomber.com.

#1 *New York Times* Bestselling Author

Debbie Macomber

Wyoming Brides

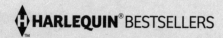

HARLEQUIN® BESTSELLERS

Recycling programs
for this product may
not exist in your area.

ISBN-13: 978-0-373-40109-3

Wyoming Brides
Copyright © 2009 by Harlequin Books S.A.

The publisher acknowledges the copyright holder
of the individual works as follows:

Denim and Diamonds
Copyright © 1989 by Debbie Macomber

The Wyoming Kid
Copyright © 2006 by Debbie Macomber

This edition published by arrangement with Harlequin Books S.A.

For questions and comments about the quality of this book,
please contact us at CustomerService@Harlequin.com.

www.Harlequin.com

Printed in U.S.A.

CONTENTS

DENIM AND DIAMONDS

To Karen Macomber, sister, dear friend
and downtown Seattle explorer

Prologue

Dusk had settled; it was the end of another cold, harsh winter day in Red Springs, Wyoming. Chase Brown felt the chill of the north wind all the way through his bones as he rode Firepower, his chestnut gelding. He'd spent the better part of the afternoon searching for three heifers who'd gotten separated from the main part of his herd. He'd found the trio a little while earlier and bullied them back to where they belonged.

That tactic might work with cattle, but from experience, Chase knew it wouldn't work with Letty. She should be here, in Wyoming. With him. Four years had passed since she'd taken off for Hollywood on some fool dream of becoming a singing star. Four years! As far as Chase was concerned, that was three years too long.

Chase had loved Letty from the time she was a teenager. And she'd loved him. He'd spent all those lazy afternoons with her on the hillside, chewing on a blade of grass, talking, soaking up the warmth of the sun, and he knew she felt something deep and abiding for him. Letty had been innocent and Chase had sworn she would stay that way until they were married. Although it'd been hard not to make love to her the way he'd wanted. But Chase was a patient man, and he was convinced a lifetime with Letty was worth the wait.

When she'd graduated from high school, Chase had come to her with a diamond ring. He'd wanted her to share his vision of Spring Valley, have children with him to fill the emptiness that had been such a large part of his life since his father's death. Letty had looked up at him, tears glistening in her deep blue eyes, and whispered that she loved him more than she'd thought she'd ever love anyone. She'd begged him to come to California with her. But Chase couldn't leave his ranch and Red Springs any more than Letty could stay. So she'd gone after her dreams.

Letting her go had been the most difficult thing he'd ever had to do. Everyone in the county knew Letty Ellison was a gifted singer. Chase couldn't deny she had talent, lots of it. She'd often talked of becoming a professional singer, but Chase hadn't believed she'd choose that path over the one he was offering. She'd kissed him before she left, with all the innocence of her youth, and pleaded with him one more time to come with her. She'd had some ridiculous idea that he could become her manager. The only thing Chase had ever wanted to manage was Spring Valley, his ranch. With ambition clouding her eyes, she'd turned away from him and headed for the city lights.

That scene had played in Chase's mind a thousand times in the past few years. When he slipped the diamond back inside his pocket four years earlier, he'd known it would be impossible to forget her. Someday she'd return, and when she did, he'd be waiting. She hadn't asked him to, but there was only one woman for him, and that was Letty Ellison.

Chase wouldn't have been able to tolerate her leaving if he hadn't believed she *would* return. The way he figured it, she'd be back within a year. All he had to do was show a little patience. If she hadn't found those glittering diamonds she was searching for within that time, then surely she'd come home.

But four long years had passed and Letty still hadn't returned.

The wind picked up as Chase approached the barnyard. He paused on the hill and noticed Letty's brother's beloved Ford truck parked outside the barn. A rush of adrenaline shot through Chase, accelerating his heartbeat. Involuntarily his hands tightened on Firepower's reins. Lonny had news, news that couldn't be relayed over the phone. Chase galloped into the yard.

"Evening, Chase," Lonny muttered as he climbed out of the truck.

"Lonny." He touched the brim of his hat with gloved fingers. "What brings you out?"

"It's about Letty."

The chill that had nipped at Chase earlier couldn't compare to the biting cold that sliced through him now.

He eased himself out of the saddle, anxiety making the inside of his mouth feel dry.

"I thought you should know," Lonny continued, his expression uneasy. He kicked at a clod of dirt with the toe of his boot. "She called a couple of hours ago."

Lonny wouldn't look him in the eye, and that bothered Chase. Letty's brother had always shot from the hip.

"The best way to say this is straight out," Lonny said, his jaw clenched. "Letty's pregnant and the man isn't going to marry her. Apparently he's already married, and he never bothered to let her know."

If someone had slammed a fist into Chase's gut it wouldn't have produced the reaction Lonny's words did. He reeled back two steps before he caught himself. The pain was unlike anything he'd ever experienced.

"What's she going to do?" he managed to ask.

Lonny shrugged. "From what she said, she plans on keeping the baby."

"Is she coming home?"

"No."

Chase's eyes narrowed.

"I tried to talk some sense into her, believe me, but it didn't do a bit of good. She seems more determined than ever to stay in California." Lonny opened the door to his truck, looking guilty and angry at once. "Mom and Dad raised her better than this. I thank God they're both gone. I swear it would've killed Mom."

"I appreciate you telling me," Chase said after a lengthy pause. It took him that long to reclaim a grip on his chaotic emotions.

"I figured you had a right to know."

Chase nodded. He stood where he was, his boots planted in the frozen dirt until Lonny drove off into the fading sunlight. Firepower craned his neck toward the barn, toward warmth and a well-deserved dinner of oats and alfalfa. The gelding's action caught Chase's attention. He turned, reached for the saddle horn and in one smooth movement remounted the bay.

Firepower knew Chase well, and sensing his mood, the gelding galloped at a dead run. Still Chase pushed him on, farther and farther for what seemed like hours, until both man and horse were panting and exhausted. When the animal stopped, Chase wasn't surprised the unplanned route had led him to the hillside where he'd spent so many pleasant afternoons with Letty. Every inch of his land was familiar to him, but none more than those few acres.

His chest heaving with exertion, Chase climbed off Firepower and stood on the crest of the hill as the wind gusted against him. His lungs hurt and he dragged in several deep breaths, struggling to gain control of himself. Pain choked off his breath, dominated his thoughts. Nothing eased the terrible ache inside him.

He groaned and threw back his head with an anguish so intense it could no longer be held inside. His piercing shout filled the night as he buckled, fell to his knees and covered his face with both hands.

Then Chase Brown did something he hadn't done in fifteen years.

He wept.

Chapter 1

Five years later

Letty Ellison was home. She hadn't been back to Red Springs in more than nine years, and she was astonished by how little the town had changed. She'd been determined to come home a star; it hadn't happened. Swallowing her pride and returning to the town, the ranch, without having achieved her big dream was one thing. But to show up on her brother's doorstep, throw her arms around him and casually announce she could be dying was another.

As a matter of fact, Letty had gotten pretty philosophical about death. The hole in her heart had been small enough to go undetected most of her life, but it was there, and unless she had the necessary surgery, it would soon be lights-out, belly up, buy the farm, kick the bucket or whatever else people said when they were about to die.

The physicians had made her lack of options abundantly clear when she was pregnant with Cricket, her daughter. If her heart defect hadn't been discovered then and had remained undetected, her doctor had assured her she'd be dead before she reached thirty.

And so Letty had come home. Home to Wyoming. Home to the Bar E Ranch. Home to face whatever lay before her. Life or death.

In her dreams, Letty had often imagined her triumphant return. She saw herself riding through town sitting in the back of a red convertible, dressed in a strapless gown, holding bouquets of red roses. The high school band would lead the procession. Naturally the good people of Red Springs would be lining Main Street, hoping to get a look at her. Being the amiable soul she was, Letty would give out autographs and speak kindly to people she hardly remembered.

Her actual return had been quite different from what she'd envisioned. Lonny had met her at the Rock Springs Airport when she'd arrived with Cricket the evening before. It really had been wonderful to see her older brother. Unexpected tears had filled her eyes as they hugged. Lonny might be a onetime rodeo champ and now a hard-bitten rancher, but he was the only living relative she and Cricket had. And if anything were to happen to her, she hoped her brother would love and care for Cricket with the same dedication Letty herself had. So far, she hadn't told him about her condition, and she didn't know when she would. When the time felt right, she supposed.

Sunlight filtered in through the curtain, and drawing in a deep breath, Letty sat up in bed and examined her old bedroom. So little had changed in the past nine years. The lace doily decorating the old bureau was the same one that had been there when she was growing up. The photograph of her and her pony hung on the wall. How Letty had loved old Nellie. Even her bed was covered with the same quilted spread that had been there when she was eighteen, the one her mother had made.

Nothing had changed and yet everything was different. Because *she* was different.

The innocent girl who'd once slept in this room was gone forever. Instead Letty was now a woman who'd become disenchanted with dreams and disillusioned by life. She could never go back to the guileless teen she'd been, but she wouldn't give up the woman she'd become, either.

With that thought in mind, she folded back the covers and climbed out of bed. Her first night home, and she'd slept soundly. *She* might not be the same, but the sense of welcome she felt in this old house was.

Checking in the smallest bedroom across the hall, Letty found her daughter still asleep, her faded yellow "blankey" clutched protectively against her chest. Letty and Cricket had arrived exhausted. With little more than a hug from Lonny, she and her daughter had fallen into bed. Letty had promised Lonny they'd talk later.

Dressing quickly, she walked down the stairs and was surprised to discover her brother sitting at the kitchen table, waiting for her.

"I was beginning to wonder if you'd ever wake up,"

he said, grinning. The years had been good to Lonny. He'd always been handsome—as dozens of young women had noticed while he was on the rodeo circuit. He'd quit eight years ago, when his father got sick, and had dedicated himself to the Bar E ever since. Still, Letty couldn't understand why he'd stayed single all this time. Then again, she could. Lonny, like Chase Brown, their neighbor, lived for his land and his precious herd of cattle. That was what their whole lives revolved around. Lonny wasn't married because he hadn't met a woman he considered an asset to the Bar E.

"How come you aren't out rounding up cattle or repairing fences or whatever it is you do in the mornings?" she teased, smiling at him.

"I wanted to welcome you home properly."

After pouring herself a cup of coffee, Letty walked to the table, leaned over and kissed his sun-bronzed cheek. "It's great to be back."

Letty meant that. Her pride had kept her away all these years. How silly that seemed now, how pointless and stubborn not to admit her name wasn't going to light up any marquee, when she'd lived and breathed that knowledge each and every day in California. Letty had talent; she'd known that when she left the Bar E nine years ago. It was the blind ambition and ruthless drive she'd lacked. Oh, there'd been brief periods of promise and limited success. She'd sung radio commercials and done some backup work for a couple of rising stars, but she'd long ago given up the hope of ever making it big herself. At one time, becoming a singer had meant the world to her. Now it meant practically nothing.

Lonny reached for her fingers. "It's good to have you home, sis. You've been away too long."

She sat across from him, holding her coffee mug with both hands, and gazed down at the old Formica tabletop. In nine years, Lonny hadn't replaced a single piece of furniture.

It wasn't easy to admit, but Letty needed to say it. "I should've come back before now." She thought it was best to let him know this before she told him about her heart.

"Yeah," Lonny said evenly. "I wanted you back when Mom died."

"It was too soon then. I'd been in California less than two years."

It hurt Letty to think about losing her mother. Maren Ellison's death had been sudden. Although Maren had begged her not to leave Red Springs, she was a large part of the reason Letty had gone. Her mother had had talent, too. She'd been an artist whose skill had lain dormant while she wasted away on a ranch, unappreciated and unfulfilled. All her life, Letty had heard her mother talk about painting in oils someday. But that day had never come. Then, when everyone had least expected it, Maren had died—less than a year after her husband. In each case, Letty had flown in for the funerals, then returned to California the next morning.

"What are your plans now?" Lonny asked, watching her closely.

Letty's immediate future involved dealing with social workers, filling out volumes of forms and having a dozen doctors examine her to tell her what she already knew. Heart surgery didn't come cheap. "The first thing I thought I'd do was clean the house," she said, deliberately misunderstanding him.

A guilty look appeared on her brother's face and Letty chuckled softly.

"I suppose the place is a real mess." Lonny glanced furtively around. "I've let things go around here for the past few years. When you phoned and said you were coming, I picked up what I could. You've probably guessed I'm not much of a housekeeper."

"I don't expect you to be when you're dealing with several hundred head of cattle."

Lonny seemed surprised by her understanding. He stood and grabbed his hat, adjusting it on his head. "How long do you plan to stay?"

Letty shrugged. "I'm not sure yet. Is my being here a problem?"

"Not in the least," Lonny rushed to assure her. "Stay as long as you like. I welcome the company—and decent meals for a change. If you want, I can see about finding you a job in town."

"I don't think there's much call for a failed singer in Red Springs, is there?"

"I thought you said you'd worked as a secretary."

"I did, part-time, and as a temp." In order to have flexible hours, she'd done what she'd had to in order to survive, but in following her dream she'd missed out on health insurance benefits.

"There ought to be something for you, then. I'll ask around."

"Don't," Letty said urgently. "Not yet, anyway."

After the surgery would be soon enough to locate employment. For the time being, she had to concentrate on making arrangements with the appropriate authorities. She should probably tell Lonny about her heart condition, she decided reluctantly, but it was too much to hit him with right away. There'd be plenty of time later, after the arrangements had been made. No point in upsetting him now. Besides, she wanted him to become acquainted with Cricket before he found out she'd be listing him as her daughter's guardian.

"Relax for a while," Lonny said. "Take a vacation. There's no need for you to work if you don't want to."

"Thanks, I appreciate that."

"What are brothers for?" he joked, and drained his coffee. "I should get busy," he said, rinsing his cup and setting it on the kitchen counter. "I should've gotten started hours ago, but I wanted to talk to you first."

"What time will you be back?"

Lonny's eyes widened, as though he didn't understand. "Five or so, I guess. Why?"

"I just wanted to know when to plan dinner."

"Six should be fine."

Letty stood, her arms wrapped protectively around her waist. One question had been burning in her mind from the minute she'd pulled into the yard. One she needed to ask, but whose answer she feared. She tentatively broached the subject. "Will you be seeing Chase?"

"I do most days."

"Does he know I'm back?"

Lonny's fingers gripped the back door handle. "He knows," he said without looking at her.

Letty nodded and she curled her hands into fists. "Is he…married?"

Lonny shook his head. "Nope, and I don't imagine he ever will be, either." He hesitated before adding, "Chase is a lot different now from the guy you used to know. I hope you're not expecting anything from him, because you're headed for a big disappointment if you are. You'll know what I mean once you see him."

A short silence followed while Letty considered her brother's words. "You needn't worry that I've come home expecting things to be the way they were between Chase and me. If he's different…that's fine. We've all changed."

Lonny nodded and was gone.

The house was quiet after her brother left. His warning about Chase seemed to taunt her. The Chase Brown she knew was gentle, kind, good. When Letty was seventeen he'd been the only one who really understood her dreams. Although it had broken his heart, he'd loved her enough to encourage her to seek her destiny. Chase had loved her more than anyone before or since.

And she'd thrown his love away.

"Mommy, you were gone when I woke up." Looking forlorn, five-year-old Cricket stood in the doorway of the kitchen, her yellow blanket clutched in her hand and dragging on the faded red linoleum floor.

"I was just downstairs," Letty said, holding out her arms to the youngster, who ran eagerly to her mother, climbing onto Letty's lap.

"I'm hungry."

"I'll bet you are." Letty brushed the dark hair away

from her daughter's face and kissed her forehead. "I was talking to Uncle Lonny this morning."

Cricket stared up at her with deep blue eyes that were a reflection of her own. She'd inherited little in the way of looks from her father. The dark hair and blue eyes were Ellison family traits. On rare occasions, Letty would see traces of Jason in their child, but not often. She tried not to think about him or their disastrous affair. He was out of her life and she wanted no part of him—except for Christina Maren, her Cricket.

"You know what I thought we'd do today?" Letty said.

"After breakfast?"

"After breakfast." She smiled. "I thought we'd clean house and bake a pie for Uncle Lonny."

"Apple pie," Cricket announced with a firm nod.

"I'm sure apple pie's his favorite."

"Mine, too."

Together they cooked oatmeal. Cricket insisted on helping by setting the table and getting the milk from the refrigerator.

As soon as they'd finished, Letty mopped the floor and washed the cupboards. Lonny's declaration about not being much of a housekeeper had been an understatement. He'd done the bare minimum for years, and the house was badly in need of a thorough cleaning. Usually, physical activity quickly wore Letty out and she became breathless and light-headed. But this morning she was filled with an enthusiasm that provided her with energy.

By noon, however, she was exhausted. At nap time, Letty lay down with Cricket, and didn't wake until early afternoon, when the sound of male voices drifted up the stairs. She realized almost immediately that Chase Brown was with her brother.

Running a brush through her short curly hair, Letty composed herself for the coming confrontation with Chase and walked calmly down the stairs.

He and her brother were sitting at the table, drinking coffee.

Lonny glanced up when she entered the room, but Chase looked away from her. Her brother had made a point of telling her that Chase was different, and she could see the truth of his words. Chase's dark hair had become streaked with gray in her absence. Deep crevices marked his forehead and grooved the sides of his mouth. In nine years he'd aged twenty, Letty thought with a stab of regret. Part of her longed to wrap her arms around him the way she had so many years before. She yearned to bury her head in his shoulder and weep for the pain she'd caused him.

But she knew she couldn't.

"Hello, Chase," she said softly, walking over to the stove and reaching for the coffeepot.

"Letty." He lowered his head in greeting, but kept his eyes averted.

"It's good to see you again."

He didn't answer that; instead he returned his attention to her brother. "I was thinking about separating part of the herd, driving them a mile or so south. Of course, that'd mean hauling the feed a lot farther, but I believe the benefits will outweigh that inconvenience."

"I think you're going to a lot of effort for nothing," Lonny said, frowning.

Letty pulled out a chair and sat across from Chase. He could only ignore her for so long. Still his gaze skirted hers, and he did his utmost to avoid looking at her.

"Who are you?"

Letty turned to the doorway, where Cricket was standing, blanket held tightly in her hand.

"Cricket, this is Uncle Lonny's neighbor, Mr. Brown."

"I'm Cricket," she said, grinning cheerfully.

"Hello." Chase spoke in a gruff unfriendly tone, obviously doing his best to disregard the little girl in the same manner he chose to overlook her mother.

A small cry of protest rose in Letty's throat. Chase could be as angry with her as he wanted. The way she figured it, that was his right, but he shouldn't take out his bitterness on an innocent child.

"Your hair's a funny color," Cricket commented, fascinated. "I think it's pretty like that." Her yellow blanket in tow, she marched up to Chase and raised her hand to touch the salt-and-pepper strands that were more pronounced at his temple.

Chase frowned and moved back so there wasn't any chance of her succeeding.

"My mommy and I are going to bake a pie for Uncle Lonny. Do you want some?"

Letty held her breath, waiting for Chase to reply. Something about him appeared to intrigue Cricket. The child couldn't stop staring at him. Her actions seemed to unnerve Chase, who made it obvious that he'd like nothing better than to forget her existence.

"I don't think Mr. Brown is interested in apple pie,

sweetheart," Letty said, trying to fill the uncomfortable silence.

"Then we'll make something he does like," Cricket insisted. She reached for Chase's hand and tugged, demanding his attention. "Do you like chocolate chip cookies? I do. And Mommy makes really yummy ones."

For a moment Chase stared at Cricket, and the pain that flashed in his dark eyes went straight through Letty's heart. A split second later he glanced away as though he couldn't bear to continue looking at the child.

"Do you?" Cricket persisted.

Chase nodded, although it was clearly an effort to do so.

"Come on, Mommy," Cricket cried. "I want to make them *now*."

"What about my apple pie?" Lonny said, his eyes twinkling.

Cricket ignored the question, intent on the cookie-making task. She dragged her blanket after her as she started opening and closing the bottom cupboards, searching for bowls and pans. She dutifully brought out two of each and rummaged through the drawers until she located a wooden spoon. Then, as though suddenly finding the blanket cumbersome, the child lifted it from the floor and placed it in Chase's lap.

Letty could hardly believe her eyes. She'd brought Cricket home from the hospital in that yellow blanket and the little girl had slept with it every night of her life since. Rarely would she entrust it to anyone, let alone a stranger.

Chase looked down on the much-loved blanket as if the youngster had deposited a dirty diaper in his lap.

"I'll take it," Letty said, holding out her hands.

Chase gave it to her, and when he did, his cold gaze locked with hers. Letty felt the chill in his eyes all the way through her bones. His bitterness toward her was evident with every breath he drew.

"It would've been better if you'd never come back," he said so softly she had to strain to hear.

She opened her mouth to argue. Even Lonny didn't know the real reason she'd returned to Wyoming. No one did, except her doctor in California. She hadn't meant to come back and disrupt Chase's life—or anyone else's, for that matter. Chase didn't need to spell out that he didn't want anything to do with her. He'd made that clear the minute she'd walked into the kitchen.

"Mommy, hurry," Cricket said. "We have to bake cookies."

"Just a minute, sweetheart." Letty was uncertain how to handle this new problem. She doubted Lonny had chocolate chips in the house, and a trip into town was more than she wanted to tackle that afternoon.

"Cricket..."

Lonny and Chase both stood. "I'm driving on over to Chase's for the rest of the afternoon," Lonny told her. He obviously wasn't accustomed to letting anyone know his whereabouts and did so now only as an afterthought.

"Can I go, too?" Cricket piped up, so eager her blue eyes sparkled with the idea.

Letty wanted her daughter to be comfortable with Lonny, and she would've liked to encourage the two of them to become friends, but the frown that darkened Chase's brow told her now wasn't the time.

"Not today," Letty murmured, looking away from the two men.

Cricket pouted for a few minutes, but didn't argue. It wouldn't have mattered if she had, because Lonny and Chase left without another word.

Dinner was ready and waiting when Lonny returned to the house that evening. Cricket ran to greet him, her pigtails bouncing. "Mommy and me cooked dinner for you!"

Lonny smiled down on her and absently patted her head, then went to the bathroom to wash his hands. Letty watched him and felt a tugging sense of discontent. After years of living alone, Lonny tended not to be as communicative as Letty wanted him to be. This was understandable, but it made her realize how lonely he must be out here on the ranch night after night without anyone to share his life. Ranchers had to be more stubborn than any other breed of male, Letty thought.

To complicate matters, there was the issue of Cricket staying with Lonny while Letty had the surgery. The little girl had never been away from her overnight.

Letty's prognosis for a complete recovery was good, but there was always the possibility that she wouldn't be coming home from the hospital. Any number of risks had to be considered with this type of operation, and if anything were to happen, Lonny would have to raise Cricket on his own. Letty didn't doubt he'd do so with the greatest of care, but he simply wasn't accustomed to dealing with children.

By the time her brother had finished washing up, dinner was on the table. He gazed down at the ample amount of food and grinned appreciatively. "I can't tell you how long it's been since I've had a home-cooked meal like this. I've missed it."

"What have you been eating?"

He shrugged. "I come up with something or other, but nothing as appetizing as this." He sat down and filled his plate, hardly waiting for Cricket and Letty to join him.

He was buttering his biscuit when he paused and looked at Letty. Slowly he put down the biscuit and placed his knife next to his plate. "Are you okay?" he asked.

"Sure," she answered, smiling weakly. Actually, she wasn't—the day had been exhausting. She'd tried to do too much and she was paying the price, feeling shaky and weak. "What makes you ask?"

"You're pale."

That could be attributed to seeing Chase again, but Letty didn't say so. Their brief meeting had left her feeling melancholy all afternoon. She'd been so young and so foolish, seeking bright lights, utterly convinced that she'd never be satisfied with the lot of a rancher's wife. She'd wanted diamonds, not denim.

"No, I'm fine," she lied as Lonny picked up the biscuit again.

"Mommy couldn't find any chocolate chips," Cricket said, frowning, "so we just baked the apple pie."

Lonny nodded, far more interested in his gravy and biscuits than in conversing with a child.

"I took Cricket out to the barn and showed her the horses," Letty said.

Lonny nodded, then helped himself to seconds on the biscuits. He spread a thick layer of butter on each half.

"I thought maybe later you could let Cricket give them their oats," Letty prompted.

"The barn isn't any place for a little girl," Lonny murmured, dismissing the suggestion with a quick shake of his head.

Cricket looked disappointed and Letty mentally chastised herself for mentioning the idea in front of her daughter. She should've known better.

"Maybe Uncle Lonny will let me ride his horsey?" Cricket asked, her eyes wide and hopeful. "Mommy had a horsey when *she* was a little girl—I saw the picture in her room. I want one, too."

"You have to grow up first," Lonny said brusquely, ending the conversation.

It was on the tip of Letty's tongue to ask Lonny if he'd let Cricket sit in a saddle, but he showed no inclination to form a relationship with her daughter.

Letty was somewhat encouraged when Cricket went in to watch television with Lonny while she finished the dishes. But no more than ten minutes had passed before she heard Cricket burst into tears. A moment later, she came running into the kitchen. She buried her face in Letty's stomach and wrapped both arms around her, sobbing so hard her shoulders shook.

Lonny followed Cricket into the room, his face a study in guilt and frustration.

"What happened?" Letty asked, stroking her daughter's head.

Lonny threw his hands in the air. "I don't know! I turned on the TV and I was watching the news, when Cricket said she wanted to see cartoons."

"There aren't any on right now," Letty explained.

Cricket sobbed louder, then lifted her head. Tears ran unrestrained down her cheeks. "He said *no,* real mean."

"She started talking to me in the middle of a story about the rodeo championships in Vegas, for Pete's sake." Lonny stabbed his fingers through his hair.

"Cricket, Uncle Lonny didn't mean to upset you," Letty told her. "He was watching his program and you interrupted him, that's all."

"But he said it *mean.*"

"I hardly raised my voice," Lonny came back, obviously perplexed. "Are kids always this sensitive?"

"Not really," Letty assured him. Cricket was normally an easygoing child. Fits of crying were rare and usually the result of being overtired. "It was probably a combination of the flight and a busy day."

Lonny nodded and returned to the living room without speaking to Cricket directly. Letty watched him go with a growing sense of concern. Lonny hadn't been around children in years and didn't have the slightest notion how to deal with a five-year-old. Cricket had felt more of a rapport with Chase than she did her own uncle, and Chase had done everything he could to ignore her.

Letty spent the next few minutes comforting her daughter. After giving Cricket a bath, Letty read her a story and tucked her in for the night. With her hand on the light switch, she acted out a game they'd played since Cricket was two.

"Blow out the light," she whispered.

The child blew with all her might. At that precise moment, Letty flipped the switch.

"Good night, Mommy."

"Night, sweetheart."

Lonny was waiting for her in the living room, still frowning over the incident between him and his niece. "I don't know, Letty," he said, apparently still unsettled. "I don't seem to be worth much in the uncle department."

"Don't worry about it," she said, trying to smile, but her thoughts were troubled. She couldn't schedule the surgery if she wasn't sure Cricket would be comfortable with Lonny.

"I'll try not to upset her again," Lonny said, looking doubtful, "but I don't think I relate well to kids. I've been a bachelor for too long."

Bachelor...

That was it. The solution to her worries. All evening she'd been thinking how lonely her brother was and how he needed someone to share his life. The timing was perfect.

Her gaze flew to her brother and she nearly sighed aloud with relief. What Lonny needed was a wife.

And Letty was determined to find him one.

Fast.

Chapter 2

It wasn't exactly the welcome parade Letty had dreamed about, with the bright red convertible and the high school marching band, but Red Springs's reception was characteristically warm.

"Letty, it's terrific to see you again!"

"Why, Letty Ellison, I thought you were your dear mother. I never realized how much you resemble Maren. I still miss her, you know."

"Glad you're back, Letty. Hope you plan to stay a while."

Letty smiled and shook hands and received so many hugs she was late for the opening hymn at the Methodist church the next Sunday morning.

With Cricket by her side, she slipped silently into a pew and reached for a hymnal. The hymn was a familiar one from her childhood and Letty knew the lyrics well. But even before she opened her mouth to join the others, tears welled up in her eyes. The organ music swirled around her, filling what seemed to be an unending void in her life. It felt so good to be back. So right to be standing in church with her childhood friends and the people she loved.

Attending services here was part of the magnetic pull that had brought her back to Wyoming. This comforting and spiritual experience reminded her that problems were like mountains. There wasn't one she couldn't handle with God's help. Either she'd climb it, pass around it or carve a tunnel through it.

The music continued and Letty reached for a tissue, dabbing at the tears. Her throat had closed up, and that made singing impossible, so she stood with her eyes shut, soaking up the words of the age-old hymn.

Led by instinct, she'd come back to Red Springs, back to the Bar E and the small Methodist church in the heart of town. She was wrapping everything that was important and familiar around her like a homemade quilt on a cold December night.

The organ music faded and Pastor Downey stepped forward to offer a short prayer. As Letty bowed her head, she could feel someone's bold stare. Her unease grew until she felt herself shudder. It was a sensation her mother had often referred to as someone walking over her grave. An involuntary smile tugged at Letty's mouth. That analogy certainly hit close to home. Much too close.

When the prayer was finished, it was all Letty could do not to turn around and find out who was glaring at her. Although she could guess…

"Mommy," Cricket whispered, loudly enough for half the congregation to hear. "The man who likes chocolate chip cookies is here. He's two rows behind us."

Chase. Letty released an inward sigh. Just as she'd suspected, he was the one challenging her appearance in church, as if her presence would corrupt the good people of this gathering. Letty mused that he'd probably like it if she wore a scarlet *A* so everyone would know she was a sinner.

Lonny had warned her that Chase was different. And he was. The Chase Brown Letty remembered wasn't judgmental or unkind. He used to be fond of children. Letty recalled that, years ago, when they walked through town, kids would automatically come running to Chase. He usually had coins for the gumball machine tucked away in his pocket, which he'd dole out judiciously. Something about him seemed to attract children, and the fact that Cricket had taken to him instantly was proof of his appeal.

An icy hand closed around Letty's heart at the memory. Chase was the type of man who should've married and fathered a houseful of kids. Over the years, she'd hoped he'd done exactly that.

But he hadn't. Instead Chase had turned bitter and hard. Letty was well aware that she'd hurt him terribly. How she regretted that. Chase had loved her, but all he felt for her now was disdain. In years past, he hadn't been able to disguise his love; now, sadly, he had difficulty hiding his dislike.

Letty had seen the wounded look in his eyes when she'd walked into the kitchen the day before. She'd known then that she'd been the one to put it there. If she hadn't been so familiar with him, he might've been able to fool her.

If only she could alter the past....

"Mommy, what's his name again?" Cricket demanded.

"Mr. Brown."

"Can I wave to him?"

"Not now."

"I want to talk to him."

Exasperated, Letty placed her hand on her daughter's shoulder and leaned down to whisper, "Why?"

"Because I bet he has a horse. Uncle Lonny won't let me ride his. Maybe Mr. Brown will."

"Oh, Cricket, I don't think so...."

"Why not?" the little girl pressed.

"We'll talk about this later."

"But I can ask, can't I? Please?"

The elderly couple in front of them turned around to see what all the commotion was about.

"Mommy?" Cricket persisted, clearly running out of patience.

"Yes, fine," Letty agreed hurriedly, against her better judgment.

From that moment on, Cricket started to fidget. Letty had to speak to her twice during the fifteen-minute sermon; during the closing hymn, Cricket turned around to wave at Chase. She could barely wait for the end of the service so she could rush over and ask about his horse.

Letty could feel the dread mounting inside her. Chase didn't want anything to do with Cricket, and

Letty hated the thought of him hurting the little girl's feelings. When the final prayer was offered, Letty added a small request of her own.

"Can we leave now?" Cricket said, reaching for her mother's hand and tugging at it as the concluding burst of organ music filled the church.

Letty nodded. Cricket dropped her hand and was off. Letty groaned inwardly and dashed after her.

Standing on the church steps, Letty saw that Chase was walking toward the parking lot when Cricket caught up with him. She must have called his name, because Chase turned around abruptly. Even from that distance, Letty could see his dark frown. Quickening her step, she made her way toward them.

"Good morning, Chase," she greeted him, forcing a smile as she stood beside Cricket.

"Letty." His hat was in his hand and he rotated the brim, as though eager to make his escape, which Letty felt sure he was.

"I asked him already," Cricket blurted out, glancing up at her mother.

From the look Chase was giving Letty, he seemed to believe she'd put Cricket up to this. As if she spent precious time thinking up ways to irritate him!

"Mr. Brown's much too busy, sweetheart," Letty said, struggling to keep her voice even and controlled. "Perhaps you can ride his horse another time."

Cricket nodded and grinned. "That's what he said, too."

Surprised, Letty gazed up at Chase. She was grateful he hadn't been harsh with her daughter. From somewhere deep inside, she dredged up a smile to thank him, but he didn't answer it with one of his own. A fresh sadness settled over Letty. The past would always stand between them and there was nothing Letty could do to change that. She wasn't even sure she should try.

"If you'll excuse me," she said, reaching for Cricket's hand, "there are some people I want to talk to."

"More people?" Cricket whined. "I didn't know there were so many people in the whole world."

"It was nice to see you again, Chase," Letty said, turning away. Not until several minutes later did she realize he hadn't echoed her greeting.

Chase couldn't get away from the church fast enough. He didn't know why he'd decided to attend services this particular morning. It wasn't as if he made a regular practice of it, although he'd been raised in the church. He supposed that something perverse inside him was interested in knowing if Letty had the guts to show up.

The woman had nerve. Another word that occurred to him was *courage;* it wouldn't be easy to face all those people with an illegitimate daughter holding her hand. That kind of thing might be acceptable in big cities, but people here tended to be more conservative. Outwardly folks would smile, but the gossip would begin soon enough. He suspected that once it did, Letty would pack up her bags and leave again.

He wished she would. One look at her the day she'd arrived and he knew he'd been lying to himself all these years. She was paler than he remembered, but her face was still a perfect oval, her skin creamy and smooth. Her blue eyes were huge and her mouth a lush curve.

There was no way he could continue lying to himself. He was still in love with her—and always would be.

He climbed inside his pickup and started the engine viciously. He gripped the steering wheel hard. Who was he trying to kid? He'd spent years waiting for Letty to come back. Telling himself he hated her was nothing more than a futile effort to bolster his pride. He wished there could be someone else for him, but there wasn't; there never would be. Letty was the only woman he'd ever loved, heart and soul. If she couldn't be the one to fill his arms during the night, then they'd remain empty. But there was no reason for Letty ever to know that. The fact was, he'd prefer it if she didn't find out. Chase Brown might be fool enough to fall in love with the wrong woman, but he knew better than to hand her the weapon that would shred what remained of his pride.

"You must be Lonny's sister," a feminine voice drawled from behind Letty.

Letty finished greeting one of her mother's friends before turning. When she did, she met a statuesque blonde, who looked about thirty. "Yes, I'm Lonny's sister," she said, smiling.

"I'm so happy to meet you. I'm Mary Brandon," the woman continued. "I hope you'll forgive me for being so direct, but I heard someone say your name and thought I'd introduce myself."

"I'm pleased to meet you, Mary." They exchanged quick handshakes as Letty sized up the other woman. Single—and eager. "How do you know Lonny?"

"I work at the hardware store and your brother

comes in every now and then. He might have mentioned me?" she asked hopefully. When Letty shook her head, Mary shrugged and gave a nervous laugh. "He stops in and gets whatever he needs and then he's on his way." She paused. "He must be lonely living out on that ranch all by himself. Especially after all those years in the rodeo."

Letty could feel the excitement bubbling up inside her. Mary Brandon definitely looked like wife material to her, and it was obvious the woman was more than casually interested in Lonny. As far as Letty was concerned, there wasn't any better place to find a prospective mate for her brother than in church.

The night before, she'd lain in bed wondering where she'd ever meet someone suitable for Lonny. If he hadn't found anyone in the past few years, there was nothing to guarantee that she could come up with the perfect mate in just a few months. The truth was, she didn't know whether he'd had any serious—or even not-so-serious—relationships during her years away. His rodeo success had certainly been an enticement to plenty of girls, but since he'd retired from the circuit and since their parents had died, her brother had become so single-minded, so dedicated to the ranch, that he'd developed tunnel vision. The Bar E now demanded all his energy and all his time, and consequently his personal life had suffered.

"Your brother seems very nice," Mary was saying.

And eligible, Letty added silently. "He's wonderful, but he works so hard it's difficult for anyone to get to know him."

Mary sent her a look that said she understood that all too well. "He's not seeing anyone regularly, is he?"

"No." But Letty wished he was.

Mary's eyes virtually snapped with excitement. "He hides away on the Bar E and hardly ever socializes. I firmly believe he needs a little fun in his life."

Letty's own eyes were gleaming. "I think you may be right. Listen, Mary, perhaps we should talk…"

Chase was working in the barn when he heard Lonny's truck. He wiped the perspiration off his brow with his forearm.

Lonny walked in and Chase immediately recognized that he was upset. Chase shoved the pitchfork into the hay and leaned against it. "Problems?"

Lonny didn't answer him right away. He couldn't seem to stay in one place. "It's that fool sister of mine."

Chase's hand closed around the pitchfork. Letty had been on his mind all morning and she was the last person he wanted to discuss. Lonny appeared to be waiting for a response, so Chase gave him one. "I knew she'd be nothing but trouble from the moment you told me she was coming home."

Lonny removed his hat and slapped it against his thigh. "She went to church this morning." He turned to glance in Chase's direction. "Said she saw you there. Actually, it was her kid, Cricket, who mentioned your name. She calls you 'the guy who likes chocolate chip cookies.'" He grinned slightly at that.

"I was there," Chase said tersely.

"At any rate, Letty talked to Mary Brandon afterward."

A smile sprang to Chase's lips. Mary had set her sights on Lonny three months ago, and she wasn't about to let up until she got her man.

"Wipe that smug look off your face, Brown. You're supposed to be my friend."

"I am." He lifted a forkful of hay and tossed it behind him. Lonny had been complaining about the Brandon woman for weeks. Mary had done everything but stand on her head to garner his attention. And a wedding ring.

Lonny stalked aggressively to the other end of the barn, then returned. "Letty's overstepped the bounds this time," he muttered.

"Oh? What did she do?"

"She invited Mary to dinner tomorrow night."

Despite himself, Chase burst out laughing. He turned around to discover his friend glaring at him and stopped abruptly. "You're kidding, I hope?"

"Would I be this upset if I was? She invited that… woman right into my house without even asking me how I felt about it. I told her I had other plans for dinner tomorrow, but she claims she needs me there to cut the meat. Nine years in California and she didn't learn how to cut meat?"

"Well, it seems to me you're stuck having dinner with Mary Brandon." Chase realized he shouldn't find the situation so funny. But he did. Chase wasn't keen on Mary himself. There was something faintly irritating about the woman, something that rubbed him the wrong way. Lonny had the same reaction, although they'd never discussed what it was that annoyed them so much. Chase supposed it was the fact that Mary came on so strong. She was a little too desperate to snare herself a husband.

Brooding, Lonny paced the length of the barn. "I told Letty I was only staying for dinner if you were there, too."

Chase stabbed the pitchfork into the ground. "You did *what?*"

"If I'm going to suffer through an entire dinner with that…that woman, I need another guy to run interference. You can't expect me to sit across the dinner table from those two."

"Three," Chase corrected absently. Lonny hadn't included Cricket.

"Oh, yeah, that's right. Three against one. It's more than any man can handle on his own." He shook his head. "I love my sister, don't get me wrong. I'm glad she decided to come home. She should've done it years ago…but I'm telling you, I like my life exactly as it is. Every time I turn around, Cricket's underfoot asking me questions. I can't even check out the news without her wanting to watch cartoons."

"Maybe you should ask Letty to leave." A part of Chase—a part he wasn't proud of—prayed that Lonny would. He hadn't had a decent night's sleep since he'd found out she was returning to Red Springs. He worked until he was ready to drop, and still his mind refused to give him the rest he craved. Instead he'd been tormented by resurrected memories he thought he'd buried years before. Like his friend, Chase had created a comfortable niche for himself and he didn't like his peace of mind invaded by Letty Ellison.

"I can't ask her to leave," Lonny said in a burst of impatience. "She's my *sister!*"

Chase shrugged. "Then tell her to uninvite Mary."

"I tried that. Before I knew it, she was reminding me how much Mom enjoyed company. Then she said that since she was moving back to the community, it was only right for her to get to know the new folks in town. At the time it made perfect sense, and a few minutes later, I'd agreed to be there for that stupid dinner. But there's only one way I'll go through with this and that's if you come, too."

"Cancel the dinner, then."

"Chase! How often do I ask you for a favor?"

Chase glared at him.

"All right, *that* kind of favor!"

"I'm sorry, Lonny, but I won't have anything to do with Mary Brandon."

Lonny was quiet for so long that Chase finally turned to meet his narrowed gaze. "Is it Mary or Letty who bothers you?" his friend asked.

Chase tightened his fingers around the pitchfork. "Doesn't matter, because I won't be there."

Letty took an afternoon nap with Cricket, hoping her explanation wouldn't raise Lonny's suspicions. She'd told him she was suffering from the lingering effects of jet lag.

First thing Monday morning, she planned to contact the state social services office. She couldn't put it off any longer. Each day she seemed to grow weaker and tired more easily. The thought of dealing with the state agency filled her with apprehension; accepting charity went against everything in her, but the cost of the surgery was prohibitive. Letty, who'd once been so proud, was forced to accept the generosity of the tax-payers of Wyoming.

Cricket stirred beside her in the bed as Letty drifted into an uneasy sleep. When she awoke, she noticed Cricket's yellow blanket draped haphazardly over her shoulders. Her daughter was gone.

Yawning, she went downstairs to discover Cricket sitting in front of the television. "Uncle Lonny says he doesn't want dinner tonight."

"That's tomorrow night," Lonny shouted from the kitchen. "Chase and I won't be there."

Letty's shoulders sagged with defeat. She didn't understand how one man could be so stubborn. "Why not?"

"Chase flat out refuses to come and I have no intention of sticking around just to cut up a piece of meat for you."

Letty poured herself a cup of coffee. The fact that Chase wouldn't be there shouldn't come as any big shock, but it did, accompanied by a curious pain.

Scowling, she sat down at the square table, bracing her elbows on it. Until that moment, she hadn't realized how much she wanted to settle the past with Chase. She needed to do it before the surgery.

"I said Chase wasn't coming," Lonny told her a second time.

"I heard you—it's all right," she replied, doing her best to reassure her brother with an easy smile that belied the emotion churning inside her. It'd been a mistake to invite Mary Brandon to dinner without consulting Lonny first. In her enthusiasm, Letty had seen the other woman as a gift that had practically fallen into her lap. How was she to know her brother disliked Mary so passionately?

Lonny tensed. "What do you mean, 'all right'? I don't like the look you've got in your eye."

Letty dropped her gaze. "I mean it's perfectly fine if you prefer not to be here tomorrow night for dinner. I thought it might be a way of getting to know some new people in town, but I should've cleared it with you first."

"Yes, you should have."

"Mary seems nice enough," Letty commented, trying once more.

"So did the snake in the Garden of Eden."

Letty chuckled. "Honestly, Lonny, anyone would think you're afraid of the woman."

"This one's got moves that would be the envy of a world heavyweight champion."

"Obviously she hasn't used them, because she's single."

"Oh, no, she's too smart for that," Lonny countered, gesturing with his hands. "She's been saving them up, just for me."

"Oh, Lonny, you're beginning to sound paranoid, but don't worry, I understand. What kind of sister would I be if I insisted you eat Mama's prime rib dinner with the likes of Mary Brandon?"

Lonny's head shot up. "You're cooking Mom's recipe for prime rib?"

She hated to be so manipulative, but if Lonny were to give Mary half a chance, he might change his mind. "You don't mind if I use some of the meat in the freezer, do you?"

"No," he said, and swallowed. "I suppose there'll be plenty of leftovers?"

Letty shrugged. "I can't say, since I'm thawing out a small roast. I hope you understand."

"Sure," Lonny muttered, frowning.

Apparently he understood all too well, because an hour later, her brother announced he probably would be around for dinner the following night, after all.

Monday morning Letty rose early. The coffee had perked and bacon was sizzling in the skillet when Lonny wandered into the kitchen.

"Morning," he said.

"Morning," she returned cheerfully.

Lonny poured himself a cup of coffee and headed for the door, pausing just before he opened it. "I'll be back in a few minutes."

At the sound of a pickup pulling into the yard, Letty glanced out the kitchen window. Her heart sped up at the sight of Chase climbing out of the cab. It was as if those nine years had been wiped away and he'd come for her the way he used to when she was a teenager. He wore jeans and a shirt with a well-worn leather vest. His dark hair curled crisply at his sun-bronzed nape and he needed a haircut. In him, Letty recognized strength and masculinity.

He entered the kitchen without knocking and stopped short when he saw her. "Letty," he said, sounding shocked.

"Good morning, Chase," she greeted him simply.

Unwilling to see the bitterness in his gaze, she didn't look up from the stove. "Lonny's stepped outside for a moment. Pour yourself a cup of coffee."

"No, thanks." Already he'd turned back to the door.

"Chase." Her heart was pounding so hard it felt as though it might leap into her throat. The sooner she cleared the air between them, the better. "Do you have a minute?"

"Not really."

Ignoring his words, she removed the pan from the burner. "At some point in everyone's life—"

"I said I didn't have time, Letty."

"But—"

"If you're figuring to give me some line about how life's done you wrong and how sorry you are about the past, save your breath, because I don't need to hear it."

"Maybe you don't," she said gently, "but I need to say it."

"Then do it in front of a mirror."

"Chase, you're my brother's best friend. It isn't as if we can ignore each other. It's too uncomfortable to pretend nothing's wrong."

"As far as I'm concerned nothing *is* wrong."

"But—"

"Save your breath, Letty," he said again.

Chapter 3

"Mr. Chase," Cricket called excitedly from the foot of the stairs. "You're here!"

Letty turned back to the stove, fighting down anger and indignation. Chase wouldn't so much as listen to her. Fine. If he wanted to pretend there was nothing wrong, then she would give an award-winning performance herself. He wasn't the only one who could be this childish.

The back door opened and Lonny blithely stepped into the kitchen. "You're early, aren't you?" he asked Chase as he refilled his coffee cup.

"No," Chase snapped impatiently. The look he shot Letty said he wouldn't have come in the house at all if he'd known she was up.

Lonny paid no attention to the censure in his neighbor's voice. He pulled out a chair and sat down. "I'm not ready to leave yet. Letty's cooking breakfast."

"Mr. Chase, Mr. Chase, did you bring your horsey?"

"It's Mr. *Brown*," Letty corrected as she brought two plates to the table. Lonny immediately dug into his bacon-and-egg breakfast, but Chase ignored the meal—as though eating anything Letty had made might poison him.

"Answer her," Lonny muttered between bites. "Otherwise she'll drive you nuts."

"I drove my truck over," Chase told Cricket.

"Do you ever bring your horsey to Uncle Lonny's?"

"Sometimes."

"Are you a cowboy?"

"I suppose."

"Wyoming's the Cowboy State," Letty told her daughter.

"Does that mean everyone who lives here has to be a cowboy?"

"Not exactly."

"But close," Lonny said with a grin.

Cricket climbed onto the chair next to Chase's and dragged her yellow blanket with her. She set her elbows on the table and cupped her face in her hands. "Aren't you going to eat?" she asked, studying him intently.

"I had breakfast," he said, pushing the plate toward her.

Cricket didn't need to be asked twice. Kneeling on the chair, she reached across Chase and grabbed his fork. She smiled up at him, her eyes sparkling.

Letty joined the others at the table. Lately her appetite hadn't been good, but she forced herself to eat a piece of toast.

The atmosphere was strained. Letty tried to avoid looking in Chase's direction, but it was impossible to ignore the man. He turned toward her unexpectedly, catching her look and holding it. His eyes were dark and intense. Caught off guard, Letty blushed.

Chase's gaze darted from her eyes to her mouth and stayed there. She longed to turn primly away from him with a shrug of indifference, but she couldn't. Years ago, Letty had loved staring into Chase's eyes. He had the most soulful eyes of any man she'd ever known. She was trapped in the memory of how it used to be with them. At one time, she'd been able to read loving messages in his eyes. But they were cold now, filled with angry sparks that flared briefly before he glanced away.

What little appetite Letty had was gone, and she put her toast back on the plate and shoved it aside. "Would it be all right if I took the truck this morning?" she asked her brother, surprised by the quaver in her voice. She wished she could ignore Chase altogether, but that was impossible. He refused to deal with the past and she couldn't make him talk to her. As far as Letty could tell, he preferred to simply overlook her presence. Only he seemed to find that as difficult as she found ignoring him. That went a long way toward raising her spirits.

"Where are you going?"

"I thought I'd do a little shopping for dinner tonight." It was true, but only half the reason she needed his truck. She had to drive to Rock Springs, which was over fifty miles west of Red Springs, so she could talk to the social services people there about her eligibility for Medicaid.

"That's right—Mary Brandon's coming to dinner, isn't she?" Lonny asked, evidently disturbed by the thought.

It was a mistake to have mentioned the evening meal, because her brother frowned the instant he said Mary's name. "I suppose I won't be needing the truck," he said, scowling.

"I appreciate it. Thanks," Letty said brightly.

Her brother shrugged.

"Are you coming to dinner with Mommy's friend?" Cricket asked Chase.

"No," he said brusquely.

"How come?"

"Because he's smart, that's why," Lonny answered, then stood abruptly. He reached for his hat, settled it on his head and didn't look back.

Within seconds, both men were gone.

"You'll need to complete these forms," the woman behind the desk told Letty, handing her several sheets.

The intake clerk looked frazzled and overburdened. It was well past noon, and Letty guessed the woman hadn't had a coffee break all morning and was probably late for her lunch. The clerk briefly read over the letter from the physician Letty had been seeing in California, and made a copy of it to attach to Letty's file.

"Once you're done with those forms, please bring them back to me," she said.

"Of course," Letty told her.

Bored, Cricket had slipped her arms around her mother's waist and was pressing her head against Letty's stomach.

"If you have any questions, feel free to ask," the worker said.

"None right now. Thank you for all your help." Letty stood, Cricket still holding on.

For the first time since Letty had entered the government office, the young woman smiled.

Letty took the sheets and sat at a table in a large lobby. One by one, she answered the myriad questions. Before she'd be eligible for Wyoming's medical assistance program, she'd have to be accepted into the Supplemental Security Income program offered through the federal government. It was a humiliating fact of life, but proud, independent Letty Ellison was about to go on welfare.

Tears blurred her eyes as she filled in the first sheet. She stopped long enough to wipe them away before they spilled onto the papers. She had no idea what she'd tell Lonny once the government checks started arriving. Especially since he seemed so confident he could find her some kind of employment in town.

"When can we leave?" Cricket said, close to her mother's ear.

"Soon." Letty was writing as fast as she could, eager to escape, too.

"I don't like it here," Cricket whispered.

"I don't, either," Letty whispered back. But she was grateful the service existed; otherwise she didn't know what she would've done.

Cricket fell asleep in the truck during the hour's

drive home. Letty was thankful for the silence because it gave her a chance to think through the immediate problems that faced her. She could no longer delay seeing a physician, and eventually she'd have to tell Lonny about her heart condition. She hadn't intended to keep it a secret, but there was no need to worry him until everything was settled with the Medicaid people. Once she'd completed all the paperwork, been examined by a variety of knowledgeable doctors so they could tell her what she already knew, then she'd be free to explain the situation to Lonny.

Until then, she would keep this problem to herself.

"Letty!" Lonny cried from the top of the stairs. "Do I have to dress for dinner?"

"Please," she answered sweetly, basting the rib roast before sliding it back in the oven for a few more minutes.

"A tie, too?" he asked without enthusiasm.

"A nice sweater would do."

"I don't own a 'nice' sweater," he shouted back.

A couple of muffled curses followed, but Letty chose to ignore them. At least she knew what to get her brother next Christmas.

Lonny had been in a bad temper from the minute he'd walked in the door an hour earlier, and Letty could see that this evening was headed for disaster.

"Mommy!" Cricket's pigtails were flying as she raced into the kitchen. "Your friend's here."

"Oh." Letty quickly removed the oven mitt and glanced at her watch. Mary was a good ten minutes early and Letty needed every second of that time. The table wasn't set, and the roast was still in the oven.

"Mary, it's good to see you." Letty greeted her with a smile as she rushed into the living room.

Mary walked into the Ellison home, her eyes curious as she examined the living room furniture. "It's good to be here. I brought some fresh-baked rolls for Lonny."

"How thoughtful." Letty moved into the center of the room. "I'm running a little behind, so if you'll excuse me for a minute?"

"Of course."

"Make yourself comfortable," Letty called over her shoulder as she hurried back to the kitchen. She looked around, wondering which task to finish first. After she'd returned from Rock Springs that afternoon and done the shopping, she'd taken a nap with Cricket. Now she regretted having wasted that time. The whole meal felt so disorganized and with Lonny's attitude, well—

"This is a lovely watercolor in here," Mary called in to her. "Who painted it?"

"My mother. She was an artist," Letty answered, taking the salad out of the refrigerator. She grabbed silverware and napkins on her way into the dining room. "Cricket, would you set the table for me?"

"Okay," the youngster agreed willingly.

Mary stood in the room, hands behind her back as she studied the painting of a lush field of wildflowers. "Your mother certainly had an eye for color, didn't she?"

"Mom was very talented," Letty replied wistfully.

"Did she paint any of the others?" Mary asked, gesturing around the living room.

"No…actually, this is the only painting we have of hers."

"She gave the others away?"

"Not exactly," Letty admitted, feeling a flash of resentment. With all her mother's obligations on the ranch, plus helping Dad when she could during the last few years of his life, there hadn't been time for her to work on what she'd loved most, which was her art. Letty's mother had lived a hard life. The land had drained her energy. Letty had been a silent witness to what had happened to her mother and swore it wouldn't be repeated in her own life. Yet here she was, back in Wyoming. Back on the Bar E, and grateful she had a home.

"How come we're eating in the dining room?" Lonny muttered irritably as he came downstairs. He buried his hands in his pockets and made an obvious effort to ignore Mary, who stood no more than five feet away.

"You know Mary, don't you?" Letty asked pointedly.

Lonny nodded in the other woman's direction, but managed to do so without actually looking at her.

"Hello, Lonny," Mary cooed. "It's a real pleasure to see you again. I brought you some rolls—hot from the oven."

"Mary brought over some homemade dinner rolls," Letty reiterated, resisting the urge to kick her brother in the shin.

"Looks like those rolls came from the Red Springs Bakery to me," he muttered, pulling out a chair and sitting down.

Letty half expected him to grab his knife and fork, pound the table with them and chant, *Dinner, dinner, dinner.* If he couldn't discourage Mary by being rude, he'd probably try the more advanced "caveman" approach.

"Well, yes, I did pick up the rolls there," Mary said, clearly flustered. "I didn't have time after work to bake."

"Naturally, you wouldn't have," Letty responded mildly, shooting her brother a heated glare.

Cricket scooted past the two women and handed her uncle a plate. "Anything else, Mommy?"

Letty quickly checked the table to see what was needed. "Glasses," she mumbled, rushing back into the kitchen. While she was there, she took the peas off the burner. The vegetable had been an expensive addition to the meal, but Letty had bought them at the market in town, remembering how much Lonny loved fresh peas. He deserved some reward for being such a good sport— or so she'd thought earlier.

Cricket finished setting the table and Letty brought out the rest of their dinner. She smiled as she joined the others. Her brother had made a tactical error when he'd chosen to sit down first. Mary had immediately taken the chair closest to him. She gazed at him with wide adoring eyes while Lonny did his best to ignore her.

As Letty had predicted earlier, the meal was a disaster, and the tension in the air was thick. Letty made several attempts at conversation, which Mary leaped upon, but the minute either of them tried to include Lonny, the subject died. It was all Letty could do to keep from kicking her brother under the table. Mary didn't linger after the meal.

"Don't ever do that to me again," Lonny grumbled as soon as Letty was back from escorting Mary to the front door.

She sank down in the chair beside him and closed her eyes, exhausted. She didn't have the energy to argue with her brother. If he was looking for an apology, she'd give him one. "I'm sorry, Lonny. I was only trying to help."

"Help what? Ruin my life?"

"No!" Letty said, her eyes flying open. "You need someone."

"Who says?"

"I do."

"Did you ever stop to think that's a bit presumptuous on your part? You're gone nine years and then you waltz home, look around and decide what you can change."

"Lonny, I said I was sorry."

He was silent for a lengthy moment, then he sighed. "I didn't mean to shout."

"I know you didn't." Letty was so tired she didn't know how she was going to manage the dishes. One meal, and she'd used every pan in the house. Cricket was clearing the table for her and she was so grateful she kissed her daughter's forehead.

Lonny dawdled over his coffee, eyes downcast. "What makes you think I need someone?" he asked quietly.

"It seems so lonely out here. I assumed—incorrectly, it appears—that you'd be happier if there was someone to share your life with. You're a handsome man, Lonny, and there are plenty of women who'd like to be your wife."

One corner of his mouth edged up at that. "I intend to marry someday. I just haven't gotten around to it, that's all."

"Well, for heaven's sake, what are you waiting for?" Letty teased. "You're thirty-four and you're not getting any younger."

"I'm not exactly ready for social security."

Letty smiled. "Mary's nice—"

"Aw, come off it, Letty. I don't like that woman. How many times do I have to tell you that?"

"—but I understand why she isn't your type," Letty finished, undaunted.

"You do?"

She nodded. "Mary needs a man who'd be willing to spend a lot of time and money keeping her entertained. She wouldn't make a good rancher's wife."

"I knew that the minute I met her," Lonny grumbled. "I just didn't know how to put it in words." He mulled over his thoughts, then added, "Look at the way she let you and Cricket do all the work getting dinner on the table. She didn't help once. That wouldn't sit well with most folks."

"She was company." Letty felt an obligation to defend Mary. After all, she hadn't *asked* the other woman to help with the meal, although she would've appreciated it. Besides, Lonny didn't have a lot of room to talk; he'd waited to be served just like Mary had.

"Company, my foot," Lonny countered. "Could you see Mom or any other woman you know sitting around making idle chatter while everyone else is working around her?"

Letty had to ackowledge that was true.

"Did you notice how she wanted everyone to think she'd made those rolls herself?"

Letty had noticed, but she didn't consider that such a terrible thing.

Lonny reached into the middle of the table for a carrot stick, chewing on it with a frown. "A wife," he murmured. "I agree that a woman would take more interest in the house than I have in the past few years." He crunched down on the carrot again. "I have to admit it's been rather nice having my meals cooked and my laundry folded. Those are a couple of jobs I can live without."

Letty practically swallowed her tongue to keep from commenting.

"I think you might be right, Letty. A wife would come in handy."

"You could always hire a housekeeper," Letty said sarcastically, irritated by his attitude and unable to refrain from saying something after all.

"What are you so irked about? You're the one who suggested I get married in the first place."

"From the way you're talking, you seem to think of a wife as a hired hand who'll clean house and cook your meals. You don't want a *wife*. You're looking for a servant. A woman has to get more out of a relationship than that."

Lonny snorted. "I thought you females need to be needed. For crying out loud, what else is there to a marriage but cooking and cleaning and regular sex?"

Letty glared at her brother, stood and picked up their coffee cups. "Lonny, I was wrong. Do some woman the ultimate favor and stay single."

With that she walked out of the dining room.

"So how did dinner go?" Chase asked his friend the following morning.

Lonny's response was little more than a grunt.

"That bad?"

"Worse."

Although his friend wouldn't appreciate it, Chase had gotten a good laugh over this dinner date of Lonny's with the gal from the hardware store. "Is Letty going to set you up with that Brandon woman again?"

"Not while I'm breathing, she won't."

Chase chuckled and loosened the reins on Firepower. Mary Brandon was about as subtle as a jackhammer. She'd done everything but throw herself at Lonny's feet, and she probably would've done that if she'd thought it would do any good. Chase wanted to blame Letty for getting Lonny into this mess, but the Brandon woman was wily and had likely manipulated the invitation out of Letty. Unfortunately Lonny was the one who'd suffered the consequences.

Chase smiled, content. Riding the range in May, looking for newborn calves, was one of his favorite chores as a rancher. All creation seemed to be bursting out, fresh and alive. The trees were budding and the wind was warm and carried the sweet scent of wildflowers with it. He liked the ranch best after it rained; everything felt so pure then and the land seemed to glisten.

"That sister of yours is determined to find you a wife, isn't she?" Chase teased, still smiling. "She hasn't been back two weeks and she's matchmaking to beat the band. Before you know it, she'll have you married off. I only hope you get some say in whatever woman Letty chooses."

"Letty doesn't mean any harm."

"Neither did Lizzy Borden."

When Lonny didn't respond with the appropriate chuckle, Chase glanced in his friend's direction. "You look worried. What's wrong?"

"It's Letty."

"What about her?"

"Does she seem any different to you?"

Chase shrugged, hating the sudden concern that surged through him. The only thing he wanted to feel for Letty was apathy, or at best the faint stirring of remembrance one had about a casual acquaintance. As it was, his heart, his head—every part of him—went into overdrive whenever Lonny brought his sister into the conversation.

"How do you mean—different?" Chase asked.

"I don't know for sure." He hesitated and pushed his hat farther back on his head. "It's crazy, but she takes naps every afternoon. And I mean *every* afternoon. At first she said it was jet lag."

"So she sleeps a lot. Big deal," Chase responded, struggling to sound disinterested.

"Hey, Chase, you know my sister as well as I do. Can you picture Letty, who was always a ball of energy, taking naps in the middle of the day?"

Chase couldn't, but he didn't say so.

"Another thing," Lonny said as he loosely held his gelding's reins, "Letty's always been a neat freak. Remember how she used to drive me crazy with the way everything had to be just so?"

Chase nodded.

"She left the dinner dishes in the sink all night. I found her putting them in the dishwasher this morning, claiming she'd been too tired to bother after Mary left. Mary was gone by seven-thirty!"

"So she's a little tired," Chase muttered. "Let her sleep if it makes her happy."

"It's more than that," Lonny continued. "She doesn't sing anymore—not a note. For nine years she fought tooth and nail to make it in the entertainment business, and now it's as if…as if she never had a voice. She hasn't even touched the piano since she's been home—at least not when I was there to hear her." Lonny frowned. "It's like the song's gone out of her life."

Chase didn't want to talk about Letty and he didn't want to think about her. In an effort to change the subject he said, "Old man Wilber was by the other day."

Lonny shook his head. "I suppose he was after those same acres again."

"Every year he asks me if I'd be willing to sell that strip of land." Some people knew it was spring when the flowers started to bloom. Chase could tell when Henry Wilber approached him about a narrow strip of land that bordered their property line. It wasn't the land that interested Wilber as much as the water. Nothing on this earth would convince Chase to sell that land. Spring Valley Ranch had been in his family for nearly eighty years and each generation had held on to those acres through good times and bad. Ranching wasn't exactly making Chase a millionaire, but he would die before he sold off a single inch of his inheritance.

"You'd be a fool to let it go," Lonny said.

No one needed to tell Chase that. "I wonder when he'll give up asking."

"Knowing old man Wilber," Lonny said with a chuckle, "I'd say never."

"Are you going to plant any avocados?" Cricket asked as Letty spaded the rich soil that had once been her mother's garden. Lonny had protested, but he'd tilled a large section close to the house for her and Cricket to plant. Now Letty was eager to get her hands in the earth.

"Avocados won't grow in Wyoming, Cricket. The climate isn't mild enough."

"What about oranges?"

"Not those, either."

"What *does* grow in Wyoming?" she asked indignantly. "Cowboys?"

Letty smiled as she used the sturdy fork to turn the soil.

"Mommy, look! Chase is here...on his horsey." Cricket took off, running as fast as her stubby legs would carry her. Her reaction was the same whenever Chase appeared.

Letty stuck the spading fork in the soft ground and reluctantly followed her daughter. By the time she got to the yard, Chase had climbed down from the saddle and dropped the reins. Cricket stood awestruck on the steps leading to the back porch, her mouth agape, her eyes wide.

"Hello, Chase," Letty said softly.

He looked at her and frowned. "Didn't that old straw hat used to belong to your mother?"

Letty nodded. "She wore it when she worked in the garden. I found it the other day." Chase made no further comment, although Letty was sure he'd wanted to say something more.

Eagerly Cricket bounded down the steps to stand beside her mother. Her small hand crept into Letty's, holding on tightly. "I didn't know horsies were so big and *pretty,*" she breathed.

"Firepower's special," Letty explained. Chase had raised the bay from a yearling, and had worked with him for long, patient hours.

"You said you wanted to see Firepower," Chase said, a bit gruffly. "I haven't got all day, so if you want a ride it's got to be now."

"I can ride him? Oh, Mommy, can I really?"

Letty's blood roared in her ears. She opened her mouth to tell Chase she wasn't about to set her daughter on a horse of that size.

Before she could voice her objection, however, Chase quieted her fears. "She'll be riding with me." With that he swung himself onto the horse and reached down to hoist Cricket into the saddle with him.

As if she'd been born to ride, Cricket sat in front of Chase on the huge animal without revealing the least bit of fear. "Look at me!" she shouted, grinning widely. "I'm riding a horsey! I'm riding a horsey!"

Even Chase was smiling at such unabashed enthusiasm. "I'll take her around the yard a couple of times," he told Letty before kicking gently at Firepower's sides. The bay obediently trotted around in a circle.

"Can we go over there?" Cricket pointed to some undistinguishable location in the distance.

"Cricket," Letty said, clamping the straw hat onto her head and squinting up. "Chase is a busy man. He hasn't got time to run you all over the countryside."

"Hold on," Chase responded, taking the reins in both hands and heading in the direction Cricket had indicated.

"Chase," Letty cried, running after him. "She's just a little girl. Please be careful."

He didn't answer her, and not knowing what to expect, Letty trailed them to the end of the long drive. When she reached it, she was breathless and lightheaded. It took her several minutes to walk back to the house. She was certain anyone watching her would assume she was drunk. Entering the kitchen, Letty grabbed her prescription bottle—hidden from Lonny in a cupboard—and swallowed a couple of capsules without water.

Not wanting to raise unnecessary alarm, she went back to the garden, but had to sit on an old stump until her breathing returned to normal. Apparently her heart had gotten worse since she'd come home. Much worse.

"Mommy, look, no hands," Cricket called out, her arms raised high in the air as Firepower trotted back into the yard.

Smiling, Letty stood and reached for the spading fork.

"Don't try to pretend you were working," Chase

muttered, frowning at her. "We saw you sitting in the sun. What's the matter, Letty? Did the easy life in California make you lazy?"

Once more Chase was baiting her. And once more Letty let the comment slide. "It must have," she said and looked away.

Chapter 4

Chase awoke just before dawn. He lay on his back, listening to the birds chirping outside his half-opened window. Normally their singing would have cheered him, but not this morning. He'd slept poorly, his mind preoccupied with Letty. Everything Lonny had said the week before about her not being herself had bounced around in his brain for most of the night.

Something *was* different about Letty, but not in the way Chase would have assumed. He'd expected the years in California to transform her in a more obvious way, making her worldly and cynical. To his surprise, he'd discovered that in several instances she seemed very much like the naive young woman who'd left nine years earlier to follow a dream. But the changes were there, lots of them, complex and subtle, when he'd expected them to be simple and glaring. Perhaps what troubled Chase was his deep inner feeling that something was genuinely wrong with her. But try as he might, he couldn't pinpoint what it was. That disturbed him the most.

Sitting on the edge of the bed, Chase rubbed his hands over his face and glanced outside. The cloudless dawn sky was a luminous shade of gray. The air smelled crisp and clean as Wyoming offered another perfect spring morning.

Chase dressed in his jeans and a Western shirt. Downstairs, he didn't bother to fix himself a cup of coffee; instead he walked outside, climbed into his pickup and headed over to the Bar E.

Only it wasn't Lonny who drew him there.

The lights were on in the kitchen when Chase pulled into the yard. He didn't knock, but stepped directly into the large family kitchen. Letty was at the stove, the way he knew she would be. She turned when he walked in the door.

"Morning, Chase," she said with a smile.

"Morning." Without another word, he walked over to the cupboard and got himself a mug. Standing next to her, he poured his own coffee.

"Lonny's taking care of the horses," she told him, as if she needed to explain where her brother was.

Briefly Chase wondered how she would've responded if he'd said it wasn't Lonny he'd come to see.

"Cricket talked nonstop for hours about riding Firepower. It was the thrill of her life. Thank you for being so kind to her, Chase."

Chase held back a short derisive laugh. He hadn't planned to let Cricket anywhere near his gelding. His intention all along had been to avoid Letty's daughter entirely. To Chase's way of thinking, the less he had to do with the child the better.

Ignoring Cricket was the only thing he could do, because every time he looked at that sweet little girl, he felt nothing but pain. Not a faint flicker of discomfort, but a deep wrenching pain like nothing he'd ever experienced. Cricket represented everything about Letty that he wanted to forget. He couldn't even glance at the child without remembering that Letty had given herself to another man, and the sense of betrayal cut him to the bone.

Naturally Cricket was innocent of the circumstances surrounding her birth, and Chase would never do anything to deliberately hurt the little girl, but he couldn't help feeling what he did. Yet he'd given her a ride on Firepower the day before, and despite everything, he'd enjoyed himself.

If the truth be known, the ride had come about accidentally. Chase had been on the ridge above the Bar E fence line when he saw two faint dots silhouetted against the landscape, far in the distance. Almost immediately he'd realized it was Letty and her daughter, working outside. From that moment on, Chase hadn't been able to stay away. He'd hurried down the hill, but once he was in the yard, he had to come up with some logical reason for showing up in the middle of the day. Giving Cricket a chance to see Firepower had seemed solid enough at the time.

"Would you like a waffle?" Letty asked, breaking into his musings.

"No, thanks."

Letty nodded and turned around. "I don't know why Cricket's taken to you the way she has. She gets excited every time someone mentions your name. I'm afraid you've made a friend for life, whether you like it or not."

Chase made a noncommital noise.

"I can't thank you enough for bringing Firepower over," Letty continued. "It meant a lot to me."

"I didn't do it for you," he said bluntly, watching her, almost wanting her to come back at him with some snappy retort. The calm way in which Letty swallowed his barbs troubled him more than anything else.

As he'd suspected, Letty didn't respond. Instead she brought butter and syrup to the table, avoiding his gaze.

The Letty Ellison he remembered had been feisty and fearless. She wouldn't have tolerated impatience or tactlessness from anyone, least of all him.

"This coffee tastes like it came out of a sewer," he said rudely, setting his cup down hard on the table.

The coffee was fine, but he wanted to test Letty's reactions. In years past, she would've flared right back at him, giving as good as she got. Nine years ago, Letty would've told him what he could do with that cup of coffee if he didn't like the taste of it.

She looked up, her face expressionless. "I'll make another pot."

Chase was stunned. "Forget it," he said quickly, not knowing what else to say. She glanced at him, her eyes large and shadowed in her pale face.

"But you just said there's something wrong with the coffee."

Chase was speechless. He watched her, his thoughts confused.

What had happened to his dauntless Letty?

Letty was working in the garden, carefully planting rows of corn, when her brother's pickup truck came barreling down the drive. When he slammed on the brakes, jumped out of the cab and slammed the door, Letty got up and left the seed bag behind. Her brother was obviously angry about something.

"Lonny?" she asked quietly. "What's wrong?"

"Of all the stupid, idiotic, crazy women in the world, why did I have to run into *this* one?"

"What woman?" Letty asked.

Lonny thrust his index finger under Letty's nose. "She—she's going to pay for this," he stammered in his fury. "There's no way I'm letting her get away with what she did."

"Lonny, settle down and tell me what happened."

"There!" he shouted, his voice so filled with indignation it shook.

He was pointing at the front of the pickup. Letty studied it, but didn't see anything amiss. "What?"

"Here," he said, directing her attention to a nearly indistinguishable dent in the bumper of his ten-year-old vehicle.

The entire truck was full of nicks and dents. When a rancher drove a vehicle for as many years as Lonny had, it collected its share of battle scars. It needed a new left fender, and a new paint job all the way around wouldn't have hurt, either. As far as Letty could tell,

Lonny's truck was on its last legs, as it were—or, more appropriately, tires.

"Oh, you mean *that* tiny dent," she said, satisfied she'd found the one he was referring to.

"Tiny dent!" he shouted. "That...woman nearly cost me a year off my life."

"Tell me what happened," Letty demanded a second time. She couldn't remember ever seeing her brother this agitated.

"She ran a stop sign. Claimed she didn't see it. What kind of idiot misses a stop sign, for Pete's sake?"

"Did she slam into you?"

"Not exactly. I managed to avoid a collision, but in the process I hit the pole."

"What pole?"

"The one holding up the stop sign, of course."

"Oh." Letty didn't mean to appear dense, but Lonny was so angry, he wasn't explaining himself clearly.

He groaned in frustration. "Then, ever so sweetly, she climbs out of her car, tells me how sorry she is and asks if there's any damage."

Letty rolled her eyes. She didn't know what her brother expected, but as far as Letty could see, Lonny was being completely unreasonable.

"Right away I could see what she'd done, and I pointed it out to her. But that's not the worst of it," he insisted. "She took one look at my truck and said there were so many dents in it, she couldn't possibly know which one our *minor* accident had caused."

In Letty's opinion the other driver was absolutely right, but saying as much could prove dangerous. "Then what?" she asked cautiously.

"We exchanged a few words," he admitted, kicking the dirt and avoiding Letty's gaze. "She said my truck was a pile of junk." Lonny walked all the way around it before he continued, his eyes flashing. "There's no way I'm going to let some *teacher* insult me like that."

"I'm sure her insurance will take care of it," Letty said calmly.

"Damn straight it will." He slapped his hat back on his head. "You know what else she did? She tried to buy me off!" he declared righteously. "Right there in the middle of the street, in broad daylight, in front of God and man. Now I ask you, do I look like the kind of guy who can be bribed?"

At Letty's questioning look, her irate brother continued. "She offered me fifty bucks."

"I take it you refused."

"You bet I refused," he shouted. "There's two or three hundred dollars' damage here. Probably a lot more."

Letty bent to examine the bumper again. It looked like a fifty-dollar dent to her, but she wasn't about to say so. It did seem, however, that Lonny was protesting much too long and loud over a silly dent. Whoever this woman was, she'd certainly gained his attention. A teacher, he'd said.

"I've got her license number right here." Lonny yanked a small piece of paper from his shirt pocket and carefully unfolded it. "Joy Fuller's lucky I'm not going to report her to the police."

"Joy Fuller," Letty cried, taking the paper away from him. "I know who she is."

That stopped Lonny short. "How?" he asked suspiciously.

"She plays the organ at church on Sundays, and as you obviously know, she teaches at the elementary school. Second grade, I think."

Lonny shot a look toward the cloudless sky. "Do the good people of Red Springs realize the kind of woman they're exposing their children to? Someone should tell the school board."

"You've been standing in the sun too long. Come inside and have some lunch," Letty offered.

"I'm too mad to think about eating. You go ahead without me." With that he strode toward the barn.

Letty went into the house, and after pouring herself a glass of iced tea, she reached for the church directory and dialed Joy Fuller's number.

Joy answered brusquely on the first ring. "Yes," she snapped.

"Joy, it's Letty Ellison."

"Letty, I'm sorry, but your brother is the rudest... most arrogant, unreasonable man I've ever encountered."

"I can't tell you how sorry I am about this," Letty said, but she had the feeling Joy hadn't even heard her.

"I made a simple mistake and he wouldn't be satisfied with anything less than blood."

"Can you tell me what happened?" She was hoping Joy would be a little more composed than Lonny, but she was beginning to have her doubts.

"I'm sure my version is nothing like your brother's," Joy said, her voice raised. "It's simple, really. I ran the stop sign between Oak and Spruce. Frankly, I don't go that way often and I simply forgot it was there."

Letty knew the intersection. A huge weeping willow partially obscured the sign. There'd been a piece in the weekly paper about how the tree should be trimmed before a collision occurred.

"I was more than willing to admit the entire incident was my fault," Joy went on. "But I couldn't even tell which dent I'd caused, and when I said as much, your brother started acting like a crazy man."

"I don't know what's wrong with Lonny," Letty confessed. "I've never seen him like this."

"Well, I'd say it has something to do with the fact that I turned him down the last time he asked me out."

"*What?* This is the first I've heard of it. You and my brother had a…relationship?"

Joy gave an unladylike snort. "I wouldn't dignify it with that name. He and I… He— Oh, Letty, never mind. It's all history. Back to this so-called accident…" She drew in an audible breath. "I told him I'd contact my insurance company, but to hear him tell it, he figures it'll take at least two thousand dollars to repair all the damage I caused."

That was ridiculous. "I'm sure he didn't mean it—"

"Oh, he meant it, all right," Joy interrupted. "Personally, I'd rather have the insurance people deal with him, anyway. I never want to see your arrogant, ill-tempered, bronc-busting brother again."

Letty didn't blame her, but she had the feeling that in Joy Fuller, her brother had met his match.

* * *

At four o'clock, Lonny came into the house, and his mood had apparently improved, because he sent Letty a shy smile and said, "Don't worry about making me dinner tonight. I'm going into town."

"Oh?" Letty said, looking up from folding laundry.

"Chase and I are going out to eat."

She smiled. "Have a good time. You deserve a break."

"I just hope that Fuller woman isn't on the streets."

Letty raised her eyebrows. "Really?"

"Yeah, really," he snapped. "She's a menace."

"Honestly, Lonny, are you still mad about that… silly incident?"

"I sure am. It isn't safe for man or beast with someone like her behind the wheel."

"I do believe you protest too much. Could it be that you're attracted to Joy? *Still* attracted?"

Eyes narrowed, he stalked off, then turned back around and muttered, "I was *never* attracted to her. We might've seen each other a few times but it didn't work out. How could it? She's humorless, full of herself and…and she's a city slicker. From the West Coast, the big metropolis of Seattle, no less."

"I've heard it's a nice place," Letty said mildly.

Lonny did not consider that worthy of comment, and Letty couldn't help smiling.

His bathwater was running when he returned several minutes later, his shirt unbuttoned. "What about you, Letty?"

"What do you mean?" she asked absently, lifting the laundry basket onto the table. The fresh, clean scent of sun-dried towels made the extra effort of hanging them on the line worth it.

"What are you doing tonight?"

"Nothing much." She planned to do what she did every Saturday night. Watch a little television, polish her nails and read.

Her brother pulled out a chair, turned it around and straddled it. "From the minute you got home, you've been talking about marrying me off. That's the reason you invited that Brandon woman over for dinner. You admitted it yourself."

"A mistake that won't be repeated," she assured him, fluffing a thick towel.

"But you said I need a woman."

"A wife, Lonny. There's a difference."

"I've been thinking about what you said, and you might be right. But what about you?"

Letty found the task of folding bath towels vitally important. "I don't understand."

"When are you going to get married?"

Never, her mind flashed spontaneously.

"Letty?"

She shrugged, preferring to avoid the issue and knowing it was impossible. "Someday...maybe."

"You're not getting any younger."

Letty supposed she had that coming. Lonny's words were an echo of her own earlier ones to him. Now she was paying the penalty for her miserable attempt at matchmaking. However, giving Lonny a few pat answers wasn't going to work, any more than it had worked with her. "Frankly, I'm not sure I'll ever marry," she murmured, keeping her gaze lowered.

"Did...Cricket's father hurt you that much?"

Purposely she glanced behind her and asked stiffly, "Isn't your bathwater going to run over?"

"I doubt it. Answer me, Letty."

"I have no intention of discussing what happened with Jason. It's in the past and best forgotten."

Lonny was silent for a moment. "You're so different now. I'm your brother—I care about you—and it bothers me to see you like this. No man is worth this kind of pain."

"Lonny, please." She held the towels against her stomach. "If I'm different it isn't because of what happened between me and Jason. It's...other things."

"What other things?" Lonny asked, his eyes filled with concern.

That was one question Letty couldn't answer. At least not yet. So she sidestepped it. "Jason taught me an extremely valuable lesson. Oh, it was painful at the time, don't misunderstand me, but he gave me Cricket, and she's my joy. I can only be grateful to Jason for my daughter."

"But don't you hate him for the way he deceived you and then deserted you?"

"No," she admitted reluctantly, uncertain her brother would understand. "Not anymore. What possible good would that do?"

Apparently absorbed in thought, Lonny rubbed his hand along the back of his neck. Finally he said, "I don't know, I suppose I want him to suffer for what he put you through. Some guy I've never even seen got you pregnant and walked away from you when you needed him most. It disgusts me to see him get off scot-free after the way he treated you."

Unexpected tears pooled in Letty's eyes at the protectiveness she saw in her brother. She blinked them away, and when she could speak evenly again, she murmured, "If there's anything I learned in all those years away from home, it's that there's an order to life. Eventually everything rights itself. I don't need revenge, because sooner or later, as the old adage says, what goes around, comes around."

"How can you be so calm about it, though?"

"Take your bath, Lonny," she said with a quick laugh. She shoved a freshly folded towel at him. "You're driving me crazy. And you say *Cricket* asks a lot of questions."

Chase arrived a couple of hours later, stepping gingerly into the kitchen. He completely avoided looking at or speaking to Letty, who was busy preparing her and Cricket's dinner. He walked past Letty, but was waylaid by Cricket, who was coloring in her book at the dining room table.

Chase seemed somewhat short with the child, Letty noted, but Cricket had a minimum of ten important questions Chase needed to answer regarding Firepower. The five-year-old didn't seem to mind that Chase was a little abrupt. Apparently her hero could do no wrong.

Soon enough Lonny appeared. He opened a can of beer, and Letty listened to her brother relate his hair-raising encounter with "the Fuller woman" at the stop sign in town as if he were lucky to have escaped with his life.

The two men were in the living room while Letty stayed in the kitchen. Chase obviously wanted to keep his distance, and that was just as well. He'd gone out of his way to irritate her lately and she'd tolerated about all she could. Doing battle with Chase now would only deplete her energy. She'd tried to square things with him once, and he'd made his feelings abundantly clear. For now, Letty could do nothing but accept the situation.

"Where do you think we should eat?" Lonny asked, coming into the kitchen to deposit his empty beer can.

"Billy's Steak House?" Chase called out from the living room. "I'm in the mood for a thick sirloin."

Letty remembered that Chase had always liked his meat rare.

"How about going to the tavern afterward?" Lonny suggested. "Let's see if there's any action to be had."

Letty didn't hear the response, but whatever it was caused the two men to laugh like a couple of rambunctious teenagers. Amused, Letty smiled faintly and placed the cookie sheet with frozen fish sticks in the oven.

It wasn't until later, while Letty was clearing away the dinner dishes, that the impact of their conversation really hit her. The "action" they were looking for at the Roundup Tavern involved women.... Although she wouldn't admit it to Lonny—and he'd never admit it himself—she suspected he might be hoping Joy Fuller would show up.

But Chase—what woman was *he* looking for? Would anyone do, so long as she wasn't Letty? Would their encounter go beyond a few dances and a few drinks?

Tight-lipped, Letty marched into the living room and threw herself down on the overstuffed chair. Cricket was playing with her dolls on the carpet and Letty pushed the buttons on the remote control with a vengeance. Unable to watch the sitcom she usually enjoyed, she turned off the set and placed a hand over her face. Closing her eyes was a mistake.

Instantly she imagined Chase in the arms of a beautiful woman, a sexy one, moving suggestively against him.

"Oh, no," Letty cried, bolting upright.

"Mommy?"

Letty's pulse started to roar in her ears, drowning out reason. She looked at Cricket, playing so contentedly, and announced curtly, "It's time for bed."

"Already?"

"Yes… Remember, we have church in the morning," she said.

"Will Chase be there?"

"I…I don't know." If he was, she'd…she'd ignore him the way he'd ignored her.

Several hours later, Cricket was in bed asleep and Letty lay in her own bed, staring sightlessly into the dark. Her fury, irrational though it might be, multiplied with every passing minute. When she could stand it no longer, Letty hurried down the stairs and sat in the living room without turning on any lights.

She wasn't there long before she heard a vehicle coming up the drive. The back door opened and the two men stumbled into the house.

"Sh-h-h," she heard Chase whisper loudly, "you'll wake Letty."

"God forbid." Lonny's slurred words were followed by a husky laugh.

"You needn't worry, I'm already awake," Letty said righteously as she stood in the doorway from the dining room into the kitchen. She flipped on the light and took one look at her brother, who was leaning heavily against Chase, one arm draped across his neighbor's neck, and snapped, "You're drunk."

Lonny stabbed a finger in her direction. "Nothing gets past you, does it?"

"I'll get him upstairs for you," Chase said, half dragging Lonny across the kitchen.

Lonny's mood was jovial and he attempted to sing some ditty, off-key, the words barely recognizable. Chase shushed him a second time, reminding him that Cricket was asleep even if Letty wasn't, but his warning went unheeded.

Letty led the way, trudging up the stairs, arms folded. She threw open Lonny's bedroom door and turned on the light.

Once inside, Lonny stumbled and fell across the bed, glaring up at the ceiling. Letty moved into the room and, with some effort, removed his boots.

Chase got a quilt from the closet and unfolded it across his friend. "He'll probably sleep for the rest of the night."

"I'm sure he will," Letty said tightly. She left Lonny's bedroom and hurried down the stairs. She was pacing the kitchen when Chase joined her.

"What's the matter with you?" he asked, frowning.

"How dare you bring my brother home in that condition," she demanded, turning on him.

"You wanted me to leave him in town? Drunk?"

If he'd revealed the slightest amount of guilt or contrition, Letty might've been able to let him go without another word. But he stood in front of her, and all she could see was the imagined woman in that bar. The one he'd danced with…and kissed and—

Fury surged up inside her, blocking out sanity. All week he'd been baiting her, wanting to hurt her for the pain she'd caused him. Tonight he'd succeeded.

"I hate you," she sobbed, lunging at him.

He grabbed her wrists and held them at her sides. "Letty, what's gotten into you?"

She squirmed and twisted in his arms, frantically trying to free herself, but she was trapped.

"Letty?"

She looked up at him, her face streaked with tears she didn't care to explain, her shoulders heaving with emotion.

"You're angry because Lonny's drunk?" he whispered.

"No," she cried, struggling again. "You went to that bar. You think I don't know what you did but—"

"*What* are you talking about?"

"You went to the Roundup to…to pick up some woman!"

Chase frowned, then shook his head. "Letty, no!"

"Don't lie to me…don't!"

"Oh, Letty," he murmured. Then he leaned down to settle his mouth over hers.

The last thing Letty wanted at that moment was his

touch or his kiss. She meant to brace her hands against his chest and use her strength to push him away. Instead her hands inched upward until she was clasping his shoulders. The anger that had consumed her seconds before was dissolving in a firestorm of desire, bringing to life a part of her that had lain dormant from the moment she'd left Chase Brown's arms nine years before.

Chapter 5

Chase kissed her again and again while his hands roved up and down the curve of her spine as though he couldn't get enough of her.

His touch began to soothe the pain and disappointment that had come into her life in their long years apart. She was completely vulnerable to him in that moment. She *wanted* him.

And Chase wanted her.

"Letty..."

Whatever he'd intended to say was lost when his mouth covered hers with a hungry groan. Letty's lips parted in eager response.

She'd been back in Red Springs for several weeks, but she wasn't truly home until Chase had taken her in his arms and kissed her. Now that she was with him, a peace settled over her. Whatever lay before her, life or death, she was ready, suffused with the serenity his embrace offered. Returning to this small town and the Bar E were only a tiny part of what made it so important to come home for her surgery. Her love for Chase had been the real draw; it was what had pulled her back, and for the first time she was willing to acknowledge it.

Letty burrowed her fingers into his hair, her eyes shut, her head thrown back. Neither she nor Chase spoke. They held on to each other as though they were afraid to let go.

A sigh eased from Letty as Chase lifted his head and tenderly kissed her lips. He brought her even closer and deepened his probing kiss until Letty was sure her knees were about to buckle. Then his mouth abandoned hers to explore the hollow of her throat.

Tears welled in her eyes, then ran unheeded down her cheeks. Chase pressed endless kisses over her face until she forgot everything but the love she'd stored in her heart for him.

When she was certain nothing could bring her any more pleasure than his kiss, he lowered his hand to her breast—

"Mommy!"

Cricket's voice, coming from the top of the stairs, penetrated the fog of Letty's desire. Chase apparently hadn't heard her, and Letty had to murmur a protest and gently push him aside.

"Yes, darling, what's wrong?" Her voice sounded weak even to her own ears as she responded to her daughter.

Chase stumbled back and raised a hand to his face,

as if he'd been suddenly awakened from a dream. Letty longed to go to him, but she couldn't.

"Uncle Lonny keeps singing and he woke me up!" Cricket cried.

"I'll be right there." Letty prayed Chase understood that she couldn't ignore her daughter.

"Mommy!" Cricket called more loudly. "Please hurry. Uncle Lonny sings terrible!"

"Just a minute." She retied her robe, her hands shaking. "Chase—"

"This isn't the time to do any talking," he said gruffly.

"But there's so much we need to discuss." She whisked the curls away from her face. "Don't you think so?"

"Not now."

"But—"

"Go take care of Cricket," he said and turned away.

Letty's heart was heavy as she started for the stairs. A dim light illuminated the top where Cricket was standing, fingers plugging her ears.

In the background, Letty heard her brother's drunken rendition of "Puff the Magic Dragon." Another noise blended with the first, as Chase opened the kitchen door and walked out of the house.

The next morning, Letty moved around downstairs as quietly as possible in an effort not to wake her brother. From everything she'd seen of him the night before, Lonny was going to have one heck of a hangover.

The coffee was perking merrily in the kitchen as

Letty brushed Cricket's long hair while the child stood patiently in the bathroom.

"Was Uncle Lonny sick last night?" Cricket asked.

"I don't think so." Letty couldn't remember hearing him get out of bed during the night.

"He sounded sick when he was singing."

"I suppose he did at that," Letty murmured. "Or sickly, anyway." She finished tying the bright red ribbons in Cricket's hair and returned to the kitchen for a cup of coffee. To her astonishment, Lonny was sitting at the table, neatly dressed in a suit and tie.

"Lonny!"

"Morning," he greeted her.

Although his eyes were somewhat bloodshot, Lonny didn't look bad. In fact, he acted as though he'd gone sedately to bed at nine or ten o'clock.

Letty eyed him warily, unsure what to make of him. Only a few hours earlier he'd been decidedly drunk— but maybe not as drunk as she'd assumed. And Chase hadn't seemed inebriated at all.

"How are you feeling?" she asked, studying him carefully.

"Wonderful."

Obviously his escapades of the night before hadn't done him any harm. Unexpectedly he stood, then reached for his Bible, wiping the dust off the leather binding.

"Well, are you two coming to church with me or not?" he asked.

Letty was so shocked it took her a moment to respond. "Yes...of course."

It wasn't until they'd pulled into the church parking

lot that Letty understood her brother's newly formed desire for religion. He was attending the morning service not because of any real longing to worship. He'd come hoping to see Joy Fuller again. The thought surprised Letty as much as it pleased her. Red Springs's second-grade teacher had managed to reignite her brother's interest. That made Letty smile. From the little Letty knew of the church organist, Joy would never fit Lonny's definition of the dutiful wife.

The congregation had begun to file through the wide doors. "I want to sit near the front," Lonny told Letty, looking around.

"If you don't mind, I'd prefer to sit near the back," Letty said. "In case Cricket gets restless."

"She'll be good today, won't you, cupcake?"

The child nodded, clearly eager for her uncle's approval. Lonny took her small hand in his and, disregarding Letty's wishes, marched up the center aisle.

Groaning inwardly, Letty followed her brother. At least his choice of seats gave Letty the opportunity to scan the church for any sign of Chase. Her quick survey told her he'd decided against attending services this morning, which was a relief.

Letty had been dreading their next encounter, yet at the same time she was eager to talk to him again. She felt both frightened and excited by their rekindled desire for each other. But he'd left her so brusquely the night before that she wasn't sure what to expect. So much would depend on his reaction to her. Then she'd know what he was feeling—if he regretted kissing her or if he felt the same excitement she did.

Organ music resounded through the church, and

once they were settled in their pew, Letty picked up a hymnal. Lonny sang in his loudest voice, staring intently at Joy as she played the organ. Letty resisted the urge to remind him that his behavior bordered on rude.

When Joy faltered over a couple of notes, Lonny smiled with smug satisfaction. Letty moaned inwardly. So *this* was her brother's game!

"Mommy," Cricket whispered, standing backward on the pew and looking at the crowd. "Chase is here."

Letty's grip on the hymnal tightened. "That's nice, sweetheart."

"Can I go sit with him?"

"Not now."

"Later?"

"No."

"How come?"

"Cricket," Letty pleaded. "Sit down and be quiet."

"But I like Chase and I want to sit with him."

"Maybe next week," she said in a low voice.

"Can I ask him after the pastor's done talking at everybody?"

Letty nodded, willing to agree to just about anything by then. The next time her brother insisted on sitting in the front pew, he would do so alone.

No worship service had ever seemed to take longer. Cricket fidgeted during the entire hour, eager to run and talk to Chase. Lonny wasn't much better. He continued to stare at Joy and did everything but make faces at her to distract the poor woman. Before the service was half over, Letty felt like giving him a good, hard shake. Even as a young girl, she'd never seen her older brother behave more childishly. The only reason he'd come to church was to make poor Joy as uncomfortable as he possibly could.

By the time Letty was outside the church, Cricket had already found Chase. From his stiff posture, Letty knew he'd planned on escaping without talking to her and the last thing he'd wanted was to be confronted by Cricket. Letty's heart swelled with fresh pain. So this was how he felt.

He regretted everything.

Letty hastened to her daughter's side and took her small hand. "Uncle Lonny's waiting for us at the truck," she said, her eyes skirting Chase.

"But I haven't asked Chase if I can sit with him next week."

"I'm sure he has other friends he'd prefer to sit with," Letty answered, hiding her impatience.

"I can answer for myself." Chase's voice was clipped and unfriendly. "As it happens, Cricket, I think your mother's right. It would be best if you sat with her in church."

"Can't you sit in the same row as us?"

"No."

"Why not?"

Chase didn't say anything for an awkward moment, but when he did, he looked past Letty. "Because I'd rather not."

"Okay," Cricket said, apparently accepting that without a problem.

"It's time to go," Letty said tersely. Only a few hours earlier, Chase had held her in his arms, kissed her and loved her with a gentleness that had fired her senses back to life. And in the light of a new day, he'd told her as plainly as if he'd shouted it from the church steps that it had all been a mistake, that nothing had changed and he didn't want anything to do with her.

After all the hurt she'd suffered in California, Letty thought she was immune to this kind of pain. In the span of a few minutes Chase had taught her otherwise.

Cricket raced ahead of Letty to Lonny's truck and climbed inside. For his part, her brother seemed to be taking his time about getting back to the ranch. He talked to a couple of men, then finally joined Cricket and Letty.

"We're ready anytime you are," Letty said from inside the truck.

"In a minute," he returned absently, glancing around before he got in.

Letty realized Lonny was waiting for Joy to make an appearance. The parking lot was nearly deserted now. There were only three other cars left, and Lonny had parked next to one of them, a PT Cruiser. Letty had no trouble figuring out that it belonged to Joy.

Lonny was sitting in the truck, with the window down, his elbow resting on the frame, apparently content to laze away in the sunshine while he waited.

"Lonny?" Letty pressed. "Can we please go?" After the way he'd behaved in church, Letty had every intention of having a serious discussion with her brother, but she preferred to do it when Cricket wasn't around to listen. She'd also prefer not to witness another embarrassing skirmish between him and Joy Fuller.

"It'll only be another minute."

He was right; the church door opened and Joy came

out. She hesitated when she saw Lonny's pickup beside her car.

"What are you going to say to her?" Letty whispered angrily.

"Oh, nothing much," Lonny murmured back, clearly distracted. When Joy approached her car, Lonny got out of the pickup and leaned indolently against the side, bracing one foot on the fender.

"I wouldn't do that if I were you," Joy said scathingly.

She was nearly as tall as Lonny, her dark hair styled so it fell in waves around her face. Her cheeks were a rosy hue and Letty couldn't help wondering if confronting Lonny again was why they were so flushed.

"Do what?" Lonny demanded.

"Put your foot on that truck. You might damage your priceless antique."

"I'll have you know, this truck isn't even ten years old!"

Joy feigned shock, opening her eyes wide while she held her hand against her chest. "Is that so? I could've sworn you claimed otherwise only yesterday. But, then, it seems you have a problem keeping your facts straight."

"You were impossible to talk to yesterday, and I can see today isn't going to be any better."

"Impossible?" Joy echoed. "Me? *You* were the one jumping up and down and acting like an idiot."

"Me?" Lonny tilted back his head and forced a loud laugh. "That's a good one."

Joy ignored him and continued to her car.

Lonny dropped his foot and yanked open the truck

door. "I thought we might be able to settle our differences, but you're being completely unreasonable."

"Perhaps I am, but at least I don't throw temper tantrums in the middle of the street."

"Yeah, but *I* know how to drive."

"Based on *what?* Taking that…that unsafe rattletrap on a public road should be an indictable offense!"

"Rattletrap? *Unsafe?*" Lonny slapped his hat against his thigh. "Just who do you think you are, talking to me like that?"

"If you don't like the way I talk, Mr. Rodeo Star, then stay away from me."

"It'll be my pleasure."

Suddenly, Lonny couldn't seem to get out of the parking lot fast enough. He gripped the steering wheel as if he was driving in the Indy 500.

"Lonny," Letty ordered, "slow down."

When he reached the end of the street, he drove off as if the very fires of hell were licking at his heels.

"Lonny!" Letty cried a second time. If he continued to drive in this manner, she'd walk home. "You're driving like a maniac. Stop the truck this minute!"

"Didn't I tell you that woman's a living, breathing menace?" he snapped, but he reduced his speed. To his credit, he looked surprised by how fast he'd been traveling. "I swear she drives me over the edge."

"Then do as she says and stay away from her," Letty advised, shaking her head in wonder. But she doubted he would.

He ignored her comment. "Did you see the way she laid into me?"

"Lonny, you provoked her."

"Then you didn't see things the way they happened," he muttered, shooting Letty a look of indignation. "I was only trying to be friendly."

Her brother was as unreasonable as he'd claimed Joy was. "I like Joy and I think you were rude to her this morning," Letty returned primly.

"When?"

"Oh, honestly! The only reason you came to church was to intimidate her into making a mistake while she was playing the organ. When you succeeded, I thought you were going to stand up and cheer."

Lonny cast her a frown that said Letty should consider counseling. "You're totally wrong, little sister."

Letty rolled her eyes. "Have you figured out *why* you feel so strongly?"

"Because she needs to be put in her place, that's why!"

"And you think you're the one to do it?"

"Damn right! I'm not about to let any woman get away with the things she said to me."

"Calling this truck an antique or—" she grinned "—a rattletrap…well, they don't exactly sound like fighting words to me."

Lonny turned into the long dusty drive leading to the house. "You women really stick together, don't you?" he asked bitterly. "No matter how stupid you act."

"Stupid?"

He pulled the truck into his usual spot. "Yeah. Like the fact that Joy Fuller doesn't know how to drive and then blames me. And what about you? You're the perfect example, taking off on some fool dream. Chase should never have let you go."

"It wasn't up to Chase to stop me or not. He couldn't have, anyway—no one could. I wasn't going to end up like Mom, stuck out here in no-man's-land, working so hard… Why, she was little more than a slave."

Lonny's eyes widened as he turned to her. "That's the way you see Mom?"

"You mean you don't?" How could her brother be so blind? Their mother had worked herself into an early grave, sacrificing her talent and her dreams for a few head of cattle and an unforgiving land.

"Of course I don't! Mom had a good life here. She loved the ranch and everything about it."

"You're so oblivious you can't see the truth, can you? Mom hated it here, only she wasn't honest enough to admit it, not even to herself."

"And you hate it, too?" he asked, his voice dangerously quiet.

"I did."

Lonny climbed out of the pickup and slammed the door. "No one asked you to come back, Letty. You could turn around and go straight back to California." With that he stormed into the house.

Fueled by her anger, Letty stayed in the truck, tears streaming down her face. She and Lonny had both been furious and the conversation had quickly gotten out of control. She should never have said the things she did. And Lonny shouldn't have, either. Now wasn't the time to deal with the past.

"Mommy?" Cricket leaned against her mother, obviously confused and a little frightened. "Why was Uncle Lonny shouting at you?"

"He was angry, honey."

"You were shouting at him, too."

"I know." She climbed out of the cab and helped Cricket clamber down. They walked into the house, and Lonny glared at her. She glared right back, surprised by how heated her response to him remained. In an effort to avoid continuing their argument, Letty went upstairs and changed her clothes. She settled Cricket with her activity book and crayons, then went outside and grabbed the hoe. Venting her frustration in the garden was bound to help. Once they'd both cooled down, they could discuss the matter rationally.

Lonny left soon afterward, barreling down the driveway as if he couldn't get away from her fast enough.

She was happy to see him go.

Chase felt as though his world had been knocked off its axis and he was struggling with some unknown force to right it again.

Letty was to blame for this. A part of him yearned to take Letty in his arms, love her, care for her and make up to her for the pain and disappointment she'd suffered. Yet something powerful within him wouldn't allow him to do it. He found himself saying and doing things he'd never intended.

Telling her he preferred not to sit beside her daughter in church was a prime example. The only reason he even attended was to be close to Letty. He rarely listened to the sermons. Instead, he sat and pretended Letty was the one sitting next to him. He thought about what it would be like to hear her lovely voice again as she sang. He imagined how it would feel to hold her hand while the pastor spoke.

Cricket had provided him with the perfect excuse to do those things. His pride wouldn't have suffered, and he'd be doing something to appease the kid. No one needed to know that being with Letty was what he'd wanted all along.

Yet he'd rejected the child's request flat out. And he'd been equally unwilling to talk to Letty last night. Chase didn't know how to explain his own actions. He was behaving like an idiot.

On second thought, his actions made perfect sense. He was protecting himself, and with good reason. He figured that if Letty really planned to make a life for herself in Red Springs, she'd be doing something about finding a decent job and settling down. She hadn't done that. Every piece of evidence pointed in the direction of her leaving again. She behaved as if this was an extended vacation and once she'd rested, she'd be on her way. Other than the garden she'd planted, he couldn't see any sign of permanence.

Chase couldn't allow his emotions to get involved with Letty a second time. He hadn't fully healed from the first. It wasn't that simple, however. He loved her, and frankly, he doubted he'd ever stop.

Rubbing his face, Chase drew in a deep, shuddering breath. He hadn't meant to touch her the night before, but her outrage, her eyes shooting sparks, had reminded him of the old Letty. The Letty who'd been naive, perhaps, but confident and self-assured, certain of her own opinions. He'd forgotten that he'd promised himself he'd never touch her again. One kiss and he'd been lost....

Even now, hours later, the memory of the way she'd melted in his embrace had the power to arouse him. He pushed it out of his mind. The best thing to do was forget it ever happened.

He went outside and got into the truck, deciding he'd go into town and do some shopping. Perhaps keeping busy would ease the ache in his heart.

Still confused, Chase wondered if he'd feel differently if Letty had made more of an effort to acknowledge their kisses. Cricket had come running up to him after the church service and Letty wouldn't even meet his eye. Obviously the memory of their encounter embarrassed her.

That pleased him.

And it infuriated him.

If Letty was disconcerted by their kissing, it said she didn't often let men touch her like that—which made him glad. The thought of another man making love to her was enough to produce a fireball of resentment in the pit of his stomach.

But her actions that morning also infuriated him, because she so obviously regretted what they'd done. While he'd spent the night dreaming of holding her and kissing her, she'd apparently been filled with remorse. Maybe she thought he wasn't good enough for her.

Telephone poles whizzed past him as he considered that bleak possibility.

A flash of red caught his attention. He looked again. It was Cricket, standing alone at the end of the Bar

E driveway, crying. She was wearing the same dress she'd worn at church.

Chase stepped on his brakes and quickly backed up. When he reached the little girl, she looked up and immediately started running to him.

"Chase...oh, Mr. Chase!"

"Cricket," he said sternly, climbing out of the truck, angry with Letty for being so irresponsible. "What are you doing here? Where's your mother?"

Sobbing, the little girl ran and hugged his waist. "Uncle Lonny and Mommy shouted at each other. Then Uncle Lonny left and Mommy went outside. Now she's sleeping in the garden and I can't wake her up."

Chapter 6

Letty sat on the porch steps, rubbing her eyes. Her knees felt weak and her eyes stubbornly refused to focus. It had been through sheer force of will that she'd made it from the garden to the back steps. She trembled with fear and alarm. Although she'd called for Cricket, the little girl was nowhere in the house or garden. Letty had to find her daughter despite the waves of nausea and weakness.

The last thing Letty remembered clearly was standing in the garden, shoveling for all she was worth, weeding because she was furious with Lonny and equally upset with herself for being drawn into such a pointless argument.

"Cricket," Letty called out again, shocked by how unsteady her voice sounded. Her daughter had been standing beside her only a few minutes before. Now she was gone.

The roar of an approaching truck was nearly deafening. Letty didn't have the strength to get up, so she sat there and waited. Whoever it was would have to come to her.

"Letty?"

"Mommy! Mommy!"

Chase leaped out of the pickup and quickly covered the space that separated them. Cricket was directly behind him, her face wet and streaked with tears.

Confused, Letty glanced up at them. She had no idea how Cricket had come to be with Chase. Even more surprising was the way he looked, as though he was ill himself. His face was gray, set and determined, but she couldn't understand why.

"What happened?" Chase demanded.

For a long moment her mind refused to function. "I...I think I fainted."

"Fainted?"

"I must have." She wiped her forehead, forcing a smile. By sheer resolve, she started to stand, but before she was fully on her feet, Chase had scooped her up in his arms.

"Chase," she protested. "Put me down...I'm perfectly all right."

"Like hell you are."

He seemed furious, as if she'd purposely fainted in a ploy to gain his sympathy. That added to her frustration and she tried to get free. Her efforts, however, were futile; Chase merely tightened his grip.

Cricket ran ahead of him and opened the back door. "Is Mommy sick?"

"Yes," Chase answered, his mouth a white line of impatience. He didn't so much as look at Letty as he strode through the house.

"I'm fine, sweetheart," Letty countered, trying to reassure her daughter, who ran beside Chase, intently studying her mother. Cricket looked so worried and frightened, which only distressed Letty more.

Chase gently deposited Letty on the sofa, then knelt beside her, his gaze roaming her face, inspecting her for any injury. Reluctantly, as if he was still annoyed, he brought his hand to her forehead. "You're not feverish," he announced.

"Of course I'm not," she shot back, awkwardly rising to an upright position. If everyone would give her a few minutes alone and some breathing room, she'd feel better. "I'm fine. I was weeding the garden, and next thing I knew I was on the ground. Obviously I got too much sun."

Cricket knelt on the carpet. "I couldn't wake you up," she murmured, her blue eyes round, her face shiny with tears.

Letty reached out to hug her. "I'm sorry I scared you, honey."

"Did you hit your head?" Chase asked.

"I don't think so." Tentatively she touched the back of her skull. As far as she could tell, there wasn't even a lump to suggest she'd hit anything besides the soft dirt.

"Cricket, go get your mother a glass of water."

The child took off running as if Chase's request was a matter of life and death.

"How did Cricket ever find you?" Letty asked, frowning. Her daughter wouldn't have known the way to Chase's ranch, and even if she had, it was several minutes away by car.

"I saw her on the road."

"The road," Letty repeated, horrified. "She got that far?"

"She was in a panic, and with Lonny gone, she didn't know what else to do."

Letty stared at Chase. "I'm grateful you stopped. Thank you."

Cricket charged into the living room with the glass of water, which was only partially full. Letty assumed the other half had spilled. She planted a soft kiss on her daughter's cheek as a thank-you.

"I think your mother could use a blanket, too," Chase murmured. His mouth was set and obstinate, but for what reason Letty could only speculate. It was unreasonable for him to be angry with her because she'd fainted!

Once more Cricket raced out of the room.

Chase continued to frown at Letty. He seemed to think that if he did that long enough, he'd discover why she'd taken ill. She boldly met his look and did her best to reassure him with a smile, but obviously failed.

Chase closed his eyes, and when he opened them again, the agony that briefly fluttered into his gaze was a shock. He turned away from her as if he couldn't bear to have her look at him.

"Letty, I didn't know what to think when I found

Cricket," he said, and dragged a breath between clenched teeth. "For all I knew you could have been dead."

Motivated by something other than reason, Letty raised her hand to his face, running the tips of her fingers along his tense jaw. "Would you have cared?" she whispered.

"Yes," he cried. "I don't want to, but heaven help me, I do."

He reached for her, kissing her awkwardly, then hungrily, his mouth roving from one side of her face to the other, brushing against her eyes, her cheek, her ears and finally her throat.

They were interrupted by Cricket, who dashed into the room.

"I brought Mommy a blankey," Cricket said. She edged her way between Letty and Chase and draped her yellow knit blanket across Letty's lap.

"Thank you, sweetheart."

Chase rose and paced the floor in front of the sofa. "I'm calling Doc Hanley."

Letty was overcome with panic. She'd purposely avoided the physician, who'd been seeing her family for as long as she could remember. Although she trusted Doc Hanley implicitly, he wasn't a heart specialist, and if she was seen going in and out of his office on a regular basis there might be talk that would filter back to Lonny or Chase and cause them concern.

"Chase," she said, "calling Doc Hanley isn't necessary. I was in the sun too long—that's all. I should've known better."

"You're in the sun every day. Something's wrong. I want you to see a doctor."

"All right," she agreed, thinking fast. "I'll make an appointment, if you want, but I can't today—none of the offices are open."

"I'll drive you to the hospital," he insisted.

"The nearest hospital's an hour from here."

"I don't care."

"Chase, please, I'm a little unsettled, but basically I'm fine. What I need more than anything is some rest. The last thing I want to do is sit in a hot, stuffy truck and ride all the way into Rock Springs so some doctor can tell me I got too much sun."

Chase paced back and forth, clearly undecided.

"I'll just go upstairs and lie down. It's about time for Cricket's nap, anyway," Letty said calmly, although her heart was racing. She really did feel terrible. Dizzy. Disoriented. Nauseous.

Chase wasn't pleased about Letty's proposal, but nodded. "I'll stay here in case you need me later."

"That really isn't necessary," she said again.

He turned and glared at her. "Don't argue with me. I'm not in the mood."

That was obvious. With some effort, although she struggled to conceal it, Letty stood and walked up the stairs. Chase followed her as though he suspected she might not make it. Letty was exhausted by the time she entered her bedroom.

"I'll take a nap and feel totally refreshed in a couple of hours. You wait and see."

"Right," Chase said tersely. As soon as she was lying down, he left.

* * *

Letty sat across the desk from Dr. Faraday the next afternoon. He'd wanted to talk to her after the examination.

"I haven't received your records from your physician in California yet, but I'm expecting them any day," he said.

Letty nodded, making an effort to disguise her uneasiness. As she'd promised Chase, she'd contacted the heart specialist in Rock Springs first thing Monday morning. She'd seen Dr. Faraday the week before and he'd asked that she come in right away. His brooding look troubled her.

"Generally speaking, how are you?"

"Fine." That was a slight exaggeration, but other than being excessively tired and the one fainting spell, she *had* felt healthy most of the time.

Dr. Faraday nodded and made a notation in her file. It was all Letty could do not to stand up and try to read what he'd written. He was a large man, his face dominated by a bushy mustache that reminded Letty of an umbrella. His eyes were piercing, and Letty doubted that much got past him.

"The results from the tests we did last week are in, and I've had a chance to review them. My opinion is that we shouldn't delay surgery much longer. I'll confer with my colleague, Dr. Frederickson, and make my report to the state. I'm going to ask that they put a rush on their approval."

Letty nodded and watched as he lifted his prescription pad from the corner of his desk. "I want you to start taking these pills right away."

"Okay," Letty agreed. "How long will I be in the hospital, Doctor?" Although she tried to appear calm, Letty was frightened. She'd never felt more alone. Her sense of humor, which had helped her earlier, seemed to have deserted her.

"You should plan on being in the hospital and then the convalescent center for up to two weeks," he replied absently, writing out a second prescription.

"Two weeks?" Letty cried. That was far longer than she'd expected.

His eyes met hers. "Is that a problem?"

"Not…exactly." It seemed foolish now, but Letty had automatically assumed that Lonny would be able to watch Cricket for her. He'd be happy to do that, she was confident, if her hospital stay was going to be only a few days. Even with the responsibilities of the ranch, he'd have found a way to look after the five-year-old, maybe hiring a part-time babysitter. True, it would have been an inconvenience for him, but Lonny was family. But two weeks was too long for Letty to even consider asking him.

Lonny and Cricket were just beginning to find their footing with each other. Cricket had accepted him, and Lonny seemed to think that as kids went, his niece was all right. Letty smiled to herself—she didn't want to do anything that would threaten their budding relationship.

A list of people who could possibly watch Cricket flashed through Letty's mind. There were several older women from church who'd been her mother's friends, women Letty would feel comfortable asking. Any one of them would take excellent care of her daughter. Whoever Letty found would have her hands full, though. Cricket had never spent much time away from Letty.

"I'd like you to make an appointment for Thursday," Dr. Faraday said, adding a couple of notes to her file. "See my receptionist before you leave and she'll give you a time."

Letty nodded, chewing on her lower lip. She wondered what she was going to say to Lonny about needing the truck again so soon.

Cricket was waiting for her in the hallway outside Dr. Faraday's office. She sat next to the receptionist and was busy coloring in her activity book. The child looked up and smiled when Letty came out. She placed her crayons neatly back in the box, closed her book and crawled down from the chair, hurrying to Letty's side.

Letty made her appointment for later in the week, then she and Cricket headed for the parking lot.

It was during the long drive home that Letty decided to broach the subject of their being separated.

"Cricket, Mommy may have to go away for a few days."

"Can I go with you?"

"Not this time. Uncle Lonny will be busy with the ranch, so you won't be able to stay with him, either."

Cricket shrugged.

Letty didn't think she'd mind not staying with Lonny. Her brother still hadn't come to appreciate the finer points of watching cartoons.

"Do you remember Mrs. Martin from church?" Letty asked. "She was my mommy's good friend." Dorothy Martin was a dear soul, although she'd aged considerably since her husband's death. Letty knew her mother's friend would agree to care for Cricket until Letty was able to do so herself.

"Does Mrs. Martin have gray hair and sing as bad as Uncle Lonny?"

"That's the one. I was thinking you could stay with her while I'm away."

"Don't want to." Cricket rejected Mrs. Martin without further comment.

"I see." Letty sighed. There were other choices, of course, but they were all women Cricket had met only briefly.

"What about—"

Cricket didn't allow her to finish.

"If you're going away and I can't go with you, then I want to stay with Chase. I bet he'd let me ride Firepower again, and we could make chocolate chip cookies."

Letty should've guessed Chase would be her first choice.

"He'd read me stories like you do and let me blow out the lights at bedtime," Cricket continued. "We'd have lots of fun together. I like Chase better than anyone 'cept you." She paused, then added as extra incentive, "We could sit in church together and everything."

A tight knot formed in Letty's throat. In making her decision to return to Red Springs, she could never have predicted that Cricket would take such a strong and instant liking to Chase Brown.

"Mommy, could I?"

"I'm afraid Chase has to work on his ranch the same way Uncle Lonny does."

"Oh." Cricket sighed in disappointment.

"Think of all the people we've met since we came to live with Uncle Lonny," Letty suggested. "Who do you like best other than Chase?"

Cricket seemed to need time to mull over the question. She crossed her legs and tugged at one pigtail, winding the dark hair around her index finger as she considered this important decision.

"I like the lady who plays the organ second-best."

Joy Fuller was the perfect choice, although Letty was certain Lonny wouldn't take Cricket's preference sitting down. "I like Ms. Fuller, too," she told her daughter. "I'll talk to her. But my going away isn't for sure yet, honey, so there's no need to say anything to anyone. Okay?"

"Is it a surprise?"

"Yes." Letty's fingers tightened on the steering wheel. She hated to mislead Cricket, but she couldn't have her daughter announce to Chase or her brother that she was going away and leaving Cricket behind.

"Oh, goody. I won't tell anyone," she said, pretending to zip her mouth closed.

"It's so nice to see you, Letty," Joy said as she stood in the doorway of her small rental house. "You, too, Cricket." A smile lit up Joy's face. "Your phone call came as a pleasant surprise."

Cricket followed Letty inside.

"I made some iced tea. Would you like some?"

"Please." Letty sat in the compact living room; as always, Cricket was at her side.

"Cricket, I have some Play-Doh in the kitchen if

you'd like to play with that. My second-graders still enjoy it. I've also got some juice just for you."

Cricket looked to her mother and Letty nodded. The child trotted into the kitchen after Joy. Letty could hear them chatting, and although it was difficult to stay where she was, she did so the two of them could become better acquainted.

Joy returned a few minutes later with frosty glasses of iced tea. She set one in front of Letty, then took the chair opposite her.

"Cricket certainly is a well-behaved child. You must be very proud of her."

"Thank you, I am." Letty's gaze fell to her fingers, which were tightly clenched on the glass of iced tea. "I take it you and Lonny have come to some sort of agreement?"

Joy sighed, her shoulders rising reflexively, then sagging with defeat. "To be honest, I think it's best if he and I don't have anything to do with each other. I don't know what it is about your brother that irritates me so much. I mean, last fall we seemed to get along okay. But—and I'm sorry to say this, Letty—he's just so *arrogant.* He acted like I was supposed to be really impressed that he was a rodeo champion back in the day. *And* he kept calling me a hopeless city slicker because I'm from Seattle." She shook her head. "Now we can't even talk civilly to each other."

Letty doubted Joy would believe her if she claimed Lonny was still attracted to her. The problem was that he was fighting it so hard.

"You may find this difficult to believe," she said, "but Lonny's normally a calm, in-control type of guy.

I swear to you, Joy, I've never seen him behave the way he has lately."

"I've known him for almost a year, but I had no idea he was that kind of hothead."

"Trust me, he usually isn't."

"He phoned me last Sunday."

At Letty's obvious surprise, Joy continued, eyes just managing to avoid her guest. "He started in about his stupid truck again. Then he mentioned something about an argument with you and how that was my fault—and then apparently you fainted, but he didn't really explain. Anyway, I hung up on him." She glanced over at Letty. "What happened to you? He sounded upset."

"He was, but mostly he was angry with himself. We got into an argument—which was *not* your fault—and, well, we both said things we didn't mean and immediately regretted. I went outside to work in the garden and...I don't know," she murmured. "The sun must've bothered me, because the next thing I knew, I'd fainted."

"Oh, Letty! Are you all right?"

"I am, thanks." Letty realized she was beginning to get good at exaggerating the state of her health.

"Did you see a doctor?"

"Yes. Everything's under control, so don't worry."

Cricket wandered in from the kitchen with a miniature cookie sheet holding several flat Play-Doh circles. "Mommy, I'm baking chocolate chip cookies for Chase."

"Good, sweetheart. Will you bake me some, too?"

The child nodded, then smiled shyly up at Joy. "Did you ask her, Mommy?"

"Not yet."

Letty's gaze followed Cricket back into the kitchen. She could feel Joy's curiosity, and wished she'd been able to lead into the subject of Cricket's staying with her a little more naturally.

"There's a possibility I'll need to be away for a week or two in the near future," she said, holding the glass with both hands. "Unfortunately I won't be able to take Cricket with me, and I doubt Lonny could watch her for that length of time."

"I wouldn't trust your brother to care for Cricket's *dolls*," Joy said stiffly, then looked embarrassed.

"Don't worry, I don't think I'd feel any differently toward my brother if I were in your shoes," Letty said, understanding her friend's feelings.

"As you were saying?" Joy prompted, obviously disturbed that the subject of Lonny had crept into the conversation.

"Yes," Letty said, and straightened. This wasn't easy; it was a lot to ask of someone she'd only known for a little while. "As I explained, I may have to go away for a couple of weeks, and since I can't leave Cricket with my brother, I'm looking for someone she could stay with while I'm gone."

Joy didn't hesitate for a second. "I'd be more than happy to keep her for you. But there's one problem. I've still got three more weeks of school. I wouldn't be able to take her until the first week of June. Would you need to leave before then?"

"No…I'd make sure of that." For the first time, Letty felt the urge to tell someone about her condition. It would be so good to share this burden with someone she considered a friend, someone who'd calm and reassure her. Someone she trusted.

But Joy was a recent friend, and it seemed wrong to shift the burden onto her shoulders. And if Lonny somehow discovered Letty's secret, he'd be justifiably angry that she'd confided her troubles in someone she barely knew and not her own flesh and blood.

"Letty…"

She looked up then and realized her thoughts had consumed her to the point that she'd missed whatever Joy had been saying. "I'm sorry," she said, turning toward her.

"I was just suggesting that perhaps you could leave Cricket with me for an afternoon soon—give us the opportunity to get better acquainted. That way she won't feel so lost while you're away."

"That would be wonderful."

As if knowing the adults had been discussing her, Cricket came into the living room. "Your chocolate chip cookies are almost cooked, Mommy."

"Thank you, sweetheart. I'm in the mood for something chocolate."

"Me, too," Joy agreed, smiling.

"Mommy will share with you," Cricket stated confidently. "She *loves* chocolate."

All three laughed.

"Since Cricket's doing so well, why don't you leave her here for an hour or two?"

Letty stood. "Cricket?" She looked at her daughter, wanting to be sure the child felt comfortable enough to be here alone with Joy.

"I have to stay," Cricket said. "My cookies aren't finished cooking yet."

"I'd be delighted with the company," Joy said so sincerely Letty couldn't doubt her words. "I haven't got anything planned for the next hour or so, and since you're already here, it would save you a trip into town later on."

"All right," Letty said, not knowing exactly where she'd go to kill time. Of course, she could drive back to the Bar E, but there was nothing for her there. She reached for her purse. "I'll be back...soon."

"Take your time," Joy said, walking her to the door. Cricket came, too, and kissed Letty goodbye with such calm acceptance it tugged at her heart.

Once inside her brother's battered pickup, she drove aimlessly through town. That was when she decided to visit the town cemetery. No doubt her parents' graves had been neglected over the years. The thought saddened her and yet filled her with purpose.

She parked outside the gates and ambled over the green lawn until she arrived at their grave sites. To her surprise they were well maintained. Lonny had obviously been out here recently.

Standing silent, feeling oppressed by an overwhelming sense of loss, Letty bowed her head. Tears gathered in her eyes, but Letty wiped them aside; she hadn't come here to weep. Her visit had been an impromptu one, although the emotions were churning inside her.

"Hi, Daddy," she whispered. "Hi, Mom. I'm back... I tried California, but it didn't work out. I never knew there were so many talented singers in the world." She paused, as though they'd have some comment to make, but there was only silence. "Lonny welcomed me home. He didn't have to, but he did. I suppose you know about my heart...that's what finally convinced me I had to be here."

She waited, not expecting a voice of authority to rain down from the heavens, yet needing something... except she didn't know what.

"What's it like...on the other side?" Letty realized that even asking such a question as if they could answer was preposterous, but after her visit with Dr. Faraday, she'd entertained serious doubts that she'd ever recover. "Don't worry, I don't actually think you're going to tell me. Anyway, I always did like surprises."

Despite her melancholy, Letty smiled. She knelt beside the tombstones and reverently ran the tips of her fingers over the names and dates engraved in the marble. Blunt facts that said so little about their lives and those who'd loved them so deeply.

"I went to the doctor today," she whispered, her voice cracking. "I'm scared, Mom. Remember how you used to comfort me when I was a little girl? I wish I could crawl into your lap now and hear you tell me that everything's going to be all right." With the back of her hand she dashed away the tears that slid unrestrained down her cheeks.

"There's so much I want to live for now, so many things I want to experience." She remembered how she'd joked and kidded with the California doctors about her condition. But the surgery was imminent, and Letty wasn't laughing anymore.

"Mom. Dad." She straightened, coming to her feet. "I know you loved me—never once did I doubt that—

and I loved you with all my heart…damaged though it is," she said with a hysterical laugh. "I wish you were with me now…I need you both so much."

Letty waited a couple of minutes, staring down at the graves of the two people who'd shaped and guided her life with such tender care. A tranquillity came to her then, a deep inner knowledge that if it had been humanly possible, her mother would have thrown both arms around her, hugged her close and given her the assurance she craved.

"I need someone," Letty admitted openly. Her burden was becoming almost more than she could bear. "Could you send me a friend?" she whispered. "Someone I can talk to who'll understand?" Names slipped in and out of her mind. The pastor was a good choice. Dorothy Martin was another.

"Letty?"

At the sound of her name, she turned and looked into Chase's eyes.

Chapter 7

"I saw Lonny's pickup on the road," Chase said, glancing over his shoulder. His hat was tipped back on his head as he studied her, his expression severe. "What are you doing here, Letty?"

She looked down at her parents' graves as a warm, gentle breeze blew over her. "I came to talk to Mom and Dad."

Her answer didn't seem to please him and he frowned. "Where's Cricket?"

"She's with Joy Fuller."

"Joy Fuller." He repeated the name slowly. "Lonny's Joy Fuller?"

"One and the same."

A sudden smile appeared on his face. "Lonny's certainly taken a dislike to that woman, although he was pretty keen on her for a while there."

"Lonny's making an utter fool of himself," Letty said.

"That's easy enough to do," Chase returned grimly. His face tightened. "Did you make an appointment with the doctor like you promised?"

Letty nodded. She'd hoped to avoid the subject, but she should've known Chase wouldn't allow that.

"And?" he barked impatiently. "Did you see him?"

"This afternoon." She would've thought that would satisfy him, but apparently it didn't. If anything, his frown grew darker.

"What did he say?"

"Not to vent my anger in the hot sun," she told him flippantly, then regretted responding to Chase's concern in such a glib manner. He was a friend, perhaps the best she'd ever had, and instead of answering him in an offhand way, Letty should be grateful for his thoughtfulness. Only minutes before she'd been praying for someone with whom she could share her burdens, and then Chase had appeared like someone out of a dream.

He could, in every sense, be the answer to her prayer.

"Chase," she said, moving between the headstones, unsure how to broach the difficult subject. "Have you thought very much about death?"

"No," he said curtly.

Strangely stung by his sharp reaction, she continued strolling, her hands behind her back. "I've thought about it a lot lately," she said, hoping he'd ask her why.

"That's sick, Letty."

"I don't think so," she said, carefully measuring

each word. "Death, like birth, is a natural part of life. It's sunrise and sunset, just the way the song says."

"Is that the reason you're wandering among the tombstones like...like some vampire?"

It took her several minutes to swallow a furious response. Did she need to hit this man over the head before he realized what she was trying to tell him? "Oh, Chase, that's a mean thing to say."

"Do you often stroll through graveyards as if they're park grounds?" he asked, his voice clipped. "Or is this a recent pastime?"

"Recent," she said, smiling at him. She hoped he understood that no matter how much he goaded her, she wasn't going to react to his anger.

"Then may I suggest you snap out of whatever trance you're in and join the land of the living? There's a whole world out there just waiting to be explored."

"But the world isn't always a friendly place. Bad things happen every day. No one said life's fair. I wish it was, believe me, but it isn't."

"Stop talking like that. Wake up, Letty!" He stepped toward her as if he'd experienced a sudden urge to shake her, but if that was the case, he restrained himself.

"I'm awake," she returned calmly, yearning for him to understand that she loved life, but was powerless to control her own destiny. She felt a deep need to prepare him for her vulnerability to death. Now if only he'd listen.

"It's really very lovely here, don't you think?" she asked. "The air is crisp and clear, and there's the faint scent of sage mingled with the wildflowers. Can't you smell it?"

"No."

Letty ignored his lack of appreciation. "The sky is lovely today. So blue… When it's this bright I sometimes think it's actually going to touch the earth." She paused, waiting for Chase to make some kind of response, but he remained resolutely silent. "Those huge white clouds resemble Spanish galleons sailing across the seas, don't they?"

"I suppose."

Her linked hands behind her back, she wandered down a short hill. Chase continued to walk with her, but the silence between them was uneasy. Just when Letty felt the courage building inside her to mention the surgery, he spoke.

"You lied to me, Letty."

His words were stark. Surprised, she turned to him and met his gaze. It was oddly impassive, as if her supposed deceit didn't matter to him, as though he'd come to expect such things from her.

"When?" she demanded.

"Just now. I phoned Doc Hanley's office and they said you hadn't so much as called. You're a liar—on top of everything else."

Letty's breath caught painfully in her throat. The words to prove him wrong burned on her lips. "You don't have any right to check up on me." She took a deep breath. "Nevertheless, I didn't lie to you. I never have. But I'm not going to argue with you, if that's what you're looking for."

"Are you saying Doc Hanley's office lied?"

"I'm not going to discuss this. Believe what you want." She quickened her steps as she turned and headed toward the wrought-iron gates at the cemetery entrance. He followed her until they stood next to the trucks.

"Letty?"

She looked at him. Anger kindled in his eyes like tiny white flames, but Letty was too hurt to appease him with an explanation. She'd wanted to reveal a deep part of herself to this man because she trusted and loved him. She couldn't now. His accusation had ruined what she'd wanted to share.

He reached out and clasped her shoulders. "I need to know. Did you or did you not lie to me?"

The scorn was gone from his eyes, replaced with a pain that melted her own.

"No...I did see a doctor, I swear to you." She held her head at a proud angle, her gaze unwavering, but when she spoke, her voice cracked.

His eyes drifted closed as if he didn't know what to believe anymore. Whatever he was thinking, he didn't say. Instead he pulled her firmly into his embrace and settled his mouth on hers.

A tingling current traveled down her body at his touch. Letty whimpered—angry, hurt, excited, pleased. Still kissing her, Chase let his hands slide down to caress her back, tugging her against him. Her body was already aflame and trembling with need.

Chase held her tightly as he slipped one hand up to tangle in her short curls. His actions were slow, hesitant, as if he was desperately trying to stop himself from kissing her.

"Letty..." he moaned, his breath featherlight against her upturned face. "You make me want you...."

She bowed her head. The desire she felt for him was equally ravenous.

Chase dragged in a heavy breath and expelled it loudly. "I don't want to feel the things I do."

"I know." It was heady knowledge, and Letty took delight in it. She moved against him, craving the feel of his arms around her.

Chase groaned. His mouth found hers once more and he kissed her tentatively, as if he didn't really want to be touching her again, but couldn't help himself. This increased Letty's reckless sensation of power.

He slid his hands up her arms and gripped her shoulders. Letty shyly moved her body against him; unfortunately the loving torment wasn't his alone, and she halted abruptly at the intense heat that surged through her.

A car drove past them, sounding its horn.

Letty had forgotten that they were standing on the edge of the road. Groaning with embarrassment, she buried her face against his heaving chest. Chase's heart felt like a hammer beating against her, matching her own excited pulse.

"Listen to me, Letty," he whispered.

He held her head between his hands and gently lifted her face upward, his breath warm and moist against her own.

"I want you more than I've ever wanted a woman in my life. You want me, too, don't you?"

For a moment she was tempted to deny everything, but she couldn't.

"Don't you?" he demanded. His hands, which were holding her face, were now possessive. His eyes, which had so recently been clouded with passion, were now sharp and insistent.

Letty opened her mouth to reply, but some part of her refused to acknowledge the truth. Her fear was that Chase would find a way to use it against her. He didn't trust her; he'd told her that himself. Desire couldn't be confused with love—at least not between them.

"Don't you?" he questioned a second time.

Knowing he wouldn't free her until she gave him an answer, Letty nodded once.

The instant she did, he released her. "That's all I wanted to know." With that he turned and walked away.

For the three days after her confrontation with Chase, Letty managed to avoid him. When she knew he'd be over at the house, she made a point of being elsewhere. Her thoughts were in chaos, her emotions so muddled and confused that she didn't know what to think or feel toward him anymore.

Apparently Chase was just as perplexed as she was, because he seemed to be avoiding her with the same fervor. Normally he stopped by the house several mornings a week. Not once since they'd met in the cemetery had he shown up for breakfast. Letty was grateful.

She cracked three eggs in a bowl and started whipping them. Lonny was due back in the house any minute and she wanted to have his meal ready when he arrived. Since her argument with her brother, he'd gone out of his way to let her know he appreciated her presence. He appeared to regret their angry exchange as much as Letty did.

The back door opened, and Lonny stepped inside and hung his hat on the peg next to the door. "Looks like we're in for some rain."

"My garden could use it," Letty said absently as she poured the eggs into the heated frying pan, stirring them while they cooked. "Do you want one piece of toast or two?"

"Two."

She put the bread in the toaster. Her back was to her brother when she spoke. "Do you have any plans for today?"

"Nothing out of the ordinary."

She nodded. "I thought you were supposed to see the insurance adjuster about having the fender on your truck repaired."

"It isn't worth the bother," Lonny said, walking to the stove to refill his coffee cup.

"But I thought—"

Lonny had made such a fuss over that minuscule dent in his truck that Letty had assumed he'd want to have it fixed, if for no other reason than to irritate Joy.

"I decided against it," he answered shortly.

"I see." Letty didn't, but that was neither here nor there. She'd given up trying to figure him out when it came to his relationship with Joy Fuller.

"I hate it when you say that," he muttered.

"Say what?" Letty asked, puzzled.

"'I see' in that prim voice, as if you know exactly what I'm thinking."

"Oh."

"There," he cried, slamming down his coffee cup. "You did it again."

"I'm sorry, Lonny. I didn't mean anything by it." She dished up his eggs, buttered the toast and brought his plate to the table.

He glanced at her apologetically when she set his breakfast in front of him, picked up his fork, then hesitated. "If I turn in a claim against Joy, her insurance rates will go up. Right?"

Letty would've thought that would be the least of her brother's concerns. "That's true. She'd probably be willing to pay you something instead. Come to think of it, didn't she offer you fifty dollars to forget the whole thing?"

Lonny's eyes flared briefly. "Yes, she did."

"I'm sure Joy would be happy to give you the money if you'd prefer to handle the situation that way. She wants to be as fair as she can. After all, she admitted from the first that the accident was her fault."

"What else could she do?"

Letty didn't respond.

"I don't dare contact her, though," Lonny said, his voice low.

As she sat down across from him, Letty saw that he hadn't taken a single bite of his eggs. "Why not?"

He sighed and looked away, clearly uncomfortable. "The last time I tried to call her she hung up."

"You shouldn't have blamed her for our argument. That was a ridiculous thing to do. Ridiculous and unfair."

A lengthy pause followed. "I know," Lonny admitted. "I was lashing out at her because I was furious with myself. I was feeling bad enough about saying the things I did to you. Then I found out you fainted soon afterward and I felt like a real jerk. The truth is, I had every intention of apologizing when I got back to the house. But you were upstairs sleeping and Chase was sitting here, madder than anything. He nearly flayed me alive. I guess I was looking for a scapegoat, and since Joy was indirectly involved, I called her."

"Joy wasn't involved at all! Directly *or* indirectly. You just wanted an excuse to call her."

He didn't acknowledge Letty's last comment, but said, "I wish I hadn't done it."

"Not only that," she went on as though he hadn't spoken, "Chase had no right to be angry with you."

"Well, he thought he did." Lonny paused. "Sometimes I wonder about you and Chase. You two have been avoiding each other all week. I mention your name and he gets defensive. I mention him to you and you change the subject. The fact is, I thought that once you got home and settled down, you and Chase might get married."

At those words, Letty did exactly what Lonny said she would. She changed the subject. "Since you won't be taking the truck in for body work, someone needs to tell Joy. Would you like me to talk to her for you?"

Lonny shrugged. "I suppose."

"What do you want me to say?"

Lonny shrugged again. "I don't know. I guess you can say I'm willing to drop the whole insurance thing. She doesn't need to worry about giving me that fifty dollars, either—I don't want her money."

Letty ran one finger along the rim of her coffee cup. "Anything else?"

Her brother hesitated. "I guess it wouldn't do any harm to tell her I said I might've overreacted just a bit the day of the accident, and being the sensitive kind of guy I am, I regret how I behaved.... This, of course, all depends on how receptive she is to my apology."

"Naturally," Letty said, feigning a sympathetic look. "But I'm sure Joy will accept your apology." Letty wasn't at all certain that was true, but she wanted to reassure her brother, who was making great leaps in improving his attitude toward her friend.

Digging his fork into his scrambled eggs, Lonny snorted softly. "Now *that's* something I doubt. Knowing that woman the way I do, I'll bet Joy Fuller demands an apology written in blood. But this is the best she's going to get. You tell her that for me, will you?"

"Be glad to," Letty said.

Lonny took a huge bite of his breakfast, as if he'd suddenly realized how hungry he was. He picked up a piece of toast with one hand and waved it at Letty. "You might even tell her I think she does a good job at church with the organ. But play that part by ear, if you know what I mean. Don't make it sound like I'm buttering her up for anything."

"Right."

"Do you want the truck today?"

"Please." Letty had another doctor's appointment and was leading up to that request herself.

Lonny stood up and carried his plate to the sink. "I'll talk to you this afternoon, then." He put on his hat, adjusted it a couple of times, then turned to Letty and smiled. "You might follow your own advice, you know."

"What are you talking about?"

"You and Chase. I don't know what's going on, but I have a feeling that a word or two from you would patch everything up. Since I'm doing the honorable thing with Joy, I'd think you could do the same with Chase."

With that announcement he was gone.

Letty sat at the table, both hands around the warm coffee mug, while she mulled over Lonny's suggestion. She didn't know what to say to Chase, or how to talk to him anymore.

More than a week had passed since Chase had seen Letty. Each day his mood worsened. Each day he grew more irritable and short-tempered. Even Firepower, who had always sensed his mood and adjusted his own temperament, seemed to be losing patience with him. Chase didn't blame the gelding; he was getting to the point where he hated himself.

Something had to be done.

The day Chase had found Letty wandering through the cemetery, he'd been driving around looking for her. She'd promised him on Sunday that she'd see Doc Hanley. Somehow, he hadn't believed she'd do it. Chase had been furious when he discovered she hadn't seen the doctor. It'd taken him close to an hour to locate Letty. When he did, he'd had to exercise considerable restraint not to blast her for her lack of common sense. She'd fainted, for crying out loud! A healthy person didn't just up and faint. Something was wrong.

But before Chase could say a word, Letty had

started in with that macabre conversation about death and dying. His temper hadn't improved with her choice of subject matter. The old Letty had been too full of life even to contemplate death. It was only afterward, when she was in his arms, that Chase discovered the vibrant woman he'd always known. Only when he was kissing her that she seemed to snap out of whatever trance she was in.

It was as though Letty was half-alive these days. She met his taunts with a smile, refused to argue with him even when he provoked her. Nothing had brought a response from her, with the exception of his kisses.

Chase couldn't take any more of this. He was going to talk to her and find out what had happened to change her from the lively, spirited woman he used to know. And he didn't plan to leave until he had an answer.

When he pulled into the yard, Cricket was the only one he saw. The child was sitting on the porch steps, looking bored and unhappy. She brightened as soon as he came into view.

"Chase!" she called and jumped to her feet.

She ran toward him with an eagerness that grabbed his heart. He didn't know why Cricket liked him so much. He'd done nothing to deserve her devotion. She was so pleased, so excited, whenever she saw him that her warm welcome couldn't help but make him feel... good.

"I'm glad you're here," she told him cheerfully.

"Hello, Cricket. It's nice to see you, too."

She slipped her small hand into his and smiled up at him. "It's been ages and *ages* since you came over to see us. I missed you a whole bunch."

"I know."

"Where've you been all this time? Mommy said I wasn't supposed to ask Uncle Lonny about you anymore, but I was afraid I wouldn't see you again. You weren't in church on Sunday."

"I've been...busy."

The child sighed. "That's what Mommy said." Then, as though suddenly remembering something important, Cricket tore into the house, returning a moment later with a picture that had been colored in with the utmost care. "This is from my book. I made it for you," she announced proudly. "It's a picture of a horsey."

"Thank you, sweetheart." He examined the picture, then carefully folded it and put it in his shirt pocket.

"I made it 'cause you're my friend and you let me ride Firepower."

He patted her head. "Where's your mother?"

"She had to go to Rock Springs."

"Who's watching you?"

Cricket pouted. "Uncle Lonny, but he's not very good at it. He fell asleep in front of the TV, and when I changed the channel, he got mad and told me to leave it 'cause he was watching it. But he had his eyes closed. How can you watch TV with your eyes closed?"

She didn't seem to expect an answer, but plopped herself down and braced her elbows on her knees, her small hands framing her face.

Chase sat down next to her. "Is that why you're sitting out here all by yourself?"

Cricket nodded. "Mommy says I'll have lots of friends to play with when I go to kindergarten, but that's not for months and months."

"I'm sure she's right."

"But you're my friend and so is Firepower. I like Firepower, even if he's a really big horse. Mommy said I could have a horsey someday. Like she did when she was little."

He smiled at the child, fighting down an emotion he couldn't identify, one that kept bobbing to the surface of his mind. He remembered Letty when she was only a few years older than Cricket. They had the same color hair, the same eyes and that same stubborn streak, which Chase swore was a mile wide.

"My pony's going to be the best pony *ever,*" Cricket prattled on, clearly content to have him sitting beside her, satisfied that he was her friend.

It hit Chase then, with an impact so powerful he could hardly breathe. His heart seemed to constrict, burning within his chest. The vague emotion he'd been feeling was unmistakable now. Strong and unmistakable. He loved this little girl. He didn't *want* to love Cricket, didn't want to experience this tenderness, but the child was Letty's daughter. And he loved Letty. In the last few weeks he'd been forced to admit that nine long years hadn't altered his feelings toward her.

"Chase—" Lonny stepped outside and joined them on the back porch. "When did you get here?"

"A few minutes ago." He had trouble finding his voice. "I came over to talk to Letty, but she's not here."

"No, she left a couple of hours ago." He checked his watch, frowning as he did. "I don't know what time to expect her back."

"Did she say where she was going?"

Lonny glanced away, his look uncomfortable. "I

have no idea what's going on with that woman. I wish I did."

"What do you mean?" Chase knew his friend well enough to realize Lonny was more than a little disturbed. "She's been needing the truck all week. She's always got some errand or another. I don't need it that much myself, so I don't mind. But then yesterday I noticed she's been putting a lot of miles on it. I asked her why, but she got so defensive and closemouthed we nearly had another fight."

"So did you find out where she's going?"

"Rock Springs," Lonny said shortly. "At least, that's what she claims."

"Why? What's in Rock Springs?"

Lonny shrugged. "She never did say."

"Mommy goes to see a man," Cricket interjected brightly. "He looks like the one on TV with the mustache."

"The one on TV with the mustache," Lonny repeated, exchanging a blank stare with Chase. "Who knows what she means by that?"

"He's real nice, too," Cricket went on to explain patiently. "But he doesn't talk to me. He just talks to Mommy. Sometimes they go in a room together and I have to wait outside, but that's all right 'cause I work in my book."

Lonny's face tensed as he looked at Chase again. "I'm sure that isn't the way it sounds," he murmured.

"Why should I care what she does," Chase lied. "I don't feel a thing for her. I haven't in years."

"Right," Lonny returned sarcastically. "The problem is, you never could lie worth a damn."

Chapter 8

The arrival of Letty's first welfare check had a curious effect on her. She brought in the mail, sat down at the kitchen table and carefully examined the plain beige envelope. Tears filled her eyes, then crept silently down her face. Once she'd been so proud, so independent, and now she was little more than a charity case, living off the generosity of taxpayers.

Lonny came in the back door and wiped his feet on the braided rug. "Mail here?" he asked impatiently.

Her brother had been irritated with her for the past couple of weeks without ever letting her know exactly why. Letty realized his displeasure was connected to her trips into Rock Springs, and her secrecy about them, but he didn't mention them again. Although he hadn't said a word, she could feel his annoyance every time they were together. More than once over the past few days, Letty had toyed with the idea of telling Lonny about her heart condition, but whenever she thought of approaching him, he'd look at her with narrow, disapproving eyes.

Without waiting for her to respond, Lonny walked over to the table and sorted through the bills, flyers and junk mail.

Letty stood and turned away from him. She wiped her cheeks, praying that if he did notice her tears he wouldn't comment.

"Mommy!" Cricket crashed through the back door, her voice high with excitement. "Chase is here on Firepower and he's got another horsey with him. Come and look." She was out the door again in an instant.

Letty smiled, tucked the government check in her pocket and followed her daughter outside. Sure enough, Chase was riding down the hillside on his gelding, holding the reins of a second horse, a small brown-and-white pinto trotting obediently behind the bay.

"Chase! Chase!" Cricket stood on the top step, jumping up and down and frantically waving both arms.

Chase slowed his pace once he reached the yard. Lonny joined his sister, trying to hide a smile. Bemused, Letty stared at him. The last time she could remember seeing him with a silly grin like that, she'd been ten years old and he was suffering through his first teenage crush.

Unable to wait a second longer, Cricket ran out to greet her friend. Smiling down at the child, Chase lowered his arms and hoisted her into the saddle beside him. Letty had lost count of the times Chase had "just happened" to stop by with Firepower in the past few weeks. Cricket got as excited as a game show winner whenever he was around. He'd taken her riding more than once. He was so patient with the five-year-old, so gentle. The only time Chase had truly laughed in Letty's presence was when he was with her daughter—and Cricket treasured every moment with her hero.

In contrast, Letty's relationship with Chase had deteriorated to the point that they'd become, at best, mere acquaintances. Chase went out of his way to avoid talking to her. It was as if their last meeting in the cemetery, several weeks before, had killed whatever love there'd ever been between them.

Letty watched from the porch as Chase slid out of the saddle and onto the ground, then lifted Cricket down. He wore the same kind of silly grin as Lonny, looking exceptionally pleased with himself.

"Well, what do you think?" Lonny asked, rocking back on his heels, hands in his pockets. He seemed almost as excited as Cricket.

"About what?" Letty felt as if everyone except her was in on some big secret.

Lonny glanced at her. "Chase bought the pony for Cricket."

"What?" Letty exploded.

"It's a surprise," Lonny whispered.

"You're telling me! Didn't it cross his mind— or yours—to discuss the matter with *me?* I'm her mother... I should have some say in this decision, don't you think?"

For the first time, Lonny revealed signs of uneasiness. "Actually, Chase did bring up the subject with me, and I'm the one who told him it was okay. After all, I'll be responsible for feeding it and paying the vet's bills, for that matter. I assumed you'd be as thrilled as Cricket."

"I am, but I wish one of you had thought to ask me first. It's…it's common courtesy."

"You're not going to make a federal case out of this, are you?" Lonny asked, his gaze accusing. "Chase is just doing something nice for her."

"I know," she sighed. But that wasn't the issue.

Chase and Cricket were standing next to the pony when Letty approached them in the yard. Apparently Chase had just told her daughter the pony now belonged to her, because Cricket threw her arms around Chase's neck, shouting with glee. Laughing, Chase twirled her in a circle, holding her by the waist. Cricket's short legs flew out and she looked like a tiny top spinning around and around.

Letty felt like an outsider in this touching scene, although she made an effort to smile and act pleased. Perhaps Cricket sensed Letty's feelings, because as soon as she was back on the ground, she hurried to her mother's side and hugged her tightly.

"Mommy, did you see Jennybird? That's the name of my very own pony."

Chase walked over and placed his hands on the little girl's shoulders. "You don't object, do you?" he asked Letty.

How could she? "Of course not. It's very thoughtful of you, Chase." She gazed down at her daughter and restrained herself from telling him she wished he'd consulted her beforehand. "Did you thank him, sweetheart?"

"Oh, yes, a hundred million, zillion times."

Letty turned back to the porch, fearing that if she stood there any longer, watching the two of them, she'd start to weep. The emotions she felt disturbed her. Crazy as it seemed, the most prominent one bordered on jealousy. How she yearned for Chase to look at her with the same tenderness he did Cricket. Imagine being envious of her own daughter!

Chase didn't hide his affection for the child. In the span of a few weeks, the pair had become great friends, and Letty felt excluded, as if she were on the outside looking in. Suddenly she couldn't bear to stand there anymore and pretend everything was fine. As unobtrusively as possible, she walked back to the house. She'd almost reached the door when Chase stopped her.

"Letty?"

She turned to see him standing at the bottom of the steps, a frown furrowing his brow.

"You dropped this." He extended the plain envelope to her.

The instant she realized what it was, Letty was mortified. Chase stood below her, holding out her welfare check, his face distorted with shock and what she was sure must be scorn. When she took the check, his eyes seemed to spark with questions. Before he could ask a single one, she whirled around and raced into the house.

It shouldn't have surprised Letty that she couldn't sleep that night, although she seemed to be the only member of the family with that problem. After all the excitement with Jennybird, Cricket had fallen asleep almost immediately after dinner. Lonny had been snoring softly when Letty had dressed and tiptoed past his bedroom on her way downstairs.

Now she sat under the stars, her knees under her chin, on the hillside where she'd so often met Chase when they were young. Chase had listened to her talk about her dreams and all the wonderful things in store for her. He'd held her close and kissed her and believed in her and with her.

That secure feeling, that sense of being loved, had driven Letty back to this spot now. There'd been no place else for her to go. She felt more alone than ever, more isolated—cut off from the people she loved, who loved her. She was facing the most difficult problem of her life and she was doing it utterly alone.

Letty knew she should be pleased with the unexpected change in Chase's attitude toward Cricket… and she was. It was more than she'd ever expected from him, more than she'd dared to hope. And yet, she longed with all her heart for Chase to love *her*.

But he didn't. That was a fact he'd made abundantly clear.

It was hard to be depressed out here, Letty mused as she studied the spectacular display in the heavens. The stars were like frosty jewels scattered across black velvet. The moon was full and brilliant, a madcap adventurer in a heaven filled with like-minded wanderers.

Despite her low spirits, Letty found she was smiling. So long ago, she'd sat under the same glittering moon, confident that nothing but good things would ever come into her life.

"What are you doing here?"

The crisp voice behind her startled Letty. "Hello, Chase," she said evenly, refusing to turn around. "Are you going to order me off your land?"

Chase had seen Letty approach the hillside from the house. He'd decided the best tactic was to ignore her. She'd leave soon enough. Only she hadn't. For more than an hour she'd sat under the stars, barely moving. Unable to resist anymore, he'd gone over to the hill, without knowing what he'd say or do.

"Do you want me to leave?" she asked. He hadn't answered her earlier question.

"No," he answered gruffly.

His reply seemed to please her and he felt her tension subside. She relaxed, clasped her bent knees and said, "I haven't seen a night this clear in...forever." Her voice was low and enticing. "The stars look like diamonds, don't they?"

They did, but Chase didn't respond. He shifted his weight restlessly as he stood behind her, gazing up at the heavens, too.

"I remember the last time I sat on this hill with you, but...but that seems a million years ago now."

"It was," he said brusquely.

"That was the night you asked me to marry you."

"We were both young and foolish," he said, striving for a flippant air. He would've liked Letty to believe the ridiculous part had been in *wanting* her for his wife, but the truth was, he'd hoped with everything in him that she'd consent. Despite all the heartbreak, he felt the same way this very moment.

To his surprise, Letty laughed softly. "Now we're both older and wiser, aren't we?"

"I can't speak for anyone but myself." Before he was even conscious of moving, Chase was on the ground, sitting next to her, his legs stretched out in front of him.

"I wish I knew then what I do now," she continued. "If, by some miracle, we were able to turn back the clock to that night, I'd like you to know I'd jump at your proposal."

A shocked silence followed her words. Chase wished he could believe her, but he couldn't.

"You were after diamonds, Letty, and all I had to offer you was denim."

"But the diamonds were here all along," she whispered, staring up at the stars.

Chase closed his eyes to the pain that squeezed his heart. He hadn't been good enough for her then, and he wasn't now. He didn't doubt for an instant that she was waiting to leave Red Springs. When the time came she'd run so fast his head would spin. In fact, he didn't know what was keeping her here now.

The crux of the problem was that he didn't trust Letty. He couldn't—not anymore, not since he'd learned she was seeing some man in Rock Springs. Unfortunately it wasn't easy to stop caring for her. But in all the years he'd cherished Letty, the only thing his love had gotten him had been pain and heartache.

When she'd first come back to Wyoming, he'd carefully allowed himself to hope. He'd dreamed that they'd find a way to turn back time, just as she'd said, and discover a life together. But in the past few weeks she'd proved to him over and over how impossible that was.

Chase's gut twisted with the knowledge. He'd done everything he could to blot her out of his life. In the beginning, when he'd recognized his feelings for Cricket, he'd thought he would fight for Letty's love, show her how things could change. But could they really? All he could offer her was a humble life on a cattle ranch— exactly what he'd offered her nine years ago. Evidently someone else had given her something better. She'd fallen for some bastard in California, someone unworthy of her love, and now, apparently she was doing it again, blatantly meeting another man. Good riddance, then. The guy with the mustache was welcome to her. All Chase wanted was for her to get out of his life, because the pain of having her so close was more than he could stand.

"I think Cricket will remember today as long as she lives," Letty said, blithely unaware of his thoughts. "You've made her the happiest five-year-old in the world."

He didn't say anything; he didn't want to discuss Cricket. The little girl made him vulnerable to Letty. Once he'd lowered his guard, it was as if a dam of love had broken. He didn't know what he'd do when Letty moved away and took the little girl with her.

"She thinks you're the sun and the moon," Letty said in a way that suggested he need not have done a thing for Cricket to worship him.

"She's a sweet kid." That was the most he was willing to admit.

"Jason reminded me of you." She spoke so softly it was difficult to make out her words.

"I beg your pardon?"

"Jason was Cricket's father."

That man was the last person Chase wanted to hear about, but before he could tell Letty so, she continued in a voice filled with pain and remembered humiliation.

"He asked me out for weeks before I finally accepted. I'd written you and asked you to join me in California, and time and again you turned me down."

"You wanted me to be your manager! I'm a rancher. What did I know about the music business?"

"Nothing…I was asking the impossible," she said, her voice level, her words devoid of blame. "It was ridiculous—I realize that now. But I was so lonely for you, so lost."

"Apparently you found some comfort."

She let the gibe pass, although he saw her flinch and knew his words had hit their mark. He said things like that to hurt her, but the curious thing was, *he* suffered, too. He hurt himself as much as he hurt Letty, maybe more.

"He took me to the best restaurants in town, told me everything I wanted to hear. I was so desperate to believe him that a few inconsistencies didn't trouble me. He pretended to be my friend, and I needed one so badly. He seemed to share my dream the way you always had. I couldn't come back to Wyoming a nobody. You understand that, don't you?"

Chase didn't give her an answer and she went on without waiting for one.

"I was still chasing my dreams, but I was so lonely they were losing their appeal.

"I never planned to go so far with Jason, but it happened, and for days afterward I was in shock. I was—"

"Letty, stop, I don't want to hear this." Her relationship with Cricket's father was a part of her life he wanted to remove completely from his mind.

Letty ignored him, her voice shaky but determined. "Soon afterward I found out I was pregnant. I wanted to crawl into a hole and die, but that wasn't the worst part. When I told Jason, he misunderstood... He seemed to think I wanted him to marry me. But I didn't. I told him because, well, because he was Cricket's father. That's when I learned he was married. *Married.* All that time and he'd had a wife."

"Stop, Letty. I'm the last person you should be telling this to. In fact, I don't want to hear any of it," Chase shouted. He clenched his fists in impotent rage, hating the man who'd used and deceived Letty like this.

"It hurts to talk about it, but I feel I have to. I want you to know that—"

"Whatever you have to say doesn't matter anymore."

"But, Chase, it does, because as difficult as you may find this to believe, I've always loved you...as much then as I do now."

"Why didn't you come home when you found out you were pregnant?"

"How could I have? Pregnant and a failure, too. Everyone expected me to make a name for Red Springs. I was so ashamed, so unhappy, and there was nowhere to go."

She turned away and Chase saw her wipe the tears from her eyes. He ached to hold and comfort her, his heart heavy with her grief, but he refused to make himself vulnerable to her again. She spoke of loving him, but she didn't mean it. She couldn't, not when there was someone else in her life.

"What changed your mind?" he asked. "What made you decide to come back now?"

Several minutes passed, far longer than necessary to answer a simple question. Obviously something had happened that had brought her running back to the Bar E when she'd managed to stay away all those years. Something traumatic.

"I suppose it was a matter of accepting defeat," she finally said. "In the years after Cricket's birth, the determination to succeed as a singer left me. I dabbled in the industry, but mainly I did temp work. As the years passed, I couldn't feel ashamed of Cricket. She's the joy of my life."

"But it took you nine years, Letty. *Nine* years."

She looked up at him, her eyes filled with pain, clearly revealed in the moonlight that seemed as bright as day.

The anger was still with him. The senselessness of it all—a dream that had ruined their lives. And for what? "I loved you once," he said starkly, "but I don't now, and I doubt I ever will again. You taught me that the only thing love brings is heartache."

She lowered her head and he saw new tears.

"I could hate you for the things you've done," he said in a low, angry voice.

"I think you do," she whispered.

Chase hadn't known what to expect, but it wasn't this calm, almost humble acceptance of his resentment.

Maybe the proud, confident Letty was gone forever, but he couldn't believe that was true. Every once in a while, he saw flashes of the old Letty. Just enough to give him hope.

"I *don't* hate you, Letty," he murmured in a tormented whisper. "I wish I could, but I can't...I can't."

Chase intended to kiss her once, then release her and send her back to the house. It was late, and they both had to get up early. But their kiss sparked, then caught fire, leaping to sudden brilliance. She sighed, and the sound was so soft, so exciting, that Chase knew he was lost even before he pressed her against the cool, fragrant grass.

Lying down beside her, Chase felt helpless, caught in a maze of love and desire. He tried to slow his breathing, gain control of his senses, but it was impossible, especially when Letty raised her hand and stroked his shoulders through the fabric of his shirt, then glided her fingers around to his back.

Chase felt engulfed by his love for her, lost, drowning, and it didn't matter, nothing did, except the warm feeling of her beside him, longing for him as desperately as he longed for her.

Again and again he kissed her, and when he paused to collect his senses, she eased her hand around his neck and gently brought his mouth back to hers.

Their need for each other was urgent. Fierce. Chase couldn't get enough of her. He kissed her eyes, her cheeks, her forehead and tenderly nuzzled her throat.

Eventually he released her and she sagged breathlessly against him. No other woman affected him the way Letty did. Why her? Of all the women in the world, why did he have to love *her*? For years she'd rewarded his loyalty with nothing but pain.

But it wasn't distress he was feeling now. The pleasure she brought him was so intense he wanted to cry out with it. He kissed her and her soft, gasping breaths mingled with his own. Chase was shaking and he couldn't seem to stop—shaking with anticipation and desire, shaking with the resolve not to make love to her, not to claim her completely, because once he did, he'd never be able to let her go. He wanted her, but he needed her to love him as much as he loved her. A love that came from their hearts and minds—not just the passionate dictates of their bodies.

His jaw tight with restraint, he closed his hands around hers and gently lifted her away from him.

"Chase?" she whispered, perplexed.

If she was confused, it was nothing compared to the emotions churning inside him. He'd always loved her, still did, yet he was turning her away again, and it was agonizing. She wanted him, and she'd let him know that. But he wouldn't make love to her. Not now.

"Letty...no."

She bowed her head. "You...don't want to make love to me?" she whispered tremulously. "Just one time..."

"No," he told her bluntly. "It wouldn't be enough."

He stroked her hair and kissed her gently. Then he realized the true significance of what she'd said. She only wanted him to love her *one time.* "You're going away, aren't you, Letty?" He felt her tense in his arms before her startled gaze found his.

"Who told you?"

Without responding, he pushed her away from him and stood.

"Chase?"

"No one told me," he said, the love and tenderness he felt evaporating in the heat of her betrayal. "I guessed."

Chapter 9

"What happened with you and Letty last night?" Lonny asked Chase early the next morning. They'd planned on repairing the fence that separated their property lines.

"What's between Letty and me is none of your business."

Lonny paused to consider this while rubbing the side of his jaw. "Normally I'd agree with you, but my sister looked really bad this morning. To be honest, I haven't been particularly pleased with her myself lately."

Lonny followed him to the pile of split cedar fence posts. "When Cricket mentioned Letty meeting some man in Red Springs," he continued, "I was madder 'n anything. But after all the fuss I made about her interfering in my life, I didn't think I had the right to ask her a whole lot of questions."

"Then why start with me now?" After that, Chase ignored his friend and loaded the posts into the back of his pickup. His mood hadn't improved since he'd left Letty only a few hours ago.

"I'm sticking my nose where it doesn't belong because you're the best friend I've got."

"Then let's keep it that way." Chase wiped the perspiration from his brow, then went back to heaving posts, still trying to pretend Lonny hadn't introduced the subject of his sister.

"You're as bad as she is," Lonny shouted.

"Maybe I am."

Lonny jerked on his gloves and walked toward the pile of wood. He pulled one long piece free, balanced it on his shoulder and headed toward the truck.

"I don't think she slept all night," Lonny muttered.

It was difficult for Chase to feel any sympathy when he hadn't, either.

"I got downstairs this morning and she was sitting in the kitchen, staring into space. I swear there were enough damp tissues on that table to insulate the attic."

"What makes you think I had anything to do with Letty crying?"

"Because she more or less told me so—well, less rather than more," Lonny muttered, shaking his head. "She wouldn't say a word at first, mind you—she's as tight-lipped as you are, but harder to reason with, Letty being a woman and all."

"Listen, if your sister wants to shed a few tears, that's her concern. Not mine. Not yours. Understand?"

Lonny tipped back the rim of his hat. "Can't say I do. Look, Chase, I know you're furious at me for butt-ing in, and I don't blame you. But the least you can do is hear me out."

"I'm a busy man, Lonny, and I'd appreciate it if you kept your thoughts to yourself."

Lonny disregarded his suggestion. "Like I said, I don't know what happened between you, but—"

"How many times do I have to tell you? It's none of your business."

"It is if it's hurting my sister," Lonny said darkly. "And she's hurting plenty."

"That's her problem." Chase had to take care of himself, protect his own heart; he couldn't worry about hers, or so he told himself.

"Why don't you talk to her?" Lonny was saying.

"What do you expect me to say? Are you going to tell me that, too? I respect you, Lonny, but I'm telling you right now to butt out. What's between Letty and me doesn't have anything to do with you." It would be a shame to ruin a lifetime friendship because of Letty, but Chase wasn't about to let Lonny Ellison direct his actions toward her.

They worked together for the next few hours without exchanging another word. Neither seemed willing to break the icy silence. They were repairing the fence, replacing the rotting posts with new ones. Normally, a day like that was an opportunity to joke and have a little fun. Today, it seemed, they could barely tolerate each other.

"I'm worried about her," Lonny said when they broke for lunch. He stared at his roast beef sandwich, then took a huge bite, quickly followed by another.

Chase sighed loudly. "Are you back to talking about

Letty again?" Although she hadn't left his mind for an instant, he didn't want to discuss her.

"I can't help it!" Lonny shouted as he leaped to his feet and threw the remains of his lunch on the ground with such force that bits of apple flew in several directions. "Be mad at me if you want, Chase. Knock me down if it'll make you feel better. But I can't let you do this to Letty. She's been hurt enough."

"That isn't my fault!"

"I've never seen her like this—as if all the life's gone out of her. She sits and stares into space with a look that's so pathetic it rips your heart out. Cricket started talking to her this morning and she hardly noticed. You know that's not like Letty."

"She's leaving," Chase shouted, slamming his own lunch against the tree. "Just like she did before—she's walking away. It nearly destroyed me the first time, and I'm not letting her do that to me again."

"Leaving?" Lonny cried. "What do you mean? Did she tell you that herself?"

"Not exactly. I guessed."

"Well, it's news to me. She enrolled Cricket in kindergarten the other day. That doesn't sound like she's planning to move."

"But…" Chase's thoughts were in chaos. He'd assumed that Letty would be leaving; she'd certainly given him that impression. In fact, she'd said so—hadn't she?

"Would it be so difficult to ask her directly?" Lonny said. "We've repaired all the fence we're going to manage today. Come to the house and ask her point-blank.

Letty doesn't lie. If she's planning to leave Red Springs, she'll admit it."

Chase expelled his breath forcefully. He might as well ask her, since Lonny wasn't going to quit bugging him until he did. And yet...

"Will you do that, at least?" Lonny urged.

"I..." Indecision tore at Chase. He didn't want any contact with Letty; he was still reeling from their last encounter. But he'd never seen Lonny behave like this. He was obviously worried about Letty. It wasn't typical of Lonny to get involved in another man's business and that alone was a more convincing argument than anything he'd said.

"You're driving me back to the house, aren't you?" Lonny asked matter-of-factly.

"What about Destiny?"

"I'll pick him up later."

Lonny said this casually, as if he often left his horse at Spring Valley. As far as Chase could remember, he'd never done so in all the years they'd been friends and neighbors.

"All right, I'll ask her," Chase agreed, but reluctantly. He'd do it, if for nothing more than to appease Lonny, although Chase wanted this issue with Letty cleared up. From what he remembered, she'd made her intentions obvious. Yet why she'd enrolled Cricket in kindergarten—which was several months away—was beyond him. It didn't make sense.

Lonny muttered something under his breath as he climbed into the cab of the truck.

The first thing Chase noticed when he rolled into the yard at Lonny's place was that his friend's battered pickup was missing. He waited outside while Lonny hurried into the kitchen.

"She's not here," Lonny said when he returned, holding a note. "She's gone into town to see Joy Fuller."

Chase frowned. Now that he'd made the decision to confront Letty, he was disappointed about the delay. "I'll ask her another time," he said.

"No." Lonny had apparently sensed Chase's frustration. "I mean...I don't think it would do any harm to drive to Joy's. I've been wanting to talk to her, anyway, and this business with Letty gives me an excuse."

"You told me it was completely over. What possible reason could you have to talk to her?"

Lonny was already in the truck. Chase couldn't help noticing the color that tinged his face. "I might've been a bit...hasty. She might not have a sense of humor, but if Letty thinks she's okay, maybe I should give her another chance."

"Well, she is cute. But does she want to give *you* another chance?"

Lonny swallowed and glanced out the window. He didn't answer Chase's question—but then, how could he? Whether or not Joy would be willing to get involved with him again was debatable. Chase suspected Lonny was a lot more interested in Joy than he'd let on; he also suspected Joy might not feel quite the same way.

"Take a right at the next corner," Lonny said as they entered town. "Her house is the first one on the left."

Chase parked under the row of elms. "I'll wait here," he said abruptly.

Lonny got out of the truck and hesitated before he shut the door. "That might not be such a good idea."

"Why not?"

"Well, I'm not sure if Joy's going to talk to me. And what about Letty? Don't you want to see her?"

Chase sighed. Now that he'd had time to think about it, running into town to find Letty wasn't that brilliant a plan.

"Come with me, okay?" Lonny said. "That way Joy might not throw me out the second she sees me."

Sighing loudly, Chase left the truck, none too pleased by any of this. He accompanied Lonny to Joy Fuller's door and watched in surprise as Lonny licked his fingertips and smoothed down the sides of his hair before ringing the bell. It was all Chase could do not to comment.

Cricket answered the door. "Hi, Uncle Lonny. Hi, Chase." She whirled around and shouted over her shoulder. "Joy, it's my uncle Lonny and Chase! You remember Chase, don't you? He's my very best friend in the whole world." Then she ran back into the house.

A minute or so passed before Joy came to the door, Cricket on her heels.

"Yes?" she said stiffly.

She wore a frilly apron tied around her waist, and traces of flour dusted her nose. She'd obviously been baking, and knowing Cricket, it was probably chocolate chip cookies.

Lonny jerked the hat from his head. "We were wondering…me and Chase, my neighbor here, if it would be convenient to take a moment of your time."

Chase had never heard his friend more tongue-tied. Lonny made it sound as though they were old-fashioned snake oil salesmen, come to pawn their wares.

"We can't seem to talk to each other without yelling, Mr. Ellison," Joy returned. Her hands were neatly clasped in front of her, and her gaze was focused somewhere in the distance.

"I'd like to talk to Letty," Chase said. The way things were going, it could be another half hour before anyone learned the reason for their visit. Not that he actually knew what his friend planned to say to Joy—or if Lonny had even figured it out himself.

"Mommy's gone," Cricket piped up.

"She left a few minutes ago," Joy explained.

"Did she say where she was going?"

"No…but I'm sure you can catch her if it's important."

"Go, man," Lonny said, poking his elbow into Chase's ribs. "I'll stay here—that is, if Miss Fuller has no objections."

"*Ms*. Fuller," Joy corrected, her eyes narrowing.

"*Ms*. Fuller," Lonny echoed.

"You can stay, but only if you promise you won't insult me in my own home. Because I'm telling you right now, Lonny Ellison, I won't put up with it."

"I'll do my best."

"That may not be good enough," she said ominously.

"Which way did Letty go?" Chase demanded, decidedly impatient with the pair.

"Toward downtown," Joy said, pointing west. "You shouldn't have any trouble finding her. She's driving that piece of junk Mr..Ellison seems so fond of."

For a moment Lonny looked as if he'd swallowed a grapefruit. His face flamed red, he swallowed hard and it was obvious he was doing everything in his power not to let loose with a blistering response. His efforts were promptly rewarded with a smile from Joy.

"Very good, Mr. Ellison. You've passed the test." She stepped aside to let him enter.

"I won't be long," Chase told them.

Lonny repeatedly twisted the brim of his hat. "Take your time," he muttered. "But go!"

Chase didn't need any more incentive and ran toward his pickup. As soon as the engine roared to life, he shifted gears and swerved out into the traffic, such as it was.

Red Springs's main street was lined with small businesses that had diagonal parking in front. Chase could determine at a single glance that Lonny's truck wasn't in sight. He drove the full length of the town and down a couple of side streets, but she wasn't there, either.

Mystified, he parked and stood outside his truck, looking down Main Street in both directions. Where could she possibly have gone?

Letty came out of Dr. Faraday's office and sat in Lonny's truck for several minutes before she started the engine. After waiting all these weeks, after stringing out the medical and financial details of her life as though they were laundry on a clothesline—after all this, she should feel some sort of release knowing that the surgery was finally scheduled.

But she didn't.

Instead she experienced an overwhelming sadness. Tears burned in her eyes, but she held her head high and drove toward the freeway that would take her back to Red Springs. Now that everything had been cleared with the doctor and the state, Letty felt free to explain what was wrong with her to her brother. She'd leave it to him to tell Chase—if he wanted.

Chase. Quickly she cast all thoughts of him aside, knowing they'd only bring her pain.

A few miles out of town, Letty saw another truck in her rearview mirror, several cars back. Her first reaction was that someone was driving a model similar to the one Chase had.

Not until the truck started weaving in and out of traffic in an effort to catch up with her did Letty realize it *was* Chase's.

Why was he following her? All she could think was that something terrible must have happened… Cricket! Oh, no, it had to be Cricket.

Letty pulled to the side of the road.

Chase was right behind her.

Shutting off the engine, she climbed out and saw him leap from his vehicle and come running toward her.

"Letty. Letty." He wrapped his arms around her, holding her with a tenderness she thought he could no longer feel.

She loosened his grip enough to raise her head. "Is anything wrong with Cricket?" she asked urgently.

He frowned. "No," he said before he kissed her with a thoroughness that left her weak and clinging.

"Then what are you doing here?"

Chase closed his eyes briefly. "That's a long story. Letty, we've got to talk."

She broke free from his embrace. "I don't think we can anymore. Every time we get close to each other, we end up arguing. I know I hurt you, Chase, but I don't know how much longer I can stand being hurt back. After last night, I decided it was best if we didn't see each other again."

"You make us sound as bad as Lonny and Joy."

"Worse."

"It doesn't have to be that way."

"I don't think we're capable of anything else," she whispered. "Not anymore."

His eyes blazed into hers. "Letty, I *know.*"

Chase wasn't making any sense. If he knew they were incapable of sustaining a relationship, then why had he been driving like a madman to catch her? Frankly, she wasn't in the mood for this. All she wanted to do was get Cricket and go home.

Chase dropped his arms and paced in front of her. "The day you fainted in the garden, I should've figured it out. For weeks before, Lonny had been telling me how tired you were all the time, how fragile you'd become." He shook his head. "I thought it was because you were depressed and California had spoiled you."

"It did. I'm a soft person, unaccustomed to anything resembling hard work."

Chase ignored her sarcasm. "Then that day in the cemetery…you tried to tell me, didn't you?" But he didn't allow her to answer his question. "You started talking about life and death, and all I could do was get angry with you because I thought you'd lied. I wasn't even listening. If I had been, I would've heard what you were trying to tell me."

Tears blurred her vision as she stood silent and unmoving before him.

"It's the reason you dragged Mary Brandon over to the house for dinner that night, isn't it?" Again he didn't wait for her response. "You figured that if Lonny was married and anything happened to you, Cricket would have a secure home."

"Not exactly," she managed. In the beginning her thoughts had leaned in that direction. But she wasn't the manipulative type, and it had soon become obvious that Lonny wanted nothing to do with her schemes.

Chase placed his hands on her shoulders. "Letty, I saw Dr. Faraday." A hint of a smile brushed the corners of his mouth. "I wanted to go over to the man and hug him."

"Chase, you're still not making any sense."

"Cricket told me that when you came to Rock Springs, you visited a man with a mustache—a man who looked like someone on TV."

"When did she tell you that?"

"Weeks ago. But more damning was that she claimed you went into a room together, and she had to stay outside and wait for you."

"Oh, dear…"

"You can imagine what Lonny and I thought."

"And you believed it?" It seemed that neither Chase nor her brother knew her. Both seemed willing to condemn her on the flimsiest evidence. If she *were* meeting a man, the last person she'd take with her was Cricket. But apparently that thought hadn't so much as entered their minds.

"We didn't know what to believe," Chase answered.

"But you automatically assumed the worst?"

Chase looked properly chagrined. "I know it sounds

bad, but there'd been another man in your life before. How was I to know the same thing wasn't happening again?"

"How were you to know?" Letty echoed, slumping against the side of the truck. "How were you to know?" she repeated in a hurt whisper. "What kind of person do you think I am?"

"Letty, I'm sorry."

She covered her eyes and shook her head.

"From the moment you returned, everything's felt wrong. For a while I thought my whole world had been knocked off its axis. Nothing I did seemed to balance it. Today I realized it wasn't my world that was off-kilter, but yours, and I couldn't help feeling the effects."

"You're talking in riddles," she said.

Once more he started pacing, running his fingers through his hair. "Tell me what's wrong. Please. I want to know—I need to know."

"It's my heart," she whispered.

He nodded slowly. "I figured that's what it had to be. Dr. Faraday's specialty was the first thing I noticed when I saw you walk into his office."

"You saw me walk into his office?"

His gaze skirted away from hers. "I followed you to Rock Springs." He continued before she could react. "I'm not proud of that, Letty. Lonny convinced me that you and I needed to talk. After last night, we were both hurting so badly…and I guess I wasn't the best company this morning. Lonny and I went back to the ranch and found your note. From there, we went to Joy's place and she said you'd just left and were heading into town. I drove there and couldn't find you anywhere. That was when I realized you'd probably driven to Rock Springs. If you were meeting a man, I wanted to find out who it was. I had no idea what I'd do—probably nothing—but I had to know."

"So...so you followed me."

He nodded. "And after you walked back to the truck, I went into the office—where I caught sight of the good doctor...and his mustache."

She sighed, shaking her head.

"Letty, you have every reason in the world to be angry. All I can do is apologize."

"No." She met his eyes. "I wanted to tell you. I've kept this secret to myself for so long and there was no one...no one I could tell and I needed—"

"Letty...please, what's wrong with your heart?"

"The doctors discovered a small hole when I was pregnant with Cricket."

"What are they going to do?"

"Surgery."

His face tightened. "When?"

"Dr. Faraday's already scheduled it. I couldn't afford it.... When you saw my first welfare check I wanted to die. I knew what you thought and there wasn't any way to tell you how much I hate being a recipient of... charity."

Chase shut his eyes. "Letty, I failed you—you needed me and I failed you."

"Chase, I'm not going to blame you for that. I've failed you, too."

"I've been so blind, so stupid."

"I've suffered my share of the same afflictions," she said wryly.

"This time I can change things," he said, taking her by the shoulders.

"How?"

"Letty." His fingers were gentle, his eyes tender. "We're getting married."

Chapter 10

"Married," Letty said, repeating the word for the twentieth time in the past hour. Chase sat her down, poured her a cup of coffee and brought it to the kitchen table. Only a few days earlier, he'd thought nothing of watching her do a multitude of chores. Now he was treating her as if she were an invalid. If Letty hadn't been so amused by his change in attitude, she would've found his behavior annoying.

"I'm not arguing with you, Letty Ellison. We're getting married."

"Honestly, Chase, you're being just a little dramatic, don't you think?" She loved him for it, but that didn't alter the facts.

"No!" His face was tormented with guilt. "Why didn't I listen to you? You tried to tell me, and I was so pigheaded, so blind." He knelt in front of her and took both her hands in his, eyes dark and filled with emotion. "You aren't in any condition to fight me on this, Letty, so just do as I ask and don't argue."

"I'm in excellent shape." Chase could be so stubborn, there were times she found it impossible to reason with him. Despite all that, she felt a deep, abiding love for this man. Yet there were a multitude of doubts they hadn't faced or answered.

Chase hadn't said he loved her or even that he cared. But then, Chase always had been a man of few words. When he'd proposed the first time, he'd told her, simply and profoundly, how much he loved her and wanted to build a life with her. That had been the sweetest, most romantic thing she'd ever heard. Letty had supposed that what he'd said that night was going to be all the poetry Chase would ever give her.

"You're scheduled for heart surgery!"

"I'm not on my deathbed yet!"

He went pale at her joke. "Letty, don't even say that."

"What? That I could die? It's been known to happen. But I hope it won't with me. I'm otherwise healthy, and besides, I'm too stubborn to die in a hospital. I'd prefer to do it in my own bed with my grandchildren gathered around me, fighting over who'll get my many jewels." She said this with a hint of dark drama, loving the way Chase's eyes flared with outrage.

In response, he shook his head. "It's not a joking matter."

"I'm going to get excellent care, so don't worry, okay?"

"I'll feel better once I talk to Dr. Faraday myself.

But when I do, I'm telling you right now, Letty Ellison, it'll be as your husband."

Letty rolled her eyes. She couldn't believe they were having this discussion. Yet Chase seemed so adamant, so certain that marrying now was the right thing to do. Letty loved him more than ever, but she wasn't nearly as convinced of the need to link their lives through marriage while the surgery still loomed before her. Afterward would be soon enough.

Her reaction seemed to frustrate Chase. "All right, if my words can't persuade you, then perhaps this will." With that he wove his fingers into her hair and brought his lips to hers. The kiss was filled with such tenderness that Letty was left trembling in its aftermath.

Chase appeared equally shaken. His eyes held hers for the longest moment, then he kissed her again. And again—

"Well, isn't this peachy?"

Lonny's harsh tone broke them apart.

"Lonny." Chase's voice sounded odd. He cast a glance at the kitchen clock.

"'I won't be long,'" Lonny mimicked, clearly agitated. "It's been *four* hours, man! Four minutes with that...that woman is more than any guy could endure."

"Where's Cricket?" Letty asked, instantly alarmed.

"With *her*." He turned to Chase, frowning. "Did you know all women stick together, even the little ones? I told Cricket to come with me, and she ran behind Joy and hid. I couldn't believe my eyes—my own niece!"

Letty sprang to her feet. "I'm going to call Joy and find out where Cricket is."

"How'd you get back here?" Chase asked his friend.

"Walked."

Letty paused in the doorway, anxious to hear more of her brother's reply.

"But it's almost twenty miles into town," she said.

"You're telling me?" Lonny moaned and slumped into a chair. The first thing he did was remove his left boot, getting it off his swollen foot with some difficulty. He released a long sigh as it fell to the floor. Next he flexed his toes.

"What happened?"

"She kicked me out! What do you think happened? Do I look like I'd stroll home for the exercise?" His narrowed eyes accused both Letty and Chase. "I don't suppose you gave me another thought after you dropped me off, did you? Oh, no. You two were so interested in playing kissy face that you conveniently forgot about *me.*"

"We're sorry, Lonny," Letty said contritely.

Lonny's gaze shifted from Letty to Chase and back again. "I guess there's no need to ask if you patched things up—that much is obvious." By this time, the second dust-caked boot had hit the floor. Lonny peeled off his socks. "Darn it, I've got blisters on my blisters, thanks to the two of you."

"We're getting married," Chase announced without preamble, his look challenging Letty to defy him.

Lonny's head shot up. "What?"

"Letty and I are getting married," Chase repeated. "And the sooner the better."

Lonny's eyes grew suspicious, and when he spoke his voice was almost a whisper. "You're pregnant again, aren't you?"

Letty burst out laughing. "I wish it was that simple."

"She's got a defective heart," Chase said, omitting the details and not giving Letty the opportunity to explain more fully. "She has to have an operation—major surgery from the sound of it."

"Your heart?" Shocked, Lonny stared at her. "Is that why you fainted that day?"

"Partially."

"Why didn't you tell me?"

"I couldn't. Not until I had everything sorted out with the government, and the surgery was scheduled. You would've worried yourself into a tizzy, and I didn't want to dump my problems on top of all your other responsibilities."

"But…" He frowned, apparently displeased with her response. "I could've helped…or at least been more sympathetic. When I think about the way you've cleaned up around here… You had no business working so hard, planting a garden and doing everything else you have. I wish you'd said something, Letty. I feel like a jerk."

"I didn't tell anyone, Lonny. Please understand."

He wiped the back of his hand over his mouth. "I hope you never keep anything like this from me again."

"Believe me, there were a thousand times I wanted to tell you and couldn't."

"I'm going to arrange for the wedding as soon as possible," Chase cut in. "You don't have any objections, do you, Lonny?" His voice was demanding and inflexible.

"Objections? Me? No…not in the least."

"Honestly, Chase," Letty said, patting her brother's

shoulder. "This whole conversation is becoming monotonous, don't you think? I haven't agreed to this yet."

"Call Joy and find out where Cricket is," he told her.

Letty moved to the phone and quickly dialed Joy's number. Her friend answered on the second ring. "Joy, it's Letty. Cricket's with you, right?"

"Yes, of course. I wouldn't let that brother of yours take her, and frankly, she wouldn't have gone with him, anyway. I'm sorry, Letty. I really am. You're my friend and I adore Cricket, but your brother is one of the most—" She stopped abruptly. "I...I don't think it's necessary to say anything else. Lonny's your brother—you know him better than anyone."

In some ways Letty felt she didn't know Lonny at all. "Joy, whatever happened, I'm sorry."

"It's not your fault. By the way, did Chase ever catch up with you? I didn't think to mention until after he'd gone that you'd said something about a doctor's appointment."

"Yes, he found me. That's the reason it's taken me so long to get back to you. I'm home now, but Chase and I have been talking for the past hour or so. I didn't mean to leave Cricket with you all this time."

"Cricket's been great, so don't worry about that. We had a great time—at least, we did until your brother decided to visit." She paused and Letty heard regret in her voice when she spoke again. "I don't know what it is with the two of us. I seem to bring out the worst in Lonny—I know he does in me."

Letty wished she knew what it was, too. Discussing this situation over the phone made her a little uncomfortable. She needed to see Joy, read her expression and her body language. "I'll leave now to pick up Cricket."

"Don't bother," Joy said. "I was going out on an errand and I'll be happy to drop her off."

"You're sure that isn't a problem?"

"Positive." Joy hesitated again. "Lonny got home all right, didn't he? I mean it *is* a long walk. When I told him to leave, I didn't mean for him to hike the whole way back. I forgot he didn't have the truck. By the time I realized it, he'd already started down the sidewalk and he ignored me when I called him."

"Yes, he's home, no worse for wear."

"I'll see you in a little while, then," Joy murmured. She sounded guilty, and Letty suspected she was bringing Cricket home hoping she'd get a chance to apologize. Unfortunately, in Lonny's mood, that would be nearly impossible.

Letty replaced the phone, but not before Lonny shouted from the kitchen, "What do you mean, 'no worse for wear'? I've got blisters that would've brought a lesser man to his knees."

"What did you want me to tell her? That you'd dragged yourself in here barely able to move?"

"Letty, I don't think you should raise your voice. It can't be good for your heart." Chase draped his arm around Letty's shoulders, led her back to the table and eased her onto a chair.

"I'm not an invalid!" she shouted, immediately sorry for her outburst. Chase flinched as if she'd attacked him, and in a way she had.

"Please, Letty, we have a lot to discuss. I want the details for this wedding ironed out before I leave." He knelt in front of her again, and she wondered if he expected her to keel over at any moment.

She sighed. Nothing she'd said seemed to have reached Chase.

"I'm taking a bath," Lonny announced. He stuffed his socks inside his boots and picked them up as he limped out of the kitchen.

"Chase, listen to me," Letty pleaded, her hands framing his worried face. "There's no reason for us to marry now. Once the surgery's over and I'm back on my feet, we can discuss it, if you still feel the same."

"Are you turning me down a second time, Letty?"

"Oh, Chase, you know that isn't it. I told you the other night how much I love you. If my feelings for you didn't change in all the years we were apart, they won't in the next few months."

"Letty, you're not thinking clearly."

"It's my heart that's defective, not my brain."

"I'll arrange for the license right away," he continued as if she hadn't spoken. "If you want a church wedding with all the trimmings, we'll arrange for that later."

"Why not bring Pastor Downey to the hospital, and he can administer the last rites while he's there," she returned flippantly.

"Don't say that!"

"If I agree to this, I'll be married in the church— the first time."

"You're not thinking."

"Chase, you're the one who's diving into the deep end here—not me. Give me one solid reason why we should get married now."

"Concern for Cricket ought to be enough."

"What's my daughter got to do with this?"

"She loves me and I love her." His mouth turned up in a smile. "I never guessed I could love her as much as I do. In the beginning, every time I saw her it was like someone had stuck a knife in my heart. One day—" he lowered his gaze to the floor "—I realized that nothing I did was going to keep me from loving that little girl. She's so much a part of you, and I couldn't care about you the way I do and *not* love her."

Hearing him talk about his feelings for Cricket lifted Letty's sagging spirits. It was the closest he'd come to admitting he loved her.

"More than that, Letty, if something did happen to you, I'd be a better parent than Lonny. Don't you agree?"

Chase was arguably more of a natural, and he had greater patience; to that extent she did agree. "But," she began, "I don't—"

"I know," he said, raising his hand. "You're thinking that you don't have to marry me to make me Cricket's legal guardian, and you're right. But I want you to consider Lonny's pride in all this. If you give me responsibility for Cricket, what's that going to say to your brother? He's your only living relative, and he'd be hurt if he felt you didn't trust him to properly raise your child."

"But nothing's going to happen!" Letty blurted out, knowing she couldn't be completely sure of that.

"But what if the worst *does* happen? If you leave things as they are now, Lonny might have to deal with a grief-stricken five-year-old child. He'd never be able to cope, Letty."

She knew he was right; Lonny would be overwhelmed.

"This situation is much too important to leave everything to fate," he said, closing his argument. "You've got Cricket's future to consider."

"This surgery is a fairly standard procedure." The doctor had told her so himself. Complicated, yes, but not uncommon.

"Yes, but as you said before, things can always go wrong. No matter how slight that chance is, we need to be prepared," Chase murmured.

Letty didn't know what to think. She'd asked Chase to come up with one good argument and he'd outdone himself. In fact, his preoccupation with morbid possibilities struck her as a bit much, considering that he wouldn't let her make even a slight joke about it. However, she understood what he was doing—and why. There were other areas Chase hadn't stopped to consider, though. If they were married, he'd become liable for the cost of her medical care.

"Chase, this surgery isn't cheap. Dr. Faraday said I could be in the hospital as long as two weeks. The hospital bill alone will run into five figures, and that doesn't include the doctor's fee, convalescent care or the pharmaceutical bills, which will add up to much, much more."

"As my wife, you'll be covered by my health insurance policy."

He said this with such confidence that Letty almost believed him. She desperately wanted to, but she was pretty sure that wouldn't be the case. "In all likelihood, your insurance company would deny the claim since my condition is preexisting."

"I can find that out easily enough. I'll phone my broker and have him check my policy right now." He left and returned five minutes later. "It's just as I thought. As my wife, you'd automatically be included for all benefits, no matter when we found out about your heart condition."

It sounded too good to be true. "Chase…I don't know."

"I'm through with listening to all the reasons we can't get married. The fact is, you've rejected one proposal from me, and we both suffered because of it. I won't let you do it a second time. Now will or won't you marry me?"

"You're *sure* about the insurance?"

"Positive." He crouched in front of her and took both her hands in his. "You're going to marry me, Letty. No more arguments, no more ifs, ands or buts." He grinned at her. "So we're getting married?"

Chase made the question more of a statement. "Yes," she murmured, loving him so much. "But you're taking such a risk…"

His eyes narrowed. "Why?"

"Well, because—" She stopped when Cricket came running through the door and held out her arms to her daughter, who flew into them.

"I'm home." Cricket hugged Letty, then rushed over to Chase and threw her arms around his neck with such enthusiasm it nearly knocked him to the floor.

Letty watched them and realized, above anything

else, how right Chase was to be concerned about Cricket's welfare in the unlikely event that something went wrong. She drew in a shaky breath and held it until her lungs ached. She loved Chase, and although he hadn't spelled out his feelings for her, she knew he cared deeply for her and for Cricket.

Joy stood sheepishly near the kitchen door, scanning the area for any sign of Lonny. Letty didn't doubt that if her brother were to make an appearance, Joy would quickly turn a designer shade of red.

"Joy, come in," Letty said, welcoming her friend.

She did, edging a few more feet into the kitchen. "I just wanted to make sure Cricket was safely inside."

"Thanks so much for watching her for me this afternoon," Letty said, smiling broadly. "I appreciate it more than you know."

"It wasn't any problem."

A soft snicker was heard from the direction of the hallway. Lonny stood there, obviously having just gotten out of the shower. His dark hair glistened and his shirt was unbuttoned over his blue jeans. His feet were bare.

Joy stiffened. "The only difficulty was when unexpected company arrived and—"

"Uncle Lonny was yelling at Joy," Cricket whispered to her mother.

"Don't forget to mention the part where she was yelling at me," Lonny said.

"I'd better go." Joy stepped back and gripped the doorknob.

"I'm not stopping you," Lonny said sweetly, swaggering into the room.

"I'm on my way out, *Mr.* Ellison. The less I see of you, the better."

"My feelings exactly."

"Lonny. Joy." Letty gestured at each of them. They were both so stubborn. Every time they were within range of each other, sparks ignited—and, in Letty's opinion, they weren't *just* sparks of anger.

"I'm sorry, Letty, but I cannot tolerate your brother."

Lonny moved closer to Joy and Letty realized why his walk was so unusual. He was doing his utmost not to limp, what with all his blisters. Lonny stopped directly in front of Joy, his arms folded over his bare chest. "The same goes for you—only double."

"Goodbye, Letty, Chase. Goodbye, Cricket." Joy completely ignored Lonny and walked out of the house.

The instant she did, Lonny sat down and started to rub his feet. "Fool woman."

"I won't comment on who's acting like a fool here, brother dearest, but the odds are high that you're in the competition."

Chase sat in the hospital waiting room and picked up a *Time* magazine. He didn't even notice the date until he'd finished three news articles and realized everything he'd read about had happened months ago.

Like the stories in the out-of-date magazine, Chase's life had changed, but the transformation had taken place within a few days, not months.

A week after following Letty into Rock Springs and discovering her secret, he was both a husband and a father. He and Letty had a small wedding at which Pastor Downey had been kind enough to officiate. And now they were facing what could be the most difficult trial of their lives together—her heart surgery.

Setting the magazine aside, Chase wandered outside to the balcony, leaning over the railing as he surveyed the foliage below.

Worry entangled his thoughts and dominated his emotions. And yet a faint smile hovered on his lips. Even when they'd wheeled Letty into the operating room, she'd been joking with the doctors.

A vision of the nurses, clad in surgical green from head to foot, who'd wheeled Letty through the double doors and into the operating room, came back to haunt him. They'd taken Letty from his side, although he'd held her hand as long as possible. Only Chase had seen the momentary look of stark fear, of panic, in her eyes. But her gaze had found his and her expression became one of reassurance.

She was facing a traumatic experience and she'd wanted to encourage *him*.

Her sweet smile hadn't fooled him, though. Letty was as frightened as he was, perhaps more; she just wouldn't let anyone know it.

She could die in there, and he was powerless to do anything to stop it. The thought of her death made him ache with an agony that was beyond description. Letty had been back in Wyoming for less than two months and already Chase couldn't imagine his life without her. The air on the balcony became stifling. Chase fled.

"Chase!" Lonny came running after him. "What's happened? Where's Letty?"

Chase's eyes were wild as he stared at his brother-in-law. "They took her away twenty minutes ago."

"Hey, are you all right?"

The question buzzed around him like a cloud of mosquitoes, and he shook his head.

"Chase." Lonny clasped his shoulders. "I think you should sit down."

"Cricket?"

"She's fine. Joy's watching her."

Chase nodded, sitting on the edge of the seat, his elbows on his knees, his hands covering his face. Letty had come into his life when he'd least expected her back. She'd offered him love when he'd never thought he'd discover it a second time. Long before, he'd given up the dream of her ever being his wife.

They'd been married less than a day. Only a few hours earlier, Letty had stood before Pastor Downey and vowed to love him—Chase Brown. Her *husband*. And here she was, her life on the line, and they had yet to have their wedding night.

Chase prayed fate wouldn't be so cruel as to rip her from his arms. He wanted the joy of loving her and being loved by her. The joy of fulfilling his dreams and building happiness with her and Cricket and whatever other children they had. A picture began to form in his mind. Two little boys around the ages of five and six. They stood side by side, the best of friends, each with deep blue eyes like Letty's. Their hair was the same shade as his own when he was about their age.

"She's going to make it," Lonny said. "Do you think my sister's going to give up on life without a fight? You

know Letty better than that. Relax, would you? Everything's going to work out."

His friend's words dispelled the vision. Chase
wished he shared Lonny's confidence regarding Letty's
health. He felt so helpless—all he could do was pray.

Chase stood up abruptly. "I'm going to the chapel,"
he announced, appreciating it when Lonny chose to
stay behind.

The chapel was empty, and Chase was grateful for
the privacy. He sat in the back pew and stared straight
ahead, not knowing what to say or do that would convince the Almighty to keep Letty safe.

He rotated the brim of his hat between his fingers
while his mind fumbled for the words to plead for her
life. He wanted so much more than that, more than
Letty simply surviving the surgery, and then felt self-
ish for being so greedy. As the minutes ticked past,
he sat and silently poured out his heart, talking as he
would to a friend.

Chase had never been a man who could speak elo-
quently—to God or, for that matter, to Letty or anyone else. He knew she'd been looking for words of love
the day he'd proposed to her. He regretted now that he
hadn't said them. He'd felt them deep in his heart, but
something had kept them buried inside. Fear, he suspected. He'd spoken them once and they hadn't meant
enough to keep her in Red Springs. He didn't know if
they'd mean enough this time, either.

An eternity passed and he stayed where he was,
afraid to face whatever would greet him upon his return. Several people came and went, but he barely noticed them.

The chapel door opened once more and Chase didn't have to turn around to know it was Lonny. Cold fear dampened his brow and he sat immobilized. The longest seconds of his life dragged past before Lonny joined him in the pew.

"The surgery went without a hitch—Letty's going to be just fine," he whispered. "You can see her, but only for a minute."

Chase closed his eyes as the tension drained out of him.

"Did you hear me?"

Chase nodded and turned to his lifelong friend. "Thank God."

The two men embraced and Chase was filled with overwhelming gratitude.

"Be warned, though," Lonny said on their way back to the surgical floor. "Letty's connected to a bunch of tubes and stuff, so don't let it throw you."

Chase nodded.

One of the nurses who'd wheeled his wife into surgery was waiting when Chase returned. She had him dress in sterile surgical garb and instructed him to follow her.

Chase accompanied her into the intensive care unit. Letty was lying on a gurney, perfectly still, and Chase stood by her side. Slowly he bent toward her and saw that her eyes were closed.

"Letty," he whispered. "It's Chase. You're going to be fine."

Chase thought he saw her mouth move in a smile, but he couldn't be sure.

"I love you," he murmured, his voice hoarse with

emotion. "I didn't say it before, but I love you—I never stopped. I've lived my life loving you, and nothing will ever change that."

She was pale, so deathly pale, that he felt a sudden sharp fear before he realized the worst of the ordeal was over. The surgery had etched its passing on her lovely face, yet he saw something else, something he hadn't recognized in Letty before. There was a calm strength, a courage that lent him confidence. She was his wife and she'd stand by his side for the rest of their days.

Chase kissed her forehead tenderly before turning to leave.

"I'll see you in the morning," he told her. *And every morning after that,* he thought.

Chapter 11

"Here's some tea," Joy said, carrying a tray into the living room, where Letty was supposed to be resting.

"I'm perfectly capable of getting my own tea, for heaven's sake," Letty mumbled, but when Joy approached, she offered her friend a bright smile. It didn't do any good to complain—and she didn't want to seem ungrateful—although having everyone wait on her was frustrating.

She was reluctant to admit that the most difficult aspect of her recovery was this lengthy convalescence. She'd been released from the hospital two weeks earlier, still very weak; however, she was regaining her strength more and more every day. According to Dr. Faraday, this long period of debility was to be expected. He was pleased with her progress, but Letty found herself becoming increasingly impatient. She yearned to go back to the life she'd just begun with Chase. It was as if their marriage had been put on hold.

They slept in the same bed, lived in the same house, ate the same meals, but they might as well have been brother and sister. Chase seemed to have forgotten that she was his *wife*.

"You're certainly looking good," Joy said as she took the overstuffed chair across from Letty. She poured them each a cup of tea and handed the first one to Letty. Then she picked up her own and sat back.

"I'm feeling good." Her eyes ran lovingly over the room with its polished oak floors, thick braided rug and the old upright piano that had once been hers. The house at Spring Valley had been built years before the one on the Bar E, and Chase had done an excellent job on the upkeep. When she'd been released from the hospital, Chase had brought her to Spring Valley and dutifully carried her over the threshold. But that had been the only husbandly obligation he'd performed the entire time she'd been home.

During her hospital stay, Lonny and Chase had packed her things and Cricket's, and moved them to the house at Spring Valley. Perhaps that had been a mistake, because Letty's frustration mounted as she hungered to become Chase's wife in every way.

She took a sip of the lemon-scented tea, determined to exhibit more patience with herself and everyone else. "I can't thank you enough for all you've done."

Joy had made a point of coming over every afternoon and staying with Letty. Chase had hired an extra man to come over in the early mornings so he could be with her until it was nearly noon. By then she'd showered and dressed and been deposited on the living room couch, where Chase and Cricket made a game of serving her breakfast.

"I've hardly done anything," Joy said, discounting Letty's appreciation. "It's been great getting better acquainted. Cricket is a marvelous little girl, and now that I know you, I understand why. You're a good mother, Letty, but even more important, you're a wonderful person."

"Thank you." Letty smiled softly, touched by Joy's tribute. She'd worked hard to be the right kind of mother, but there were plenty of times when she had her doubts, as any single parent did. Only she wasn't single anymore....

"Speaking of Cricket, where is she?"

"Out visiting her pony," Letty said, and grinned. Cricket thought that marrying Chase had been a brilliant idea. According to her, there wasn't anyone in the whole world who'd make a better daddy. Chase had certainly lived up to her daughter's expectations. He was patient and gentle and kind to a fault. The problem, if it could be termed that, was the way Chase treated *her,* which was no different from the way he treated Cricket. But Letty yearned to be a wife. A real wife.

"What's that?" Joy asked, pointing at a huge box that sat on the floor next to the sofa.

"Lonny brought it over last night. It's some things that belonged to our mother. He thought I might want to sort through them. When Mom died, he packed up her belongings and stuck them in the back bedroom. They've been there ever since."

Joy's eyes fluttered downward at the mention of

Lonny's name. Letty picked up on that immediately. "Are you two still not getting along?" she asked, taking a chance, since neither seemed willing to discuss the other.

"Not exactly. Didn't you ask me to write down the recipe for that meatless lasagna? Well, I brought it along and left it in the kitchen."

From little things Letty had heard Lonny, Chase and Joy drop, her brother had made some effort to fix his relationship with Joy while Letty was in the hospital. Evidently whatever he'd said or done had worked, because the minute she mentioned Joy's name to Lonny he got flustered.

For her part, Joy did everything but stand on her head to change the subject. Letty wished she knew what was going on, but after one miserable attempt to involve herself in her brother's love life, she knew better than to try again.

"Mommy," Cricket cried as she came running into the living room, pigtails skipping. "Jennybird ate an apple out of my hand! Chase showed me how to hold it so she wouldn't bite me." She looped her small arms around Letty's neck and squeezed tight. "When can you come and watch me feed Jennybird?"

"Soon." At least, Letty hoped it would be soon.

"Take your time," Joy said. "There's no reason to push yourself, Letty."

"You're beginning to sound like Chase," Letty said with a grin.

Joy shook her head. "I doubt that. I've never seen a man more worried about anyone. The first few days after the surgery, he slept at the hospital. Lonny finally dragged him home, fed him and insisted he get some rest."

Joy wasn't telling Letty anything she didn't already know. Chase had been wonderful, more than wonderful, from the moment he'd learned about her heart condition. Now, if he'd only start treating her like a wife instead of a roommate....

"I want you to come and see my new bedroom," Cricket said, reaching for Joy's hand. "I've got a new bed with a canopy and a new bedspread and a new pillow and everything."

Joy turned to Letty. "Chase again?"

Letty nodded. "He really spoils her."

"He loves her."

"He loves me," Cricket echoed, pointing a finger at her chest. "But that's okay, because I like being spoiled."

Letty sighed. "I know you do, sweetheart, but enough is enough."

Chase had been blunt about the fact that Cricket was his main consideration when he asked Letty to marry him. His point had been a valid one, but Letty couldn't doubt for an instant that Chase loved them both. Although he hadn't said the words, they weren't necessary; he'd shown his feelings for her in a hundred different ways.

"I'd better go take a gander at Cricket's room, and then I should head back into town," Joy said as she stood. "There's a casserole in the refrigerator for dinner."

"Joy!" Letty protested. "You've done enough."

"Shush," Joy said, waving her index finger under

Letty's nose. "It was a new recipe, and two were as easy to make as one."

"You're going to have to come up with a better excuse than that, Joy. You've been trying out new recipes all week." Although she chided her friend, Letty was grateful for all the help Joy had given her over the past month. Her visits in the afternoons had brought Chase peace of mind so he could work outside without constantly worrying about Letty. The casseroles and salads Joy contributed for dinner were a help, too.

Chase wouldn't allow Letty to do any of the household chores yet and insisted on preparing their meals himself. Never in a thousand years would Letty have dreamed that she'd miss doing laundry or dishes. But there was an unexpected joy in performing menial tasks for the people she loved. In the past few weeks, she'd learned some valuable lessons about life. She'd experienced the nearly overwhelming need to do something for someone else instead of being the recipient of everyone else's goodwill.

The house was peaceful and still as Joy followed Cricket up the stairs. When they returned a few minutes later, Cricket was yawning and dragging her blanket behind her.

"I want to sleep with you today, Mommy."

"All right, sweetheart."

Cricket climbed into the chair across from Letty, which Joy had recently vacated, and curled up, wrapping her blanket around her. Letty knew her daughter would be asleep within five minutes.

Watching the child, Letty was grateful that Cricket

would be in the morning kindergarten class, since she still seemed to need an afternoon nap.

Joy worked in the kitchen for a few minutes, then paused in the doorway, smiled at Cricket and waved goodbye. Letty heard the back door close as her friend left the house.

In an hour or so Chase would come to check her. Letty cherished these serene moments alone and lay down on the couch to nap, too. A few minutes later she realized she wasn't tired, and feeling good about that, she sat up. The extra time was like an unexpected gift and her gaze fell on the carton her brother had brought. Carefully Letty pried open the lid.

Sorting through her mother's personal things was bound to be a painful task, Letty thought as she lovingly removed each neatly packed item from the cardboard container.

She pulled out a stack of old pattern books and set those aside. Her mother had loved to sew, often spending a winter evening flipping through these pages, planning new projects. Letty had learned her sewing skills from Maren, although it had been years since she'd sat down at a sewing machine.

Sudden tears welled up in Letty's eyes at the memories of her mother. Happy memories of a loving mother who'd worked much too hard and died far too young. A twinge of resentment struck her. Maren Ellison had given her life's blood to the Bar E ranch. It had been her husband's dream, not hers, and yet her mother had made the sacrifice.

Letty wiped away her tears and felt a surge of sorrow over her mother's death, coming so soon after her father's. Maren had deserved a life so much better than the one she'd lived.

Once Letty's eyes had cleared enough to continue her task, she lifted out several large strips of brightly colored material in odd shapes and sizes and set them on the sofa. Bits and pieces of projects that had been carefully planned by her mother and now waited endlessly for completion.

Then Letty withdrew what had apparently been her mother's last project. With extreme caution, she unfolded the top of a vividly colored quilt, painstakingly stitched by hand.

Examining the patchwork piece produced a sense of awe in Letty. She was astonished by the time and effort invested in the work, and even more astonished that she recognized several swatches of the material her mother had used in the quilt. The huge red star at the very center had been created from a piece of leftover fabric from a dress her mother had made for Letty the summer she'd left home. A plaid piece in one corner was from an old Western shirt she'd worn for years. After recognizing one swatch of material after another, Letty realized that her mother must have been making the quilt as a Christmas or birthday gift for her.

Lovingly she ran the tips of her fingers over the cloth as her heart lurched with a sadness that came from deep within. Then it dawned on her that without too much difficulty she'd be able to finish the quilt herself. Everything she needed was right here. The task would be something to look forward to next winter, when the days were short and the nights were Arctic-cold.

After folding the quilt top and placing it back in the box, Letty discovered a sketchbook, tucked against the side of the carton. Her heart soared with excitement as she reverently picked it up. Her mother had loved to draw, and her talent was undeniable.

The first sketch was of a large willow against the backdrop of an evening sky. Letty recognized the tree immediately. Her mother had sketched it from their front porch years ago. The willow had been cut down when Letty was in her early teens, after lightning had struck it.

Letty had often found her mother sketching, but the opportunity to complete any full-scale paintings had been rare. The book contained a handful of sketches, and once more Letty felt a wave of resentment. Maren Ellison had deserved the right to follow her own dreams. She was an artist, a woman who'd loved with a generosity that touched everyone she knew.

"Letty." Chase broke into her thoughts as he hurried into the house. He paused when he saw Cricket asleep in the chair. "I saw Joy leave," he said, his voice a whisper.

"Chase, there's no need to worry. I can stay by myself for an hour or two."

He nodded, then wiped his forearm over his brow and awkwardly leaned over to brush his lips over her cheek. "I figured I'd drop in and make sure everything's under control."

"It is." His chaste kiss only frustrated Letty. She wanted to shout at him that the time had come for him to act like a married man instead of a saint.

"What's all this?" Chase asked, glancing around her.

Letty suspected he only slept three hours a night. He never went to bed at the same time she did, and he was always up before she even stirred. Occasionally, she heard him slip between the sheets, but he stayed so far over on his side of the bed that they didn't even touch.

"A quilt," Letty said, pointing at the cardboard box.

"Is that the box Lonny brought here?"

"Yes. Mom was apparently working on it when she died. She was making it for me." Letty had to swallow the lump in her throat before she could talk again. She turned and pointed to the other things she'd found. "There's some pieces of material in here and pattern books, as well."

"What's this?"

"A sketch pad. Mom was an artist," Letty said proudly.

His eyebrows drew together. "I didn't realize that," he said slowly. He flipped through the book of pencil sketches. "She was very talented."

Chase sounded a little surprised that he hadn't known about her mother's artistic abilities. "Mom was an incredible woman. I don't think anyone ever fully appreciated that—I know I didn't."

Chase stepped closer and massaged Letty's shoulders with tenderness and sympathy. "You still miss her, don't you?"

Letty nodded. Her throat felt thick, and she couldn't express everything she was feeling, all the emotion rising up inside her.

Chase knelt in front of her, his gaze level with hers. He slipped his callused hands around the nape of her neck as he brought her into his arms. Letty rested her head against his shoulder, reveling in his warm embrace. It had been so long since he'd held her and even longer since he'd kissed her...really kissed her.

Raising her head slightly, she ran the moist tip of her tongue along the side of his jaw. He filled her senses. Chase tensed, but still Letty continued her sensual movements, nibbling at his earlobe, taking it into her mouth...

"Letty," he groaned, "no."

"No what?" she asked coyly, already knowing his answer. Her mouth roved where it wanted, while she held his face in her hands, directing him as she wished. She savored the edge of his mouth, teasing him, tantalizing him, until he moaned anew.

"Letty." He brought his hands to her shoulders.

Letty was certain he'd meant to push her away, but before he could, she raised her arms and slid them around his neck. Then she leaned against him. Chase held her there.

"Letty." Her name was a plea.

"Chase, kiss me, please," she whispered. "I've missed you so much."

Slowly, as if uncertain he was doing the right thing, Chase lowered his mouth to touch her parted lips with his. Letty didn't move, didn't breathe, for fear he'd stop. She would've screamed in frustration if he had. His brotherly pecks on the cheeks were worse than no kisses at all; they just made her crave everything she'd been missing. Apparently Chase had been feeling equally deprived, because he settled his mouth over hers with a passion and need that demanded her very breath.

"What's taken you so long?" she asked, her voice urgent.

He answered her with another fiery kiss that robbed her of what little strength she still had. Letty heard a faint moan from deep within his chest.

"Letty…this is ridiculous," he murmured, breaking away, his shoulders heaving.

"What is?" she demanded.

"My kissing you like this."

He thrust his fingers through his hair. His features were dark and angry.

"I'm your *wife,* Chase Brown. Can't a man kiss his wife?"

"Not like this…not when she's— You're recovering from heart surgery." He moved away from her and briefly closed his eyes, as though he needed an extra moment to compose himself. "Besides, Cricket's here."

"I'm your wife," Letty returned, not knowing what else to say.

"You think I need to be reminded of that?" he shot back. He got awkwardly to his feet and grabbed his hat and gloves. "I have to get to work," he said, slamming his hat on top of his head. "I'll be home in a couple of hours."

Letty couldn't have answered him had she tried. She felt like a fool now.

"Do you need anything before I go?" he asked without looking at her.

"No."

He took several steps away from her, stopped abruptly, then turned around. "It's going to be months before we can do—before we can be husband and wife in the full sense," he said grimly. "I think it would be best if we avoided situations like this in the future. Don't you agree?"

Letty shrugged. "I'm sorry," she whispered.

"So am I," he returned grimly and left the house.

"Mommy, I want to learn how to play another song," Cricket called from the living room. She was sitting at the upright piano, her feet crossed and swinging. Letty had taught her "Chopsticks" earlier in the day. She'd been impressed with how easily her daughter had picked it up. Cricket had played it at least twenty times and was eager to master more tunes.

"In a little while," Letty said. She sat at the kitchen table, peeling potatoes for dinner and feeling especially proud of herself for this minor accomplishment. Chase would be surprised and probably a little concerned when he realized what she'd done. But the surgery was several weeks behind her and it was time to take on some of the lighter responsibilities. Preparing dinner was hardly an onerous task; neither was playing the piano with her daughter.

Seeking her mother's full attention, Cricket headed into the kitchen and reached for a peeler and a potato. "I'll help you."

"All right, sweetheart."

The chore took only a few minutes, Letty peeling four spuds to Cricket's one. Next the child helped her collect the peelings and clean off the table before leading her back into the living room.

"Play something else, Mommy," the little girl insisted, sitting on the bench beside Letty.

Letty's fingers ran lazily up and down the keyboard in a quick exercise. She hadn't touched the piano until after her surgery. Letty supposed there was some psychological reason for this, but she didn't want to analyze it now. Until Cricket's birth, music had dominated her life. But after her daughter's arrival, her life had turned in a different direction. Music had become a way of entertaining herself and occasionally brought her some paying work, although—obviously—*that* was no longer the case.

"Play a song for me," Cricket commanded.

Letty did, smiling as the familiar keys responded to her touch. This piano represented so much love and so many good times. Her mother had recognized Letty's musical gift when she was a child, only a little older than Cricket. Letty had started taking piano lessons in first grade. When she'd learned as much as the local music instructors could teach her, Maren had driven her into Rock Springs every week. A two-hour drive for a half-hour lesson.

"Now show me how to do it like you," Cricket said, completely serious. "I want to play just as good as you."

"Sweetheart, I took lessons for seven years."

"That's okay, 'cause I'm five."

Letty laughed. "Here, I'll play 'Mary Had a Little Lamb' and then you can move your fingers the way I do." Slowly she played the first lines, then dropped her hands on her lap while Cricket perfectly mimicked the simple notes.

"This is fun," Cricket said, beaming with pride.

Ten minutes later, she'd memorized the whole song. With two musical pieces in her repertoire, Cricket was convinced she was possibly the most gifted musical student in the history of Red Springs.

The minute Chase was in the door, Cricket flew to his side. "Chase! Chase, come listen."

"Sweetie, let him wash up first," Letty said with a smile.

"What is it?" Chase asked, his amused gaze shifting from Cricket to Letty, then back to Cricket again.

"It's a surprise," Cricket said, practically jumping up and down with enthusiasm.

"You'd better go listen," Letty told him. "She's been waiting for you to come inside."

Chase washed his hands at the kitchen sink, but hesitated when he saw the panful of peeled potatoes. "Who did this?"

"Mommy and me," Cricket told him impatiently.

"Letty?"

"And I lived to tell about it. I'm feeling stronger every day," she pointed out, "and there's no reason I can't start taking up the slack around here a little more."

"But—"

"Don't argue with me, Chase," she said in what she hoped was a firm voice.

"It hasn't been a month yet," he countered, frowning.

"I feel fine!"

It looked as if he wanted to argue, but he apparently decided not to, probably because Cricket was tugging anxiously at his arm, wanting him to sit down in the living room so he could hear her recital.

Letty followed them and stood back as Cricket directed Chase to his favorite overstuffed chair.

"You stay here," she said.

Once Chase was seated, she walked proudly over to the piano and climbed onto the bench. Then she looked over her shoulder and ceremoniously raised her hands. Lowering them, she put every bit of emotion her five-year-old heart possessed into playing "Chopsticks."

When she'd finished, she slid off the seat, tucked her arm around her middle and bowed. "You're supposed to clap now," she told Chase.

He obliged enthusiastically, and Letty stifled a laugh at how seriously Cricket was taking this.

"For my next number, I'll play—" She stopped abruptly. "I want you to guess."

Letty sat on the armchair, resting her hand on his shoulder. "She's such a ham."

Chase grinned up at her, his eyes twinkling with shared amusement.

"I must have quiet," Cricket grumbled. "You aren't supposed to talk now...."

Once more Cricket gave an Oscar-quality performance.

"Bravo, bravo," Chase shouted when she'd slipped off the piano bench.

Cricket flew to Chase's side and climbed into his lap. "Mommy taught me."

"She seems to have a flair for music," Letty said.

"I'm not as good as Mommy, though." Cricket sighed dramatically. "She can play anything...and she sings pretty, too. She played for me today and we had so much fun."

Letty laughed. "I'm thinking of giving Cricket piano lessons myself," Letty said, sure that Chase would add his wholehearted approval.

To her surprise, Letty felt him tense beneath her fingers. It was as if all the joy had suddenly and mysteriously disappeared from the room.

"Chase, what's wrong?" Letty whispered.

"Nothing."

"Cricket, go get Chase a glass of iced tea," Letty said. "It's in the refrigerator."

"Okay," the child said, eager as always to do anything for Chase.

As soon as the little girl had left, Letty spoke. "Do you object to Cricket taking piano lessons?"

"Why should I?" he asked, without revealing any emotion. "As you say, she's obviously got talent."

"Yes, but—"

"We both know where she got it from, don't we," he said with a resigned sigh.

"I would think you'd be pleased." Chase had always loved it when she played and sang; now he could barely stand it if she so much as looked at the piano.

"I *am* pleased," he declared. With that, he walked into the kitchen, leaving Letty more perplexed than ever.

For several minutes, Letty sat there numbly while Chase talked to Cricket, praising her efforts.

Letty had thought Chase would be happy, but he clearly wasn't. She didn't understand it.

"Someday," she heard him tell Cricket, his voice full of regret, "you'll play as well as your mother."

Chapter 12

Astride Firepower at the top of a hill overlooking his herd, Chase stared vacantly into the distance. Letty was leaving; he'd known it from the moment he discovered she'd been playing the piano again. The niggling fear had been with him for days, gnawing at his heart.

Marrying her had been a gamble, a big one, but he'd accepted it, grateful for the opportunity to have her and Cricket in his life, even if it was destined to be for a short time. Somehow, he'd find the courage to smile and let her walk away. He'd managed it once and, if he had to, he could do it again.

"Chase."

At the sound of his name, carried softly on the wind, Chase twisted in the saddle, causing the leather to creak. He frowned as he recognized Letty, riding one of his mares, advancing slowly toward him. Her face was lit with a bright smile and she waved, happy and elated. Sadly he shared little of her exhilaration. All he could think about was his certainty that she'd soon be gone.

Letty rode with a natural grace, as if she'd been born to it. Her beauty almost broke his heart.

Chase swallowed, and a sense of dread swelled up inside him. Dread and confusion—the same confusion that being alone with Letty always brought. He wanted her, and yet he had to restrain himself for the sake of her health. He wanted to keep her with him, and yet he'd have to let her go if that was her choice.

Sweat broke out across his upper lip. He hadn't touched Letty from the moment he'd learned of her heart condition. Now she needed to recover from her surgery. It was debatable, however, whether he could continue to resist her much longer. Each day became more taxing than the one before. Just being close to her sapped his strength. Sleeping with her only inches away had become almost impossible and as a result he was constantly tired…as well as frustrated.

Chase drew himself up when she joined him. "What are you doing here?" he asked. He sounded harsher than he'd intended.

"You didn't come back to the house for lunch," she murmured.

"Did it occur to you that I might not be hungry?" He was exhausted and impatient and hated the way he was speaking to her, but he felt himself fighting powerful emotions whenever he was near her.

"I brought you some lunch," Letty said, not reacting to his rudeness. "I thought we…we might have a picnic."

"A picnic?" he echoed with a short sarcastic laugh.

Letty seemed determined to ignore his mood, and smiled up at him, her eyes gleaming with mischief. "Yes," she said, "a picnic. You work too hard, Chase. It's about time you relaxed a little."

"Where's Cricket?" he asked, his tongue nearly sticking to the roof of his mouth. It was difficult enough keeping his eyes off Letty without having to laze around on some nice, soft grass and pretend he had an appetite. Oh, he was hungry, all right, but it was Letty he needed; only his wife would satisfy his cravings.

"Cricket went into town with Joy," she said, sliding down from the mare. "She's helping Joy get her new classroom ready, although it's questionable how much help she'll actually be. School's only a couple of weeks away, you know."

While she was speaking, Letty emptied the saddlebags. She didn't look back at him as she spread a blanket across the grass, obviously assuming he'd join her without further argument. Next she opened a large brown sack, then knelt and pulled out sandwiches and a thermos.

"Chase?" She looked up at him.

"I…I'm not hungry."

"You don't have to eat if you don't want, but at least take a break."

Reluctantly Chase climbed out of the saddle. It was either that or sit where he was and stare down her blouse.

Despite the fact that Letty had spent weeks inside the house recuperating, her skin was glowing and healthy, Chase noted. Always slender, she'd lost weight and had worked at putting it back on, but he'd never guess it, looking at her now. Her jeans fit snugly, and her lithe, elegant body seemed to call out to him....

"I made fresh lemonade. Would you like some?" She interrupted his tortured thoughts, opening the thermos and filling a paper cup, ready to hand it to him.

"No...thanks." Chase felt both awkward and out of place. He moved closer to her, drawn by an invisible cord. He stared at her longingly, then dropped to his knees, simply because standing demanded so much energy.

"The lemonade's cold," she coaxed. As if to prove her point, she took a sip.

The tip of her tongue came out and she licked her lips. Watching that small action, innocent yet sensuous, was like being kicked in the stomach.

"I said I didn't want any," he said gruffly.

They were facing each other, and Letty's gaze found his. Her eyes were wide, hurt and confused. She looked so beautiful.

He realized he should explain that he knew she was planning to go back to California, but his tongue refused to cooperate. Letty continued to peer at him, frowning slightly, as though trying to identify the source of his anger.

At that instant, Chase knew he was going to kiss her and there wasn't a thing he could do to stop himself. The ache to touch her had consumed him for weeks. He reached out for her now, easing her into his embrace. She came willingly, offering no resistance.

"Letty..."

Intuitively she must have known his intent, because she closed her eyes and tilted back her head.

At first, as if testing the limits of his control, Chase merely touched his mouth to hers. The way her fingers curled into his chest told him she was as eager for his touch as he was for hers. He waited, savoring the taste and feel of her in his arms, and when he could deny himself no longer, he deepened the kiss.

With a soft sigh, Letty brought her arms around his neck. Chase's heart was pounding and he pulled back for a moment, breathing in her delectable scent—wildflowers and some clean-smelling floral soap.

He ran his fingers through her hair as he kissed her again. He stopped to breathe, then slowly lowered them both to the ground, lying side by side. Then, he sought her mouth once more. He felt consumed with such need, yet forced himself to go slowly, gently....

Since Letty had returned to Red Springs, Chase had kissed her a number of times. For the past few weeks he'd gone to sleep each night remembering how good she'd felt in his arms. He had treasured the memories, not knowing when he'd be able to hold her and kiss her again. *Soon,* he always promised himself; he'd make love to her soon. Every detail of every time he'd touched her was emblazoned on his mind, and he could think of little else.

Now that she was actually in his arms, he discovered that the anticipation hadn't prepared him for how perfect it would be. The reality outdistanced his memory—and his imagination.

His mouth came down hard on hers, releasing all the tension inside him. Letty's breathing was labored and harsh and her fingers curled more tightly into the fabric of his shirt, then began to relax as she gave herself completely over to his kiss.

Chase was drowning, sinking fast. At first he associated the rumbling in his ears with the thunder of his own heartbeat. It took him a moment to realize it was the sound of an approaching horse.

Chase rolled away from Letty with a groan.

She sat up and looked at him, dazed, hurt, confused.

"Someone's riding toward us," he said tersely.

"Oh."

That one word bespoke frustration and disappointment and a multitude of other emotions that reflected his own. He retrieved his gloves and stood, using his body to shield Letty from any curious onlooker.

Within seconds Lonny trotted into view.

"It's your brother," Chase warned, then added something low and guttural that wasn't meant for her ears. His friend had quite the sense of timing.

Chase saw Letty turn away and busy herself with laying out their lunch.

As Lonny rode up, pulling on his horse's reins, Chase glared at him.

More than a little chagrined, Lonny muttered, "Am I interrupting something?"

"Of course not," Letty said, sounding unlike herself. She kept her back to him, making a task of unfolding napkins and unwrapping sandwiches.

Chase contradicted her words with a scowl. The last person he wanted to see was Lonny. To his credit, his brother-in-law looked as if he wanted to find a hole to hide in, but that didn't help now.

"Actually, I was looking for Letty," Lonny explained, after clearing his throat. "I wanted to talk to her about…something. I stopped at the house, but there wasn't anyone around. Your new guy, Mel, was working in the barn and he told me she'd come out here. I guess, uh, I should've figured it out."

"It would've been appreciated," Chase muttered savagely.

"I brought lunch out to Chase," Letty said.

Chase marveled that she could recover so quickly.

"There's plenty if you'd care to join us," she said.

"You might as well," Chase said, confirming the invitation. The moment had been ruined and he doubted they'd be able to recapture it.

Lonny's gaze traveled from one to the other. "Another time," he said, turning his horse. "I'll talk to you later, sis."

Letty nodded, and Lonny rode off.

"You should go back to the house yourself," Chase said without meeting her eyes.

It wasn't until Letty had repacked the saddlebags and ridden after her brother that Chase could breathe normally again.

Lonny was waiting for Letty when she trotted into the yard on Chase's mare. His expression was sheepish, she saw as he helped her down from the saddle, although she was more than capable of doing it on her own.

"I'm sorry, Letty," he mumbled. Hot color circled his ears. "I should've thought before I went traipsing out there looking for you."

"It's all right," she said, offering him a gracious smile. There was no point in telling him he'd interrupted a scene she'd been plotting for days. Actually, her time with Chase told her several things, and all of them excited her. He was going crazy with desire for her. He wanted her as much as she wanted him.

"*You* may be willing to forgive me, but I don't think Chase is going to be nearly as generous."

"Don't worry about it," she returned absently. Her brother had foiled Plan A, but Plan B would go into action that very evening.

"Come on in and I'll get you a glass of lemonade."

"I could use one," Lonny said, obediently following his sister into the kitchen.

Letty could see that something was troubling her brother, and whatever it was appeared to be serious. His eyes seemed clouded and stubbornly refused to meet hers.

"What did you want to talk to me about?"

He sat down at the scarred oak table. Removing his hat, he set it on the chair beside him. "Do you remember when you first came home you invited Mary Brandon over to the house?"

Letty wasn't likely to forget it; the evening had been a catastrophe.

"You seemed to think I needed a wife," Lonny continued.

"Yes...mainly because you'd become consumed by the ranch. Your rodeo days are over—"

"My glory days," he said with a self-conscious laugh.

"You quit because you had to come back to the Bar E when Dad got sick. Now you're so wrapped up in the ranch, all your energy's channeled in that one direction."

He nodded, agreeing with her, which surprised Letty.

"The way I see it, Lonny, you work too hard. You've given up—been forced to give up—too much. You've grown so...short-tempered. In my arrogant way I saw you as lonely and decided to do something about it." She was nervous about her next remark but made it anyway. "I was afraid this place was going to suck the life out of you, like I thought it had with Mom."

"Are you still on that kick?" he asked, suddenly angry. Then he sighed, a sound of resignation.

"We had a big fight over this once, and I swore I wouldn't mention it again, but honestly, Letty, you're seeing Mom as some kind of martyr. She loved the ranch...she loved Wyoming."

"I know," Letty answered quietly.

"Then why are you arguing with me about it?"

Letty ignored the question, deciding that discretion was well-advised at the moment. "It came to me after I sorted through the carton of her things that you brought over," she said, toying with her glass. "I studied the quilt Mom was making and realized that her talent *wasn't* wasted. She just transferred it to another form—quilting. At first I was surprised that she hadn't used the sewing machine to join the squares. Every stitch in that quilt top was made by hand, every single one of them."

"I think she felt there was more of herself in it that way," Lonny suggested.

Letty smiled in agreement. "I'm going to finish it this winter. I'll do the actual quilting—and I'll do it by hand, just like she did."

"It's going to be beautiful," Lonny said. "Really beautiful."

Letty nodded. "The blending of colors, the design—it all spells out how much love and skill Mom put into it. When I decided to leave Red Springs after high school, I went because I didn't want to end up like Mom, and now I realize I couldn't strive toward a finer goal."

Lonny frowned again. "I don't understand. You left for California because you didn't want to be a rancher's wife, and yet you married Chase...."

"I know. But I love Chase. I always have. It wasn't being a rancher's wife that I objected to so much. Yes, the life is hard. But the rewards are plentiful. I knew that nine years ago, and I know it even more profoundly now. My biggest fear was that I'd end up dedicating my life to ranching like Mom did and never achieve my own dreams."

"But Mom was happy. I never once heard her complain. I guess that's why I took such offense when you made it sound as if she'd wasted her life. Nothing could be farther from the truth."

"I know that now," Letty murmured. "But I didn't understand it for a long time. What upset me most was that I felt she could never paint the way she wanted to. There was always something else that needed her attention, some other project that demanded her time. It wasn't until I saw the quilt that I understood.... She sketched for her own enjoyment, but the other things she made were for the people she loved. The quilt she was working on when she died was for me, and it's taught me perhaps the most valuable lesson of my life."

Lonny's face relaxed into a smile. "I'm glad, Letty. In the back of my mind I had the feeling that once you'd recuperated from the surgery, you'd get restless. But you won't, will you?"

"You've got to be kidding," she said with a laugh. "I'm a married woman, you know." She twisted the diamond wedding band around her finger. "My place is here, with Chase. I plan to spend the rest of my life with him."

"I'm glad to hear that," he said again, his relief evident.

"We got off the subject, didn't we?" she said apologetically. "You wanted to talk to me." He hadn't told her why, but she could guess....

"Yes.... Well, it has to do with..." He hesitated, as if saying Joy Fuller's name would somehow conjure her up.

"Joy?" Letty asked.

Lonny nodded.

"What about her?"

In response, Lonny jerked his fingers through his hair and glared at the ceiling. "I'm telling you, Letty, no one's more shocked by this than me. I've discovered that I like her. I...mean I *really* like her. The fact is, I can't stop thinking about Joy, but every time I try to talk to her, I say something stupid, and before I know it, we're arguing."

Letty bent her head to show she understood. She'd witnessed more than one of her brother's clashes with Joy.

"We don't just argue like normal civilized people," Lonny continued. "She can make me so angry I don't even know what I'm saying anymore."

Letty lowered her eyes, afraid her smile would annoy her brother, especially since he'd come to her for help. Except that, at the moment, she didn't feel qualified to offer him any advice.

"The worst part is," he went on, "I was in town this morning, and I heard that Joy's agreed to go out with Glen Brewster. The thought of her dating another man has me all twisted up inside."

"Glen Brewster?" That surprised Letty. "Isn't he the guy who manages the grocery store?"

"One and the same," Lonny confirmed, scowling. "Can you imagine her going out with someone like Glen? He's all wrong for her!"

"Have you asked Joy out yourself?"

The way the color streaked his face told Letty what she needed to know. "I don't think I should answer that." He lifted his eyes piteously. "I want to take her out, but everyone's working against me."

"Everyone?"

He cleared his throat. "No, not everyone. I guess I'm my own worst enemy—I know that sounds crazy. I mean, it's not like I haven't had girlfriends before. But she's different from the girls I met on the rodeo circuit."

He stared down at the newly waxed kitchen floor. "All I want you to do is tell me what a woman wants from a man. A woman like Joy. If I know that, then maybe I can do something right—for once."

The door slammed in the distance. Lonny's gaze flew up to meet Letty's. "Joy?"

"Probably."

"Oh, great," he groaned.

"Don't panic."

"Me?" he asked with a short, sarcastic laugh. "Why should I do that? The woman's told me in no uncertain terms that she never wants to see me again. Her last words to me were—and I quote—'take a flying leap into the nearest cow pile.'"

"What did you say to her, for heaven's sake?"

He shrugged, looking uncomfortable. "I'd better not repeat it."

"Oh, Lonny! Don't you ever learn? She's not one of your buckle bunnies—but you already know that. Maybe if you'd quit insulting her, you'd be able to have a civil conversation."

"I've decided something," he said. "I don't know how or when, but I'm going to marry her." The words had no sooner left his lips than the screen door opened.

Cricket came flying into the kitchen, bursting to tell her mother about all her adventures with Joy at the school. She started speaking so fast that the words ran together. "I-saw-my-classroom-and-I-got-to-meet-Mrs.-Webber…and I sat in a real desk and everything!"

Joy followed Cricket into the kitchen, but stopped abruptly when she saw Lonny. The expression on her face suggested that if he said one word to her—one word—she'd leave.

As if taking his cue, Lonny reached for his hat and stood. "I'd better get back to work. Good talking to you, Letty," he said stiffly. His gaze skipped from his sister to Joy, and he inclined his head politely. "Hello, *Ms.* Fuller."

"*Mr.* Ellison." Joy dipped her head, too, ever so slightly.

They gave each other a wide berth as Lonny stalked out of the kitchen. Before he opened the screen door, he sent a pleading glance at Letty, but she wasn't sure what he expected her to do.

Chase didn't come in for dinner, but that didn't surprise Letty. He'd avoided her so much lately that she rarely saw him in the evenings anymore. Even Cricket had commented on it. She obviously missed him, although he made an effort to work with her and Jennybird, the pony.

The house was dark, and Cricket had been asleep for hours, when Letty heard the back door open. Judging by the muffled sounds Chase was making, she knew he was in the kitchen, washing up. Next he would shower.

Some nights he came directly to bed; others he'd sit in front of the TV, delaying the time before he joined her. In the mornings he'd be gone before she woke. Letty didn't know any man who worked as physically hard as Chase did on so little rest.

"You're later than usual tonight," she said, standing barefoot in the kitchen doorway.

He didn't turn around when he spoke. "There's lots to do this time of year."

"Yes, I know," she answered, willing to accept his lame excuse. "I didn't get much of a chance to talk to you this afternoon."

"What did Lonny want?"

So he was going to change the subject. Fine, she'd let him. "Joy problems," she told him.

Chase nodded, opened the refrigerator and took out a carton of milk. He poured himself a glass, then drank it down in one long swallow.

"Would you like me to run you a bath?"

"I'd rather take a shower." Reluctantly he turned to face her.

This was the moment Letty had been waiting for. She'd planned it all night. The kitchen remained dark; the only source of light was the moon, which cast flickering shadows over the wall. Letty was leaning against the doorjamb, her hands behind her back. Her nightgown had been selected with care, a frothy see-through piece of chiffon that covered her from head to foot, yet revealed everything.

Letty knew she'd achieved the desired effect when the glass Chase was holding slipped from his hand and dropped to the floor. By some miracle it didn't shatter. Chase bent over to retrieve it, and even standing several yards away, Letty could see that his fingers were trembling.

"I saw Dr. Faraday this morning," she told him, keeping her voice low and seductive. "He gave me a clean bill of health."

"Congratulations."

"I think this calls for a little celebration, don't you?"

"Celebration?"

"I'm your wife, Chase, but you seem to have conveniently forgotten that fact. There's no reason we should wait any longer."

"Wait?" He was beginning to sound like an echo.

Letty prayed for calm.

Before she could say anything else, he added abruptly, "I've been out on the range for the past twelve hours. I'm dirty and tired and badly in need of some hot water."

"I've been patient all this time. A few more minutes won't kill me." She'd never thought it would come to this, but she was going to have to seduce her own husband. So be it. She was hardly an expert in the techniques of seduction, but instinct was directing her behavior—instinct and love.

"Letty, I'm not in the mood. As I said, I'm tired and—"

"You were in the mood this afternoon," she whispered, deliberately moistening her lips with the tip of her tongue.

He ground out her name, his hands clenched at his sides. "Perhaps you should go back to bed."

"Back to bed?" She straightened, hands on her hips. "You were supposed to take one look at me and be overcome with passion!"

"I was?"

He was silently laughing at her, proving she'd done an excellent job of making a fool of herself. Tears sprang to her eyes. Before the surgery and directly afterward, Chase had been the model husband—loving, gentle, concerned. He couldn't seem to spend enough time with her. Lately just the opposite was true. The man who stood across from her now wasn't the same man she'd married, and she didn't understand what had changed him.

Chase stood where he was, feet planted apart, as if he expected her to defy him.

Without another word, Letty turned and left. Tears blurred her vision as she walked into their room and sank down on the edge of the bed. Covering her face with both hands, she sat there, her thoughts whirling, gathering momentum, until she lost track of time.

"Letty."

She vaulted to her feet and wiped her face. "Don't you *Letty* me, you…you arrogant cowboy." That was the worst thing she could come up with on short notice.

He was fresh from the shower, wearing nothing more than a towel around his waist.

"I had all these romantic plans for seducing you— and…and you made me feel I'm about as appealing as an old steer. So you want to live like brother and sister? Fine. Two can play this game, fellow." She pulled the chiffon nightie over her head and yanked open a drawer, grabbing an old flannel gown and donning that. When she'd finished, she whirled around to face him.

To her chagrin, Chase took one look at her and burst out laughing.

Chapter 13

"Don't you *dare* laugh at me," Letty cried, her voice trembling.

"I'm not," he told her. The humor had evaporated as if it had never been. What he'd told her earlier about being tired was true; he'd worked himself to the point of exhaustion. But he'd have to be a crazy man to reject the very thing he wanted most. Letty had come to him, demolished every excuse not to hold and kiss her, and like an idiot he'd told her to go back to bed. Who did he think he was? A man of steel? He wasn't kidding anyone, least of all himself.

Silently he walked around the end of the bed toward her.

For every step Chase advanced, Letty took one away from him, until the backs of her knees were pressed against the mattress and there was nowhere else to go.

Chase met her gaze, needing her love and her warmth so badly he was shaking with it.

Ever so gently he brought his hands up to frame her face. He stroked away the moisture on her cheeks, wanting to erase each tear and beg her forgiveness for having hurt her. Slowly, he slid his hands down the sides of her neck until they settled on her shoulders.

"Nothing in my life has been as good as these past months with you and Cricket," he told her, although the admission cost him dearly. He hadn't wanted to tie her to him with words and emotional bonds. If she stayed, he wanted it to be of her own free will, not because she felt trapped or obliged.

"I can't alter the past," he whispered. "I don't have any control of the future. But we have now…tonight."

"Then why did you…laugh at me?"

"Because I'm a fool. I need you, Letty, so much it frightens me." He heard the husky emotion in his voice, but didn't regret exposing his longing to her. "If I can only have you for a little while, I think we should take advantage of this time, don't you?"

He didn't give her an opportunity to respond, but urged her toward him and placed his mouth on hers, kissing her over and over until her sweet responsive body was molded against him. He'd dreamed of holding Letty like this, pliable and soft in his arms, but once again reality exceeded his imagination.

"I was beginning to believe you hated me," she whimpered against his mouth. Then, clinging to him, she resumed their kiss.

"Let's take this off," he said a moment later, tugging at the flannel gown. With a reluctance that excited him all the more, Letty stepped out of his arms just far enough to let him pull the gown over her head and discard it.

"Oh, Letty," he groaned, looking at her, heaving a sigh of appreciation. "You're so beautiful." He felt humble seeing her like this. Her beauty, so striking, was revealed only to him, and his knees went weak.

"The scar?" Her eyes were lowered.

The red line that ran the length of her sternum would fade in the years to come. But Chase viewed it as a badge of courage. He leaned forward and kissed it, gently, lovingly, breathing her name.

"Oh, Chase, I thought…maybe you found me ugly and that's why…you wouldn't touch me."

"No," he said. "Never."

"But you *didn't* touch me. For weeks and weeks you stayed on your side of the bed, until…until I thought I'd go crazy."

"I couldn't be near you and not want you," he admitted hoarsely. "I had to wait until Dr. Faraday said it was okay." If those weeks had been difficult for Letty, they'd been doubly so for him.

"Do you want to touch me now?"

He nodded. From the moment they'd discarded her gown, Chase hadn't been able to take his eyes off her.

"Yes. I want to hold you for the rest of my life."

"Please love me, Chase." Her low, seductive voice was all the encouragement he needed. He eased her onto the bed, securing her there with his body. He had to taste her, had to experience all the pleasure she'd so unselfishly offered him earlier.

Their lovemaking was everything he could've hoped

for—everything he *had* hoped for. She welcomed him
readily and he was awed by her generosity, lost in her
love.

Afterward, Chase lay beside Letty and gathered her
in his arms. As he felt the sweat that slid down her face,
felt the heavy exhaustion that claimed his limbs, he
wondered how he'd been able to resist her for so long.

Letty woke at dawn, still in Chase's arms. She felt
utterly content—and excited. Plan B hadn't worked
out exactly the way she'd thought it would, but it had
certainly produced the desired effect. She felt like sitting up and throwing her arms in the air and shouting
for sheer joy. She was a wife!

"Morning," Chase whispered.

He didn't look at her, as if he half expected her to
be embarrassed by the intimacies they'd shared the
night before. Letty's exhilarated thoughts came to an
abrupt halt. Had she said or done something a married
woman shouldn't?

She was about to voice her fears when her husband
turned to her, bracing his arms on either side of her
head. She met his eyes, unsure of what he was asking.
Slowly he lowered his mouth to hers, kissing her with
a hungry need that surprised as much as delighted her.

"How long do we have before Cricket wakes up?"
he whispered.

"Long enough," she whispered back.

In the days that followed, Letty found that Chase
was insatiable. Not that she minded. In fact, she was
thrilled that his need to make love to her was so great.

Chase touched and held her often and each caress made her long for sundown. The nights were theirs.

Cricket usually went to bed early, tired out from the long day's activities. As always, Chase was endlessly patient with her, reading her bedtime stories and making up a few of his own, which he dutifully repeated for Letty.

Cricket taught him the game of blowing out the light that Letty had played with her from the time she was a toddler. Whenever she watched Chase with her daughter, Letty was quietly grateful. He was so good with Cricket, and the little girl adored him.

Letty had never been happier. Chase had never told her he loved her in so many words, but she was reassured of his devotion in a hundred different ways. He'd never communicated his feelings freely, and the years hadn't changed that. But the looks he gave her, the reverent way he touched her, his exuberant lovemaking, told her everything she needed to know.

The first week of September Cricket started kindergarten. On the opening day of school, Letty drove her into town and lingered after class had begun, talking to the other mothers for a few minutes. Then, feeling a little melancholy, she returned to the ranch. A new world was opening up for Cricket, and Letty's role in her daughter's life would change.

Letty parked the truck in the yard and walked into the kitchen. Chase wasn't due back at the house until eleven-thirty for lunch; Cricket would be coming home on the school bus, but that wasn't until early afternoon, so Letty's morning was free. She did some housework, but without much enthusiasm. After throwing a load of clothes in the washer, she decided to vacuum.

Once in the living room, she found herself drawn to the old upright piano. She stood over the keys and with one finger plinked out a couple of the songs she'd taught Cricket.

Before she knew it, she was sitting on the bench, running her fingers up and down the yellowing keys, playing a few familiar chords. Soon she was singing, and it felt wonderful, truly wonderful, to release some of the emotion she was experiencing in song.

She wasn't sure how long she'd been sitting there when she looked up and saw Chase watching her. His eyes were sad.

"Your voice is still as beautiful as it always was," he murmured.

"Thank you," she said, feeling shy. It had been months since she'd sat at the piano like this and sung.

"It's been a long time since I've heard you," he told her, his voice flat.

She slipped off the piano bench and closed the keyboard. She considered telling him she didn't do this often; she knew that, for some reason, her playing made him uncomfortable. That saddened Letty—even more so because she didn't understand his feelings.

An awkward silence passed.

"Chase," she said, realizing why he must be in the house. "I'm sorry. I didn't realize it was time for lunch already."

"It isn't," he said.

"Is something wrong?" she asked, feeling unnerved and not knowing why.

"No." The look in his eyes was one of tenderness... and fear? Pain? Either way, it made no sense to her.

Without a word, she slipped into his arms, hugging him close. He was tense and held himself stiffly, but she couldn't fathom why.

Tilting her head, Letty studied him. He glided his thumb over her lips and she captured it between her teeth. "Kiss me," she said. That was one sure way of comforting him.

He did, kissing her ravenously. Urgently. As if this was the last opportunity they'd have. When he ended the kiss, Letty finally felt him relax, and sighed in relief.

"I need you, Letty," he murmured.

Chase's mouth was buried in the hollow of her throat. She burrowed her fingers in his hair, needing to continue touching him.

He kissed her one more time, then drew back. "I want to have you in my arms and in my bed as often as I can before you go," he whispered, refusing to meet her gaze.

"Before I go?" she repeated in confusion. "I'm not going anywhere—Cricket's taking the bus home."

Chase shook his head. "When I married you, I accepted that sooner or later you'd leave," he said, his voice filled with resignation.

Letty was so stunned, so shocked, that for a second she couldn't believe what she was hearing. "Let me see if I understand you," she said slowly. "I married you, but you seem to think I had no intention of staying in the relationship and that sooner or later I'd fly the coop? Am I understanding you correctly?" It was an effort to disguise her sarcasm.

"You were facing a life-or-death situation. I offered you an alternative because of Cricket."

Chase spoke as if that explained everything. "I love you, Chase Brown. I loved you when I left Wyoming. I loved you when I came back.... I love you even more now."

He didn't look at her. "I never said I felt the same way about you."

The world seemed to skid to a halt; everything went perfectly still except for her heart, which was ramming loudly against her chest.

"True," she began when she could find her voice. "You never *said* you did. But you *show* me every day how much you love me. I don't need the words, Chase. You can't hide what you feel for me."

He was making his way to the door when he turned back and snorted softly. "Don't confuse great sex with love, Letty."

She felt unbelievably hurt and fiercely angry.

"Do you *want* me to leave, Chase? Is that what you're saying?"

"I won't ask you to stay."

"In...in other words, I'm free to walk out of here anytime?"

He nodded. "You can go now, if that's what you want."

"Generous of you," she snapped.

He didn't respond.

"I get it," she cried sharply. "Everything's falling into place now. Every time I sit down at the piano, I can feel your displeasure. Why did you bring it here if it bothered you so much?"

"It wasn't my bright idea," he said curtly. "Joy thought it would help you recuperate. If I'd had my way, it would never have left Lonny's place."

"Take it back, then."

"I will once you're gone."

Letty pressed her hand against her forehead. "I can't believe we're having this conversation. I love you, Chase... I don't ever want to leave you."

"Whatever you decide is fine, Letty," he said, and again his voice was resigned. "That decision is yours." He walked out of the house, letting the back door slam behind him.

For several minutes, Letty did nothing but lean against the living room wall. Chase's feigned indifference infuriated her. Hadn't the past few weeks meant *anything* to him? Obviously that was what he wanted her to think. He was pretending to be so damn smug... so condescending, that it demanded all her restraint not to haul out her suitcases that instant and walk away from him just to prove him right.

His words made a lie of all the happiness she'd found in her marriage. Angry tears scalded her eyes. For some reason she didn't grasp, Chase wanted her to think he was using her, and he'd paid a steep price for the privilege—he'd married her.

Letty sank down onto the floor and covered her face with her hands, feeling wretched to the marrow of her bones.

Like some romantic fool, she'd held on to the belief that everything between her and Chase was perfect now and would remain that way forever after. It was a blow to discover otherwise.

When she'd first come back to Wyoming, Letty had been afraid her life was nearly over and the only things awaiting her were pain and regret. Instead Chase had given her a glimpse of happiness. With him, she'd experienced an immeasurable sense of satisfaction and joy, an inner peace. She'd seen Chase as her future, seen the two of them as lifelong companions, a man and a woman in love, together for life.

Nearly blinded by her tears, she got up and grabbed her purse from the kitchen table. She had to get away to think, put order to her raging thoughts.

Chase was in the yard when she walked out the door. He paused, and out of the corner of her eye, Letty saw that he moved two steps toward her, then abruptly stopped. Apparently he'd changed his mind about whatever he was going to say or do. Which was just as well, since Letty wasn't in the mood to talk to him.

His gaze followed her as she walked toward the truck, as if he suspected she was leaving him right then and there.

Perhaps that was exactly what she should do.

Chapter 14

Letty had no idea where she was going. All she knew was that she had to get away. She considered driving to town and waiting for Cricket. But it was still a while before the kindergarten class was scheduled to be dismissed. In addition, Cricket was looking forward to riding the bus home; to her, that seemed the height of maturity. Letty didn't want to ruin that experience for her daughter.

As she drove aimlessly down the country road, Letty attempted to put the disturbing events of the morning in perspective. Leaving Chase, if only for a day or two, would be an overreaction, but she didn't know how else to deal with this situation. One moment she had everything a woman could want; the next it had all been taken away from her for reasons she couldn't understand or explain. The safe harbor she'd anchored in—her marriage to Chase—had been unexpectedly invaded by an enemy she couldn't even identify.

Without realizing where she'd driven, Letty noticed that the hillside where she'd so often sat with Chase was just over the next ridge. With an ironic smile, she stopped the truck. Maybe their hillside would give her the serenity and inner guidance she sought now.

With the autumn sun warm on her back, she strolled over to the crest of the hill and sat down on a soft patch of grass. She saw a few head of cattle resting under the shade of trees near the stream below, and watched them idly while her thoughts churned. How peaceful the animals seemed, how content. Actually, she was a little surprised to see them grazing there, since she'd heard Chase say that he was moving his herd in the opposite direction. But where he chose to let his cattle graze was the least of her worries.

A slow thirty minutes passed. What Letty found so disheartening about the confrontation with Chase was his conviction that she'd leave him and, worse, his acceptance of it. Why was he so certain she'd pack up and move away? Did he trust her so little?

To give up on their love, their marriage and all the happiness their lives together would bring was traumatic enough. For her and, she was convinced, for him. But the fact that he could do so with no more than a twinge of regret was almost more than Letty could bear. Chase's pride wouldn't let him tell her he loved her and that he wanted her to stay.

Yet he *did* love her and he loved Cricket. Despite his heartless words to the contrary, Letty could never doubt it.

Standing, Letty let her arms hang limply at her sides. She didn't know what she should do. Perhaps getting away for a day or two wasn't such a bad plan.

The idea started to gather momentum. It was as she turned to leave that Letty noticed one steer that had separated itself from the others. She paused, then stared at the brand, surprised it wasn't Chase's. Before she left Spring Valley she'd let Chase know that old man Wilber's cattle were on his property.

Chase was nowhere to be seen when Letty got back to the house. That was fine, since she'd be in and out within a matter of minutes. She threw a few things in a suitcase for herself and dragged it into the hallway. Then she rushed upstairs to grab some clothes for Cricket. Letty wasn't sure what she'd tell her daughter about this unexpected vacation, but she'd think of something later.

Chase was standing in the kitchen when she reached the bottom of the stairs. His eyes were cold and cruel in a way she hadn't seen since she'd first returned home. He picked up her suitcase and set it by the back door, as if eager for her to leave.

"I see you decided to go now," he said, leaning indolently against the kitchen counter.

His arms were folded over his chest in a gesture of stubborn indifference. If he'd revealed the least bit of remorse or indecision, Letty might have considered reasoning with him, but it was painfully apparent that he didn't feel anything except the dire satisfaction of being proven right.

"I thought I'd spend a few days with Lonny."

"Lonny," Chase repeated with a short, sarcastic laugh. "I bet he'll love that."

"He won't mind." A half-truth, but worth it if Chase believed her.

"You're sure of that?"

It was obvious from Chase's lack of concern that he wasn't going to invite her to stay at the ranch so they could resolve their differences—which was what Letty had hoped he'd do.

"If Lonny *does* object, I'll simply find someplace in town."

"Do you have enough money?"

"Yes…" Letty said, striving to sound casual.

"I'll be happy to provide whatever you need."

Chase spoke with such a flippant air that it cut her to the quick. "I won't take any money from you."

Chase shrugged. "Fine."

Everything in Letty wanted to shout at him to give her some sign, anything, that would show her he wanted her to stay. It was the whole reason she was staging this. His nonchalant response was so painful, that not breaking down, not weeping, was all Letty could manage.

"Is this what you really want?" she asked in a small voice.

"Like I said before, if you're set on leaving, I'm not going to stop you."

Letty reached down for her suitcase, tightening her fingers around the handle. "I'll get Cricket at school. I'll think up some excuse to tell her." She made it all the way to the back door before Chase stopped her.

"Letty…"

She whirled around, her heart ringing with excitement until she saw the look in his eyes.

"Before you go, there's something I need to ask you," he said, his face drawn. "Is there any possibility you could be pregnant?"

His question seemed to echo against the walls.

"Letty?"

She met his gaze. Some of his arrogance was gone, replaced with a tenderness that had been far too rare these past few hours. "No," she whispered, her voice hardly audible.

Chase's eyes closed, but she didn't know if he felt regret or relief. The way things had been going, she didn't want to know.

"I...went to the hillside," she said in a low voice that wavered slightly despite her effort to control it. She squared her shoulders, then continued. "There were several head of cattle there. The brand is Wilber's."

Chase clenched his jaw so tightly that the sides of his face went pale under his tan. "So you know," he said, his voice husky and filled with dread. His gaze skirted hers, fists at his sides.

Letty was baffled. Chase's first response to the fact that she'd seen his neighbor's cattle on his property made no sense. She had no idea why he'd react like that.

Then it struck her. "You sold those acres to Mr. Wilber, didn't you? Why?" That land had been in Chase's family for over three generations. Letty couldn't figure out what would be important enough for him to relinquish those acres. Not once in all the weeks they'd been married or before had he given her any indication that he was financially strapped.

"I don't understand," she said—and suddenly she did. "There wasn't any insurance money for my surgery, was there, Chase?"

She'd been so unsuspecting, so confident when he'd told her everything had been taken care of. She should've known—in fact, did know—that an insurance company wouldn't cover a preexisting condition without a lengthy waiting period.

"Chase?" She held his eyes with her own. Incredulous, shocked, she set the suitcase down and took one small step toward her husband. "Why did you lie to me about the insurance?"

He tunneled his fingers through his hair.

"Why would you do something like that? It doesn't make any sense." Very little of this day had. "Didn't you realize the state had already agreed to cover all the expenses?"

"You hated being a charity case. I saw the look in your eyes when I found your welfare check. It was killing you to accept that money."

"Of course I hated it, but I managed to swallow my pride. It was necessary. But what you did wasn't. Why would you sell your land? I just can't believe it." Chase loved every square inch of Spring Valley. Parting with a single acre would be painful, let alone the prime land near the creek. It would be akin to his cutting off one of his fingers.

Chase turned away from her and walked over to the sink. His shoulders jerked in a hard shrug as he braced his hands on the edge. "All right, if you must know. I did it because I wanted you to marry me."

"But you said the marriage was for Cricket's sake...

in case anything happened to me…. Then you could raise her."

"That was an excuse." The words seemed to be wrenched from him. After a long pause, he added, "I love you, Letty." It was all the explanation he gave her.

"I love you, too…I always have," she whispered, awed by what he'd done and, more importantly, the reason behind it. "I told you only three hours ago how I felt about you, but you practically threw it back in my face. If you love me so much," she murmured, "why couldn't you let me know it? Would that have been so wrong?"

"I didn't want you to feel trapped."

"Trapped?" How could Chase possibly view their marriage in such a light? He made it sound as if he'd taken her hostage!

"Sooner or later I realized you'd want to return to California. I knew that when I asked you to marry me. I accepted it."

"That's ridiculous!" Letty cried. "I don't ever want to go back. There's nothing for me there. Everything that's ever been good in my life is right here with you."

Chase turned to face her. "What about the fight you and Lonny had about your mother? You said—"

"I realized how wrong I was about Mom," she interrupted, gesturing with her hands. "My mother was a wonderful woman, but more significant than that, she was fulfilled as a person. I'm not going to say she had an easy life—we both know differently. But she loved the challenge here. She loved her art, too, and found ways to express her talent. I was just too blind to recognize it. I was so caught up in striving toward my dreams, I failed to see that my happiness was right here in Red Springs with you. The biggest mistake I ever made was leaving you. Do you honestly believe I'd do it again?"

A look of hope crept into Chase's eyes.

"Telling me I'm free to walk away from you is one thing," Letty said softly. "But you made it sound as if you wanted me gone—as if you couldn't wait to get me out of your life. You weren't even willing to give us a chance. That hurt more than anything."

"I was afraid to," he admitted, his voice low.

"Over and over again, you kept saying that you wouldn't stop me from leaving. It was almost as if you'd been waiting for it to happen because I'd been such a disappointment to you."

"Letty, no, I swear that isn't true."

"Then why are you standing way over there—and I'm way over here?"

"Oh, Letty." He covered the space between them in three giant strides, wrapping his arms around her. When he lifted his head, their eyes melted together. "I love you, Letty, more than I thought it was possible to care about anyone. I haven't told you that, and I was wrong. You deserve to hear the words."

"Chase, you didn't need to say them for me to know how you feel. That's what was so confusing. I couldn't doubt you loved me, yet you made my leaving sound like some long-anticipated event."

"I couldn't let you know how much I was hurting."

"But I was hurting, too."

"I know, my love, I know."

He rained hot, urgent kisses down upon her face.

She directed his mouth to hers, and his kiss intensified. Letty threaded her fingers through his hair, glorying in the closeness they shared. She was humbled by the sacrifice he'd made for her. He could have given her no greater proof of his love.

"Chase." His name was a broken cry on her lips. "The land...you sold...I can't bear to think of you losing it."

He caressed her face. "It's not as bad as it sounds. I have the option of buying it back at a future date, and I will."

"But—"

He silenced her with his mouth, kissing away her objections and concerns. Then he tore his mouth from hers and brought it to the hollow of her throat, kissing her there. "I would gladly have sold all of Spring Valley if it had been necessary."

Letty felt tears gather in her eyes. Tears of gratitude and joy and need.

"You've given me so much," he whispered. "My life was so empty until you came back and brought Cricket with you. I love her, Letty, as if she were our own. I want to adopt her and give her my name."

Letty nodded through her tears, knowing that Cricket would want that, too.

Chase inhaled deeply, then exhaled a long, slow breath. "As much as I wanted you to stay, I couldn't let you know that. When I asked if you might be pregnant, it was a desperate attempt by a desperate man to find a way to keep you here, despite all my claims to the contrary. I think my heart dropped to my feet when you told me you weren't."

Letty wasn't sure she understood.

He stared down at her with a tender warmth. "I don't know if I can explain this, but when I mentioned the possibility of you being pregnant, I had a vision of two little boys."

Letty smiled. "Twins?"

"No," Chase said softly. "They were a year or so apart. I saw them clearly, standing beside each other, and somehow I knew that those two were going to be our sons. The day you had the surgery—I saw them then, too. I wanted those children so badly.... Today, when you were about to walk out the door, I didn't know if you'd ever come back. I knew if you left me, the emptiness would return, and I didn't think I could bear it. I tried to prepare myself for your going, but it didn't work."

"I couldn't have stayed away for long. My heart's here with you. You taught me to forgive myself for the past and cherish whatever the future holds."

His eyes drifted shut. "We have so much, Letty." He was about to say more when the kitchen door burst open and Cricket came rushing into the room.

Chase broke away from Letty just in time for the five-year-old to vault into his arms. "I have a new friend, and her name's Karen and she's got a pony, too. I like school a whole bunch, and Mrs. Webber let me hand out some papers and said I could be her helper every day."

Chase hugged the little girl. "I'm glad you like school so much, sweetheart." Then he put his hand on Letty's shoulder, pulling her to him.

Letty leaned into his strength and closed her eyes,

savoring these few moments of contentment. She'd found her happiness in Chase. She'd come home, knowing she might die, and instead had discovered life in its most abundant form. Spring Valley was their future—here was where they'd thrive. Here was where their sons would be born.

Cricket came to her mother's side, and Letty drew her close. As she did, she looked out the kitchen window. The Wyoming sky had never seemed bluer. Or filled with greater promise.

* * * * *

THE WYOMING KID

To the Peninsula Chapter
of Romance Writers of America—gutsy girls all.

Chapter 1

His truck shuddering as he hit a rut, Lonny Ellison pulled into the ranch yard at Spring Valley and slammed on the brakes. He jumped out of the cab, muttering furiously. In pure frustration, he kicked the side of his Ford Ranger with one scuffed boot. His sister, who was hanging clothes on the line, straightened and watched him approach. No word of greeting, not even a wave, just a little smile. As calm as could be, Letty studied him, which only irritated him more. He blamed her for this. She was the one who had her heart set on Lonny's dating that…that woman. She was also the one who'd been busy trying to do some matchmaking—not that she'd had any success. She'd even promised a year ago that she wouldn't do it again. Ha!

It wasn't like Lonny to let a woman rattle him, but

Joy Fuller certainly had. This wasn't the first time, either. Oh, no. Far from it.

He had plenty of cause to dislike her. Two years ago, when she'd moved to Red Springs to take a teaching job, he'd gone out of his way to make her feel welcome in the community. They'd gone out a few times, and they'd argued—he couldn't even remember why— and he hadn't spoken to her until Letty came back on the scene last summer. He'd—briefly—rediscovered some interest in her, but it hadn't ended well. Now *this!* Friend of Letty's or not, he wasn't about to let Joy Fuller escape the consequences of what she'd done.

What bothered him most was the complete disrespect Joy had shown him and his vehicle. Why, his truck was in prime condition, his pride and— No, under the circumstances, he couldn't call it his pride and *joy.* But he treasured that Ford almost as much as he did his horse.

"What's gotten into you?" Letty asked, completely unruffled by his actions.

"Why did it have to be *her?* Again?"

"And who would that be?" his sister asked mildly.

"Your...your teacher friend. She—" Lonny struggled to find the words. "It's outrageous!"

Letty's expressive eyes widened and she gave a deep sigh. "Okay, what did Joy do this time?"

"Here!" He motioned toward the front of his pickup so his sister could see for herself.

"Oh, oh. This sounds like déjà vu." Letty scanned the bumper. "Looks like it, too."

He pointed, his finger shaking as he directed her attention to the most recent dent.

"Where?" Letty asked, bending over to examine it more carefully, squinting hard.

"There." If she assumed that being obtuse was amusing him, she was wrong. He stabbed his finger at it again. All right, he'd admit the truck had its share of nicks and dents. The pickup could use a new front fender, and a paint job wouldn't be a bad idea, but in no way did that minimize what Joy had done.

"Oh, give it up, Lonny. This thing is ready for the scrap heap."

"You're joking, aren't you? There's at least another decade left in the engine." He should've known better than to discuss this with his sister. As he'd learned to his sorrow, women always stuck together.

"You don't mean this tiny little dent, do you?" she asked, poking it with her finger.

"Tiny little dent!" he repeated, shocked that she didn't see this for what it was.

"Come on," Letty said, "and just tell me what Joy supposedly did." She shook her head. "I don't understand why you're so upset."

To say he was *upset* was an understatement. He was fit to be tied, and it was Joy Fuller's fault. Lonny liked to think of himself as an easygoing guy. Very rarely did a woman, any woman, rile him the way Joy had. Not only that, she seemed to enjoy it.

"Joy Fuller ran a stop sign," he explained. "Just like she did last year. Different stop sign, though," he muttered in disgust. "Not that it makes things any better."

"Joy crashed into you?"

"Almost. By the grace of God, I was able to avoid a collision, but in the process I hit the pole."

"Then this really *is* déjà vu," Letty said delightedly.

That was not the response he was looking for.

Lonny jerked the Stetson off his head and smacked it hard against his thigh. Wincing, he went on with his story. "Then Joy gets out of her car, tells me she's *sorry* and asks if there's any damage."

"Gee, I hope you slugged her for that," Letty murmured, rolling her eyes.

Lonny decided to ignore the sarcasm. "I showed her the dent," he said, not even trying to keep the indignation out of his voice. "She said there were even more dents on my truck than last year, so how could she tell which one she'd caused?" His voice rose as his agitation grew.

"What did you say next?" Letty asked.

Lonny stared down at the ground. "We…argued." That was Joy's fault, too. Just like last year. She seemed to expect him to tell her that all was forgiven. Well, he wasn't forgiving her anything, least of all the damage she'd caused.

When he hadn't fallen under her spell once again— as she'd obviously expected—their argument had quickly heated up. Within minutes her true nature was revealed. "She said my truck was a piece of crap." Even now the statement outraged him. Lonny looked at his Ford, muttering, "That's no way for a lady to talk. Not only did Joy insult my vehicle, she insulted *me*."

This schoolteacher, this city slicker, had no appreciation of country life. That was what you got when the town hired someone like Joy Fuller. You could take the woman out of the city but there was plenty of city left in her.

"Why don't you let Joy's insurance take care of it?" Letty said in that soothing way of hers. "It was really nice of you to let it go last year."

Lonny scowled. Joy had a lot to atone for as far as he was concerned, and he wasn't inclined to be as generous this time. "And get this. She tried to buy me off—again!" Even now, the suggestion offended him.

Letty raised her eyebrows and Lonny muttered, "She said she'd give me fifty bucks."

"So she didn't increase her offer? Wasn't that the amount she wanted to give you before?"

His sister's mouth quivered, and if he didn't know better, Lonny would've thought she was laughing. "You refused?" she murmured.

"Oh, yeah," he told her. "I'm gonna get an estimate from the body shop. Fifty bucks," he spat. "Fifty bucks!"

"Hmm." Letty grinned. "Seems to me Joy's managed to get your attention. Hasn't she?"

Lonny decided to ignore that comment, which he considered unworthy of his sister. All right, he had some history with Joy Fuller, most of it unpleasant. But the past was the past and had nothing to do with the here and now. "I wrote down her license plate number." He pulled a small piece of paper from his shirt pocket and brandished it under her nose. "This time I *am* going to report her to the police."

"You most certainly will not!" Letty snatched the paper out of his hand. "Joy is one of my best friends and I won't let you treat her so rudely."

His sister hadn't encountered the same side of the teacher he had. "You haven't seen that evil look about her—I suspect she normally keeps that PT Cruiser in the garage and travels by broomstick."

His sister didn't appreciate his attempt at humor. "Oh, for heaven's sake, Joy plays the organ at church on Sundays, as you very well know. Don't try to pretend you don't."

"That's all a front," he said darkly.

"You have unfinished business with Joy, which is why you're blowing this *incident* out of all proportion."

Lonny thought it best to ignore that comment, too. He'd finished with Joy a long time ago—and she with him—which suited him just fine. "I'd say she's one scary woman. Mean as a rattlesnake." He gave an exaggerated shiver. "Probably shrinks heads as a hobby."

Letty had the grace to smile. "Would you stop it? Joy's probably the sweetest person I've ever met."

"*Sweet?*" Lonny hadn't seen any evidence of a gentle disposition, not in the past year, and not now. He shuddered to think he'd once wanted to marry Joy. Man, had he dodged *that* bullet.

Hands on her hips, Letty shook her head sadly. "Come in and have some iced tea."

"Nah. You go on without me." Shaking his head, he strolled toward the barn. Joy Fuller was his sister's friend. One of her best friends. That meant he had to seriously question Letty's taste—and good sense. Years ago, when he was young and foolish, Lonny had ridden broncos and bulls and been known as The Wyoming Kid. He darn near got himself killed a time or two. But he'd rather sit on one of those beasts again than tangle with the likes of Joy Fuller.

Chapter 2

Joy Fuller glanced out the window of her combination third-and-fourth-grade classroom and did a quick double take. It couldn't be! But it was—Lonny Ellison. She should've known he wouldn't just let things be. The real problem was that they'd started off on the wrong foot two years ago. She'd been new to the community, still learning about life in Red Springs, Wyoming, when she'd met Lonny through a mutual acquaintance.

At first they'd gotten along well. He'd been a rodeo cowboy and had an ego even bigger than that ridiculously big belt buckle he'd shown her. Apparently, she hadn't paid him the homage he felt was his due. After a month or two of laughing, with decreasing sincerity, at his comments about city slickers, the joke had worn thin. She'd made it clear that she wasn't willing to be another of his buckle bunnies and soon after, they'd agreed not to see each other anymore. Not that their relationship was serious, of course; they'd gone out for dinner and dancing a few times—that was about it. So she hadn't thought their disagreement was a big deal, but apparently it had been to Lonny. It seemed no woman had ever spoken her mind to the great and mighty Wyoming Kid before.

Lonny had said he appreciated her honesty, and that was the last she'd heard from him. Joy had been surprised by his reaction. However, if that was how he felt, it was fine with her. He hadn't asked her out again and she hadn't contacted him, either. She saw him around town now and then, but aside from a polite nod or a cool "hello," they'd ignored each other. It was a rather disappointing end to what had begun as a promising relationship. But that was nearly two years ago and she was long past feeling any regrets. Their minor collision soon after Letty's return had seemed fitting somehow, the perfect finishing touch to their so-called relationship.

Then she'd had to miss that blasted stop sign the other day—but at least it was a different one, not the sign she'd missed last year, the one at Oak and Spruce. Naturally he had to be the one who slammed into the post. Again. The shock and embarrassment still upset her. Worse, Joy hadn't recovered yet from their verbal exchange. Lonny was completely and totally unreasonable, and he'd made some extremely unpleasant accusations. All right, in an effort to be fair, she'd admit that Lonny Ellison was easy to look at—tall and rangy with wide, muscular shoulders. He had strikingly rich, dark eyes and a solid jaw, and he reminded her a little of a young Clint Eastwood. However, appearances weren't everything.

Letty, who was a romantic, had wanted to match Joy with her brother. Letty had only moved back to the area a year ago and at first she hadn't realized that they'd already dated for a brief time. Joy had done her best to explain why a relationship with Lonny just wouldn't work. He was too stubborn and she was… well, a woman had her pride. They simply weren't compatible. And if she hadn't known that before, their first near-collision had proven it. This second one just confirmed it.

She peeked surreptitiously out the window again. Lonny was leaning against his rattletrap truck, ankles crossed to highlight his dusty boots. Chase Brown, Letty's husband, and Lonny owned adjoining ranches and shared a large herd of cattle. According to Letty, that was a recent enterprise; they'd joined forces last fall and were now raising hormone-free cattle. In any case, one would think a working rancher had better things to do than hang around outside a schoolyard. He was there to pester her; she was convinced of it. His lanky arms were crossed and his head bowed, with his Stetson riding low on his forehead, as if he didn't have a care in the world. His posture resembled that neon sign of a cowpoke in downtown Vegas, she thought.

She knew exactly why Lonny had come to the school. He was planning to cause her trouble. Joy rued the day she'd ever met the man. He was rude, unreasonable, juvenile, plus a dozen other adjectives she didn't even want to *think* about in front of a classroom full of young children.

Children.

Sucking in a deep breath, Joy returned her attention to her class, only to discover that all the kids were watching her expectantly. Seeing Lonny standing outside her window had thrown her so badly that she'd forgotten she was in the middle of a spelling test. Her students were waiting for the next word.

"Arrogant," she muttered.

A dozen hands shot into the air.

"Eric," Joy said, calling on the boy sitting at the front desk in the second row.

"Arrogant isn't one of our spelling words," he said, and several protests followed.

"This is an extra-credit word," she said. Squinting, she glared out the window again.

No sooner had the test papers been handed in than the bell rang, signaling the end of the school day. Her students dashed out the door a lot faster than they'd entered, and within minutes, the entire schoolyard was filled with youngsters. As luck would have it, she had playground duty that afternoon. This meant she was required to step out of the shelter of the school building and into the vicinity of Lonny Ellison.

Because Red Springs was a ranching community, most children lived well outside the town limits. Huge buses lumbered down country roads every morning and afternoon. These buses delivered the children to school and to their homes, some traveling as far as thirty miles.

Despite Lonny's dire predictions, Joy was surprised

by how successfully she'd adjusted to life in this small Wyoming community. Born and raised in Seattle, she'd hungered for small-town life, eager to experience the joys of living in a close, family-oriented community. Red Springs was far removed from everything familiar, but she'd discovered that people were the same everywhere. Not exactly a complicated insight, but it was as profound as it was simple. Parents wanted the best for their children in Red Springs, the same way they did back home. Neighbors were friendly if you made the effort to get to know them. Wyoming didn't have the distinctive beauty associated with Puget Sound and the two mountain ranges; instead, it possessed a beauty all its own. Joy had done her research and was fascinated to learn that this was the land where dinosaurs had once roamed and where more than half the world's geysers were located, in Yellowstone National Park. Much of central Wyoming had been an ancient inland sea, and she'd gone on a few fossil-hunting expeditions with friends from school.

It was true that Joy didn't have access to all the amenities she did in a big city. But she'd found that she could live without the majority of convenient luxuries, such as movie theaters and the occasional concerts. Movies went to DVD so quickly these days, and if the small theater in town didn't show it, Joy could rent it a few months after its release, via the internet.

As for shopping, virtually everything she needed was available online. Ordering on the internet wasn't the same as spending the day at the mall, but that, too, had its compensations. If Joy couldn't step inside a shopping mall, then she didn't squander her money on impulse buys.

The one thing she did miss, however, was her family and friends. She talked to her parents every week, and regularly emailed her brother and her closest friends. At Christmas or during the summer, she visited Seattle to see everyone. Several of her college classmates were married now. Three years after receiving her master's in education, Joy was still single. While she was in no rush, she did long for a husband and family of her own one day. Red Springs was full of eligible men; unfortunately, most of them were at least fifty. The pickings were slim, as Letty was eager to remind her. She'd dated, but none of the men had interested her the way Lonny once had.

Since there was no avoiding it, Joy left the school and watched as the children formed neat rows and boarded the buses. She folded her arms and stood straight and as tall as her five-foot-ten-inch frame would allow. Thankfully she'd chosen her nicest jumper that morning, a denim one with a white turtleneck. She felt she needed any advantage she could get if she had to face Lonny Ellison. The jumper had buckle snaps and crisscrossed her shoulders, helping to disguise her slight build.

"Ms. Fuller, Ms. Fuller," six-year-old Cricket Brown shouted, racing across the playground to her side. The little girl's long braids bounced as she skipped over to Joy. Her cherub face was flushed with excitement.

"Hello, Cricket," Joy said, smiling down at the youngster. She'd witnessed a remarkable change in the little girl since Letty's marriage to Chase Brown.

Despite her friendship with Letty, Joy wasn't aware of all the details, but she knew there was a lengthy romantic history between her and Chase, one that had taken place ten years earlier. Letty had moved away and when she'd returned, she had a daughter and no husband.

Letty was gentle, kind, thoughtful, the exact opposite of her brother. Out of the corner of her eye, Joy noticed he was striding toward her.

Cricket wasn't in the lineup for the bus, which explained Lonny's presence. He'd apparently come to pick up his niece. Preferring to ignore him altogether, Joy turned her back to avoid looking in Lonny's direction. The students were all aboard the waiting buses. One had already pulled out of the yard and was headed down the street.

"My uncle Lonny's here." Cricket grinned ecstatically.

"I know." Joy couldn't very well say she hadn't seen him, because she had. The hair on the back of her neck had stood on end the minute he'd parked outside the school. The radar-like reaction her body continued to have whenever he made an appearance confused and annoyed her.

"Look! He's coming now," Cricket cried, waving furiously at her uncle.

Lonny joined the two of them and held Joy's look for a long moment. Chills ran down her spine. It was too much to hope that Lonny would simply collect Cricket and then be on his way, too much to hope he wouldn't mention the stop sign incident. The *second* stop sign incident. Oh, no, this man wouldn't permit an opportunity like that to pass him by.

"Mr. Ellison," she said, unwilling to blink. She kept her face as expressionless as possible.

"Ms. Fuller." He touched the brim of his Stetson with his index finger.

"Yes?" Crossing her arms, she boldly met his gaze, preferring to let him do the talking. She refused to be intimidated by this ill-tempered rancher. She'd made one small mistake and run a stop sign, causing a *minor* near-accident. The stop sign at Grove and Logan was new and she'd been so accustomed to not stopping that she'd sailed through the intersection.

She'd driven at the legal speed limit, forgetting about the newly installed stop sign. She'd noticed it at the last possible second; it was already too late to stop but she'd immediately slowed down. Unfortunately, Lonny Ellison had entered the same intersection at the same time and they'd experienced a *trivial* mishap. Once again, Joy had been more than willing to admit that she was the one at fault, and she would gladly have accepted full responsibility if he hadn't behaved like an escaped lunatic. In fact, Lonny had carried this incident far beyond anything sane or reasonable. Not that—based on past experience—this was surprising.

It didn't help that he was a good five inches taller than she was and about as lean and mean as a wolverine. Staring up at him now, she changed her mind about his being the slightest bit attractive. Well, he *could* be if not for his dark, beady eyes. Even when Joy and Lonny had dated he hadn't smiled all that often, and only at his own jokes, which were usually about city slickers and absurd rodeo exploits. Since then, he seemed to wear a perpetual frown, glaring at her as if she were a stinkbug he wanted to stomp.

"I got the estimate on the damage to my truck," he announced, handing her a folded sheet.

Damage? What damage? The dent in his fender was barely visible. Joy concluded it was better not to ask. "I'll take a look at it," she said, struggling not to reveal how utterly irritating she found him. As far as she could see, his precious truck was on its way to the scrap yard.

"You'll want to pay particular attention to the cost of repairing that section of the fender," he added.

She might as well pay him off and be done with it. Unfolding the yellow sheet, she glanced down. Despite her best efforts to refrain from any emotion, she gasped. "This is a joke, right?"

"No. You'll see I'm not asking you to replace the *whole* bumper."

"They don't replace half a bumper or even a small section. This…this two hundred and fifty dollars seems way out of line."

"A new bumper, plus installation, costs over five hundred dollars. Two hundred and fifty is half of that."

Joy swallowed hard. Yes, she'd been at fault, and yes, it wasn't the first time, but even dividing the cost of the bumper, that amount was ridiculous. She certainly hadn't done five hundred dollars' worth of damage—or even fifty dollars, in her opinion.

To his credit, Lonny had done an admirable job of preventing any serious repercussions. She'd been badly shaken by the incident, which could easily have been much worse, and so had Lonny. She'd tried to apologize, sincerely tried, but Lonny had leaped out of his pickup in a rage.

Because he'd been such a jerk about it, Joy had responded in anger, too. From that moment on, they'd had trouble even being civil to each other. Joy was convinced his anger wasn't so much about this so-called accident as it was about their former relationship. He was the one who'd broken it off, not her. Well, okay, it'd been a mutual decision.

Now he was insisting that a mere scratch would cost hundreds of dollars to repair. It was hard to tell which dent the collision had even caused. His truck had at least ten others just like it, including the one from last year's *incident,* and most of them were much worse. She suspected he was punishing her for not falling under the spell of the Great Rodeo Rider. *That* was the real story here.

Joy marched over to where Lonny had parked his vehicle. "You can't expect me to pay that kind of money for one tiny dent." She gestured at the scratched and battered truck. "That's highway robbery." She stood her ground—easy to do because she didn't *have* an extra two hundred and fifty dollars. "What about all the other dents? They don't seem to bother you, but this one does. And why is that, I wonder?"

Anger flashed from his eyes. "That *tiny dent* does bother me. So does the other *tiny dent* you caused. But what bothers me more is unsafe drivers. In my view, you should have your driver's license revoked."

"I forgot about the stop sign," Joy admitted. "And

I've apologized a dozen times. I don't mean to be difficult here, but this just seems wrong to me. You're angry about something else entirely and we both know what that is."

"You're wrong. This has nothing to do with you and me. This is about my truck."

"Who do you think you're kidding?" she burst out. "You're angry because I'm a woman with opinions that didn't happen to agree with yours. You didn't want a relationship, you wanted someone to flatter your ego and I didn't fall into line the way other women have." She'd never met any of those women, but she'd certainly heard about them....

His eyes narrowed. "You're just a city girl. I'm surprised you stuck around this long. If you figure that arguing will convince me to forget what you did to my truck, you're dead wrong." He shook his head as if she'd insulted him.

Joy couldn't believe he was going to pursue this.

"You owe me for the damage to my vehicle," he insisted.

"You...you..." she sputtered at the unfairness of it all. "I'm not paying you a dime." If he wanted to be unreasonable, then she could be, too.

"Would you rather I had my insurance company contact yours?"

"Not really."

"Then I'd appreciate a check in the amount of two hundred and fifty dollars."

"That's practically blackmail!"

"Blackmail?" Lonny spat out the word as if it left a bad taste in his mouth. "I went to a lot of time and effort to get this estimate. I wanted to be as fair and amicable as possible and *this* is what I get?" He threw his arms up as if completely disgusted. "You're lucky I was willing to share the cost with you, which I didn't have to do."

"You think you're being *fair?*"

"Yes." He nodded. "I only want to be fair," he said in self-righteous tones.

Joy relaxed. "Then fifty dollars should do it."

Lonny's eyes widened. "Fifty dollars won't even begin to cover the damage."

"I don't see you rushing out for estimates on any of the other damage to your truck." She pointed at a couple of deep gouges on the driver's door. "And they had nothing to do with *me.*"

"I admit I was responsible for those," he said. "I'll get around to taking care of them someday."

"Apparently *someday* has arrived and you're trying to rip me off."

They were almost nose to nose now and tall as he was, Joy didn't even flinch. This man was a Neanderthal, a knuckle-dragging throwback who didn't know the first thing about civility or common decency.

"Ms. Fuller? Uncle Lonny?"

The small voice of a child drifted through the fog of Joy's anger. To her horror, she'd been so upset, she'd forgotten all about Cricket.

"You're yelling," the little girl said, staring up at them. Her expression was one of uncertainty.

Joy immediately crouched down so she was level with the six-year-old. "Your uncle Lonny and I let our emotions get the better of us," she said and laughed as if it was all a joke.

Frowning, Cricket glanced from Joy to her uncle. "Uncle Lonny says when you aren't teaching school you shrink heads. When I asked Mommy about it, she said Uncle Lonny didn't mean that. You don't really shrink heads, do you?"

Lonny cleared his throat. "Ah, perhaps it's time we left, Cricket." He reached for the little girl's hand but Cricket resisted.

"Of course I don't shrink heads," Joy said, standing upright. Her irritation continued to simmer as she met Lonny's gaze. "Your uncle was only teasing."

"No, I wasn't," Lonny muttered under his breath.

Joy sighed. "*That* was mature."

"I don't care what you think of me. All I want from you is two hundred and fifty dollars to pay for the damage you did to my truck."

"My fifty-dollar offer stands anytime you're willing to accept it."

His fierce glare told her the offer was, and would remain, unacceptable.

"If you don't cooperate, I'll go to your insurance company," he warned.

If it came to that, then so be it. Surely a claims adjustor would agree with her. "You can threaten me all you want. Fifty dollars is my best offer—take it or leave it."

"I'll leave it." This was said emphatically, conviction behind each syllable.

Joy handed him back the written estimate. "That's

perfectly fine by me. You can contact me when you're prepared to be reasonable."

"You think *I'm* the one who's being unreasonable?" he asked, sounding shocked and hurt.

She rolled her eyes. Lonny should've had a career as a B-movie actor, not a bull-rider or whatever he'd been. Bull *something*, anyway.

"As a matter of fact, I do," she said calmly.

Lonny had the audacity to scowl.

This man was the most outrageous human being she'd ever had the misfortune to meet. Remembering the child's presence, Joy bit her tongue in an effort to restrain herself from arguing further.

"You haven't heard the last of me," he threatened.

"Oh, say it isn't so," Joy murmured ever so sweetly. If she never saw Lonny Ellison again, it would be too soon.

Lonny whirled around and opened the door on the passenger side for his niece.

"Be careful not to scratch this priceless antique," Joy called out to the little girl.

After helping Cricket inside, Lonny closed the door. "Very funny," he said. "You won't be nearly as amused once your insurance people hear from mine."

Joy was no longer concerned about that. Her agent would take one look at Lonny Ellison's beaten-up vehicle and might, if the cowpoke was lucky, offer him fifty bucks.

Whatever happened, he wasn't getting a penny more out of her. She'd rather go to jail.

Chapter 3

"You've got a thing for Ms. Fuller, don't you?" Cricket asked as she sat beside Lonny in the cab of his truck. "That's what my mommy says."

Lonny made a noncommittal reply. If he announced his true feelings for the teacher, he'd singe his niece's ears. Joy was right about something, though. His anger was connected to their earlier relationship, if he could even call it that. The first few dates had gone well, and he'd felt encouraged. He'd been impressed with her intelligence and adventuresome spirit. For a time—more than once, actually—he'd even thought Joy might be the one. But it became apparent soon enough that she couldn't take a joke. That was when her uppity, know-it-all, schoolmarm side had come out. She seemed to think his ego was the problem. Not so! He was a kidder and she had no sense of humor. He'd been glad to end it right then and there.

His sister had tried to play the role of matchmaker after she returned to Red Springs and became friends with Joy. Lonny wasn't interested, since he'd had a private look into the real Joy Fuller, behind all her sweetness and charm.

"Mom says sometimes people who really like each other pretend they don't, 'cause they're afraid of their feelings," Cricket continued, sounding wise beyond her years. He could hear the echo of Letty's opinions in her daughter's words.

Leave it to a female to come up with a nonsensical notion like that.

"Do you like Ms. Fuller the way Mom said?" Cricket asked again.

Lonny shrugged. That was as much of a comment as he cared to make. He was well aware of his sister's opinions. Letty hoped to marry him off. He was thirty-five now, and the pool of eligible women in Red Springs was quickly evaporating. His romantic sister had set her sights on him and Joy, but as far as he was concerned, hell would freeze over first.

Lonny figured he'd had his share of women on the rodeo circuit and he had no desire for that kind of complication again. Most of those girlfriends had been what you'd call short-term—some of them *very* short-term. They'd treated him like a hero, which was gratifying, but he'd grown bored with their demands, and even their adulation had become tiresome after a while. Since he'd retired eight years earlier, he'd lived alone and frankly, that was how he liked it.

Just recently he'd hired Tom, a young man who'd drifted onto his ranch. That seemed to be working out all right. Tom had a room in the barn and kept mostly to himself. Lonny didn't want to pry into his business, but he had checked the boy's identification. To his relief, Tom was of age; still, he seemed young to be completely on his own. Lonny had talked to the local sheriff and learned that Tom wasn't wanted for any crimes. Lonny hoped that, given time, the boy would trust him enough to share what had prompted him to leave his family. For now, he was safer living and working with Lonny than making his own way in the world.

Despite his sister's claims, Lonny was convinced that bringing a woman into his life would cause nothing but trouble. First thing a wife would want to do was update his kitchen and the appliances. That stove had been around as long as he could remember—his mother had cooked on it—and he didn't see any need to buy another. Same with the refrigerator. Then, as soon as a wife had sweet-talked him into redoing the kitchen, sure as hell she'd insist on all new furniture. It wouldn't end there, either. He'd be forking out for paint and wallpaper and who knows what. After a few months he wouldn't even recognize his own house—or his bank account. No, sir, he couldn't afford a wife, not with the financial risk he and Chase were taking by raising their cattle without growth hormones.

A heifer took five years to reach twelve hundred pounds on the open range, eating a natural diet of grass. By contrast, commercial steers, who were routinely given hormones, reached that weight in eighteen to twenty months. That meant he and Chase were feeding and caring for a single head of beef nearly three years longer than the average cattleman. Penned cattle were corn-fed and given a diet that featured protein supplements. Lonny had seen some of those so-called supplements, and they included chicken feathers and rot like that. Furthermore, penned steers were on a regimen of antibiotics to protect them from the various diseases that ran rampant in such close quarters.

Yup, they were taking a risk, he and Chase, raising natural beef, and the truth was that Lonny was on a tight budget. But he could manage, living on his own, even with Tom's wages and the room and board he provided. Lonny was proud of their cattle-ranching venture; not only were they producing a higher quality beef, for which the market was growing, but their methods were far more humane.

Cricket sang softly to herself during the rest of the ride. Lonny pulled into the long dirt drive that led to Chase and Letty's place, leaving a plume of dust in his wake.

When he neared the house, he was mildly surprised to find Chase's truck parked outside the barn. His sister had phoned him a couple of days earlier and asked him to collect Cricket after school. Letty had an appointment with the heart specialist in Rock Springs, sixty miles west of Red Springs. Chase had insisted on driving her. Of course Lonny had agreed to pick up his niece.

Letty had undergone heart surgery a little less than a year ago. While the procedure had been a success, she required regular physicals. Lonny was happy to help in any way he could. He knew Letty was fine health-wise, and in just about every other way, too. In fact, he'd never seen his sister happier. Still, it didn't do any harm to have that confirmed by a physician.

As soon as he brought the truck to a stop, Cricket bounded out of the cab and raced off to look for her mother. Lonny climbed out more slowly and glanced around. He walked into the barn, where Chase was busy with his afternoon chores. For a while, he'd had an older ranch hand working with him, but Mel had retired in December. Now the two of them, Chase and Lonny, managed alone, with the addition of Tom's help.

"Cricket's with you?" Chase asked, looking up from the stall he was mucking out.

Lonny nodded. "Letty asked me to pick her up today."

Straightening, Chase leaned against the pitchfork and slid back the brim of his hat. "Why'd she do that?" he asked, frowning slightly. "The school bus would've dropped her off at your place. No need for you to go all the way into town."

"I had other business there," Lonny said, but he didn't explain that his real reason had to do with Joy Fuller and the money she owed him.

"Hey, Lonny," Letty called. Bright sunlight spilled into the barn as Letty swept open the door. Cricket stayed close to her mother's side. "I wondered if I'd find you here."

"I thought you might want your daughter back," he joked. "How'd the appointment go?"

"Just great." She raised her eyebrows. "Cricket tells me you got into another argument with Joy."

He frowned at his niece. He should've guessed she'd run tattling to her mother. "The woman's being completely unreasonable. Personally, I don't know how you can get along with her."

"Really?" Letty exchanged a knowing look with her husband.

"Just a minute here!" Lonny waved his finger at them. "None of that."

"None of what?" His sister was the picture of innocence.

"You know very well what I mean. You've got this sliver up your fingernail about me being attracted to your friend, and how she'd be the perfect wife."

"As I've said before, you protest too much." Letty seemed hard put to keep from rubbing her hands together in satisfaction. His sister was in love and it only made sense, he supposed, for her to see Cupid at work between him and Joy. Only it wasn't happening. He didn't even like the woman. And she didn't like him.

Not that there was any point in saying another word. Arguing with his sister was like asking an angry bronc not to throw you. No matter what Lonny said or did, it wouldn't change Letty's mind. Despite his brief and ill-fated romance with Joy, something—he couldn't imagine what—had convinced his softhearted little sister that he was head-over-heels crazy about *Ms.* Fuller.

"What did you say to her this time?" Letty demanded.

"Me?"

"Yes, you!" She propped her hands on her hips, and judging by her stern look, there'd be no escaping the wrath of Letty. The fact that Joy had managed to turn his own sister against him was testament to the evil power she possessed.

"If you must know, I took her the estimate for the damage she did to my truck."

"You're kidding!" Letty cried. "You actually got an estimate?"

"Damn straight I did." Okay, so maybe he was carrying this a bit far, but someone needed to teach the woman a lesson, and that someone might as well be him.

"But your truck…"

Lonny already knew what she was going to say. It was the same argument Joy had given him. "Yes, there are plenty of other dents on the bumper—including the *previous* one she caused. All I'm asking is that she make restitution for the *second* one. I don't understand why everyone wants to argue about this. She caused the dent. The least she can do is pay to have it fixed."

"Lonny, you've got to be joking."

He wasn't. "What about assuming personal responsibility? You'd think a woman teaching our children would *want* to make restitution." According to Letty, the entire community thought the sun rose and set on Ms. Fuller. Not him, though. He'd seen the woman behind those deceptive smiles.

"What did Joy have to say to that?" Chase asked, and his mouth twitched in a smile he couldn't quite hide.

Lonny resisted the urge to ask his brother-in-law what he found so darned amusing. "She made me an insulting offer of fifty dollars. The woman's nuts if she thinks I'll accept that."

Letty uttered a rather unfeminine-sounding snort. "I can't say I blame her."

"What about my truck? What about me? That woman's carelessness nearly gave me a heart attack!"

"You said she apologized."

Granted, after the accident, Joy had been all sweet and apologetic. However, it didn't take long for her dark side to show, just like it had a year ago.

Since everyone was taking sides with Joy, Lonny considered dropping the entire matter. Or he considered it for a moment, anyway... When he presented Joy with the bill, he'd hoped she'd take all the blame and tell him how sorry she was...and sound as if she meant it. At that point, he would've felt good about absolving her and being magnanimous. He'd figured they could talk like adults, maybe meet for a friendly drink—see what happened from there.

That, however, wasn't how things had gone. Joy had exploded. His impetuous little fantasy shriveled up even more quickly than it had appeared, to be replaced by an anger that matched hers.

"What are you planning to do now?" Letty asked, checking her watch.

Lonny looked to his brother-in-law and best friend for help, but Chase was staying out of this one. There was a time Chase would've leaped to Lonny's defense. Not now; marriage had changed him. "I don't know yet. I was thinking I should file a claim with her insurance company." He didn't actually plan to do that, but the threat sounded real and he'd let Letty believe he just might.

"Don't even think about it," his sister snapped.

He shrugged, afraid now that he was digging himself into a hole. But pride demanded he not back down.

"One look at your truck and I'm afraid the adjuster would laugh," Chase told him.

That hole was getting deeper by the minute.

Shaking her head, Letty sighed. "I'd better call Joy and see if she's okay."

Lonny stared at her. "Why wouldn't she be okay?"

Letty patted his shoulder. "Sometimes you don't know how intimidating you can be, big brother."

As Lonny stood there scratching his head, wondering how everything had gotten so confused, Letty walked out of the barn.

Utterly baffled, Lonny muttered, "Did I hear her right? Is she actually going to phone Joy? Isn't that like consorting with the enemy? What about family loyalty, one for all and all for one, that kind of stuff?"

Chase seemed about to answer when Letty turned back. "Do you want to stay for dinner?" she asked.

Invitations on days other than Sunday were rare, and Lonny had no intention of turning one down. He might be upset with his sister but he wasn't stupid. Letty was a mighty fine cook. "Sure."

A half hour or so later, Lonny accompanied his brother-in-law to the house. After washing up, Chase brought out two cans of cold beer. Then, just as they had on so many other evenings, the two of them sat on the porch, enjoying the cool breeze.

"The doc said Letty's going to be all right?" Lonny asked his friend.

Chase took a deep swallow of beer. "According to him, Letty's as good as new."

That was what Lonny had guessed. His sister had come home after almost ten years without telling him why. Her heart was in bad shape, and she'd needed an expensive surgery, one she couldn't afford. She'd trusted Lonny to raise Cricket for her if she died. Cricket's father had abandoned Letty before the little girl was even born. Letty hadn't told Lonny any more than that, and he'd never asked. Thankfully she'd had the surgery, for which Chase had secretly paid, and it'd been successful. She'd been married to him since last summer. Even for a guy as cynical about marriage as Lonny, it was easy to see how much she and Chase loved each other. Cricket had settled down, too. For the first time in her life, the little girl had a father and a family. Lonny was delighted with the way everything had turned out for his sister and his best friend.

"You like married life, don't you?" he asked. Although he knew the answer, he asked the question anyway. Lonny couldn't think of another man who'd be completely honest with him.

Chase looked into the distance and nodded.

"Why?"

Chase smiled. "Well, marriage definitely has its good points."

"Sex?"

"I'm not about to discount that," his friend assured him, his smile widening. "But there's more to marriage than crawling into bed with a warm body."

"Such as?"

Chase didn't take offense at the question, the way another guy might have. "I hadn't realized how lonely it was around this place since my dad died," Chase said. His expression was sober and thoughtful as he stared out at the ranch that had been in his family for four generations. "Letty and Cricket have given me purpose. I have a reason to get out of bed in the morning—a reason other than chores. That's the best I can explain it."

Lonny leaned back and rested his elbows on the step. He considered what his friend had said and, frankly, he didn't see it. "I like my life the way it is."

Chase nodded. "Before Letty returned, I thought the same thing."

At least *one* person understood his feelings.

"Is it okay if I join you?" Letty asked from behind the screen door before moving on to the porch. She held a glass of lemonade.

"Sure, go ahead," Lonny said agreeably.

His sister sat on the step beside Chase, who slid his arm around her shoulder. She pressed her head against him, then glanced at Lonny.

"Did you phone her?" he muttered. It probably wasn't a good idea to even ask, but he had to admit he was curious.

"I will later," Letty said. "I was afraid if I called her now, she might be too distressed to talk."

"I'm the one who's distressed," he muttered, not that anyone had asked about *his* feelings.

Letty ignored the comment. "You've really got a thing for her, don't you?"

"No, I don't." Dammit, he wished his sister would stop saying that. Even his niece was parroting her words. Lonny didn't want to argue with Letty, but the fact was, he knew his own feelings. "I can guess what you're thinking and I'm here to tell you, you're wrong."

"You seem to talk about her quite a bit," she said archly.

No argument there. "Now, listen, I want you to give me your solemn word that you won't do anything stupid."

"Like what?" Letty asked.

"Like try to get me and Joy together again. I told you before, I'm not interested and I mean it."

"You know, big brother, I might've believed you earlier, but I don't anymore."

Not knowing what to say, Lonny just shook his head. "I want your word, Letty. I'm serious about this."

"Your brother doesn't need your help." Chase kissed the top of her head.

"He's right," Lonny said.

"But—"

"I don't need a woman in my life."

"You're lonely."

"I've got plenty of friends, plus you guys practically next door," he told her. "Besides, Tom's around."

At this reminder of the teenage boy living at the ranch, Letty asked, "How's that going?"

Lonny shrugged. "All right, I guess." He liked the kid, who was skinny as a beanpole and friendly but still reserved. "He's a hard worker."

Letty reached for Chase's hand. "It was good of you to give him a job."

Lonny didn't think of it that way. "I was looking for seasonal help. He showed up at the right time." When Lonny found him in the barn, Tom had offered to work in exchange for breakfast. The kid must've been half-starved, because he gobbled down six eggs, half a pound of bacon and five or six slices of toast, along with several cups of coffee. In between bites, he brushed off Lonny's questions about his history and hometown. When Lonny mentioned that he and Chase were hoping to hire a ranch hand for the season, Tom's eyes had brightened and he'd asked to apply for the job.

"I'm worried about you," his sister lamented, refusing to drop the subject. "You do need someone."

"I do not."

Letty studied him for a long moment, then finally acquiesced. "Okay, big brother, you're on your own."

And that was exactly how Lonny wanted it.

Chapter 4

Tom Meyerson finished the last of his nightly chores and headed for his room in the barn. Stumbling onto this job was the best thing that'd happened to him in years. He'd been bone-weary and desperate when Lonny Ellison found him sleeping in his barn. That day, three months ago now, he'd walked twenty or twenty-five miles, and all he'd had to eat was an apple and half a candy bar. By the time he saw the barn far off in the distance, he'd been thirsty, hungry and so exhausted he could barely put one foot in front of the other. He didn't think he'd make it to the next town by nightfall, so he'd hidden in the barn and fallen instantly asleep.

Life had been hell since his mother died. The doctor had said she had a weak heart, and Tom knew why: his dad had broken it years before. His father was a no-good drunk. There'd been nothing positive in Tom's life except his mother. Fortunately, he was an only child, so at least there wasn't a younger brother or sister to worry about. Shortly after he graduated from high school last spring, nearly a year ago, it became apparent that his father's sole interest in him was as a source of beer money. He'd stolen every penny Tom had tried to save.

The last time his money had mysteriously disappeared, Tom had confronted his father. They'd had a vicious argument and his old man had kicked him out of the house. At first Tom didn't know what to do, but then he'd realized this was probably for the best. He collected what was due him from the hardware store where he worked part-time and, with a little less than fifty dollars in his pocket, started his new life. He'd spent twenty of those dollars on a bus ticket to the town of Red Springs, then walked from there. All Tom wanted was to get away from Thompson, Wyoming, as far and fast as he could. It wasn't like his father would be looking for him.

Life on the road was hard. He'd hitchhiked when he could, but there'd been few vehicles on the routes he'd traveled. Most of the time he'd hoofed it. He must have walked a hundred miles or more, and no matter what happened, he never wanted to go back.

When Lonny Ellison discovered him, Tom was sure the rancher would file trespassing charges. Instead, Lonny had given him a job, a room and three square meals a day, which was more than he'd had since his mother's death.

The phone in the barn rang, and Tom leaped out of

his bunk where he'd been reading yesterday's paper and hurried to answer it. Lonny wasn't back from town yet, because his truck wasn't parked out front.

He lifted the receiver and offered a tentative "Hello."

A short silence followed. "Tom?"

Tom's heart began to pound. It was Michelle, a girl he'd met at the feed store soon after he'd started working for Lonny. Like him, she was shy and although they hadn't said more than a few words to each other, he enjoyed seeing her. Whenever he went to the store with Lonny, she made an excuse to come out of the office and hang around outside.

"Hi." Tom couldn't help being excited that she'd phoned.

"You didn't come in this afternoon," Michelle said, sounding disappointed.

Tom had looked forward to seeing her all week, only to be thwarted. "Lonny decided to drive into town by himself." Tom had searched for an excuse to join him, but none had presented itself, so he'd stayed on the ranch. He liked the work, although he'd never lived on a ranch before, and Lonny and Chase were teaching him a lot.

His afternoon had been spent repairing breaks in the fencing along the road. The whole time he was doing that, he was thinking about Michelle and how pretty she was.

"I wondered," Michelle whispered, then hesitated as if there was more she wanted to tell him.

Her father owned Larson's Feed, and she helped out after school. The last time he was in town, he'd casu-

ally mentioned that he'd be back on Tuesday and hoped
to see her then. He wanted to ask her out on a date but
didn't have any way of getting into Red Springs without borrowing Lonny's truck and he was reluctant to
ask. Lonny had already done plenty for him, and it
didn't seem right to take advantage of his generosity.

"Lonny had to pick up his niece after school," Tom
added.

"Oh."

Michelle didn't appear to be much of a conversa-
tionalist, which could be a problem because he wasn't,
either.

"I was hoping, you know…" She let the rest fade.
Then, all at once, she blurted out, "There's a dance
the last day of school. It's a pretty big deal. The whole
town throws a festival and the high school has this
big dance and I was wondering if you'd go with me."

She said it all so fast, she couldn't possibly have
taken a breath. After she finished speaking, it took
Tom a few seconds to realize what she'd asked him.
He felt an immediate surge of regret.

The silence seemed endless as he struggled with
what to tell her. In the end, he told the simple truth.
"I can't."

"Why not?"

Tom didn't want to get into that. "I just…can't." He
hated to disappoint her, but there was nothing more
he could say.

"I shouldn't have asked…I wouldn't have, but— Oh,
never mind. I'm sorry.…" With that, she hung up as if
she couldn't get off the line fast enough.

Tom felt wretched. He didn't have the clothes he'd

need for a dance; in fact, he'd never attended a dance in his life, even in high school. Those kinds of social events were for other kids. He was sorry to refuse Michelle, sorrier than she'd ever know, but there wasn't any alternative.

As he returned to his room, Tom lay back on the hard mattress and tucked his hands behind his head, staring up at the ceiling. It would've been nice, that school dance with Michelle. All they'd done so far was talk a few times. The thought of holding her in his arms imbued him with a sense of joy—a joy that was new and unfamiliar to him.

Tom gave himself a mental shake. He might as well forget about the dance right then and there, because it wasn't going to happen.

Just back from school, Joy was still furious over her confrontation with Lonny Ellison. The man had his nerve. In an effort to forget that unfortunate episode, Joy tried to grade the spelling-test papers, but she soon discovered she couldn't concentrate. The only thing she seemed able to do with all this pent-up anger was pace her living room until she'd practically worn a pattern in the carpet.

When the phone rang, Joy nearly jumped out of her skin. Her heart still hadn't stopped hammering when she picked up the portable telephone on the kitchen counter.

"Joy, it's Letty. Lonny dropped Cricket off and he's beside himself. What happened?"

"Your brother," Joy answered from between gritted teeth, "is the most egotistical, unpleasant, arrogant man I've ever met." Then she proceeded to describe the entire scene in the schoolyard, which was burned in her memory.

"You mean to say you didn't *really* come after him with a pitchfork?" Letty asked.

"Is that what he said?" Joy asked. She wouldn't put it past Lonny to fabricate such a ridiculous story.

"No, no, I was just teasing," Letty assured her. "But I will say his version of events is only vaguely similar to yours."

"He's exaggerating, of course."

"I'm sorry," Letty said, sounding genuinely contrite. "My guess is Lonny's still attracted to you and isn't sure how to deal with it. What went wrong with you two, anyway?"

"I don't know, and furthermore, I don't care." That wasn't completely true. She did care and, despite her annoyance at his current attitude, wished the situation between them was different.

Letty hesitated briefly before she continued. "I have no idea how else to explain my brother's behavior. All I can tell you is that this isn't like Lonny."

"In other words, it's me he dislikes," she said starkly.

"No," Letty said. "Just the opposite. I think this is his nutty way of getting back together with you. Like I said, he's attracted to you. There's no question in my mind about that."

Her ego would like to believe it, but she'd seen the look in Lonny's eyes and it wasn't admiration or attraction.

"Lonny can be a little stubborn but—"

"A little?" Joy broke in. "A *little?*"

"I apologize on his behalf," Letty said. "I'm hoping you'll be able to look past his perverse behavior and recognize the reason for it. Be gentle with him, okay? I'm fairly certain my brother is smitten."

"He's *what?*"

"Smitten," Letty repeated. "It's an old-fashioned word, one my mother would've used. It means—well, you know what it means. The sad part is, Lonny isn't smart enough to figure this out."

"Then I hope he never does, because any spark of interest I might've felt toward him is dead. No one's ever made me so mad!" Joy felt her anger regain momentum and crowd out her other feelings for Lonny.

"You're *sure* you're not interested in my brother?"

"Positive. I don't want to see him again as long as I live. Every time I do, my blood pressure rises until I feel like my head's going to explode. I've never met a more irritating man in my life."

Letty's regretful sigh drifted through the phone line. "I was afraid of that."

They spoke for a few more minutes and then Joy replaced the receiver. She felt better after talking to Letty—only she wasn't sure why. Maybe venting her aggression with someone who understood both her and Lonny had helped. It would be nice, flattering really, if all this craziness was indeed related to Lonny's overpowering attraction, as Letty seemed to think, but Joy doubted it.

She hadn't been on a date in so long that she was actually considering one of those online dating services. School would be out in a couple of weeks; this summer, when she had some free time, Joy planned to develop a social life. She didn't have a strategy yet, beyond the vague possibilities offered by the internet, nor did she have much romantic experience. Her only serious romance had been with Josh Howell in her last year of college. Their relationship was relegated to casual-friends status after she'd accepted the teaching job in Wyoming. They'd kept in touch, usually by email. Since she'd moved away, he'd been involved in an increasingly serious relationship. She hadn't heard from him in more than two months, and Joy surmised that his current girlfriend was soon to become his wife.

Josh lived in Seattle, where he worked for an investment firm. He went on—in detail—about the woman he was seeing every time he emailed her. Lori Something-or-Other was apparently blonde, beautiful and a power to be reckoned with in the investment industry. Or maybe it was insurance… In any case, Joy sometimes wondered why he kept in touch with her at all when he was so enamored of someone else.

She microwaved a frozen entrée for dinner, ate while watching the national news, corrected her spelling papers and then logged on to the internet. She immediately noticed Josh's email. How ironic that she'd get this message when she'd just been thinking about him!

From: Josh Howell
Sent: May 16
To: Joy Fuller
Subject: I'm going to be in your area!
Hi, Joy,
We haven't exchanged emails in a while, and I was

wondering what you've been up to lately. The company's sending me on a business trip to Salt Lake City, which I'm combining with a few vacation days. When I looked at the map, I noticed that Red Springs isn't too far away. I'd love to stop by and catch up with you. After the conference, I'll rent a car, and I should be in your area the first or second of June. Would that work for you?

Look forward to hearing from you! I've missed your emails.

Love,

Josh

P.S. Did I mention that Lori and I broke up?

With her hand pressed to her mouth to contain her surprise and happiness, Joy read the email twice. Josh wasn't seeing Lori anymore! Interesting that he'd mentioned it in a postscript, as if he'd almost forgotten the fact. This made her wonder. Had she misinterpreted the extent of his feelings for the other woman? Did he still see Joy as more than just a friend? Was he suggesting they might want to pick up the relationship where they'd left off? She was certainly open to the possibility. Josh was a man who knew how to treat a woman. He could teach Lonny Ellison a thing or two.

Another interesting fact—Josh had said he'd be in the area, but Red Springs was a little out of his way. Like about two hundred miles... Not that she was complaining. What she suspected, what she wanted to believe, was that he'd go a *lot* out of his way in order to see her.

Joy quickly emailed Josh back. In the space of a

single evening, her emotions had veered from fury to eager anticipation. Earlier she'd had to resist the urge to burst into tears, and now she was bubbling with delight.

Just before hitting Send, Joy paused. Maybe she should phone Josh instead. It wouldn't hurt. Calling him meant he'd know without a doubt how pleased she was to hear from him.

She hesitated, suddenly worried that she might seem too eager. But she was. In fact, she was thrilled....

Her mind made up, she reached for the phone. If he didn't answer, she could always send the email she'd already composed. Receiver in hand, Joy realized she no longer remembered his number. She'd written it down, but had no idea exactly where. Still, she found it easily enough, at the very back of her personal phone directory. In pencil, which implied that she'd expected to erase it....

Josh answered right away.

"Josh, it's Joy. I just opened your email."

"Joy!" She could hear the smile in his voice.

"I'd love it if you came to Red Springs, but I need to warn you we're in the middle of nowhere. Well, not really... There *are* other towns, but they're few and far between." She was chattering, but it felt so good to talk to him. "One of my teaching friends said we may not be at the end of the world, but you can see it from here."

Josh responded with a husky laugh. "How are you?"

"Great, just great." Especially now that she'd heard from him.

"Do those dates work for you?" he asked.

Joy had been so excited, she hadn't even checked the calendar. A glance at the one on her desk showed her that June first fell on a Thursday and the second...

"June second is the last day of school," she told him, her hopes deflating.

"That's fine. I'll take you out to dinner and we can celebrate."

"There's a problem. On the evening of the last day, we have a carnival. The whole town shows up. It's sort of a big deal, and this year they've even managed to get a real carnival company to set up rides. Everyone's looking forward to it."

"So we'll attend the carnival."

That sounded good, except for one thing. "I'm working the cotton candy machine." She'd taken that task the year before, too. While it'd been fun, she'd worn as much of the sugary pink sweetness as she'd managed to get onto the paper tubes.

"Not to worry, I'll find something to occupy myself while you're busy. If the school needs another volunteer, sign me up. I'm game for just about anything."

"You'd do that?" This was better than Joy would have dreamed. "Thanks! Oh, Josh, I can't tell you how glad I am to hear from you."

"I feel the same way."

"I'm sorry about you and Lori," she said, carefully broaching the subject.

His hesitation was only slight; still, Joy noticed. "Yeah," he said. "Too bad it didn't work out."

He didn't supply any details and Joy didn't feel it would be right to question him. Later, when they were able to meet and talk face-to-face, he'd probably be more comfortable discussing the circumstances of their parting.

"How's life in cowboy town?" Josh asked, changing the subject. When she'd been offered the teaching position, he'd discouraged her from accepting it. Josh had told her she shouldn't take the first job offered. He was convinced that if she waited, there'd be an opening in the Seattle area. He couldn't understand why Joy had wanted to get away from the big city and live in a small town.

The truth was, she loved her job and Red Springs. This was the second year of a two-year contract and, so far, she'd enjoyed every minute. That didn't mean, however, that she wouldn't be willing to move if the opportunity arose—such as renewing a promising relationship, with the hope of a marriage proposal in the not-so-distant future.

"They seem to grow cowboys by the bushel here," she said with a laugh. "Most of the kids are comfortable in the saddle by the time they're in kindergarten. I like Red Springs, but I'm sure that to outsiders, the town isn't too impressive. There are a couple of nice restaurants, the Mexican Fiesta and Uncle Dave's Café, but that's about it."

He murmured a noncommittal response.

"The town seemed rather bleak when I first arrived." She didn't mention the disappointing relationship with Lonny Ellison—then or now. "That didn't last long, though. It's the people here who are so wonderful." With one exception, she mused. "We've got a motel—I'll make you a reservation—a couple of bars, a great church, a theater and—"

"Do you still play the church organ?"

"I do." She was surprised he'd remembered that.

"Anything else I should know about Red Springs?"

"Not really. I'll be happy to give you the grand tour." The offer was sincere. She'd love showing off the town and introducing him to the friends she'd made. "Maybe we can visit a real working ranch—my friend Letty's, for example. We could even do that on horseback."

"Don't tell me you're riding horses yourself?"

"I have," she answered, smiling. "But I don't make a habit of it." Getting onto the back of a horse had been daunting the first time, but Joy discovered she rather enjoyed it. Well…she didn't hate it. Her muscles had been sore afterward and she hadn't felt the urge to try it again for quite a while. She'd gone out riding with friends three times in the last nine months, and that was enough for her.

"I don't suppose any of those cowpokes have caught your interest," Josh said casually.

Lonny Ellison flashed across her mind. She squeezed her eyes shut, unnerved by the vividness of his image.

"So there *is* someone else," Josh said when she didn't immediately respond.

"No." She nearly swallowed her tongue in her eagerness to deny it. "Not at all."

"Good," Josh said. It seemed he'd decided to accept her denial at face value, much to Joy's relief. She *wasn't* interested in Lonny Ellison, so she hadn't lied.

Annoyed by him, yes. Interested? No, no, no! "I'll be in touch again soon," he was saying.

"I'll see you in a couple of weeks." Joy could hardly wait.

Chapter 5

Saturday morning, Lonny woke in a surprisingly good mood. For some reason, he'd dreamed about Joy Fuller, although it'd been several days since he'd run into her. He was reluctant to admit it, but he hadn't been nearly as annoyed by their confrontation as he'd let her believe.

He frowned at the thought. Could it be that Letty was right and he was still attracted to Joy? Nah. Still, the possibility stayed in his mind. One thing was certain; he'd felt invigorated by their verbal exchanges and he seemed to think of her all too frequently.

He poured his first cup of coffee and stepped outside, taking a moment to appreciate the early-morning sunlight that greeted him. A rooster's crowing accentuated the feeling of peace and contentment. This was his world, the only place he wanted to be.

The one thing that troubled him on what should've been a perfect spring day was the way Joy Fuller lingered in his mind. He couldn't stop remembering how pretty she was and how animated she got when she was all riled up. He shouldn't be thinking about her at all, though. He had chores to do, places to be and, most importantly, cattle to worm. But with Tom's help, they'd make fast work of it. Chase had already done some of the herd the day before.

It was unfortunate that he and Joy had gotten off on the wrong foot, he thought as he scattered grain for the chickens. He discovered a dozen eggs waiting for him, and that made him smile.

But he was irritated when he found himself continuing to smile—smiling for no real reason. Well, there *was* a reason and her name was Joy Fuller and that was even worse. He was a little unnerved by his own amusement at the way she'd reacted to his outrageous comments. He'd never had any intention of contacting his insurance company or hers, and in the light of day, he realized how irrational he'd sounded. But even if *he* knew he wasn't following through with that threat, she didn't.

He almost laughed out loud at the image of her sputtering and gesticulating the day of their accident. Okay, *incident.* She wasn't likely to forgive him for making such a fuss over that fender-bender.

He collected the eggs and returned to the house. With an efficiency born of long practice, he scrambled half a dozen eggs, fried bacon and made toast. In the middle of his domestic efforts, Tom came in. They sat down to breakfast, exchanging a few words as they listened to the radio news, then headed out.

The morning sped by, and they finished the worming by eleven o'clock. Lonny drove into Red Springs to do errands; normally Tom liked to join him, but he'd been keeping to himself lately. During the past few days, he'd seemed more reserved than usual. Whatever the problem, the boy chose not to divulge it, which was fine. If and when he wanted to talk, Lonny was willing to listen.

Tom didn't have much to say at the best of times. The kid put in a good day's work, and that was all Lonny could expect. If Tom preferred to stay at the ranch, that was his business. Come to think of it, though, Tom had been mighty eager to get into town every chance he got—until recently. Lonny suspected Michelle Larson at the feed store had something to do with that. He couldn't help wondering what was going on there. It was probably as obvious as it seemed—a boy-girl thing. In that case, considering his own relationship difficulties, he wouldn't have much advice to offer.

As he drove toward town, Lonny turned the radio up as loud as he could stand it, listening to Johnny and Willie and Garth, even singing along now and then. As he approached the intersection at Grove and Logan, he remembered reading in the *Red Springs Journal* that the new stop sign had caused a couple of accidents in the past week. Real accidents, too, not just minor collisions. If this continued, the town was likely to order a traffic light. There was already one on Main Street, and in his opinion, one light was enough.

The first of his errands took him to the feed store. Lonny backed his pickup to the loading dock and tossed in a fifty-pound sack of chicken feed. The owner's daughter hurried out as soon as he pulled into the lot. When Michelle saw that he was alone, her face fell and she wandered back into the store.

Lonny paid for his purchase and stayed to have a cup of coffee with Charley Larson. They talked about the same things they always discussed. The weather, followed by the low price of cattle and the prospects for naturally raised beef. Then they rounded off their conversation with a few comments about the upcoming community carnival.

Lonny wasn't really surprised when Charley asked him, "What do you know about that hand you hired?"

"Tom?" Lonny said with a shrug. "Not much. He's of age, if that's what you're wondering. I checked, and as far as I can see, he's not in any trouble. He keeps to himself and he's a hard worker. What makes you ask?" Although Lonny could guess.

Charley glanced over his shoulder toward the store. "My Michelle likes him."

"That bother you?"

"Not in the least," Charley muttered. "I think Michelle might've asked him to the school dance. He seems to have turned her down."

So *that* was the reason Tom was so gloomy these days. Lonny couldn't imagine why he'd said no to Michelle when he was so obviously taken with the girl. Apparently his hired hand was as inept at relationships as Lonny was himself. Granted, he'd never had difficulties during his rodeo days, but Joy Fuller was a different proposition altogether. "I'll ask Tom about it and get back to you."

Charley hesitated. "If you do, be subtle about it, okay? Otherwise, Michelle will get upset with me."

"I will," Lonny promised, considering his options.

There was the school carnival, for starters. Lonny figured he'd go around suppertime—and while he was at it, he'd bring Tom. The dance was later that night, so if Tom was already in town, he'd have no excuse not to attend. These events weren't for another two weeks, but his sister had roped him into volunteering for the cleanup committee, which meant he'd be picking up trash and sweeping the street. She'd said something about him frying burgers with Chase, too. There was no point in arguing with her. Besides, he enjoyed the festivities.

Last year Joy had been working the cotton candy machine. He'd hoped to have a conversation with her, but he hadn't done it. For one thing, she'd been constantly busy, chatting with a crowd of people who all seemed to like her and have lots to say. For another, he'd felt uncharacteristically tongue-tied around her. He sure didn't want a bunch of interested onlookers witnessing his stumbling, fumbling attempts at conversation.

When he'd finished talking to Charley and climbed into the cab of his pickup, Lonny noticed a flash of green outside the town's biggest grocery store, situated across the street.

Lonny's eyes locked on Joy Fuller's green PT Cruiser. She pulled into the lot, parked and headed into the store.

Groceries were on Lonny's list of errands. Nothing much, just the basics. Unexpectedly, the happy feeling he'd experienced while driving into town with the radio blasting came over him again. A carefree, what-the-hell feeling...

Lonny parked and jumped out of his pickup. His steps were light as he entered the store and grabbed a cart. His first stop was the vegetable aisle. It was too soon to expect much produce from Letty's garden. Last year, she'd seen to it that he got healthy portions of lettuce, green beans, fresh peas and zucchini. He was counting on her to do the same this summer. Until then, he had no choice but to buy a few vegetables himself.

Glancing around, he was disappointed not to see Joy. He tossed a bag of carrots in his cart, then threw in some lettuce and made his way to the meat department. She wasn't there. So he wheeled his cart to the back of the store, to the dairy case. He'd heard that a lot of women ate yogurt. But Joy wasn't in that section, either.

Then he heard her laugh.

Lonny smiled. The sound came from somewhere in the middle of the store. Turning his cart around, he trotted toward the frozen food. He should've known that was where he'd find her.

Here was proof that, unlike Letty, who cooked for her family, Joy didn't take much time to prepare meals. Neither did he, come to think of it—breakfast was his one and only specialty—which was why dinner invitations from Letty were appreciated. Tom and Lonny mostly fended for themselves. A can of soup or chili, a sandwich or two, was about as fancy as either of them got.

Sure enough, the instant Lonny turned into the aisle, he saw Joy. Her back was to him, and the three Wilson kids were chatting with her, along with their mom, Della. Lonny had gone to school with Della Harrison; she'd married Bobby Wilson, a friend of his, and had three kids in quick succession. Lonny didn't know whether to envy Bobby and Della or pity them.

He strolled up to the two women. "Hi, Della," he said, trying to seem casual and nonchalant. He nodded politely in Joy's direction and touched the brim of his Stetson.

The smile faded from Joy's face. "Mr. Ellison," she returned primly.

Lonny had trouble keeping his eyes off Joy. He had to admit she looked mighty fine in a pair of jeans. Both women gazed at him expectantly, and he didn't have a clue what to say next. Judging by her expression, Joy would rather be just about anywhere else at that moment.

"Good to run into you, Lonny," Della said pleasantly. "Bobby was saying the other day that we don't see near enough of you."

"Yeah, we'll get together soon." Lonny manufactured an anxious frown. "But I've been having problems with my truck. I had an accident recently and, well, it hasn't run the same since."

"Really?" Della asked.

"That's right," he said, wondering if he'd overdone the facade of wounded innocence.

"Ms. Fuller is my teacher," a sweet little girl announced proudly.

Della was looking suspiciously from him to Joy. Lonny decided that was his cue to move on, and he would have, except that he made the mistake of glancing into Joy's grocery cart. It was just as he'd expected—frozen entrées. Only she'd picked the diet ones. She didn't need to be on any diet. In fact, her figure was about as perfect as a woman's could get. No wonder she'd snapped at him and been so irritable. The woman was starving herself.

"That's what you intend to eat this week?" he asked, reaching for one of the entrées. He felt suddenly hopeful. If she was hungry, the way he suspected, then she might accept an invitation to dinner. They could talk everything out over enchiladas and maybe a Corona or two at the Mexican Fiesta. Everything always seemed better on a full stomach.

"What's wrong with that?" she demanded, yanking the frozen entrée out of his hand and tossing it back in her cart.

"You shouldn't be on a diet," he insisted. "If that's what you're having for dinner, it's no wonder you're so skinny—or so mad."

"Lonny," Della gasped.

Oh, boy, he'd done it again. That comment hadn't come out quite as he'd intended. "I—you… I—" He tried to backtrack, but all he could manage was a bad imitation of a trout. As usual, his mouth had operated independently of his brain.

He turned to Della, but she glared at him with the same intensity as Joy. Instinct told him to hightail it out of the store before he made the situation worse than it already was.

"I didn't mean that like it sounded," he muttered. "You look fine for being underweight." Again he glanced at Della for help, but none was forthcoming. "You're a little on the thin side, that's all. Not much, of course. In fact, you're just about right."

"It's a male problem," Della said, speaking to Joy. She scowled. "They don't know when to keep their mouths shut."

"Uh, it was nice seeing you both," he said. He'd thought he was complimenting her, but to his utter astonishment, Joy's eyes had filled with tears.

Lonny's gut twisted. He couldn't imagine what he'd said that was bad enough to make her cry. "Joy, I…"

Della looked at him with open contempt. He swallowed, not knowing how to fix this mess. He was aghast as Joy abruptly left the aisle, her grocery cart rattling.

"See what you've done?" Della hissed at him under her breath. "You idiot."

"What's wrong with Ms. Fuller?" the little girl asked. "What did that man do?" She focused her blue eyes on him and had he been a lesser man, Lonny would've backed off. If looks could kill, his sister would be planning his burial service about now.

"I—I didn't mean anything," Lonny stammered, feeling as low as a man could get.

"You're hopeless," Della said, shaking her head.

The girl shook her head, too, eyes narrowed.

"I…I—"

"The least you can do is apologize." Della's fingers gripped the cart handle.

"I tried." He motioned helplessly.

"You didn't try hard enough." With that Della sped away, her children in tow. The little girl marched to the end of the aisle, then turned back and stuck her tongue out at him.

A sick feeling attacked the pit of his stomach. He should've known better. He'd decided not to pursue a relationship with Joy and then, next thing he knew, he was trying to invite her for dinner. He couldn't even do *that* without making a mess of it.

He felt dreadful, worse than dreadful. He'd actually made Joy cry, but God's honest truth, he couldn't believe a little comment like that was worthy of tears.

He walked up to the front of the store only to see Joy dash out, carrying two grocery bags. Abandoning his cart, he hurried after her.

"Joy," he called, sprinting into the parking lot.

At the sound of his voice she whirled around and confronted him. "In case you hadn't already guessed, I'm not interested in speaking to you."

"I—ah…" In his entire life, Lonny had never backed down from a confrontation. Served him right that the first time it happened would be with a woman.

"You were trying to embarrass me. Trying to make me feel stupid."

"I…I—" For some reason, he couldn't make his tongue form the words in his brain.

"You poked fun at me, called me skinny. Well, maybe I am, but—"

"You aren't," he cried. "I just said that because…

because it didn't look like you were eating enough and I thought maybe I could feed you."

"Feed me?"

"Dinner."

"Just leave me alone!" Joy left him and bolted for her car.

Lonny exhaled sharply. Following her was probably a bad idea—another in a long list of them. He would've preferred to simply go home, but he couldn't make himself do it. Unable to come up with any alternative, Lonny jogged after her. He wouldn't sleep tonight if he didn't tell her how sorry he was.

He knew she'd heard his footsteps, because the instant she set the groceries in the Cruiser's trunk, she whirled around. They were practically nose to nose. "I don't need you to feed me or talk to me or anything else," she said. "All I want you to do is *leave me alone*."

"I will, only you have to listen to me first." Darn, this was hard. "I didn't mean to suggest you were unattractive, because you are."

"Unattractive?" she cried. "I'm *unattractive?* This is supposed to be an apology? Is that why you decided not to see me two years ago? You thought I was too skinny?"

"No, no, I meant you're attractive." Could this possibly get any worse? "Anyway, that has nothing to do with now. Can't you just accept my apology? Are you always this hotheaded?"

Eyes glistening, she turned and slammed the trunk lid. The noise reverberated around the parking lot.

Nothing he said was going to help; the situation

seemed completely out of his control. "I think you're about as beautiful as a girl can get." There, he'd said it.

She stared at him for a long moment. "What did you say?"

"You're beautiful," he repeated. He hadn't intended to tell her that, even if it was true. Which it was.

The fire in her eyes gradually died away, replaced by a quizzical look that said she wasn't sure she could believe him. But then she smiled.

Lonny felt a burst of sheer happiness at that smile.

She glanced down at the asphalt. "When I was growing up, I had knobby knees and skinny legs and I was teased unmercifully. The other kids used to call me Skel. Short for skeleton."

That explained a lot.

"I had no idea."

"You couldn't have," she assured him. "When you said I was skinny, it brought back a lot of bad memories."

In an effort to comfort her, Lonny pulled her close. That was when insanity took over for the second time that day. Even knowing they were in the middle of town in the grocery-store parking lot, even knowing she'd told him in no uncertain terms to leave her alone, Lonny bent forward and kissed her.

Kissing Joy felt good. She seemed to be experiencing the same wonderful sensation, because she didn't object. He knew he was right when she wound her arms around his neck and she opened to him, as naturally as could be.

Lonny groaned. They kissed with a passion that was as heated as any argument they'd ever had. He wanted to tell her again how sorry he was, how deeply he regretted everything he'd said, and he prayed his kisses were enough to convey what was in his heart.

Then all at once Joy's hands were pushing him away. Caught off guard, Lonny stumbled back. He would've landed squarely on his butt if not for some quick shuffling.

"What did you do *that* for?" She brought one hand to her mouth.

"I don't know," he admitted quietly. "I wanted to tell you I was sorry, and that seemed as good a way as any."

She backed toward the driver's door as if she didn't trust him not to reach for her a second time.

He might have, too, if he'd felt he had the slightest chance of reasoning with her—or resuming their previous activity.

"Well, don't do it again."

"Fine," he said. She made it sound as if that kiss had been against her will. Not so. She could deny it, but he knew the truth. Joy Fuller had wanted that kiss as much as he had.

Chapter 6

Joy couldn't figure out how that kiss had ever happened. As she drove home, she touched her finger to her swollen lips. What shocked her most was how much she'd *enjoyed* his kiss. They'd kissed before, back in their dating days, but it certainly hadn't affected her like this. Her irritation rose. Lonny Ellison had insulted her, and in response, she'd let him *kiss* her?

Upset as she was, Joy nearly ran through the stop sign at Grove and Logan. Again. She slammed on her brakes hard, which jolted her forward with enough force to lock her seat belt so tightly she couldn't breathe. Just as quickly, she was thrown back against the seat. When she did manage to catch her breath, she exhaled shakily as her pulse hammered in her ears.

Once she got home, Joy unpacked her groceries and

tried hard to put that ridiculous kiss out of her mind. The fact that Lonny had apologized was a lame excuse for what he'd done—what she'd allowed. Standing in her kitchen, Joy covered her face with both hands. For heaven's sake, they'd been in a parking lot! Anyone driving by or coming out of the store might have witnessed that…that torrid scene.

Her face burned at the mere thought of it. She'd worked hard to maintain a solid reputation in the community, and now Lonny Ellison and her own reckless behavior threatened to destroy it.

Thankfully, her afternoon was busy; otherwise she would've spent the rest of the day worrying. She had choir practice at two o'clock at the church and there was a carnival committee meeting at school immediately following that. Joy's one desperate hope was that no one she knew had been anywhere near the grocery store that morning.

By the time she arrived at the church, her stomach was in turmoil. As she took her place at the organ, she surreptitiously watched the choir members. Fortunately, no one seemed to pay her any particular attention. That was promising, although she supposed the last person they'd say anything to would be her. Once she was out of sight, the gossip would probably spread faster than an August brush fire.

To her relief, practice went well. Joy stayed on when everyone had left and played through the songs, which helped settle her nerves. Music had always had a calming effect on her, and that was exactly what she needed.

Kissing in public. Dear heaven, what was she thinking? Of course, that was the problem. She *hadn't* been thinking. All reason had flown from her brain. But regardless of her own role in this, she cast the greater part of the blame at Lonny Ellison's feet. His sole purpose in commenting on her diet had been to embarrass her.

At three, the school parking lot started to fill up for the meeting. The committees had been formed months earlier, and their main purpose now was to raise funds for the end-of-school carnival. Bringing in professional carnival rides had put a definite strain on their limited budget. But everyone in town was excited about it, and the committee would do whatever was necessary to finance the rides, for which they planned to charge only a nominal fee.

A number of women had already gathered in the high school gymnasium when Joy slipped into the meeting. She sat in the back row, where she was soon joined by Letty Brown. Involuntarily, Joy tensed, afraid Lonny might have mentioned their kiss to his sister. Apparently not, because Letty smiled at her, and they made small talk for several minutes. That didn't prove anything, though.

"When's the last time you talked to your brother?" Joy asked when she couldn't stand the suspense anymore.

Letty frowned. "A couple of days ago. Why?"

It demanded all of Joy's acting skills to give a nonchalant shrug. "No reason."

A moment later, Doris Fleming banged the gavel to bring the meeting to order. After the preliminaries and the reading of the minutes, Doris announced, "I have all the game prizes ordered, I've paid for the carnival,

and—I'm shocked to tell you—our finances have been
entirely depleted. We need to raise funds and we need
to do it fast, otherwise we'll have no operating budget. We still have to buy food, drinks and so forth."

Janice Rothchild's hand shot into the air. "We could
do a bake sale. That's always good for raising money."

A few women groaned. Muttering broke out until
Doris banged the gavel again.

"A bake sale's always been our best money-raiser,"
Janice reminded the other women. She should know
because she'd been the carnival treasurer for as long
as Joy had been in town.

"Well, yes, Della's pies sell out right away, and Flor-
ence Williams's sourdough biscuits, too, of course."

"Don't forget Sally's chocolate cake," Myrtle Jameson shouted out. "That's one of the first to go. But last
year, *everything* sold out in under two hours."

"Order, please," Doris said. She held her index finger to her lips. "Myrtle, you're right. Remember how,
at the last bake sale, there was a line outside the door
even before we opened? And, Betty," she said, pointing her gavel at a woman who sat in the front row. "Tell
the ladies what happened to you."

Betty Sanders, who was well into her eighties,
stood, using her cane for balance. "One of the men
stopped me in the parking lot and bought all my butterhorn rolls the second I got out of my car."

"See what I mean?" Janice said, looking around for
confirmation. "That's why I suggested we do a bake
sale. They're *very* popular."

"I have another idea," Letty said, leaping to her feet.
The women twisted around to see who was speaking.

"If the bake sale's so popular and we sell out right away, why don't we auction off the baked goods?"

Letty sat back down and the room instantly erupted into discordant chatter.

Doris pounded the gavel and Joy could see that she was keen on Letty's idea.

"That's a fabulous suggestion," Doris said. "We'd raise a lot more cash—and our treasury could sure use it."

"But where would we hold an auction?" someone called out. "Especially at this late date? Don't forget, the carnival's only two weeks away."

A variety of suggestions followed. Finally someone else brought forth the idea of having the auction during Friday-night bingo at the community center. Expressions of approval rippled across the room.

"An auction's a perfect idea." Joy leaned close in order to whisper to her friend.

"I don't know why someone hasn't thought of it before," Letty said, shrugging off the praise.

"Bingo is the most popular event of the week," Lois Franklin reminded the group. "And Bill told me he always needs entertainment for intermission. I know he'll welcome this idea."

"It helps that you're married to him," Doris said, chuckling. "So we can count on holding the auction at bingo?"

Lois nodded. "I'll make sure of it." And she would, since Bill was the caller—and the man in charge of bingo in Red Springs.

"It's as good as done, then," Doris said. "Thank you, Lois."

"When?" another woman asked. "Next Friday?"

Doris glanced around. "Does a week give everyone enough time to get the word out?"

There were nods of assent.

Although she'd hoped to remain inconspicuous during this meeting, Joy didn't feel she could keep silent. She raised her hand and stood. "That only gives us seven days—including today—to let people know." They'd need to have signs made and posted around town right away.

After another round of muttered rumblings, Doris slammed the gavel yet again. "That's true, but there's nothing we can do about it. The bake sale auction is set for next Friday night."

"We'll tell everyone," Betty said, leaning on her cane.

"No problem." Honey Sue Jameson got to her feet. "I'll make it my business to tell the entire town about this." Honey Sue was Myrtle's daughter-in-law. She and her husband, Don, owned the local radio station, so she was on the radio every morning, announcing the news and reading the farm report. Honey Sue had come by her name because her voice was as sweet and smooth as honey. Although Joy had no interest in the price of beef or soybeans, she sometimes tuned in just to hear Honey Sue, who could actually make a list of prices sound almost poetic.

"That's terrific," Doris said, beaming at the prospect of filling the committee's coffers. "I'll put out sheets of paper for sign-up lists. Ladies, please indicate what you're bringing and how you can help publicize our bake sale."

"Just a minute," Betty said, returning everyone's attention to the front of the room. "Who'll be the auctioneer?"

"We could always ask Don," Lois Franklin suggested.

"If he won't do it, I will," Honey Sue volunteered. Once again Doris nodded her approval.

"Will the name of whoever contributed the baked item be mentioned?" someone else wanted to know.

Doris frowned. "I…" She looked to Honey Sue for advice. "What do you think?"

Honey Sue smiled. "I don't suppose it could hurt."

"The name of the donor will be announced at the time the baked item is brought up for auction," Doris stated decisively.

"That might generate even higher bids," Letty murmured. "Chase is crazy for Betty's butterhorn rolls. He doesn't know it, but Betty gave me the recipe. I just haven't gotten around to baking them yet."

Joy whispered in Letty's ear. "So it was Chase who stopped her in the parking lot?"

"I'm not sure, but knowing Chase, it probably was."

Several sheets of paper were set up on the front table, and the women stepped forward to write down their donations.

Joy and Letty joined the line. "What are you going to bake?" Joy asked her friend.

"Pecan pie," Letty said without hesitation. "What about you?"

Several ideas ran through Joy's mind. No doubt Lonny thought she purchased frozen entrées because she didn't know how to cook. Well, that wasn't the case. She should arrive with Cherries Jubilee, toss on the brandy and light it up. She could just imagine Lonny Ellison's expression when he saw flames leaping into the air. Or perhaps Baked Alaska. That would make a point, too.

"I haven't decided yet," she murmured.

"Remember the last time you watched Cricket for me?" Letty said. "The two of you baked peanut butter cookies. They were wonderful."

"You think so?" Joy didn't mean to sound so insecure. The cookies were fine, but they didn't provide the dramatic statement she was hoping to make. She shouldn't worry about impressing anyone, least of all Lonny. Still, the thought flitted through her mind. She would derive great satisfaction from seeing his face when she presented Crêpes Suzette.

Joy didn't have a single thing to prove to Lonny, or anyone else for that matter, and yet she *wanted* to impress him. It was all about pride. This…this cowpoke was taking up far too much of her time and energy. She didn't want to be attracted to him. Josh was coming back into her life and he was someone she knew, someone she felt comfortable with. Lonny made her angry every time she thought about him, he'd embarrassed her publicly more than once, *and* they had absolutely nothing in common.

"Peanut butter cookies are so…" Joy paused, searching for the right word. "*Ordinary,*" she finished.

Letty grinned. "In case you haven't noticed, most everyone around these parts prefers ordinary. We're a meat-and-potatoes kind of community. You won't see anyone signing up to bring Crêpes Suzette."

"Ah…" So much for that idea.

"It's a lesson I learned when I came back after living in California all those years," Letty went on. "I didn't need to impress anyone. All I had to do was be myself."

Even though Joy longed to see the look on Lonny's face when the auctioneer brought forth her fabulously exclusive dessert and read her name, she realized she'd only embarrass herself. No one would bid on it; no doubt they'd feel sorry for her, the city girl who'd tried to show off her superior baking skills.

"Peanut butter cookies it is," she said with a sigh.

Letty reached the front of the line and wrote down pecan pie. Joy added her cookies to the list, noticing that only one other woman had offered to bake them.

Letty waited for her, and together they walked to the parking lot. Several other cars were pulling out.

"Is something going on between my brother and you?" Letty asked unexpectedly.

Joy almost couldn't swallow her gasp of alarm. "Wh-what do you mean?"

"Well, you *did* ask about him," Letty said. "You wanted to know if I'd talked to my brother recently."

"Oh, that." Joy brushed off the question. "No reason." It was the same response she'd made earlier, but she couldn't come up with a more inventive excuse on the spur of the moment.

Letty regarded her as if she knew there *was* a reason. "Well, regardless, we'll see him soon enough."

"We will?" Joy widened her eyes. She'd sincerely hoped to avoid him.

"Of course," Letty said matter-of-factly. "You can bet he'll be at the auction." And with that simple statement, she both confirmed Joy's fears and ignited her hopes.

Chapter 7

Lonny had plenty to do around the ranch. Early in the afternoon, after he got back from town, he rode out to the herd, seeking any cattle that showed signs of sickness. Chase had found one heifer with a runny nose and isolated her for the time being.

Lonny felt a sense of pride as his gaze fell on the rows of wheat, stretching as far as the eye could see. The stalks were still slender and light green. He and Chase had planted three hundred acres, another three hundred in soybeans and nearly that much in natural grasses. The wheat was grown for grazing and for seed. They grew everything their cattle ate. The herd now numbered about four hundred, and their goal was to eventually increase it to fifteen hundred head.

A herd that size would take years to develop, depending on the public's response to natural beef. He had to believe that once health-conscious consumers realized they had a choice, they'd prefer a product devoid of potentially harmful chemicals. Both Chase and Lonny had staked their financial future on this hope.

Thinking about their plans for the herd distracted him from Joy Fuller—but not for long. Following that scene this morning, he was half-afraid his sister might be right. He *was* attracted to Joy. He had been earlier, too, when they'd first dated, only it had all blown up in his face. The woman was opinionated and argumentative—but then, so was he. Together, they were like a match striking tinder. Saturday's kiss had shown him how quickly that could lead to combustion.

He understood now why he'd reacted so irrationally at the time of the accident. He knew why he'd insisted she take responsibility for the damage to his truck. The truth had hit him squarely between the eyes when he kissed her. It shook him, mainly because he didn't *want* to be attracted to Joy. They'd already tried a relationship and he'd decided it wasn't going to work. It wouldn't this time, either, and now...now, he thought, looking over the cattle scattered across the green land, he had other considerations, other worries.

Tom came into view on Dolly, the brown-and-white mare he preferred to ride. He was unusually mature for nineteen and, to Lonny's relief, didn't require much supervision. He gave Tom a few instructions, then rode back to the barn. He should check the fence line, which needed continual attention. Yet whenever he started a task, he had to struggle not to get sidetracked by thoughts of Joy...and that kiss.

Twice he'd actually climbed inside his truck, intending to go into town so he could talk to her. He didn't know what he could possibly say that would make a shred of difference. He was convinced that she'd enjoyed their kiss as much as he had, but she'd insisted she didn't want him touching her.

For a moment there, for one of the most wonderful interludes of his life, she'd kissed him back. Then she'd suddenly broken it off.

Once he'd finished rubbing down his horse, Lonny walked resolutely toward the truck. He would go to Joy, he decided, take his hat off and ask if they could talk man to man—no, that wouldn't work. Man to woman, then. They'd clear up past misunderstandings and perhaps they could start fresh.

He'd apologize, too, for the way he'd behaved after the accident, and tell her she didn't need to pay him a dime to repair that dent. It added character to his truck, he'd say. He wouldn't mention their kiss, though. If he apologized, he'd be lying and she'd see right through him.

Determined now, even though it was already late afternoon, he got into his pickup. It was at this point that he'd changed his mind twice before. But based on his frustrating inability to forget about Joy for more than a few minutes, he could only conclude that it wouldn't do any good to stick around the ranch. In his current emotional state, he wasn't worth a plugged nickel, anyway.

The twenty-minute drive into town seemed to pass in five. Before he had a chance to think about what he intended to say, he'd reached Joy's house. At least he assumed she still lived in the same place she'd rented when she moved to town. He parked outside and clutched the steering wheel for probably three minutes before he found the gumption to walk to the front door. Checking the contents of the mailbox confirmed that this was, indeed, her home.

Lonny wasn't fond of eating crow and he was about to swallow a sizable portion. He was willing to do it, though, if that would set things straight between him and Joy.

Squaring his shoulders, he cleared his throat and removed his Stetson. He shook his head in case his hair was flat, took a deep breath and braced his feet apart. Then he rang her doorbell.

Nothing.

He pressed it again, harder and longer this time.

Still nothing.

Lonny peeked in the front window. There didn't appear to be anyone home. Now that he thought about it, her little green PT Cruiser was nowhere in sight.

Disappointed, Lonny went back to his own vehicle. It seemed important to let her know he'd made an effort to contact her. Digging around in his glove compartment, he found a slip of paper—an old gas station receipt—and a pencil stub. He spent a moment thinking about what to say. After careful consideration, he wrote: *I came to talk. I think we should, don't you? Call me. Lonny J. Ellison.* Then he wrote down his phone number.

He'd added his middle initial so she'd realize he was serious. His father had chosen Jethro as his middle name, and he usually avoided any reminder of it. For

Joy, he'd reveal his embarrassing secret—because if she asked what the *J* stood for, he'd tell her.

As he pulled away from the curb and turned the corner, he glanced in his rearview mirror and saw her green car coming from the opposite direction.

Lonny made a quick U-turn and parked just out of sight. Leaning over his steering wheel, he managed to get a glimpse of Joy's front porch. Sure enough, it was her.

His best course of action, he decided, was to wait and see what happened when she found his note.

Lonny watched Joy walk slowly toward the house. He noticed that her shoulders were hunched as if she wasn't feeling well. She opened the screen door and the slip of paper he'd tucked there dropped to the porch.

Lonny almost called out, afraid she hadn't seen it. She had, though. Bending down, she picked up the note he'd folded in half. He held his breath as she read it. Then he saw her take his heartfelt message, crumple it with both hands and shove it inside her pocket. After that, she unlocked the front door, slammed it shut and drew her drapes.

Lonny sighed. Perhaps now wasn't a good time to approach her, after all.

On the drive back to his ranch, Lonny wondered how his plan could have gone so wrong. Joy's reaction to his note made it clear that she wasn't interested in anything he had to say. He could take a hint. But in his opinion, she wasn't being honest with herself; otherwise, she would've acknowledged how much she'd liked that kiss. Fine. He could deal with it.

The rest of the day was shot, so Lonny stopped at

Chase and Letty's. As soon as his truck rolled into the yard, Cricket came running out of the house, bouncing down the porch steps.

Lonny was out of his vehicle just in time to catch her in his arms and swing her around. Now, *this* was a gratifying reception—exactly the type he'd hoped to get from Joy. That, however, was not to be.

"Mom's baking pecan pie," Cricket announced.

"For dinner?" he asked, setting his niece down on the ground.

Cricket frowned. "I don't think so."

"Your mommy makes the best pecan pie I ever tasted." If he hung around a while, she might offer him a piece.

Chase stepped out of the barn, wiping his brow with his forearm. "What are you doing here?" he asked. "I thought you were going to finish the worming."

"Good to see you, too," Lonny teased. They'd been best friends their entire lives. Friends, partners, neighbors—and now, brothers-in-law. "Tom and I finished the worming early." Early enough to race into town and make an idiot of himself over Joy. But that was information he planned to keep private.

"Aren't you and Tom driving the herd to the lower pasture this weekend?"

"I decided against it," Lonny said. "There's still plenty of grass in the upper pasture. I meant to tell you...."

Letty came out onto the back porch and waved when she saw him. "Hi, Lonny," she said. She didn't look as if she'd been baking.

"What's this I hear about a pecan pie?" he asked,

moving closer. If he was lucky, she'd offer him a piece *and* invite him to dinner. In that case, he'd casually bring up the subject of Joy and get his sister's opinion. Maybe he needed a woman's perspective.

"I'm not baking the pie until later in the week. It's for an auction. Want to stay for dinner? I'm just setting the table."

"What're you making?"

"Roast chicken, scalloped potatoes, green bean casserole."

He grinned. "It'd be my pleasure." Letty's cooking was downright inspired, and this meal reminded him of one their mother might have made. Toward the end of her life, though, she'd taken more interest in quilting than in the culinary arts. Letty had inherited their mother's abilities in the kitchen, and she could do artistic stuff, too—singing and knitting and other things, like the dried herb wreath that hung on the kitchen door.

"I'll wash up and join you in a few minutes," Chase said.

"Cricket, go add another place setting to the table," Letty instructed her daughter.

"Can Uncle Lonny sit next to me?"

"I wouldn't sit anywhere else," Lonny said as the six-year-old followed her mother up the steps.

"Were you in town today?" Letty asked.

Lonny paused, unsure how much to tell his sister. "I just made a quick trip," he said cautiously. He'd actually made two trips, but he didn't point *that* out.

"Did you happen to run into Joy?"

He froze in midstep. "Why do you ask?"

Letty eyed him speculatively. "What is it with you two?" she demanded, hands on hips. "I asked Joy about you and she clammed right up."

"Really?" Lonny played it cool. If she wasn't talking, then he wasn't, either. He didn't know how many people had caught sight of the spectacle they'd made of themselves—and whether someone had tattled to Letty.

"I wish you and Joy would talk," she said, in the same sisterly tone she'd used when they were kids. "It's ridiculous the way you keep circling each other. *One* of you needs to be adult enough to discuss this."

"I agree with you." His response seemed to surprise her. What Letty didn't know was that Lonny had already tried, and it hadn't gotten him anywhere. He held open the screen door. "It's obvious," he said, tossing Letty a cocky smile. "The woman wants me."

"The only thing that's obvious to me, big brother, is that you're so in love with her you can't think straight."

He laughed that off—but he was man enough to admit there was *something* between him and Joy. However, exactly what it was and how deep it went, not to mention how he should handle it, remained a mystery.

Letty walked into the kitchen and got him a cup of coffee. "You tried talking to her?"

Lonny took the mug and shook his head. He hadn't spoken to Joy, not technically; he'd left her a note. Rather than explain, he didn't answer the question. "Tell me about the auction. What's it for?"

Letty studied him as he added sugar to his coffee. "I signed up to bring a pecan pie for a bake sale auction. The carnival committee needs operating capital, and we have to raise it quickly."

"You aren't going to sell the goodies the way you normally do?" That was a disappointment. An auction would drive up the prices. Lonny had a sweet tooth and he was generally first in line for a bake sale. This pie might prove to be expensive.

"If you want the pecan pie, you're going to have to bid on it like everyone else," his sister gleefully informed him. "Otherwise, you'll have to wait until next Thanksgiving."

Head down, Lonny muttered a few words he didn't want Cricket or his sister to hear.

"I was at a meeting about the bake sale this afternoon," Letty said as he leaned his hip against the kitchen counter. "Joy was there, too."

That remark caught his attention; Lonny suddenly lifted his head and realized his little sister had just baited him. He'd fallen for it, too, hook, line and sinker. In an effort to cover his interest, he laughed. "You're telling me Joy's contributing to the bake sale?" Apparently his sister was unaware that the woman's meals came from the freezer section of the grocery store.

His sister didn't see the humor in it, so he felt he needed to enlighten her. "Do you seriously think she can bake?"

"Why not?" Letty asked, eyebrows raised.

Lonny could see he was getting more involved in the subject than was really prudent. He considered telling Letty about seeing Joy earlier, then promptly decided against it. With a quick shrug, he said, "Oh, nothing."

Lonny wondered what was taking Chase so long to wash up. He could use a diversion. Sighing, he thought he might as well get Letty's advice now. The hell with being sensible or discreet. "I blew it with Joy," he said in a low voice.

His confession didn't come easy. Before he could think better of it, Lonny described the incident inside the store—stopping short of the kiss. It wasn't that he was opposed to telling his sister the full truth...eventually. If he and Joy had been seen, the gossip would find its way to Letty soon enough; in fact, he was surprised she hadn't heard anything yet. But that kiss was special. For as long as possible, he wanted to keep those moments to himself.

"You said *what?*" his sister exploded after listening to the whole sad story.

Lonny pulled out a chair and sat down. "I feel bad about it now. She said she got teased about being thin as a kid, and I stepped in it with both feet."

"Lonny!"

It didn't help having his sister yell at him. He knew he'd made a mistake; she didn't need to beat up on him all over again. Della and her daughters had done an adequate job of that already.

"I apologized," he muttered, rubbing his hands over his eyes. "Well, I tried."

Letty frowned.

"What?" he snapped. If Chase didn't arrive soon, he'd go and search for the guy himself.

"Here's what you're going to do," his sister said, speaking slowly and clearly, as though he were hard of hearing—or deficient in understanding.

"Now, Letty…"

"You're going to bid on Joy's peanut butter cook-ies." His sister wouldn't allow him to interrupt. Letty was still frowning, her eyes narrowed. "And you're going to be the highest bidder."

"Okay." That much he could do.

She nodded, evidently approving his willingness to fall in with her scheme. Well, he supposed she couldn't get him into worse trouble with Joy than he was now.

"And then," Letty continued, "you're going to *taste* Joy's cookies and declare they're the best you've ever had in your entire life."

"I am?" This seemed a little overboard to Lonny.

"Yes, you will, and you're going to mean it, too."

Lonny wasn't so sure about that, but he'd hear his sister out. He'd asked for her opinion, and the least he could do was listen.

Fortunately, Chase clattered down the stairs at that moment, putting a temporary end to Letty's career as a romantic adviser.

Chapter 8

Wednesday afternoon Joy hurried home from school, planning to do some baking. She'd spent far too much time reading through cookbooks and searching websites on the internet, looking for a spectacular dessert that would knock the boots off a certain rancher.

Every time she found a recipe she was sure would impress Lonny, Joy remembered the scorn in his eyes when he'd picked up her frozen dinner. He'd probably fall over in a dead faint when he realized that not only could she bake, she was good at it.

Since she'd wasted so many hours on research, Joy had yet to make her peanut butter cookies, a recipe handed down from her grandmother. This recipe was an old family favorite.

She turned on the radio and arranged her ingredients. Flour, sugar, peanut butter... She lined them up along the counter in order of use. Bowls, measuring cups and utensils waited on the kitchen table; the oven was preheating and the cookie sheet greased. She was nothing if not organized.

The doorbell rang just as she was measuring the flour. Joy set the bag down and hurried into the front hall, curious to find out who her visitor might be.

Letty stood there, with Cricket at her side, and Joy immediately opened the screen door. "Come in," she said, glad of the company.

"Thanks," Letty said, smiling as she stepped into the house. "I was in town to buy pecans and thought I'd come over and see how you're doing."

"I'm baking," Joy announced. "Or at least, I'm getting started."

Letty hesitated. "I don't want to interrupt...."

"I haven't actually begun, so your timing's perfect," she said, ushering Letty and Cricket into the kitchen.

"Can I play on your computer?" Cricket asked when her mother sat down at the table.

Joy glanced at Letty, who nodded, and Cricket loped eagerly toward the spare bedroom. Apparently, Chase had taught her solitaire.

With a sweep of her hand, Letty indicated the half-dozen cookbooks Joy had spread out on the table and on two of her four chairs. In addition, she had a six-inch stack of recipes she'd printed off the internet.

"What's all this?" Letty asked, as Joy cleared a chair and sat down across from her.

"Dessert recipes," Joy admitted a bit sheepishly.

Letty reached for one on the stack she'd gotten off the internet. "Cannoli?" she read, and Joy watched her friend's face as she scanned the directions. "This sounds complicated."

Joy had thought so herself. "I could probably manage it, but I was afraid I'd waste a lot of time shaping them and then I'd need to fill them, too. Besides, they're deep-fried and I don't know how well they'd keep."

"You said you were baking peanut butter cookies."

"I am," Joy was quick to tell her, motioning toward the counter, "but I also wanted to bring something more…impressive. I'm a good cook and…" She let the rest fade. Since Letty was Lonny's sister, she couldn't very well confess what she was trying to prove and why. The less Letty knew about her most recent encounter with Lonny, the better.

"Tiramisu?" Letty cocked her head as she read the recipe title in a cookbook that was open directly in front of her. She looked skeptical when she returned her attention to Joy.

"I rejected that one, too," Joy confessed. "I wasn't sure I could get all the ingredients without having to drive into Red Rock or Cheyenne."

"Baklava?" Letty asked next, pointing at another recipe.

"I had no idea whether anyone in town would even know what that was," Joy said. "There isn't a large Greek population in the area, is there?"

"No." Letty confirmed what Joy already suspected.

"The Raspberry Truffle Torte Bombe had possibilities," Joy said, gesturing at yet another of the cookbooks. "However, I was afraid the ice cream would melt."

"Joy, what's wrong with peanut butter cookies?" Letty asked.

"Nothing. I just wanted to bake more than one thing."

"Then bake a cake, and not a chocolate truffle one, either," she said, reaching for another of the pages Joy had printed out. "Just a plain, simple cake. That'll generate more interest than anything with melting ice cream in the middle."

"It will?"

Letty nodded and seemed surprised that she had to remind Joy of the obvious. "You've been part of this community long enough to know this," she said mildly. "You don't need to impress anyone."

Least of all Lonny Ellison, Joy mused. "You're right," she agreed. Actually, she was relieved. Although she was willing to try, she wasn't convinced she could pull off a culinary masterpiece before Friday night. She was a little out of practice.

She shouldn't be thinking about Lonny at all. Josh would be here soon, and there'd be a chance to renew that relationship.

"You're bringing more than the pecan pie, though, aren't you?" Joy asked, determined not to think about either man.

Letty nodded. "Chase suggested I bake a Lemonade Cake, which is one of his favorites. I suspect he wants to bid on it himself." She smiled as she said it.

Joy envied Letty the warm, loving relationship she had with her husband. She couldn't imagine Chase saying or doing any of the things Lonny Ellison had said and done to her. More and more, she thought about their earlier relationship and how they'd walked away from each other after some ridiculous, forgettable argument. Maybe she was partly to blame. If she was honest, she'd have to admit there was no *maybe* about it. And, still being honest, she regretted the lost opportunity. But it was too late, especially with Josh showing up.

Letty and Chase shared a special love story, and now that they were married, it seemed as if they'd always been together. Chase had loved Letty from the time he was a teenager; in fact, he'd loved her enough to let her leave Wyoming without guilt so she could pursue her dream of becoming a singer. For almost ten years Letty had worked hard at creating a musical career, with moderate success, getting fairly steady gigs as a background singer and doing a few commercials that still paid residuals from time to time. When she returned to Wyoming, she came back with a daughter and a heart ailment that threatened to shorten her life. She'd been born with it but had never known there was a problem; it had been discovered during her pregnancy. She'd come home, possibly to die, or at least that was what she'd believed. But she'd had the required surgery and could live a normal life now.

"Other than cookies, what do you enjoy baking?" Letty asked.

Because she lived alone and generally cooked for one, Joy hadn't done much baking since her arrival in Red Springs. Before college, she used to spend hours in the kitchen, often with her mother. "My mom taught me a great apple pie recipe," Joy said after a moment.

"Then bake an apple pie."

Apple pie—it felt as if a weight had been lifted from her shoulders. "That's what I'll do," she said triumphantly.

"My brother's got a real sweet tooth," Letty murmured.

Joy shrugged, implying that was of little concern to her. She supposed this was Letty's way of reminding her that Lonny would be attending the auction. Joy wasn't sure how to react.

Her feelings on the subject of Lonny were decidedly mixed, and no one else had ever had such a confusing effect on her. Joy genuinely liked all the people who were close to him—Letty, of course, and Chase, who was Lonny's best friend. Not to mention Cricket, who talked nonstop about her wonderful uncle Lonny. He was obviously popular with the other ranchers and townsfolk, too. In other words, no one except her seemed to have a problem with him.

She was tempted to ask Letty about it. She hesitated, unsure how to introduce her question, but before she could say anything, Letty said it was time she left.

"Thanks for coming over," Joy said as she walked Letty and Cricket to the front door.

"Bake that pie," Letty advised yet again. "*After* you make those cookies."

"I will," Joy promised.

"See you Friday night. Do you want Chase and me to pick you up?"

Joy shook her head. "Honey Sue called and asked me to help with the setup, so I'll need to be there early."

Letty nodded, and Joy was grateful she had an excuse for declining the ride. If Lonny came into town for the auction, he'd sit with the couple, and if she joined them, too, the situation might be awkward for everyone.

Joy didn't want to think about Lonny anymore, but it was hard to avoid. She'd found his message in her screen door on Saturday, after the carnival committee meeting. At the time she'd been so angry and upset, she'd tossed it without even considering his suggestion. But perhaps he was right. Perhaps it would be a good idea to clear the air. Then again, to what end? They'd already learned that their personalities and beliefs were diametrically opposed, and that wasn't likely to change. Besides, Josh was coming. No, she'd better forget about Lonny—once she'd impressed him with her culinary aptitude.

The evening news was on when Joy finished baking a double batch of the peanut butter cookies. This was a tried and true recipe, tested a million times over the years, and there was no question that these were some of her best. They came out of the oven looking perfect. Her grandmother had used fork tines to create a crisscross pattern on each one, and Joy followed tradition. Once they'd cooled, she carefully arranged them in a couple of tin boxes left over from Christmas and stored them in the cupboard until Friday night.

Just as she was flipping through her family cookbook, searching for her grandmother's apple pie recipe, the phone rang. The interruption annoyed her. She'd been fantasizing about the bidding war over the cookies and the apple pie and was busy picturing Lonny's shocked face, an image she wanted to hold on to as long as she could.

"Hello," she answered on the third ring, hoping her frustration wasn't evident.

"Joy, it's Josh."

Caught up as she was in her dream world, it took her a second to remember who Josh was.

"Josh! Hi," she said quickly.

"Am I calling at a bad time?"

"No, no, of course not." It wasn't as if she could admit she'd been obsessively thinking about another man.

"Is someone there?" Josh asked after a brief hesitation.

"No, what makes you ask?"

"You sound preoccupied."

"I'm in the middle of baking."

"You bake?" He asked this as if it were a big joke.

She sighed. Not another one. "Yes, I know how to bake." Joy was unable to keep the irritation out of her voice. "I didn't mean that the way it came across," she added hastily. "There's a bake sale auction in town this Friday and—well, never mind, it isn't important."

Those remarks were followed by a short pause. "Joy," he said solemnly, "are you involved with anyone?"

"Involved, as in a relationship?" She made her voice as light and carefree as possible. "No, not at all. I already told you that. Why do you ask?"

"I got the impression you might be."

She laughed as if she found his statement humorous. Fortunately, this sounded more genuine than her previous denial. "No, Josh, I'm not involved, I promise you, but the fact that you asked has definitely brightened my day. Okay, there was someone early on, two years ago, but we only went out for a few months and then decided to drop the whole thing."

"Really?"

"Yes, it was nothing," she assured him. "Wait until you see Red Springs," she continued excitedly. "It's small-town America, just the way I always thought it would be. Everyone's so friendly and caring."

"It seems like a nice place," he said politely.

"It is. The folks around here are good salt-of-the-earth people."

"Actually…" He paused again. "I, uh, wondered if it might be a little boring—hardly any restaurants or clubs. I mean, what do you do for entertainment? Besides, I thought you were a city girl."

"I am…. I was. And for entertainment, we have bingo and the county fair and—"

"If you had the opportunity, you'd move back to the city, right?" He made it more statement than question.

"Oh, sure," she responded without much consideration. Almost as soon as the words were out of her mouth, she wondered if that was true. Joy loved Wyoming and everything she'd learned about life in a town like Red Springs. She'd made friends and felt she'd become part of the community.

"I phoned to let you know my travel plans have been confirmed," Josh said. He seemed to expect her to comment.

Joy tore her gaze away from the empty pie tin. "That's good news," she said, adding, "I look forward to seeing you," although that seemed oddly formal. Tucking the portable phone between her shoulder and ear, she walked over to the refrigerator and opened the bottom bin, where she found a bag of Granny Smith apples. She counted out six.

"Joy?"

If Josh had asked her something, she hadn't heard it. "I'm sorry, I missed what you said."

"Perhaps I should call another time. Or I'll email you."

"Fine," she said.

"Bye."

She set the apples on the counter. "Bye," she echoed, and realized Josh had hung up. He hadn't even waited until she'd said goodbye. Then again, maybe she'd kept *him* waiting a little too long.

Chapter 9

"Are you going into town?" Tom asked Lonny late Friday afternoon as they rode toward the barn.

"I guess so," Lonny said. He'd been in the saddle from dawn, they both had, and he wasn't in any mood to shower and drive all the way into Red Springs. He'd prefer something cold to drink and a long hot soak. Still, Letty would have his hide if he didn't show up for that auction. The entire town would be there. The bake sale auction had been hyped on the radio all week by Honey Sue Jameson, and Chase told him the original idea had been Letty's. Nope, he wouldn't dare disappoint her, or he'd have Chase mad at him, too. Not to mention that it was his one chance to make things right with Joy.

"If you do, could I tag along?" Tom asked.

This surprised Lonny, since Tom didn't often ask

for favors. Little by little, he'd revealed some of what his home life had been like. Lonny knew it was a sign of trust that the boy had confided in him at all. Based on what Tom had said, he was much better off not living with his father. Lonny wanted to help him in whatever way he could. Tom was smart and should be in college or trade school. The best person to talk to was a high school counselor—or maybe Joy. She related well to kids and knew a lot more than he did about scholarships and educational opportunities.

Tom had a real knack for horsemanship and an intuitive connection with animals. His patience and skill impressed Lonny; without much difficulty he could see Tom as a veterinarian. He'd mentioned it one evening and Tom had gotten flustered and quickly changed the subject. Later Tom had said it was best not to get his hopes up about anything like that. He had no chance of ever going to school, no matter how long he worked or how much money he saved. But Lonny felt there had to be a solution, and he was determined to find it.

"You can come along if you want," Lonny told him. He didn't ask for an explanation but suspected Tom's interest had to do with Michelle Larson. Which reminded him—he'd promised Charley Larson he'd speak to the boy about that dance.

"Thanks," Tom mumbled as he headed off to his room in the barn.

"Be ready in an hour," Lonny shouted after him.

Tom half turned, nodding.

Lonny finished tending to Moonshine, his gelding, and then hurried into the house for a long, hot shower. The mirror was fogged when he got out and began to shave. Normally he took care of that in the morning, but tonight he wanted his skin to be smooth in case—his thoughts came to a shuddering halt. In case he had the opportunity to kiss Joy again. It wasn't likely to happen, but he couldn't help hoping. He frowned. He'd rather tussle with a porcupine, he told himself, than cross her again.

Lonny snickered out loud. That wasn't true and it was time he fessed up. Not once had he stopped thinking about Joy. She was on his mind every minute of every day. It was her face, her eyes, that he saw when he drifted off to sleep at night, and her rose-scented perfume he thought about. When he woke in the morning, the first thing that popped into his mind was the memory of holding her and the kisses they'd shared. She was there all the times in between, too. Lonny didn't like it. Not thinking about her was a losing battle, so he figured he'd give in and try to win her over. As he'd told Letty, he'd blown it with Joy. Lonny Ellison wasn't a quitter, though. He hadn't gotten all those rodeo buckles by walking away from a challenge, and he wasn't about to start now. Not that he'd compare Joy Fuller to an ornery bull or an angry bronc. Well, not really. He chuckled at the thought.

By the time he'd shaved—fortunately without nicking himself—changed into a clean pair of Levi's and a stiff new shirt Letty had bought him last Christmas, Lonny figured he was well on his way to showing off his better side. No matter what Joy said or did, Lonny was determined not to lose his temper.

Tom was outside, leaning against the pickup, when Lonny stepped out of the house and bounded down the back steps. The boy had dressed in his best clothes, too. As soon as Lonny appeared, Tom hopped into the passenger seat.

"You goin' to the bake auction?" Lonny asked conversationally.

Tom had the window rolled down, his elbow resting on the narrow ledge. "I was thinking about it," he admitted.

"Me, too. I got a hankering for something sweet."

Tom didn't comment.

"Nothing like home-baked goods."

Tom offered him a half smile and nodded in agreement.

"Will Michelle Larson be there?" Lonny asked. That question got an immediate rise out of Tom. He jerked his elbow back inside the truck and straightened abruptly.

"Maybe," he answered, glaring at Lonny as if he resented the question. "What about Ms. Fuller?"

That caught Lonny unawares. Apparently Tom knew more about him than he'd assumed. "I suppose she might be," he grumbled in reply. His hired hand's message had been received, and Lonny didn't ask any further questions.

In fact, neither of them said another word until they reached town. Lonny suspected there'd be a good audience for the charity event, but he hadn't expected there'd be so much traffic around the community center that he'd have trouble getting a parking spot. As soon as they found a vacant space—ten minutes later—and parked, Tom climbed out of the truck. With a quick wave, he disappeared into the crowd.

Lonny didn't know how Tom intended to get home, but if his hired hand wasn't worried about it, then he wasn't, either.

When Lonny entered the community center, it was hard to tell there was a bingo game in progress. People roamed about the room, chatting and visiting, while Bill Franklin struggled to be heard over the chatter. A table, loaded with a delectable display of homemade goodies, was set up on stage.

Bill did his best to call out the bingo numbers but ended up having to shout into the microphone. This was possibly the biggest turnout for a bingo event in Red Springs history.

Goldie Frank stood up and shouted, "Bingo!" then proceeded to wave her card wildly.

Bill seemed downright relieved. There was scattered applause as Goldie came forward to accept her prize.

"That's the end of the first round of bingo for the evening," Bill said loudly, the sound system reverberating as he did. "There will now be a baked goods auction to raise funds for the carnival. Don Jameson from 1050 AM radio is our auctioneer."

That announcement was followed by another polite round of applause. Don Jameson stepped up to the front of the room and Bill handed him the microphone.

Lonny saw Letty and Chase and noticed there was an empty chair at their table. Weaving his way through the crowd, he took the opportunity to search for Joy, trying not to be too obvious. He half hoped she'd be sitting with his sister. She wasn't. When he did find her, she was with Carol Anderson. The two women sat near the back, and Joy seemed to be enjoying her-self, chatting animatedly with Carol and her husband.

Lonny nearly stumbled over his own feet. It'd been nearly a week since he'd seen Joy. For the life of him, he couldn't remember her being that pretty. He took a second look. Hot damn! His sister was easy on the eyes and so were other women in town; Joy, however, was striking. In fact, she was beautiful.

"Lonny?" Someone tugged at his sleeve.

Letty's voice broke into his thoughts, and he re-alized he'd stopped dead in the middle of the room, staring at Joy Fuller with his mouth practically hang-ing open.

"Chase and I saved you a seat."

Despite Letty's insistent tone, he couldn't drag his eyes from Joy. Unfortunately she happened to glance up just then. The room's noise seemed to fade as they stared at each other.

A few seconds later, Joy narrowed her eyes and de-liberately turned away. He blinked and finally dropped his gaze.

"Lonny," his sister said again, tugging at his arm. "Did you hear me?"

"I'm coming," he muttered. He didn't need to look back at Joy to know she was watching him. He could sense that she didn't want him there.

Her attitude didn't bode well for any conciliatory effort on his part. Still, he was up to the challenge, no matter how difficult she made it.

After exchanging greetings with Chase, Lonny took the chair next to Letty and focused his attention on the table of baked goods. As he studied the display, it occurred to him that he might not know what Joy had baked.

"Those peanut butter cookies look appetizing, don't they?" his sister whispered, leaning toward him.

"I suppose." Plenty of the other goodies did, as well.

"The apple pie, too."

There appeared to be several apple pies.

"The pie closest to the front is the one you should notice."

"Oh." It took Lonny longer than it should have to understand what his sister was trying to tell him. He brightened. "Peanut butter, you say."

Letty winked and he smiled back conspiratorially.

Generally speaking, a cookie was a cookie, as far as Lonny was concerned. Right then and there, however, he had the worst hankering for peanut butter. Of course, they could've been made with sawdust and Lonny wouldn't have cared.

The first item up for auction was Betty Sanders's butterhorn rolls. Chase made the first bid of twenty dollars for the entire batch. Another hand went up, and there were three or four other bids in quick succession. In the end Chase got the rolls but it cost him nearly fifty bucks.

He stood and withdrew his wallet, grumbling all the while that he preferred it when he could meet Betty in the parking lot and buy what he wanted before anyone else had a chance.

The next item up was a coconut cake baked by Mary and Michelle Larson. It didn't come as any surprise when Tom made the opening bid. Two or three others entered the bidding, but just when it seemed that Tom was about to walk away with the cake, someone else doubled the bid. Lonny whirled around and saw that it was Al Brighton's boy, Kenny, who'd stepped in at the last minute. Kenny got to his feet, glaring across the room at Tom, who stood at the back of the hall. Tom shrugged and bid again. The room watched as the two teenage boys squared off. When the bid reached a hundred dollars, Mary Larson hurried up to the stage and whispered in Don Jameson's ear.

"Mary has offered to bake a second coconut cake," Don announced, "so you can each have one. Is that agreeable?"

Kenny's body language said it wasn't. He looked at Tom, and Tom nodded.

"All right," Kenny conceded with bad grace.

Don's gavel hit the podium as he said into the microphone, "Two coconut cakes for one hundred dollars each."

The room erupted into chaotic noise.

"This is getting a little rich for my blood," Letty whispered to Lonny.

As luck would have it, Joy's peanut butter cookies came on the auction block next. Don hadn't even begun to describe them when Lonny's hand shot into the air. "Fifty dollars," he called out.

The room went quiet.

After the two previous bids, no one seemed interested in raising the amount and that suited him just fine. Lonny sighed with relief.

"Fifty-one," a female voice said.

Frowning, Lonny craned his neck to see who was

bidding against him. To his utter astonishment, it was Joy Fuller.

"Sixty," he shouted, annoyed that she'd do this.

"Sixty-one," was her immediate response.

Don glanced from one to the other. "Just a minute, Ms. Fuller, aren't you the one who donated these cookies?"

"I am," she told him. "Now I want them back."

What she wanted was to make sure Lonny didn't buy them. "What's she doing that for?" he asked his sister.

Letty looked as puzzled as he did. "I don't have a clue."

"Seventy dollars," Lonny offered. If she wanted to bid him up, then there was nothing he could do about it, except to keep going. The money would benefit the community. His sister seemed to think this would help in his efforts to settle his dispute with Joy, so her bidding against him made no sense.

"Seventy-one," she called back.

Letty frowned and covered Lonny's hand with her own. "Let Joy have them," she whispered.

"But…" Lonny hated to lose, and it bothered him to let her have those cookies. Surely Joy could see what he was trying to do here! Lonny didn't understand her actions; still, he figured he should trust Letty. He backed down so Joy could have the winning bid on her own peanut butter cookies.

He saw her come forward and collect the cookies. Then she immediately made her way to the exit.

"I'll be right back," he whispered to Letty as he quickly got up and followed.

It took him a few minutes to find her in the community center parking lot, which was dark and quiet. Lonny could hear the auction taking place inside, could hear Don's amplified voice and the din of laughter and bursts of applause. By the time he reached her, Joy had unlocked her car.

"Joy, wait," Lonny called. Then, thinking he should tread lightly, he amended his greeting. "Ms. Fuller." He felt as if he were back in grade school and didn't like it.

She tensed, standing outside her little green PT Cruiser. Her purse and the tin of cookies were inside, resting on the passenger seat.

"What do you want *now?*" she demanded, crossing her arms.

She was already mad at him, and he hadn't done a damned thing wrong. "Why'd you do that?" he asked, genuinely curious. "Why'd you bid against me?"

She didn't answer him; instead she asked a question of her own. "Why can't you just leave me alone?"

"I don't know," he said with a shrug. "I guess I've gotten used to having you around."

She cracked a smile. "I couldn't let you buy those cookies."

"Why not?" Lonny didn't get this at all. Frowning, he shoved his hands inside his jeans pockets. "Do you dislike me that much?"

Her eyes shot up to meet his and she slowly shook her head. "No." Her voice was barely audible. "I don't dislike you, Lonny. I never have. It's just that—"

"Is it because I called you skinny?"

She assured him that wasn't the reason. "And it isn't because of the accident," she said. "Either one."

"Do you mind giving me a clue, then?"

For a moment he thought she was going to ignore his question. "I forgot the salt," she finally told him.

"Excuse me?"

"The salt," she said, more loudly this time. "Just before the auction today, I took out a cookie to sample. I hadn't tasted one earlier and when I did, I realized what I'd done. It was too late to withdraw them or to bake a new batch." She sighed despondently. "I was working so hard to impress you and then to do something stupid like that…"

She wanted to impress him? This was exactly the kind of news he'd been hoping to hear. He propped one foot against her car bumper. "Really?"

Her gaze narrowed. "Get that smug look off your face," she snapped.

Now he knew why she'd given him the evil eye earlier. That had been a warning not to bid on her cookies, only he hadn't been smart enough to figure it out. Actually he was glad he'd bid; at least he'd shown her how interested he was.

Her eyes glistened as if she were about to cry. Lonny had dealt with his share of difficult situations over the years. He'd delivered calves in the middle of a lightning storm, dealt with rattlesnakes, faced drunken cowboys—but he couldn't handle a weeping woman.

"I would've eaten every one of those cookies and not said a word," he told Joy. Then, wanting to comfort her, he gently drew her into his arms.

Joy stared wordlessly up at him. She started to say something, then stopped. Frankly he'd rather she didn't speak because he could tell from the look in her eyes that she wanted the same thing he did. He brought his mouth to hers.

He heard her moan or maybe that was him. This—holding her in his arms, kissing her—was what he'd been thinking about all week, what he'd been dreaming about, too.

Her mouth was soft and pliable and responsive. She raised her arms and circled his neck, and that was all the encouragement Lonny needed. Immediately he deepened the kiss, locking his arms around her waist.

She moaned again, quietly at first, and then a bit louder. Lonny pulled her tight against him so she'd know exactly what she was doing to him and how much he wanted her.

Suddenly, without the slightest hint, she broke off the kiss and took two paces back. At first Lonny was too stunned to react. He stared at her, hardly knowing what to think.

She was frowning. "That shouldn't have happened," she muttered.

"Why not?" He found her reaction incomprehensible because his was entirely the opposite. As far as he was concerned, this was the best thing that had happened to him in two years.

"We—we don't get along."

"It seems to me we're getting along just great. Okay, so we had a rocky start, an argument or two, but we're over that. I'm willing to give it another shot if you are."

"I…I—"

She seemed to be having a problem making up her mind. That got him thinking she could use a little help, so he kissed her again.

When the kiss ended, he gave her a questioning look; wide-eyed, she blinked up at him.

Just to be on the safe side, he brought her into his embrace a third time. Once he'd finished, she was trembling in his arms.

"Let me know when you decide," he whispered, then turned and walked away.

Pleased with himself, Lonny strolled toward his pickup. As he neared the Ford, he saw his ranch hand leaning against the fender, head lowered.

"You ready to go?" Lonny asked.

Tom nodded, climbing into the truck. Only when the interior light went on did Lonny notice that he had a bloody nose. A bruise had formed on his cheek, too.

"You been fighting?" he asked, shocked by the boy's appearance.

Tom didn't answer.

"What happened?"

Tom remained silent.

"You don't want to talk about it?"

Tom shrugged.

"I'm guessing this involves a woman," Lonny said, starting the engine. His guess went further than that—Michelle Larson and Kenny Brighton were part of the story. Was Michelle having trouble choosing between Tom and Kenny? It struck him as highly possible. Because he knew from the events of this evening that women seldom seemed to know what they wanted.

Chapter 10

Joy couldn't believe she'd let Lonny Ellison kiss her again—and again. She didn't understand why she hadn't stopped him. It was as if her brain had gone to sleep or something and her body had taken over. As she lay in bed on Saturday morning after a restless night's sleep, she was aghast at her own behavior. Groaning, with the blankets pulled all the way up to her chin, she relived the scene outside the community center.

She could only imagine what Lonny must be thinking. She hadn't even been able to answer a simple question! He'd as much as said he was willing to start their relationship over and asked if she wanted that, too. She should've said she didn't want anything to do with him, although her heart—and her hormones— were telling her *yes*.

As soon as they were kissing—okay, be honest, *heatedly* kissing—she'd panicked. First, she and Lonny Ellison had nothing in common, and second…well, second— She put a halt to her reasoning because the truth was, she had no logical explanation for her response to his kisses. It wasn't like this two years ago. Okay, their kisses back then had been pleasant but not extraordinary. Not at all.

Maybe she'd gone without tenderness or physical affection for too long. That, however, wasn't true. She'd received no shortage of invitations and had dated various men in the past year. There'd been Earl Gross and Larry Caven and George Lewis. And Glen Brewster. She'd dated all four of them for short periods of time. She'd kissed each of them, too. Unfortunately, there hadn't been any spark and they'd seemed to recognize it just as Joy had. She remained friendly with all of them, and they with her. Of course, two years ago, there hadn't been what she'd call sparks with Lonny Ellison, either. Unless that referred to their arguments….

Now Lonny was back in her life and this couldn't have come at a worse time. Not only would Josh be visiting, he seemed interested in resuming their relationship. Once he was in town and they'd had a chance to talk, she'd know if there was a chance for them. Until then, she'd have to deal with her ambivalent feelings for Lonny.

Tossing aside her covers, she prepared a pot of coffee and while she waited, she logged on to her computer. She checked her email, scrolling down the entries, and paused when she came to a message from

Josh. Another entry caught her attention, too, one from Letty. She read Letty's first.

From: Letty Brown
Sent: Saturday, May 27, 6:45 a.m.
To: Joy Fuller
Subject: Where Did You Go?

Joy:
I looked for you last night after the auction and couldn't find you. My brother disappeared about the same time you did.

Joy groaned and wondered if anyone else had noticed that they'd both left just after the bidding on her peanut butter cookies.

In case you're wondering, the auction was a big hit. Your apple pie sold for $30.00 to Clem Russell, but the highest price paid for any one item was Myrtle Jameson's chocolate cake, which went for a whopping $175.00. (Unless you count the Larsons' coconut cake, which sold twice, to Tom and Kenny Brighton.) All in all, we raised more than a thousand dollars, which makes this the most successful fund-raising event ever. I wish you'd been there to the end.

Is everything all right? My brother didn't cause any problems, did he? Oh, did you hear about the fight? Tom, Lonny's ranch hand, got beaten up—three against one. Apparently Kenny and a couple of other boys were involved. I think it might've had something to do with Michelle Larson. Did you see or hear anything? That happened around the time you left. Bill Franklin broke it up and told Chase about it later.

I'll be in town later this morning. If I have time, I'll drop by. Chase and Lonny will be gone most of the day, since they're moving the cattle, trying to get the herd to the best pastureland.

Hope to catch up with you later.

Letty

Joy quickly answered her friend and told Letty she'd be in and out of the house all day, so if she did stop by Joy couldn't guarantee she'd be home. In her response, Joy ignored the subject of the auction and why she'd left.

Joy said she didn't know about the teenagers fighting; she didn't add that she'd heard something as she hurried to the parking lot. That was just before Lonny caught up with her. Needless to say, she didn't mention that, either. The less said about Friday night, the better.

As she hit the Send key, Joy realized she was avoiding her friend because of Lonny. That was a mistake. Letty had become her best friend in Red Springs, and Joy was determined not to let Letty's brother come between them.

At least Letty's email assured her that Lonny would be on the range all day. Knowing there was no possibility of running into him, she was free to do her errands without worrying about seeing him every time she turned a corner.

Her first order of business was stocking up on gro-

ceries. Last week, in her effort to escape Lonny, she'd
purchased the bare essentials and fled. Now she was
out of milk, bread, peanut butter and almost everything else.

After downing a cup of coffee, Joy dressed in jeans
and a light blue cotton shirt. At a little after nine, she
headed out the door, more carefree than she'd felt in
weeks. As usual, she saw a number of her students
and former students on Main Street and in the grocery store. She enjoyed these brief interactions, which
reminded her how different her life was compared to
what it would've been if she'd stayed in Seattle.

Not until she'd loaded her groceries did she remember that she hadn't even read or responded to Josh's
email. It was only natural to blame that on Lonny, too.
Preoccupied with him as she was, she'd forgotten all
about Josh.

One thing was certain—this kissing had to stop.
Both times they'd been standing in a parking lot, exposed to the entire community.

Oh, no!

The potential for embarrassment overwhelmed her
as she slammed the trunk lid of her PT Cruiser. There'd
been a fight near the community center—which meant
people had been outside, maybe more than a few. So it
was possible that…oh, dear…that someone had seen
her and Lonny wrapped in each other's arms. At the
time it had seemed so…so private. There they were, the
two of them, in this…this passionate embrace, practically devouring each other. Her face burned with
mortification.

No—she was overreacting. People kissed in public

all the time. Red Springs was a conservative town, but she hadn't done anything worthy of censure. The only logical course of action was to put the matter out of her mind. If, by chance, she and Lonny had been seen, no one was likely to ask her about it.

"Hello, Ms. Fuller." Little Cassie Morton greeted her as she skipped past Joy.

Cassie had been her student the year before and Alicia, her mother, was a classroom volunteer. Joy liked Alicia and appreciated the many hours she'd helped in class.

"Hi," Joy said cheerfully. "I see you two are out and about early on this lovely Saturday morning."

"We're going grocery shopping," Cassie explained, hopping from one foot to the other. The nine-year-old never stood still if she could run, jump or skip.

Smiling, Alicia strolled toward Joy. "Looks like you and Lonny Ellison are an item these days," the other woman said casually as she reached inside her purse and withdrew a sheaf of store coupons.

"Who told you that?" Joy asked, hoping to sound indifferent and perhaps slightly amused.

Alicia glanced up. "You mean you aren't?"

"I…I used to date Lonny. We went out a couple of years ago, but that's it." Joy nearly stuttered in her rush to broadcast her denial.

"Really?" Alicia's face took on a confused expression. "Sorry. I guess I misunderstood."

Joy hurried after her. "Who said we were seeing each other, if you don't mind my asking?"

"No one," Alicia told her. "I saw Lonny watching

you at the auction last night and he had the *look,* if you know what I mean. It was rather sweet."

"Lonny?" Joy repeated with forced joviality. "I'm sure he was staring at someone else."

Alicia shrugged. "Maybe. You could do worse, you know. Folks around here are fond of Lonny. People still talk about his rodeo days. The Wyoming Kid was one of the best bull-riders around before he retired. I think he was smart to get out while he could still walk." She flashed a quick grin. "Actually, he was at the top of his form. That takes courage, you know, to give up that kind of money and fame. His dad wasn't doing well, so he was needed at home. Lonny came back, and he hasn't left since. I admire him for that."

"I do, too," Joy said, and it was true. She'd heard plenty about Lonny's successes, riding broncs as well as bulls. In fact, when they first dated, he'd proudly shown her his belt buckles. He wasn't shy about letting her know exactly how good he'd been. And yet, he'd abandoned it all in order to help his family. Walked away from the fame and the glory without question when his parents needed him. But he'd never mentioned *that* to her, not once.

"Lonny's a real sweetheart," Alicia said warmly.

Joy nodded, unable to come up with an appropriate response, and returned to her car. Her next stop was the cleaners, where she picked up her pink pantsuit, the one she planned to wear the day Josh arrived. From there, she went to Walmart for household odds and ends. By the time she'd finished, it was after twelve, and Joy was famished.

Eating a container of yogurt in front of her computer, she logged back on to the internet and answered Josh. He'd be in Red Springs in six days. There was a lot riding on this visit—certainly for her, and maybe for him, too.

The rest of her day was uneventful. In between weekly tasks like mopping the kitchen floor and dealing with accumulated clutter, she did three loads of wash, mowed her lawn and washed her car. By dinnertime, she was pleasantly tired. She wouldn't have any problem sleeping tonight; she'd made sure of it.

The phone rang only once, late in the afternoon. It was Patsy Miller, president of the PTA. Patsy asked Joy if she'd be willing to serve as a chaperone for the high school's end-of-the-year dance.

"I'll have company," she explained reluctantly, hating to turn Patsy down. Patsy had provided consistent support to every teacher in town, and Joy wanted to repay that.

"Bring your guest," Patsy suggested.

"You wouldn't mind?"

"Not at all."

"That would be great. I'll ask him and let you know." As soon as Joy hung up, she went back online and told Josh about the dance. It would be the perfect end to a perfect day, or so she hoped. Joy couldn't think of any better way to show him the town she'd grown to love than to have him accompany her to the carnival and then the dance.

Climbing into bed, Joy went instantly to sleep—the contented sleep of a hardworking woman.

The next morning, she discovered that Josh had answered her two emails. Both the carnival and the dance sounded like fun to him, he said. He emphasized how eager he was to see her again—a mutual feeling, she thought with a smile.

When Joy arrived at church on Sunday morning, her spirits were high. Sitting in the front pew for easy access to the organ, Joy couldn't see who was and wasn't in attendance. Normally she wouldn't care. But her weekend so far had been relatively stress-free, and she wanted to keep it that way. If Lonny Ellison was at church, she needed to know for her own self-protection.

When the opening hymns were over, Joy slid off the organ bench and took the opportunity to scan the congregation. Letty and Chase sat in a middle pew; Cricket would be at the children's service in the church basement.

Without being obvious—at least she hoped not—Joy took one more look around the congregation. As far as she could tell, there was no Lonny. It seemed to her that he usually attended, so perhaps he'd decided to stay away for a week to give them both some much-needed breathing space. Her sense of well-being increased.

At the end of the announcements and just before the sermon, the choir, all dressed in their white robes, gathered at the front of the church. Joy returned to the organ bench and poised her hands over the keyboard, her eyes focused on Penny Johnson, the choir director. With a nod of her head, Penny indicated that Joy should begin.

Just as she lowered her hands, she glanced over her shoulder at the church doors. At that very instant, they opened and in stepped Lonny Ellison. He stood at the back, staring directly at her. Naturally there weren't any seats available except in front; everyone knew you had to come early if you wanted to sit in the back. After a slight hesitation, Lonny started up the left-hand side—the side where Joy sat. She watched him and nearly faltered. It took all her control to play the first chord.

He'd *planned* this, darn him. Joy didn't know how he'd managed it, but he'd timed his entrance to coincide with the music. He'd done it to unnerve her and he'd succeeded. This exact thing had happened last year, too; thanks to him she'd faltered and missed a couple of notes. Anger spread through her like flames in dry grass.

When she turned the sheet music, she inadvertently turned two pages instead of one. Her mistake was immediately obvious. He'd done it again! Penny threw her a shocked look and to her credit, Joy recovered quickly. She hoped Penny was the only person who'd noticed. Still, Joy cringed in embarrassment and her heart pounded loudly. Thud. Thud. Thud. It seemed, to her ears, like a percussive counterpoint to the chords she was playing.

The rest of the service remained a blur in Joy's mind. She didn't hear a word of Pastor Downey's sermon. Not a single word.

Thankfully, the closing song was "What a Friend We Have in Jesus," which she could've played in her sleep. As the congregation filed out, Joy finished the last refrain. She took several minutes to turn off the organ and cover the keyboard, then collect her sheet music and Bible. Normally she finished two or three minutes after the church emptied; however, this Sunday, she was at least six minutes longer than usual.

By now, she hoped, Lonny Ellison would be gone. He wasn't.

Instead, he stood on the lawn by the church steps— waiting for her. He was chatting with a couple of other ranchers, but Joy wasn't fooled. He'd purposely hung around to talk to her.

When she walked down the steps, he broke away from his group.

Joy froze, one foot behind her on the final step, the other on the sidewalk. With a fierce look, she dared him to utter even a word. It was a glare she'd perfected in the classroom, and it obviously worked as well on adult men as it did on recalcitrant little boys. Lonny stopped dead in his tracks.

Then, as if she hadn't a care in the world, Joy casually greeted her friends and left.

Chapter 11

Sunday morning before he drove to church, Lonny had come into the barn to ask Tom if he wanted to attend services with him. Tom had gone a couple of Sundays, mainly because he'd hoped to see Michelle. The bruise on his cheek had turned an ugly purple and was even more noticeable now. Still, it looked worse than it felt. Kenny had sucker punched him with the aid of two of his friends, who'd distracted Tom.

Tom had declined Lonny's invitation. He didn't want Michelle to see the bruise, didn't want her to think Kenny was tougher than he was.

Tom hated fights, but he wouldn't back down from one, either. Kenny had started it, and while Tom might be small and wiry, he knew how to defend himself. He guessed Kenny Brighton had gotten the shock of his life when Tom's first punch connected. In fact, he would've smiled at the thought—except that it hurt to smile. If Bill Franklin hadn't broken up the fight, Tom would've won, despite the assistance provided by Kenny's friends. His drunk of an old man had taught him a thing or two in that department; by the time he was fifteen, Tom had learned to hold his own. Even three to one, he figured he'd stand a chance.

Lonny drove off, and Tom busied himself sweeping the barn floor. Ten mintues later, he heard another car coming down the drive and glanced out. When he saw who it was, he sucked in his breath.

Michelle.

He hesitated, then reluctantly stepped into the yard. He stood there stiffly, hands tucked in his back pockets.

She parked the car and when she got out, he realized that she'd brought him the coconut cake, protected by a plastic dome like the kind they had in diners. Catching sight of him, she frowned. Her pretty blue eyes went soft with concern as she looked at the bruise on his cheek. "Oh, Tom," she said, walking toward him.

She reached out to stroke his cheek, but he averted his face, jerking his chin away before she could touch him. At his rejection, pain flashed in her eyes. "I—I brought the cake you bought at the bake sale."

"Thanks." He took it carefully from her hands.

He figured she'd leave then, but she didn't.

"I'll put it in the house," he mumbled.

"Okay."

Tom hurried into the kitchen, depositing the cake on the table. She and her mother had done a good job

with it, making it almost double the size of the one
Kenny had claimed Friday night. That pleased Tom.

"What are you still doing here?" he asked gruffly
when he returned to the yard. He didn't want her to
know how happy he was to see her—despite his injury and his disfigured face.

"I came to find out if Kenny hurt you."

She should worry about the other guy, not him, he
thought defiantly. "He didn't."

Her eyes refused to leave his face and after a moment, she nearly dissolved into tears. "I'm so sorry,
Tom."

"For what? You weren't to blame."

"Yes, I was," she cried, and her voice quavered. "It
was all my fault."

Tom shook his head, angry that she'd assume responsibility. Kenny Brighton was the jerk, not Michelle.

"Kenny asked me to the dance and I told him no.
He wanted to know why I wouldn't go with him and
I...I said I...I was going with you."

Tom felt his throat close up. "I already told you I
can't take you to the dance." He didn't mean to sound
angry, but he couldn't help it.

"I know, and I'm truly sorry, but I had to tell Kenny
something, otherwise he'd pester me. He wouldn't leave
me alone until I gave in and I...I know I shouldn't have
lied. But because I did, he had it in for you and when
you bid on the cake, he was mad and started that fight."

She was crying openly now. The tears ran down her
face and Tom watched helplessly. He'd only seen one
other woman cry—his mother—and he hadn't been

able to stand it. He'd always tried to protect her, to comfort her. So Tom did what came naturally, and that was to hold Michelle.

They'd never touched. All their relationship amounted to was a few conversations at the feed store. He'd liked other girls back home, but he'd never had strong feelings for any of them the way he did Michelle.

When she slipped so easily into his arms, it was all Tom could do to hold in a sigh. She brought her arms about his waist and pressed her face against his shirt. Tom shyly put his own arms around her and rested his jaw against her hair. She smelled fresh and sweet and he'd never felt this good.

Michelle sniffled, then dropped her arms. He did the same. "I should go," she whispered.

Tom didn't say anything to stop her, but he didn't want her to leave.

She started walking toward her car. "I didn't tell my parents where I was going and..." She kept her head lowered and after a short pause blurted out, "Why won't you go to the dance with me?"

Dread sat heavily on his chest. "I...can't."

"You don't like me?"

He laughed, not because what she asked had amused him, but because it was so ludicrous, so far removed from the truth. "Oh, I like you."

She gazed up at him and he swore her eyes were the pure blue of an ocean he'd never seen, and deep enough to dive straight into. "I like you, too," she told him in a whisper. "I like you a *lot*. I wait for you every week, just hoping you'll stop by with Lonny. Dad thinks

I'm working all these extra hours because I'm saving money for college. That's not the real reason, though. I'm there on the off-chance you'll come into town."

Although he was secretly thrilled, Tom couldn't allow her to care for him. He had nothing to offer her. He had no future, and his past…his past was something he hoped to keep buried for the rest of his life. "I'm nothing, Michelle, you hear me? Nothing."

"Don't say that," she countered with a firmness that surprised him. "Don't *ever* say that, because it's not true. I've seen you with people and with animals, too. You're respectful and caring and kind. You don't want anyone to see it, but you are. You're not afraid of work, either. Kenny comes to the store with his dad, but he lets other people load up the truck. You're the first one there, willing to help. I've noticed many things about you, Tom. *Many* things," she emphasized. "You're as honorable as my father."

That appeared to be the highest compliment she could pay him. Tom didn't say it, but he'd noticed many things about Michelle Larson, too. What he liked most was the way she believed in him. No one ever had, except his mother. By the time she died, though, she'd been beaten down and miserable. Tom had been determined to get away from the man who'd done that to her—his father—the man who'd tried to destroy him, too. There was no turning back now.

The pressure on his chest increased. "I'll see what I can do about that dance," he said. He couldn't make her any promises. More than anything, he wanted to go there with Michelle. More than anything he wanted an excuse to hold her again, and smell her hair and maybe even kiss her.

"Thank you," she whispered.

Then before he could stop her, she pressed the palm of her hand against his cheek. His jaw still ached a bit. Not much; just enough to remind him that Kenny Brighton was a dirty fighter and not to be trusted. Taking her wrist, Tom brought her hand to his lips and kissed it.

Michelle smiled and it seemed—it really did—as if the sun had come out from behind a dark cloud and drenched him in warmth and light. But when she left soon afterward, the sensation of buoyant happiness quickly died. He should never have told her he'd think about the dance.

An hour later, Lonny returned from church and without a word to Tom marched directly into the house. Tom didn't know what was wrong and Lonny hadn't confided in him. Lonny was fair and a good boss, but he hadn't been in a particularly good mood for the last week or so. Not that it made him rude or unpleasant. Just kind of remote.

At twelve-thirty, Tom went inside. They took turns preparing meals, and this one was his. Tom found Lonny sitting at the kitchen table, his head in his hands, almost as if he was praying.

"You feel okay?" Tom asked, wondering what he could do to help.

Lonny shrugged. "I guess."

Tom opened the refrigerator and took out a slab of cheese. Grilled cheese sandwiches were easy enough.

That and a can of soup would take care of their appetites.

"How many sandwiches you want?" he asked.

"Just one."

Tom nodded and took bread out of the plastic container on the kitchen counter. "I heard there's going to be a dance in town," he said, hoping he sounded casual and only vaguely interested.

"You thinking of going?" Lonny asked, showing the first hint of curiosity.

Tom shrugged, imitating Lonny. "I was thinking about it. Only…" He didn't finish.

"Only what?"

Tom lifted his shoulders again. "All I brought with me is work clothes." That was all he had, period, but he didn't mention that part.

Lonny stood up from the table and looked Tom up and down. "How much you weigh?"

Tom told him, as well as he could remember.

"That's about right. I've got an old suit you're welcome to have if it fits you."

Tom's heart shot straight into his throat. No one had ever given him anything without expecting something in return. "I'll pay you for it—I insist. How much you want for that suit? If it fits," he qualified.

"Fine, pay if you want," Lonny agreed. "I'll take a big fat slice of that as payment," he said, gesturing toward the coconut cake.

Tom grinned, satisfied with his response. "You got it."

"Fair trade. If you need a ride into town Friday night, let me know."

Tom laid the bread, butter side down, in the heated pan. "I'd appreciate it."

"You taking Michelle Larson to that dance?" Lonny asked next.

With his back to the other man, moving the sandwiches around with a spatula, Tom smiled. "Like I said, I was thinking about it."

"You do that. She's a good girl."

"I know." He frowned then, because having something decent to wear was just the first hurdle. It didn't come easy, letting anyone know how inadequate he was when it came to a situation like this. He glanced over his shoulder and saw that Lonny was watching him. "I've never been to a dance before," he muttered.

"You'll enjoy yourself," Lonny said, reaching for a knife and a couple of plates to serve slices of the cake.

"I said, I've never been to a dance before," Tom repeated, louder this time. He turned around to properly face his employer.

Lonny frowned and looked mildly guilty about slicing into Tom's coconut cake. "There's nothing to worry about. They might have a real band, or there could be someone playing CDs—I'm not sure how it'll work this year. The school will arrange to have a few adults there as chaperones."

It was plain that Tom would need to spell it out for him. "I don't know how to dance," he murmured, breaking eye contact. "What am I supposed to do when the music starts?"

"Ah." Lonny nodded sagely. "I see your problem."

"Do *you* know how to dance?" He wouldn't come right out and ask, but if Lonny volunteered to teach him, Tom would be willing to take lessons, as long as they didn't interfere with work.

"Me, dance?" Lonny asked in a jovial tone. "Not really. Mostly I fake it."

"Anyone can do that?" Tom wasn't sure he believed this.

"I do. I just sort of shuffle my feet and move my arms around a lot and no one's ever said anything. You like music, don't you?"

Tom did. He listened to the country-western station on the radio. "What kind of music do they play at school dances?"

The question appeared to be difficult because it took Lonny a long time to answer. "Regular music," he finally said.

Tom didn't know what regular music was. He frowned.

"I've got some old movies in the living room somewhere that you might want to watch. They might help you."

"What kind of movies?"

Lonny thought about that for a few minutes. "There's a couple with John Travolta and one with Kevin Bacon. Hey, that movie might interest you because it's got a farm boy in it who doesn't know how to dance, either. Kevin knows a few moves and takes him under his wing. It's a good movie, great music. Why don't you watch it?"

"Okay." Tom would do just about anything to keep from making a fool of himself in front of Michelle. He needed to learn quickly, too; the dance was only five days away.

The phone rang then, and Lonny went into the other room to answer it. While he was on the phone, Tom finished preparing the cheese sandwiches. He heated a can of tomato soup and had it dished up and on the table by the time Lonny returned.

When Lonny came back into the kitchen, he was frowning.

"Problems?" Tom asked, instantly alert.

Lonny shook his head. "I'm going to volunteer as a chaperone at that dance."

Tom's suspicions were instantly raised. "Any particular reason?"

Lonny bit into his grilled cheese sandwich and nodded. "Sounds like Kenny Brighton might be looking for trouble, especially if you turn up with Michelle."

Tom bristled. "I can take care of myself."

"I don't doubt it, but Kenny will think twice about starting something if I'm there."

Tom didn't like the idea of Lonny having to hang around the school dance because of him.

Lonny seemed to sense his reaction. "What about Michelle?" he added. "How's *she* going to feel if Kenny beats up on you again?"

Tom saw the wisdom of what Lonny was saying. "You'd do that for me?" he asked.

"I offered, didn't I?"

Tom's chest tightened, and he stared down at his plate while he struggled with the emotion that hit him out of nowhere. This rancher, whom he'd known for only a few months, was more of a parent to him than his own father had ever been.

"Let me see about that suit," Lonny said when he'd

eaten his lunch. He set his dirty dishes in the sink and went upstairs; within minutes he'd returned, holding out a perfectly good brown suit.

"What do you think?" Lonny asked.

The suit was far better than Tom had expected. It didn't look as if it'd ever been worn. "What I think is I should give you that entire coconut cake."

Lonny laughed. "Go try this on, and if there's any of that cake left when you get back, consider yourself fortunate."

Tom already knew he was fortunate. He didn't need a slice of coconut cake to tell him that.

Chapter 12

Letty and Chase often invited Lonny, and now Tom, to join them for dinner on Sunday evenings. Tom had accepted twice, but this week he declined. Before Lonny left, Tom asked if it would be all right if he watched a few of those movies Lonny had mentioned earlier.

Lonny had no objection to that. He smiled as he pulled out of the yard in his pickup and headed for Chase and Letty's. He was glad to be able to help the boy, hoping it worked out, with the dance and Michelle and all.

Lonny drove the short distance to Chase's ranch, still feeling confused about Joy. He counted on Letty to have some insights on what he should do about his feelings for her. He knew he could be stubborn, but until recently he hadn't recognized how much his attitude had cost him. For nearly two years, he'd allowed his relationship with Joy to lie fallow. During that time he'd watched her develop friendships in the community, and he knew that everything he'd accused her of was wrong. She was no city slicker; from the first, she'd done her best to become part of the community. Lonny hadn't wanted to accept that because she'd wounded his pride. He'd wanted her to fail just to prove how right he was. It bothered him to admit that, but it was the truth. He swallowed hard and his hands tightened around the steering wheel. Because of his stubbornness, he'd done a great disservice to Joy—and to himself.

Plain and simple, Lonny was attracted to Joy—more than attracted. Their kisses over the past few days confirmed what he already knew. Another uncomfortable truth: not once in the last two years had Joy been far from his thoughts. Following their most recent traffic *incident*—as she'd correctly described it—the potency of that attraction had all but exploded in his face.

Lonny could acknowledge it now. For two years he'd been in love with Joy. The near-collision had simply brought everything to the surface, and it explained his overreaction to the events of that afternoon. He grinned, thinking about the way he'd stormed at her as if she'd nearly caused a fatal accident. No wonder she was wary of him.

Deep in thought, Lonny missed the turnoff to Spring Valley Ranch. He must've driven here ten thousand times and not once overshot the entrance. The fact that he had today said a lot about his preoccupation with Joy.

As Lonny drove into the yard, he noticed that Chase was giving Cricket a riding lesson on Jennybird. The little girl rode her pony around the corral while Chase held the lead rope. Chase gave him a quick wave and continued his slow circuit. Meanwhile, Letty sat in a rocking chair on the porch, watching.

Lonny crossed the yard and joined his sister, claiming the chair next to hers.

Letty raised her glass of lemonade in greeting. "Tom won't be coming?" she asked.

Lonny shook his head. "Not tonight."

Letty stood and went inside the house, reappearing a minute later with a second glass of lemonade, which she handed him.

"Thanks." Lonny took a long, thirst-quenching drink, then set down the glass with a disconsolate sigh.

Letty turned to him. "What's wrong?"

His state of mind obviously showed more than Lonny had realized. Rather than blurt out what was troubling him, he shrugged. "I've been doing some thinking about Joy and me."

His sister sat down again and started rocking. "I've been telling you for a whole year that you're an idiot." Her smile cut the sharpness of her words.

"I can't disagree," he muttered. Even after being in the rodeo world and dating dozens of women, he was as naive as a twelve-year-old kid about romancing a woman like Joy.

"Listen," he said, deciding to speak openly with his sister. "Would you be willing to advise me? Maybe you could even help me—speak to Joy on my behalf." He wouldn't normally ask that of Letty, and requesting this kind of favor didn't come easy.

Letty hesitated; she rocked back and forth, just the way their mother used to. When she spoke he heard her regret. "Lonny, as much as I'd like to, I can't do that."

He nodded. Actually, that was what he'd expected, but it didn't hurt to ask.

"I'll be happy to offer my opinion, though."

He made a noncommittal sound. Letty had never been shy about sharing her opinions, especially when they concerned him.

"There's something you should probably know. Something important I learned just today."

He tensed. "About Joy?"

Letty sipped her lemonade. "Josh Howell contacted her."

"The college boyfriend?" Lonny's jaw tightened. Right now, this was the worst piece of news he could hear. When they'd first started dating, Joy had casually mentioned Josh a few times; Lonny had read between the lines and understood that this relationship had played an important role in her past.

She'd stayed in touch with Josh and although their romance had cooled, Joy still had feelings for the other man. It was early in their own relationship, and Lonny hadn't wanted Joy to think he was the jealous type, so he'd said nothing. But the fact was, he *had* been jealous and he hadn't liked knowing that Joy and this city boy were continuing some kind of involvement, even a diminished one from a distance.

"Well?" Letty pressed. "Doesn't it concern you?"

Lonny made an effort to disguise his views on the matter. "What does Josh want?"

"All I heard is he's coming to visit."

"Here? In Red Springs?"

"That's what she said. My guess is that he wants to revive their relationship."

"She told you that?" His jaw went even tighter.

"Not in so many words, but think about it. Why else would Josh come here? It isn't like he has some burning desire to visit a ranching community. He's coming because of Joy." She paused, tilting her head toward Lonny. "I find his timing rather suspicious, don't you?"

"How?" Lonny asked bluntly.

"Joy's teaching contract is up for renewal."

"So, you think he's hoping to lure her back to Seattle?" His voice fell as he took in the significance of the timing. Right then and there, Lonny decided he wasn't letting her go without a fight. Not physical, of course— that would be stupid and unfair; Josh wouldn't stand a chance against him, if he did say so himself. And knowing Joy, she'd be furious with Lonny and immediately side with the city guy. A physical showdown would be the worst possible move. No, this challenge was mental. Emotional. And it had more to do with convincing Joy than scaring off Josh.

"When will he be here?" he asked urgently.

Letty must've seen that determined look in his eyes, because she reached over and patted his hand reassuringly. "I'm not sure, but I believe it's sometime this week."

He nodded.

"What are you thinking?" she asked.

That should be obvious. "I've only got a few days to talk Joy into staying here." Although he knew darn well that more than talk would be involved...

Letty frowned at him. "Why do you care if she leaves or not?"

Lonny didn't appreciate the question. Nevertheless, he gave her an honest answer. He could pretend he hadn't heard—or he could tell Letty the words that burned to be spoken. "Because I love her."

"I know," Letty replied, leaning back with a satisfied grin. "You have for a long time."

Lonny expected more of an I-told-you-so and was mildly surprised when Letty didn't lay into him for his foolishness or recite a litany of rules on how to persuade Joy to make her life in Red Springs, with him.

"So what are you going to do about it?" Letty asked next.

The answer to that wasn't clear. "I don't know."

Letty frowned again, a worried frown. "Promise me you won't say anything stupid."

"Like what?" he demanded.

She rolled her eyes. "Like you're going to charge her insurance company for the so-called damage to your truck."

"I never really intended to do that. It was a ploy, that's all."

"A ploy to infuriate and anger Joy. Because of it— and because of other stupid things you've said—you have a lot of ground to recover."

Lonny didn't need his sister telling him what he already knew. "I'll talk to her." But that didn't seem to be working, either. He'd left her a note, and she'd thrown it away. Joy wasn't interested in talking to him, yet every time they were together, they ended up in each other's arms. The fact was, those few kisses gave him hope and encouragement. They told him that while Joy might deny it, she *did* have feelings for him, feelings as intense as his were for her. Feelings she wasn't ready to acknowledge.

His sister turned to stare at him as if he were a stranger. "Can I make a suggestion?" she asked.

"Sure." He'd been counting on it.

"A woman likes to know she's wanted and needed and treasured," she told him. Lonny understood what she was saying—that this was exactly how Chase felt about her. Lonny had seen it happen. His friend had come alive the moment Letty returned to Red Springs. It was the same way Lonny felt about Joy. All he had to do now was figure out how to protect her pride, while keeping his own intact.

"I'll tell her," Lonny said, suspecting this might be his only route to Joy.

"Go slow," Letty murmured.

"Slow," he repeated. "But I haven't got time to hang around, not with this other guy hot on her heels."

"Yes, you do, otherwise Joy will assume you're only interested now because Josh is about to make an appearance in her life. She's got to believe your actions are motivated by sincerity, not competitiveness."

"Oh." Letty was right about that, too.

This was getting complicated. "Should I approach her with gifts?" He felt at a distinct disadvantage. Joy wasn't like the girls he'd met in his rodeo days; he'd rarely ever given them gifts, beyond maybe buying them a beer.

Letty nodded approvingly. "That's a good place to start."

Lonny rather liked the idea of bringing Joy things. He had a freezer full of meat, some of his best. None of that hormone-laden stuff sold in the grocery stores, either. He'd explain that his and Chase's cattle were lean, and fed on grass, and he'd make sure she recognized the significance of that. "I could take her some steaks from my freezer," he said, pleased with himself.

"Uh…" Letty cocked her head to one side, as if she was trying to come up with a way to tell him that wasn't quite what she had in mind.

"What?"

"Bringing her a few steaks is a nice thought," his sister informed him. "But women tend to prefer gifts that are more…*personal.*"

Lonny cast a desperate look at Letty. "Help me out here."

"Flowers are always nice," she said.

Flowers from a shop were expensive and died within a few days. "What about perfume?"

"Yes, but that poses a problem. Most women have preferences. They develop their own favorites. A particular scent smells different depending on who wears it, you know."

Lonny wasn't sure what his sister had just said, other than that he shouldn't buy perfume. Well, if there was no better alternative, he'd go with her first suggestion. "Flowers I can do."

"Start there."

"I will," he promised. "Then you'll help me figure out what I should get her next?" he said, relying on his sister's assistance. He considered her the strategist; he'd simply follow her directions.

"Don't be in too big a rush," Letty reminded him. "If you run into her by accident, be polite and respectful, and then go about your business."

Lonny saw the brilliance of his sister's words. He hoped he could restrain himself enough to do that. Every time he saw Joy, all he could think about was how much he wanted to hold her and kiss her. It went without saying that there was more to a relationship between a man and a woman than the physical. Mutual desire was important and necessary, but no more so than mutual respect, honesty and genuine caring. He felt all of that for Joy. Unfortunately, it was easier to convey the holding and kissing part.

"Other than getting Joy gifts, what else should I do?"

Letty's brow creased in thought.

"Do I have to learn to talk pretty?" Lonny asked, a bit embarrassed. Like most cowboys, he tended to be plainspoken. Besides, it was hard enough not to trip over his tongue saying normal things to Joy, let alone anything poetic.

"She needs to know how much she means to you," Letty said.

Lonny gestured helplessly as a sick feeling settled in the pit of his stomach. "I'm not sure how to tell her that."

"Tell me what you like about her physically," Letty

said. "And I suggest you not say anything about her weight."

"Okay…" A picture of Joy formed in his mind, and he relaxed. "She's just the right height."

"For what?"

Lonny shifted uncomfortably in his seat. "Kissing."

"Okay…anything else?"

"Oh, sure." But now that he'd said it, he couldn't come up with a single thing.

"Do you like her eyes?"

He nodded. "They're blue." He said that so Letty would know he'd been paying attention. "A real pretty shade of blue."

"Good." She clearly approved. "You can tell her that."

"Sort of a Roquefort-cheese blue."

Her face fell.

"That's not a good comparison?" he muttered.

"Think flowers instead," she hinted.

"Okay." But he'd have to give it some consideration. He wasn't that knowledgeable about flowers. Especially *blue* flowers.

"If you can persuade her, you and Joy will make a wonderful couple."

"If?" he repeated, taking offense at the qualifier. His sister seemed to forget that at one time he'd ridden bulls and broncos. It was the sheer force of his determination, along with—of course—his innate skill, that had kept him in prize money. Joy was the biggest prize of his life and he was going to cowboy up and do whatever he had to—even if he got thrown or trampled in the process.

"What took you so long, big brother?" Letty teased. "You've been crazy about Joy for two years."

Earlier, he would've denied that, but the time for pretense was past. "Pride mostly." However, he'd seen the error of his ways. No doubt Letty was happy with his decision, and Lonny's heart felt lighter and more carefree than it had in years. He felt good. Better than good, he felt *terrific*.

Lonny followed his sister's gaze as she watched Chase and Cricket with the spotted pony. He was moved to see how much Chase loved Cricket. He might not be her biological father, but in every way that mattered, Chase was Cricket's daddy.

His sister's eyes grew soft and full of love. One day, if everything went as Lonny hoped, he'd have a son or daughter of his own. It would please him beyond measure if Joy was the mother of his children. The thought quickened a desire so powerful that his chest constricted with emotion. He loved Joy. He sincerely loved her and the sun would fall from the sky before he lost her to anyone, least of all an old boyfriend.

Chapter 13

The alarm rang at six o'clock Monday morning and with a groan, Joy stretched out her arm and flipped the switch to the off position. She was warm and comfortable, and a sense of happiness spread through her. In five days, Josh would be in Red Springs. With her!

He'd phoned on Sunday afternoon, and they'd talked for an hour. Toward the end of their conversation, he'd admitted that Red Springs was two-hundred-plus miles out of his way; in other words, he was letting her know that he wanted to renew their relationship. That meant he'd missed her and was willing to invest time, effort and expense in seeing her again. She felt the glow of that knowledge even now. Lonny drifted into her mind and she made a determined effort to chase him away. Her willingness to accept his kisses—and kiss him back—mortified her.

In fact, it was Lonny's kisses that had prompted her to tell Letty about Josh's visit. Letty would certainly mention it to Lonny, which was exactly what she wanted. It was the coward's way out, she freely admitted that, but she was apprehensive over what might happen when Josh arrived.

She was afraid Lonny might force a confrontation with her, and she hoped this news would discourage him. She didn't *want* to think about Lonny or worry about her reaction to him. She felt so positive about Josh and their future together, and the only person who might ruin that was Lonny.

Josh was thoughtful and generous and as different from Lonny Ellison as a man could get. Just the thought of him incited her to toss aside the warm covers and bolt upright, irritated that this disagreeable rancher kept making unwanted appearances in her life. He was irrational, bad-tempered and, well... It didn't matter, because she wouldn't be having anything more to do with him.

Joy got to school early and had just parked her car in the employee lot when she saw Letty Brown drive to the student drop-off area. Either Letty had business in town this morning, or Cricket had missed the bus.

The back passenger door opened and Cricket popped out, greeted Joy with an exuberant "Hi, Ms. Fuller!" and then skipped over to the playground.

Letty rolled down her car window and waved at Joy.

Joy waved back. Strangely reluctant to see her friend, she trotted over to Letty's car. Thankfully no one had pulled in behind her. In the next twenty minutes the driveway would be seething with activity.

"Morning," Letty said from inside her car.

"Isn't this a beautiful day?" It could be raining buckets and it would still be an absolutely perfect day as far as Joy was concerned. As long as she could avoid seeing, hearing or thinking about one annoying man…

"You seem in a very good mood for a Monday morning."

"I am," Joy said, resting one hand on the window frame.

Letty laughed. "Me, too." She lowered her voice. "Can you keep a secret?"

"Of course."

Letty bit her lip. "Chase doesn't even know. Cricket, either." Then her eyes brightened and she placed her hand on Joy's. "I'm pregnant!"

Joy gasped. "Oh, Letty! That's incredible news!" Because of her medical condition, pregnancy could be a risk. Letty had told Joy that Chase was concerned about the strain a pregnancy would put on her heart.

"I won't say anything to Chase until the doctor officially confirms it," she continued, "but I know my own body. And just to be sure, I took one of those home tests. Chase will want to hear what the doctor says, though."

"But I thought—" Joy closed her mouth abruptly, afraid to say anything about the worries and fears that might accompany a pregnancy.

Letty must have sensed what Joy was thinking, because she added, "I went to see Dr. Faraday, the heart specialist, a little while ago."

Joy remembered that visit. It was the day Lonny had come to pick up Cricket.

"The doc gave me a clean bill of health," Letty exclaimed with unrestrained happiness. "The surgery was one hundred percent successful, and he couldn't see any reason I shouldn't have a second baby."

Joy knew how badly Letty wanted another child. Seeing her friend's wild joy nearly brought tears to her own eyes. "I'm so thrilled for you."

"Now, promise me, not a word to anyone," Letty warned.

"My lips are sealed." Half leaning into the front of the vehicle through the open window, Joy hugged her friend's shoulders. Straightening, she said, "I have some news, too—although it isn't as momentous as yours."

"Is this a secret or am I free to broadcast it?"

"So you're the town crier?"

"No," Letty said with a laugh, "that would be Honey Sue, but I run a close second."

Joy waited a moment for effect, then nearly burst out laughing at the expression on Letty's face. "Josh and I talked for over an hour yesterday, and I'm thinking of moving back to Seattle." She hated to leave Red Springs. But if she and Josh decided to resume their relationship in a serious way, she'd have to return to the Puget Sound area. A few internet inquiries had assured her there were teaching positions available.

The joy faded from Letty's eyes. "You'd actually move back to Seattle for Josh?"

Joy nodded. "Of course, everything hinges on what happens this weekend. But at this point, I'd say there's plenty of reason to believe I would."

Letty made an effort to smile. "I'd hate to see you go."

"I'd hate it, too, but I can't ask Josh to give up his career and move to Wyoming when there are no job opportunities for him. I can get a teaching position nearly anywhere."

"That makes sense." Letty's words were filled with poorly concealed disappointment.

Joy took a deep breath, realizing this had to be said. "I know you always hoped that things would work out between Lonny and me. Unfortunately that's not the case."

"My brother can be stubborn, that's for sure."

"I can be, too," Joy admitted. "The two of us don't really get along. I feel bad about it, because I genuinely like Lonny. I always have, but it's best to bow out now before either of us gets hurt."

"You're certain about that?" Letty's gaze pleaded with hers.

"Yes," Joy said quickly. Although she was confident and hopeful about her relationship with Josh, she wouldn't leave Red Springs without a few regrets. And one of those regrets was Lonny Ellison....

"When will Josh arrive?" Letty asked.

Joy braced her hands against the window frame. "Friday. He's driving from Salt Lake City and should get here sometime in the afternoon."

"That's...great."

Joy could tell that Letty was trying hard to sound pleased for her; at the same time, the concern in her eyes sent a conflicting message.

"So Josh will be with you at the school carnival?" she asked casually.

"He's looking forward to it, and so am I."

When Letty didn't respond, Joy asked, "Do you think that'll be a problem?" Although she'd lived in the community for two years, there seemed to be a lot she didn't understand about people's expectations. Perhaps bringing a male friend to what was technically a school function would be frowned upon.

Letty gave her a slight smile. "No, everything's fine. Don't worry."

Joy smiled back but felt tears gather in her eyes.

"I'll miss you," Letty whispered.

"There's always a chance I might not leave," Joy said honestly. "The school board's offered me a new contract and I've asked for time to think it over. I'll know more after this weekend. Oh, I shouldn't have said anything," she muttered fretfully. "It's too soon."

Letty shrugged and then sighed. "We'll keep in touch no matter what happens."

"Absolutely," Joy concurred. "We'll always be friends."

Letty nodded and glanced over her shoulder. Another car had pulled into the school's circular driveway. "You're right, of course. Anyway, I should go."

"See you later," Joy said, stepping back from the curb.

Letty checked her rearview mirror and drove carefully out of the slot.

Joy went on to her class, excited and happy for her friend. Despite his worries, Chase would be ecstatic when Letty told him about her pregnancy. Joy had watched Chase with Cricket and marveled at how deeply he cared for the child. Lonny was a good uncle, too. In time, when he found the right woman, Lonny would make a good father himself. But she didn't want to think about Lonny with another woman and pushed that thought from her mind.

Her day went relatively smoothly, considering that this was the last week of school and the children were restless and eager to be outside. When classes were dismissed that afternoon, Joy drove down Main Street to Franklin Rentals. She needed to double-check that the cotton candy machine would be there in time for the carnival.

"Good afternoon, Joy," Bill Franklin greeted her .when she entered the store.

She stepped around air compressors, spray paint equipment and a dozen other machines of uncertain purpose on her way to the counter. "Hello, Bill."

"I bet I know why you're here. Rest assured, everything will be in well before Friday. If not, I'm afraid I'd be ridden out of town on a rail," he said with a laugh.

"Thanks, Bill." She smiled at his mild joke. "I'll tell the other committee members."

"Thanks, Joy."

After another few minutes, she retraced her steps through the maze of equipment that littered the floor.

She was headed toward her car when she saw Lonny Ellison strolling in the direction of Franklin Rentals. She stopped in her tracks.

He saw her, too, and froze.

Neither moved for at least a minute.

Lonny broke out of the trance first and walked, slowly and deliberately, toward her.

Joy's heart felt as if it were attempting to break free of her chest, it pounded that hard and fast. Despite her reaction, she pretended to be unaffected. As Lonny neared, she lowered her head and said in a stiff, formal tone, "Mr. Ellison."

Lonny paused, touching the brim of his Stetson. "Ms. Fuller," he returned just as formally. Then he removed his hat and held it in both hands.

Lonny had stopped a few feet away. Joy stood there, rooted to the sidewalk. She couldn't summon the resolve to take a single step, although her nerves were on full alert and adrenaline coursed through her bloodstream.

"You look…pretty…today," Lonny said after an awkward moment.

Not once had Lonny ever complimented her appearance. Well, except for that embarrassing, backhanded attempt in the grocery store… "Thank you. You do, too."

His eyes widened. "I look…pretty?"

She almost managed a smile. "Not exactly."

"That's a relief."

This was ridiculous, she told herself, the two of them standing in the middle of the sidewalk like this, just staring at each other. "Have a good afternoon," she said abruptly and started to walk away.

"Joy," Lonny choked out.

"Yes?" Joy maintained a healthy distance for fear they'd find an excuse to kiss again, and in broad daylight, too.

He hesitated. "I—I hope the two of us will remain friends."

At first Joy wasn't sure how to respond. His evident sincerity took her by surprise. "I do, too," she finally said.

His eyes crinkled with a half smile and he nodded once, then cleared his throat. "Also, I wish to apologize if I offended you by my actions."

"Actions?"

He lowered his voice. "Those…kisses."

"Oh." Her cheeks instantly flushed with heat. He appeared to be awaiting her response, so she said, "Apology accepted."

"Thank you."

Her car wasn't far away now and when she used the remote to unlock it, Lonny rushed over and held open the driver's door.

Slipping inside the Cruiser, she blinked up at him. "Who are you and what have you done with Lonny Ellison?"

He chuckled. "I'm not nearly as bad as you think."

She wanted to say she doubted that, but it would've been impolite—and untrue.

"I'm through with pretending, Joy," he told her. "I cared about you two years ago, and I care about you now." He took a step back from her vehicle. "I let foolish pride stand in the way and I regret it." Having said that, he smiled, replacing his Stetson. "Have a good evening."

"Thank you, I will." Her fingers trembled as she inserted the key in the ignition. When she looked up again, Lonny was walking into Franklin Rentals.

Joy mulled over their short exchange during her drive home, still feeling confused. There was an unreal quality about it, almost as if she'd dreamed the entire episode. This strained politeness wouldn't last; of that, she was sure. Sooner or later Lonny would return to his dictatorial ways.

She poured herself a glass of iced tea and sat at her kitchen table while she mentally reviewed her day, starting with Letty's news. This evening would be a very special one for Letty and Chase.

Without warning, Joy felt a sharp twinge of emotion. One day that same pleasure would be hers, when she'd be able to tell the man she loved that she was pregnant with his child. A yearning, a deep and silent longing, yawned inside her. She felt the desire to be loved, to experience that kind of love. Out of nowhere, tears filled her eyes and she bit hard on her lower lip, trying to control the emotion.

Someday... She had to believe that someday it would be her turn.

Chapter 14

Tom Meyerson eagerly anticipated Lonny's next trip into Red Springs. Fortunately, he didn't have long to wait. At breakfast on Wednesday morning, Lonny announced that he had several errands to run that afternoon.

"Would you mind if I came along?" Tom asked as nonchalantly as he could. It was a habit from the years of living with his father. If his old man knew that Tom wanted or needed something, he went out of his way to make sure Tom didn't get it. Through the years, Tom had gotten good at hiding his feelings.

He had to see Michelle and talk to her. He wouldn't *ask* Lonny to take him, to make a special trip for him, nor would he borrow the truck. But if Lonny was going anyway… Sure, he could phone Michelle and he probably should have, but he wanted to see her eyes light up when he told her he'd be taking her to the dance, after all. At night, as he drifted into sleep, he imagined her smile and it made him feel good inside.

He waited for Lonny to answer, almost fearing his employer would turn him down.

Lonny shrugged. "As long as you're finished your chores, I don't have a problem with you hitching a ride."

Tom smiled, unable to disguise his happiness. He cleared his throat. "Thanks, I appreciate it."

Lonny slapped him on the back in an affectionate gesture. Before he could stop himself, Tom flinched. After years of avoiding his father's brutal assaults, the reaction was instinctive. He held his breath, hoping Lonny wouldn't comment.

Lonny noticed, all right, but to Tom's relief, didn't say anything. Instead, he checked his watch. "I want to leave around four."

Michelle would be out of school by then and at the store, working in the office for her dad. Happy expectation carried Tom the rest of the day.

He'd watched the movies Lonny had mentioned two or three times each and had practiced a few moves in front of the mirror. No one was going to confuse him with Kevin Bacon or John Travolta, that was for sure. But he didn't feel like a complete incompetent, either.

He'd been listening to the radio more, too, and was beginning to think he could handle a dance. Deep down, he sensed that his mother would be pleased if she knew. Perhaps she did....

At ten to four, Tom changed his shirt and combed

his hair. When he came out of the barn, he saw that Lonny was already in the truck.

Tom hopped into the pickup beside him.

Lonny wrinkled his nose and sniffed the air. "That you?" he asked.

Tom frowned; maybe he should've taken the time to shower.

"You're wearing cologne," Lonny chided.

Tom's face turned beet-red, and Lonny chuckled. After a moment, Tom smiled, too, and then he made a loud sniffing sound himself. "Hey, I'm not the only one. Who are *you* going to see?"

Lonny's laughter faded quickly enough, and he grumbled an unintelligible reply.

"I'll bet it's Joy Fuller."

Lonny ignored him, and Tom figured he'd better not push the subject. He'd learned to trust Lonny, but he wasn't sure yet how far that trust went. Still, he found he was gradually lowering his guard. Being with Lonny, talking to him about Michelle, had felt good. He liked Letty and Chase, too. Twice now he'd joined the family for Sunday dinner, and those times were about as close as he'd gotten to seeing a real family in action. He hadn't known it could be like that, hadn't realized people related to each other in such a caring and generous manner. Tom was grateful for whatever circumstances had led him to Red Springs and Lonny's barn. It was, without question, the best thing that had happened to him in his whole life.

"Would you mind if I turned on the radio?" Tom asked as a companionable silence grew between them.

"Go ahead."

Tom leaned forward and spun the dial until he found a country-western station. He looked at Lonny, who nodded. Tom relaxed against the seat and before long, his foot was tapping and his hand was bouncing rhythmically on his knee.

Lonny turned the volume up nearly full blast. After only a moment or two, they were both singing at the top of their lungs. Tom was sure anyone passing them on the highway would cringe, because neither of them could sing on key. Tom didn't care, though. This was about as good as it got for someone like him. Cruising down the highway with the windows open, music blaring—and, for this one day, he didn't have a worry in the world other than what kind of flowers to buy his girl for the dance.

The radio was playing at a more discreet volume by the time they reached the outskirts of Red Springs. Lonny pulled up across from Larson's Feed, and Tom opened the passenger door and jumped out.

"I shouldn't be longer than an hour," Lonny told him.

"I'll wait for you here."

With a toot of his horn, Lonny drove off.

Tom jogged across the street and when he walked into the store, Michelle was behind the cash register, smiling at him.

"Hi," she said shyly.

"Hi," Tom answered, having trouble finding his tongue. She was so pretty, it was hard not to just stand there and stare at her.

"Would you like a Coke?" she asked.

"Uh, sure."

"Dad has some in the office. I'll be right back."

"That's fine." He'd wait all day if she asked him to.

Tom leaned against the long counter, then straightened when Michelle's father came in. Tom immediately removed his hat. "Good afternoon, Mr. Larson."

"Tom," the other man said, inclining his head toward him. Then, as if he had important business to attend to, he left almost as suddenly as he'd appeared.

Michelle was back a minute later, holding two cans of soda. "Dad said it'd be okay if we sat out front," she said. The feed store had a porch with two rocking chairs and a big community bulletin board. The porch had weathered with time, and the red-painted building had seen better days, but there was a feeling of comfort here, and even of welcome.

They sat down, and Tom opened his soda and handed it to Michelle. At first she didn't seem to understand that he was opening hers and they needed to exchange cans. When she did, she offered him the biggest, sweetest smile he'd ever seen. Tom thought he'd be willing to open a thousand pop cans for one of her smiles.

"Did you decide about the dance?" she asked, her eyes wide and hopeful.

Tom took his first swallow of Coke, then lowered his head. When he glanced up, he discovered Michelle watching him closely, and she seemed to be holding her breath. He smiled and said, "It looks like I'll be able to go."

Just as he'd anticipated, Michelle nearly exploded with happiness. "You *can?* Really? You're not teasing me, are you?"

He simply shook his head.

She set her drink aside and pressed her fingers to her lips. "I think I'm going to cry."

"Don't do that," he nearly shouted. Every time he'd seen tears in his mother's eyes, he'd been shaken and scared. And he'd always felt it was his duty to make things right, even though he wasn't the one who'd made her cry.

"I'm just so happy."

"I am, too." Tom wasn't accustomed to this much happiness. He felt he should be on his guard, glance over his shoulder every once in a while, because disappointment probably wasn't far behind.

Michelle picked up her drink. "Thank you," she whispered.

Tom thought *he* should be thanking her. "I need to know what color your dress is," he managed to say instead.

Her lips curved in a smile, and her eyes were alight with joy. "It's pale yellow with little white flowers. It's the prettiest dress I've ever had. I bought it even before I asked you to take me to the dance."

Tom made a mental note of the color. He'd ask Letty what kind of flower he should buy for the corsage. He didn't know much about flowers—or about any of the other things that seemed important to women.

He wouldn't even have known about the corsage if Lonny hadn't mentioned it. That'd brought up a flurry of questions on Tom's part. Having never attended a school dance, or any other dance for that matter, he had no idea what to expect. He was afraid he might inadvertently say or do something embarrassing. He wanted this one night to be as perfect as he could make it. For Michelle, yes, and in a way he could barely understand, for his mother, too.

They sat in silence for a while, and Tom searched for subjects to discuss. His mind whirled with questions and comments.

"The weather will be nice for the carnival and the dance," Michelle said conversationally.

"That's good."

"Dad says not to worry about—" She hesitated and looked away.

Tom frowned, wondering if Michelle's father had said something derogatory about him. "What?" he asked, his heart sinking. He'd barely spoken more than a few words to Mr. Larson. Her father probably didn't need a reason to dislike him, though. Tom had learned early in life that people often didn't. Being poor, being a drunkard's son—those had been reasons enough back home.

"I thought I should tell you."

"Then do it," Tom said, stiffening.

"Kenny's dad phoned mine last Sunday."

Tom didn't like the sound of this. "About what?"

"Mr. Brighton said Kenny's pretty upset about you seeing me. He said he's afraid if you and I go to the dance together, there might be trouble."

Tom relaxed, grateful this situation didn't involve Mr. Larson's feelings toward him. "Kenny Brighton doesn't scare me."

"It bothered my dad. He's afraid Kenny might try to pull something at the dance. Mostly, he doesn't want me caught in the middle."

Tom hadn't really considered that. "Your dad's right." He hated to suggest it, but he couldn't see any alternative. "Maybe we'd better not attend the dance."

Michelle's reaction was immediate. "No way are we missing that dance! Not after everything I went through to get you to be my date."

Tom started to protest, but Michelle was adamant. "I'm not letting Kenny Brighton ruin the last dance of high school. And…and you aren't half the man I thought you were if *you* let him. Besides, Dad and I came to an understanding."

Her words stung Tom's pride. "What do you mean, half the man you thought I was?"

She shook her head. "I didn't mean that part."

He eyed her skeptically.

"Don't you want to know how Dad and I compromised?" she asked, obviously eager to tell him.

"All right."

She smiled again, one of those special smiles that made his mouth go dry. "I had to get Mom on my side first, and then the two of us talked to Dad. After a couple of hours, he finally saw reason." She paused long enough to draw in a deep breath. "Dad phoned Lonny last Sunday afternoon and asked him to volunteer as a chaperone for the dance."

"I know." He'd been thinking about it, and although he appreciated Lonny's support, he'd begun to feel a little humiliated. Scowling, he said, "I don't need anyone to do my fighting for me."

"That's just it, don't you see?" Michelle insisted, her eyes pleading with his for understanding. "If Lonny's at the dance, there won't *be* any fight."

Maybe, but Tom wasn't convinced. Kenny and a couple of his friends could come looking for trouble, and if that was the case, Tom wouldn't back down. He didn't want Lonny leaping in to rescue him, either. Tom would take care of the situation, in his own time and his own way.

"Tom?" Michelle whispered.

He tried to reassure her with a smile, but he didn't think it worked, because her expression grew even more distraught. "Don't worry, okay?" he murmured.

"I can't help it. You have this…this look like you're upset and angry, and it's frightening me."

As much as possible, Tom relaxed. "It'll be fine."

"I shouldn't have said anything. But at least if Kenny does start a fight, Lonny will make sure it's fair." She paused. "I hope there isn't one, though."

Tom didn't respond.

Michelle leaned toward him and took his hand, clasping it between both of hers. Her hold was surprisingly strong.

"Look at me," she pleaded.

At first he resisted. He knew he couldn't refuse her, and he wouldn't put himself in a position where he'd be bound by his word.

"Please," she whispered, raising his hand to her lips and kissing his knuckles.

Hot sensation shot up his arm, straight to his heart. Tom closed his eyes rather than get lost in her completely.

"Don't ask me not to fight, Michelle, because I can't promise you that." His words contained a steely edge as he braced himself against the power she had over him.

"You'll let Lonny chaperone the dance, right?"

He nodded.

"That's all I ask, except…"

"Except what?"

"Except…" She smiled again. "Except that I want you to dance every dance with me."

Now, that was a promise Tom could keep.

Chapter 15

Lonny couldn't stop thinking about his conversation with Joy last Monday afternoon. He'd wanted to tell Letty about it, but hadn't had the chance. What surprised him was the wealth of feeling he'd experienced just seeing her. Perhaps the thought that he might lose her to another man had escalated the intensity of his emotions. He didn't think so, though. These feelings had always been there, hidden by pride, perhaps, but definitely there.

After dropping Tom off at Larson's, he drove over to the school. Joy's car wasn't in the lot. Then he remembered her mentioning something about early dismissal for the rest of the week. That put a dent in his plans. He'd hoped to meet her on the school grounds, figuring they'd be able to talk freely because she'd feel safe in a familiar environment.

He wanted to follow up on their previous conversation. He'd given her a couple of days to contemplate his apology. He hadn't discussed this with his sister, but Lonny felt certain Letty would approve. Lonny was a businessman who preferred to be straightforward and honest in his dealings.

Still, he was prepared to go slow, the way Letty had suggested. He needed to earn Joy's trust all over again. But he believed that she knew him, knew the person he really was.

The more Lonny thought about Joy becoming a part of his life—not just for now, but forever—the stronger his desire to make it happen. They'd have a good marriage, he was sure of it, and, if she was willing, he'd like to start a family soon. He wanted the same happiness Chase and Letty had.

Letty was pregnant. Chase had nearly shouted his ear off Monday night. He'd called after dinner, and when Lonny heard Chase yelling, he'd been afraid some disaster had occurred. It took him a moment to grasp what his friend was telling him—that he was about to become a father and Lonny an uncle for the second time. Apparently Letty had broken the news to Chase over dinner.

Lonny smiled, recalling his reaction. In the same situation, he knew he'd feel exactly the same way. Since he was already at the school, he parked and walked inside, only to find Joy's classroom empty, pretty much as he'd expected.

Lonny tried to decide what to do next. He could always swing by her place, he supposed, climbing back in his truck.

Sure enough, her car was parked on the street in front of her house, and she was in the yard watering her flower beds. She wore denim shorts and a tank top and her feet were bare. The sight of her, dressed so casually, nearly caused him to drive over the curb. She had long, shapely legs and the figure he'd once considered skinny made him practically swallow his tongue.

Lonny parked his truck directly behind her Cruiser and turned off the engine. He hesitated, wondering if he should've gotten Letty's advice first. But it was too late now. Joy had seen him.

She stood there glaring at him and holding the hose as if it were a weapon she might use against him.

Lonny got out of the truck and walked over to the sidewalk by her house.

She still clutched the hose, water jetting out, almost daring him to take one step on her green lawn.

"Good afternoon," he said, as politely as he could. He held his hat in his hands, smiling.

"Hello." Her greeting was cool, her tone uninflected. "What are you doing here?"

That was an important question. If he had his way, his answer would be to start the marriage negotiations.... Well, perhaps *negotiations* wasn't quite the right word. He'd broach the subject directly—except he knew Letty would tell him that was a mistake.

"I stopped by to see how your day went," he answered, hoping he looked relaxed.

"Why?" she asked bluntly, raising the hose. He was just outside the line of fire—or water.

"Put the hose down, Joy."

She slowly lowered it, pointing it at the ground.

"Why are you here?" she demanded again. Despite her hostility, her eyes told him she was pleased he'd come to see her.

"Wait," he said. He ran to his truck and grabbed a large bunch of wildflowers from the passenger seat. He'd picked them by the side of the road; there were yellow ones and blue ones and some pink and white ones, too. He didn't have a vase, so he'd wrapped the stems in a plastic bag with water.

Joy looked as if she didn't know what to say. In the months they'd dated, he'd never brought her flowers.

She was speechless for a long moment. "That was a lovely thing to do." She almost managed a smile— almost.

Joy set the hose on the lawn and hurried to the side of the house to turn off the water. Then she returned to accept his flowers and tucked them in the crook of her arm.

The silence stretched between them.

Feeling naked without his hat, Lonny set it back on his head. "I went to see you at school."

"My last parent-teacher appointment was over by two," she explained.

He nodded.

More silence.

She wasn't in a talkative mood, and once again Lonny recalled his sister's advice about going slow. Hard as it was to walk away, he decided he had to. "I hope you enjoy the flowers," he mumbled, trying to hide his disappointment.

Joy offered him a tentative smile. "Would you care for a glass of iced tea?" she asked in a friendly voice.

"Sure." He tried to sound nonchalant but was secretly delighted. This, finally, was progress. "That would be nice. I'd also like your opinion on something if you don't mind." He had an idea for supplementing his and Chase's income and genuinely wanted to hear what she thought. She had the advantage of living in a ranching community, while having a big-city background, both of which were relevant to his plan. He'd like her advice on how to help Tom, too.

"All right." Joy led the way into her kitchen. The sliding glass door opened onto a patio, which she'd edged with large containers holding a variety of flowers. She retrieved a large jar and arranged the wildflowers—some of which were probably weeds, he thought, slightly embarrassed as he compared them to her array of plants. After filling their glasses, she suggested they enjoy their tea outside.

Lonny held open the sliding glass door and followed her outside. Discussing this idea with her had been a spur-of-the-moment thing. But he sensed that Joy would have a valuable perspective he should hear before he approached Chase and Letty with his suggestion.

He sipped his tea and set the tall glass on the patio table. "I figure by now you've learned something about raising cattle," he began.

"A little," she agreed.

Lonny nodded encouragingly.

"I know you and Chase raise grass-fed cattle versus taking your herd to a feedlot," she continued.

"Right," he said, impressed by her understanding. "Basically, that means the animal's main diet is grass.

We supplement it with some other roughage, otherwise there can be problems. Our cattle are leaner and the beef has less saturated fat."

"I think that's admirable."

"The thing is, the economics of ranching, especially with a small herd, just doesn't work anymore. Chase and I are just too ornery to admit it." He smiled as he said that. "I suffer from an unfortunate streak of stubbornness, as you might already know." He let those words sink in, so she'd realize again how much he regretted their past differences. "Now that Letty's pregnant, Chase is worried. He sold off a large chunk of his land. When he did, he figured on buying it back one day, but the truth is, that doesn't seem possible now." Lonny wasn't sure Chase had admitted that even to himself.

"What are you going to do?" Joy asked, sounding concerned.

"I've been giving this a lot of thought. I could always let Tom go. As it is, I'm barely paying him a living wage—I can't afford to. It's hard just to make enough to keep the ranch going." Granted, Lonny still had some savings from his rodeo days, although he'd invested most of that cash in buying their herd.

"Have you considered selling?"

That was probably a solution he *should* consider, but no matter how bad the situation got, he couldn't see himself doing it. "Ranching is more than an occupation—and selling isn't really an option, at least not for me and Chase. This land came to us through our families. It's our inheritance and what we hope to pass on to our children and their children. It's more than land." He didn't know if Joy would understand this part. She hadn't been born into ranching the way he and Chase and Letty had. Perhaps he'd been wrong to bring up the subject. He felt foolish now, uncertain. This wasn't all that different from declaring his feelings for her—and proposing marriage. At least now, she'd know what she was getting when he did ask.

"You said you've got an idea. Does it have to do with this?"

"Yeah. I haven't talked to anyone else about it and, well, it's pretty much off the top of my head."

"Go on," she urged.

"I was looking through a magazine the other day and came across an article about guest ranches. I guess they used to be called dude ranches, and according to this article they're more popular than ever. The owners put people up for maybe a week and take them on cattle drives and so on. I nearly fell off my chair when I saw what they were charging."

Joy frowned thoughtfully. "I've heard of them. Like in that movie *City Slickers?* It came out in the nineties. I really enjoyed it."

"So did I, and the rest of us in town, too. I'm not laughing now, though."

Joy raised her hand. "Do you mean to say—are you actually thinking of taking on a bunch of…city slickers?"

He ducked one shoulder. "I am. I don't have a bunkhouse, but Chase does, and his place is right next to mine. It seems there are people out there willing to pay top dollar for the experience of being on a ranch."

"Sounds promising," Joy said. "How much would it add to your workload?"

"For now, the brunt of the operation would fall on Chase and Letty because they have the facilities to put folks up and I don't." He paused. "The whole idea is still in its infancy."

"For that kind of enterprise, you'd need to have a sociable personality. Which you do. You get along well with people," she said, then added, "with a few exceptions."

He smiled because he knew she was talking about the two of them. "I generally don't have a problem," he said, "unless my pride gets in the way."

"You're not the only one with that problem."

In other words, Joy was acknowledging her part in their falling-out.

"What do you think?" he asked eagerly. He hadn't used this as a ploy to get her to confess her own failings; that wasn't the point. As far as he was concerned, the past was the past, and this was now. They sat on her patio, two friends sharing ideas.

"I love it. I really do." Joy beamed at him. "You'd have to advertise," she said, "when you're ready to launch this."

He smiled back, even more excited now about the guest ranch idea. He couldn't explain why, but it'd seemed right—natural—to discuss it with Joy first.

"I'd like to bring Tom in on the deal," he said, "but only in the summers when he's out of school. That's something I want to talk to you about later."

"Tom's still in school?"

"No, but I hope he'll go to college. We've been looking at scholarships online, and he's already applied for a few in the state. He's definitely got the brains and the drive."

"What about his family?"

Lonny brushed off the question. The truth was, he still didn't know much about Tom's family other than that his mother was dead and his father was a drunk—facts Tom had only recently, and reluctantly, divulged. "He doesn't have any."

"So you're helping him?"

"I'm trying to. Tom deserves a break in life."

"I think you're doing a wonderful thing. And I'd be happy to help in any way I can."

"Thanks." Her praise flustered him. "Getting back to the guest ranch…"

She glanced away. "Letty's a fabulous cook. I imagine part of the attraction would be the meals."

"I'd want to appeal to families," Lonny said, throwing out another idea.

"You'll need activities for children, then," Joy said.

"Yeah." Lonny was glad she'd followed his thought to its logical conclusion.

"I'd be able to help you with that," she told him. "I could write out a list of suggestions."

That was precisely what he'd wanted to hear. "Great!" He could see she was catching his enthusiasm.

"Did you check to see if there are other guest ranches in the area?"

"I did. There are a few in different parts of the state, but there aren't any within a hundred miles of

Red Springs." Nor were there any operated by former rodeo champions.

Their eyes met, and Lonny realized they were smiling at each other. Again. Really smiling. "I'd appreciate any help you could give us," Lonny said, forcing himself to look away. He could feel his pulse quickening, and it didn't have anything to do with his excitement about the guest ranch, either.

"If you'll excuse me a moment," Joy said abruptly, "I—I'll get us refills on the tea."

"Sure."

She stood as if she was in a rush and Lonny wondered if he'd said or done something to offend her. On impulse, he downed the last of his tea and hurried inside.

The darkness of her kitchen, after the sunlight outside, momentarily blinded him. When he could focus, he found Joy standing by the sink with her back to him. Letty would be pretty mad if she knew what he was thinking just then. Regardless, Lonny walked up behind Joy and placed his hands lightly on her shoulders.

His heart reacted wildly when she leaned against him, and Lonny breathed in the clean, warm scent of her hair.

"Don't be angry with me," he whispered close to her ear.

"Angry? Why?" she whispered back.

"I want to kiss you again."

She released a soft indefinable moan. Then she turned and slid her arms around his neck. A moment later, his mouth was on hers with a hunger and a need that threatened to overwhelm him. Arms about her waist, he lifted her from the floor and devoured her mouth with his. He couldn't take enough or give enough.

When she tore her mouth from his, he immediately dropped his arms and stepped away, fearing she'd rant at him like she had before, when he'd kissed her in the parking lot.

She didn't.

Instead, she stared up at him with a shocked expression. She'd rested one arm on the counter as if she needed to maintain her balance, and held her free hand over her heart.

Lonny waited. He couldn't even begin to predict what she'd say or do next.

"I...I—thank you for the f-flowers," she stammered. "They're l-lovely."

"Can I take you to dinner?" he asked, not wanting to leave.

She blinked slowly. "It's a little early, isn't it?"

"An early dinner, then." He was finding it difficult to remember Letty's advice about going slow.

She didn't answer for a long time. "Not tonight."

Lonny swallowed his disappointment and nodded. "I guess I'll be going."

"Okay."

Joy walked him to the front door and held open the screen. "Thank you for stopping by."

He touched the brim of his hat and left. But as he approached the truck, his steps grew heavier. He'd completely forgotten about Josh! But then he brightened. Judging by the way she'd kissed him, Joy had, too.

Chapter 16

"Stupid, stupid, stupid!" Joy wanted to bang her head against the wall in frustration. Not only had she invited Lonny Ellison into her home, she'd allowed him to kiss her. *Again.* Worse, she'd practically *begged* him to. Then, complicating matters even more, she'd kissed him back. The man made her crazy and here she was, kissing him with an abandon that had left her nerves tingling. Instead of avoiding him, she was encouraging him.

One hand on her forehead, Joy closed the front door and, for good measure, emphatically turned the lock. She didn't know if she was keeping Lonny out or keeping herself from running after him.

This was a disaster! Josh was due in two days. Two days. Because of their emails and telephone conversations, he was coming with the expectation of resuming their relationship.

Josh was perfect for her. His future was secure, he was handsome and congenial. They had a lot in common and their parents were good friends. At one time, he was everything she'd ever wanted in a man.

At one time—what was she thinking? She'd broken up with Lonny almost two years ago, after a relationship that had lasted barely three months. The fact that he was back in her life now could only be described as bad timing. She didn't want him to invade her every waking moment—or to take up residence in her dreams, as he'd begun to do.

Totally confused about her feelings for Lonny, Joy returned to the kitchen and rearranged the wildflowers in their vase. She was touched by the image of him scrambling in ditches to collect them; it was quite possibly the sweetest gesture she'd ever received from a man. Anyone could call a florist and read off a credit card number, she told herself; not every man would go and pick his own flowers.

When she'd finished, Joy set the bouquet in the center of her kitchen table and stepped back to admire the flowers. Lonny was proud and stubborn, but he'd let her know he was sorry about what had happened two years earlier.

"The jerk," she muttered. "He did that on purpose."

The doorbell rang and Joy went rigid. If it was Lonny again, she didn't want him seeing her like this. She was an emotional mess. And even though she preferred to blame him for that, she knew she couldn't.

"Who is it?" she called out.

"Petal Pushers," Jerry Hawkins shouted back.

The local florist shop! Surprised, Joy unlatched the dead bolt and threw open the door to discover Jerry standing on the front step, holding a lovely floral arrangement protected by cellophane. "Mom asked me to drop these by," he explained.

Sally owned the shop and her son made deliveries after school.

"Who'd be sending me flowers?" Joy asked. Considering her previous thoughts, she was all too conscious of the irony.

"Mom said they're from a man."

Joy's eyes widened as she accepted the arrangement. It consisted of pink lilies, bright yellow African daisies, sweet williams and gladioli, interspersed with greenery and beautifully displayed in an old-fashioned watering can.

"Do I need to sign anything?" she asked.

"No," Jerry was quick to tell her. "Enjoy."

"I will, thank you." She closed the door with her foot and carried the large arrangement into the kitchen, placing it on the counter. As she unpinned the card from the bright yellow ribbon, she shook her head. The flowers had to be from Josh.

She was right. The card read: *I'm looking forward to this weekend. Josh.*

Until that very afternoon, Joy had been looking forward to seeing him, too. No—she still was, but not with the same unalloyed pleasure. She put the formal arrangement next to the glass jar filled with the wildflowers Lonny had brought her. Once again, the irony didn't escape her. Businessman and rancher. One as polished and smooth as the satin ribbon wrapped about the watering can and the other as unsophisticated as...the plastic grocery bag in which he'd presented his flowers.

These were the two men in her life. They didn't know it, but they were fast coming to a showdown. Josh would arrive for the school carnival and, sure as anything, Lonny would be in town at the same time. Already her stomach was in knots. Joy had no idea what to do; the only person she could talk to was Letty.

She waited until she'd calmed down before she reached for the phone and hit speed dial to connect with Letty, who answered on the first ring.

"Joy, it's so good to hear from you," she said enthusiastically.

"Can you talk for a minute?" Joy asked, too unnerved to bother with the normal pleasantries.

"Of course." Letty's voice was concerned. "Is everything all right?"

"No...I don't know," she mumbled before blurting out, "Lonny came by earlier."

Letty's hesitation was long enough for Joy to notice.

"He brought me a bouquet of wildflowers and, Letty, it was just so sweet of him."

"Lonny brought you flowers," Letty repeated, as if she had trouble believing it herself. "Really?"

"Yes. I'm looking at them right now." She didn't mention the second bouquet she was looking at, too. Sighing, Joy sank into a kitchen chair and propped her elbow on the table. She supported her forehead with one hand as she closed her eyes, suddenly feeling tired. "I should've told him Josh was coming. I wanted to, but I didn't." Granted, it would've been a bit awkward when she was in his arms kissing him. *Not* that she planned to mention that scene in the kitchen.

"Joy," her friend gently chastised, "don't you realize how much my brother cares about you?"

She swallowed hard because she did know and it distressed her. "I sort of guessed.... The last couple of times we've met, he's been so cordial and polite. He's even told me he feels sorry about our disagreement, and I never thought he'd do anything like that."

Letty released a deep sigh and said in a soft voice, "I didn't, either. Oh dear, I feel terrible."

Joy's eyes flew open. "Is it the pregnancy?"

"I'm perfectly healthy. No, this has to do with Lonny. He...asked for my help."

"Your help in what?" Joy was already confused and this wasn't making things any easier.

"My brother asked for my advice on how to win you back and...I'm the one who suggested he bring you flowers."

"Oh."

"Lonny's always cared about you, only he was too stubborn to admit it. Now it's hitting him between the eyes. Josh wants you back, too, and you're going to have to make a decision. Either way, someone's going to be disappointed."

"You're right."

Silence fell between them as they both mulled over the significance of this. Letty spoke first.

"Listen, Joy, you're my friend but Lonny's my brother, and I don't think I'm the best person to be talking to about this," she said.

"There isn't anyone else," Joy cried. "Letty, please, just hear me out?"

"I'll try, but you need to know I'm not exactly a neutral observer. It's a mess," she said, "and to some extent I blame myself."

"You didn't do anything."

"I did, though," Letty confessed, sounding thoroughly miserable. "I encouraged Lonny, built up the idea of a relationship with you. You know I think the world of you and in my enthusiasm—well, never mind. None of that's important now."

"Oh dear," Joy murmured. Things seemed to get more complicated all the time.

"Do you still have feelings for my brother?" Letty asked, her voice elevated with what could have been hope.

That was the million-dollar question. "I…I'm not sure." At the moment, Joy was too bewildered to know how she felt about either man.

"Okay, fair enough," Letty said, exhaling a lengthy sigh.

"The thing is, Josh is coming this weekend."

"Believe me, I'm well aware of that," Letty said.

Joy pressed the phone harder against her ear. "I don't want any trouble."

"What do you mean?"

"Lonny's going to the carnival, isn't he?"

"Of course."

"Is there any way you could distract him?" Joy pleaded. "Keep him away until after Josh leaves?" As soon as she said the words, she realized how ridiculous that sounded—as if these two men were a couple of bulls or stallions that had to be separated to prevent a dangerous confrontation.

Letty gave a short, cheerless laugh. "Lonny won't cause any trouble, if that's what you're thinking," she assured Joy. "That's not his style. Besides, he already knows."

"Lonny knows? About Josh?"

"Yes, I told him."

Involuntarily her foot started tapping. "That explains it, then."

"Explains what?"

"The flowers, the apology, everything." So Josh's pending visit was the reason for Lonny's abrupt change in behavior.

"You're wrong," Letty insisted. "He came to talk to me *before* he knew about Josh."

"He did?" That didn't really improve the situation; however, at least it cleared up his motives. "Oh…"

"What?" Letty asked.

"Nothing. Just…he has a wonderful idea for the ranch. He wanted to hear my opinion before he brought it to you and Chase. I think it's brilliant."

"What is it?"

"I can't tell you. Lonny will when he's ready. I like it, though, I really do. I even told him I'd be willing to help. I was sincere about that." However, if her relationship with Josh progressed the way she'd once hoped, that would be impossible. For the first time since he'd contacted her, Joy regretted that he was coming to Red Springs. His timing couldn't have been worse—or better. The problem was, she couldn't decide which.

Letty added, "Don't hurt my brother, Joy. He might be the most stubborn man you've ever met in your life, but he's decent and hardworking and he genuinely cares for you."

"I know," Joy said, and she meant it. "I'll talk to him tomorrow." She needed time to work out what to say, and yet, no matter how prepared she was, this would be one of the most difficult conversations she'd ever had.

Chapter 17

The next evening, Lonny reflected that his day had gone very well indeed. He'd awakened in a fine mood and it was still with him. He felt inspired, motivated and challenged, all at once. His goal was to win Joy's heart, and he believed he'd made some strides toward it. He wasn't going to let some fast-talking business-man steal her away, even if he was an old boyfriend. Lonny didn't know exactly what Josh did for a living but picturing him as some high-and-mighty company mogul suited his purposes.

Joy loved *him*. She might not realize it yet, but she would soon. His mission was to convince her that she belonged right here in Red Springs—with him.

Lonny hadn't fully appreciated his sister's dating advice until yesterday. Those wildflowers had worked better than he'd ever imagined. He could almost see

Joy's heart melt the instant she laid eyes on that bunch of flowers.

After dinner, feeling good about life in general, Lonny sat out on his porch, in the rocking chair that had once been his father's. He couldn't remember the last time he'd lazed away an evening like this. He sometimes joined Letty and Chase on the porch over at their place, but he seldom sat here on his own. Music sounded faintly from inside the barn, where Tom was practicing his dance moves. Given all the time and effort the boy had put into getting ready for this dance, he should be pretty confident by now.

Lonny relaxed and linked his fingers behind his head. He was feeling downright domestic. He'd waited a lot of years to consider marriage. He hadn't been in any rush to settle down, because marriage meant responsibilities, and he already had enough of those.

Funny, he didn't think like that anymore. He was actually looking forward to living the rest of his life with Joy. Marriage to her was bound to be interesting, not to mention passionate and satisfying in every conceivable way.

So far, his sister's advice to "go slow" had been right on the money. Come Friday, he'd be in town for the carnival and later the dance. He could visualize it now. By this time tomorrow night, he'd be holding her hand and later he'd be dancing with her, and that was all it would take to tell everyone in Red Springs how he felt about Joy Fuller.

A cloud of swirling dust alerted him to the fact that there was a car coming down the long driveway. Lonny stood, and when he did, Joy's PT Cruiser came into view. A sensation of happiness stole over him. The last person he'd expected to see here, at his place, was Joy, and at the same time, she was the one person he most wanted it to be.

He'd hurried down the steps and was walking across the yard as she parked. At that moment, Tom stuck his head out of the barn. He smiled at Lonny and gave him a thumbs-up, then returned to his practicing.

Lonny greeted Joy from halfway across the yard. "This is a pleasant surprise."

Her eyes didn't quite meet his. "Would it be all right if we talked?"

"It would be more than all right." With his hand at the small of her back, he steered her toward the porch. "My parents used to sit out here in the evenings. I'd consider it an honor to have you join me." He hoped she picked up on his subtle hint about the two of them sitting together in the space once reserved for a long-married couple....

Lonny reached for the second rocking chair and dragged it closer to his own. "Can I get you anything? A pillow? Something to drink?" he asked, minding his manners in a way that would've made his mother proud.

"Nothing, thanks," she said before sitting down.

She seemed nervous, but Lonny wanted her to know there wasn't any reason to be. He sat next to her and they both rocked for a few minutes.

"It's quite a coincidence that you should stop by," he commented casually. "I was just thinking about you."

"You were?"

"Yup, I spent most of my day thinking about you."

He'd dreamed about her, too, and awakened with the warmest, most delicious feeling. He couldn't recall everything his dream had entailed, but he remembered the gist of it—they were married and there were three youngsters running around. Two boys and a cute little girl. He was feeding the youngest in a high chair, while Joy was busy getting dinner on the table for the rest of the family. She interrupted what she was doing to kiss him—and then the alarm blared.

She frowned. "Lonny, please just listen."

"I'll listen to anything you want to tell me," he said, matching the seriousness of her expression.

She closed her eyes and kept them tightly shut. Lonny turned his chair so they sat facing each other, their knees touching. He took both of her hands and held them in his.

"Joy?" he asked. "What's wrong?"

She opened her eyes and gave him a tentative smile. "You know Josh Howell's coming to town, don't you? My college boyfriend?"

He nodded. "Letty mentioned it." He didn't care. Joy loved *him*—didn't she?—and he loved her. As far as he was concerned, the other man was a minor inconvenience.

"But—"

Rather than listen to her extol Josh's virtues, or even say his name, he leaned forward and gently pressed his lips to hers. Her mouth softened and instantly molded and shaped to his, as if she wanted this as badly as he did. Cradling the back of her neck, he deepened the kiss. The tantalizing sensations tormented and delighted him. Joy, too, he guessed, because after a moment, she twisted her head, breaking the contact.

"I need to talk to you and you're making it impossible," she moaned.

"Good." He wanted her as caught up in this whirlwind of feeling as he was. More importantly, he wanted her to understand that they were meant to be together, the two of them. Josh might be her past, but *he* was her future.

"Please, Lonny, just listen, all right?"

"If you insist." But then he brought his lips back to hers. This second round was even more delectable than the first....

"Please stop! I can't think when you're kissing me," she pleaded and seemed to have difficulty breathing normally.

She wasn't the only one. "It's hard to refuse you anything, but I don't know if I can stop."

"Try. For the sake of my sanity, would you kindly try?"

He pushed his chair back and motioned for her to stand. When she did, his arms circled her waist and he pulled her into his lap. Her eyes widened with surprise. She hardly seemed aware that her arms had slipped around his neck. She stared at him. "Why did you do that?"

"Isn't it obvious?" He longed to have her close, needed her close. She must know how deeply their kisses had affected him.

"I have something important to tell you," she said but without the conviction of earlier.

"Okay," he murmured as he spread soft kisses down

the side of her neck. She sighed and inclined her head. Apparently what she had to tell him wasn't that important, after all.

"I've reached a decision...." Her voice held a soft, beseeching quality.

A sense of exhilaration and triumph shot through him. "Okay, no kissing for..." He checked his watch. "Five minutes, and then all bets are off." He returned his mouth to the hollow of her throat, savoring the feel of her smooth skin.

Joy moved her head to one side. "That's kissing," she said breathlessly.

"I'm staying clear of your lips. Tell me what's so important that you had to drive all the way out here."

She caught his earlobe between her teeth. Hot sensation coursed through him like a powerful electric shock. She was quickly driving him beyond reason, and in self-defense, he seized her by the waist. To his surprise, his hands came upon bare flesh. Her light sweater had ridden up just enough to reveal her midriff. Her skin felt so smooth, so warm.... He'd never intended to take things this far, but now there was no stopping him. He slid his hand higher and cupped her breast. As his palm closed around it, he heard her soft intake of breath.

Joy buried her face in his neck and took several deep breaths. His own breathing had grown labored.

"You keep doing that and I'm going to embarrass us both," he said.

She instantly went still.

"Joy," he said, although he found it difficult to speak

at all. "I don't care why you're here or what you came to tell me. I love—"

She brought her index finger to his lips. "Don't say it." Pain flashed from her eyes.

"Okay." He sobered. "I think you'd better explain." He made an effort to focus on her words.

"Josh Howell is coming tomorrow," she said.

"Yes, I know. We talked about that. I'm not worried."

"I've decided not to renew my teaching contract. I'm moving back to the Puget Sound area."

A sense of unreality gripped him. He blinked. "What?"

"I—I've decided not to renew my teaching contract."

When the words did sink in, he stared into her eyes, but she couldn't hold his gaze.

"Say something," she pleaded. "Don't look at me like—like you don't believe I'll do it. I've made my decision."

"Okay," he said, his thoughts chaotic. "That decision is yours to make. I don't want you to go, but I can't kidnap you and keep you in the root cellar until you change your mind."

She frowned unhappily. "I know this upsets you. I haven't told anyone else yet. I wanted to tell you first."

"Any particular reason you're confiding in me?"

She nodded several times. "Considering everything that's happened, I felt I should."

"So you're in love with Josh?"

Joy bit her lip. "I don't know."

"But you've already decided you're leaving with

424	The Wyoming Kid

him?" Lonny asked, not understanding her logic. Joy didn't seem to notice that he was still caressing her back.

"I won't leave right away."

"Of course," he agreed quietly.

"Josh and I...we've been talking and emailing and—" She let the rest fade.

"Renewing your acquaintance," he finished.

"Exactly." Her eyes were half-closed as she spoke.

"And you're thinking that because of Josh, you'll leave Red Springs?"

"Yes." Slowly exhaling, she looked directly at him. "The thing is, I hate to go."

"The town will miss you. So will I."

"I'll miss you, too," she whispered.

It was exactly what Lonny had hoped to hear. "Then don't go."

She didn't respond.

"I'm hoping you'll reconsider."

"I...I don't think I can."

"If you stay here, we could get married," he suggested.

Apparently he'd shocked her into speechlessness. "I've been doing a lot of thinking about what went wrong with our relationship earlier," he said, "and I realize now I was the problem."

"You?"

"It was my fault. I reacted the same way then as I did when we had the traffic accident—I mean incident—the first time. And again last month." He grimaced comically. "I guess I'm a slow learner."

"You were unreasonable and high-handed and—"

He stopped her before she could continue with the list of his faults. "I love you, Joy, and I don't want you to move away."

She scrambled off his lap, nearly stumbling in her eagerness to get off the porch. "You're trying to confuse me!"

"No. I'm telling you right now, it'd be a big mistake to make such an important decision while you're unsure of what you want. That's what I did, and it cost me two years I might've spent with you."

"I...I've already made up my mind."

She was fighting herself just as hard as she was fighting him. He longed to kiss her again, but he knew that would only infuriate her.

"I'm...l-leaving," she said, stuttering as she turned away. "I can see it wasn't a good idea to talk to you about this."

He didn't make a move to stop her. "You might want to straighten your sweater before you go," he said in a reasonable tone.

Embarrassed and flustered, she whirled around and fumbled with her clothes.

It occurred to Lonny that she might have expected a different reaction to her announcement. "Do you want me to be jealous?" he asked. He was prepared to act as if he was, and it wouldn't be that big a stretch. He'd never even met Josh Howell, but he didn't like the man.

"No!" she blurted out irritably.

"Good. Because I will if that's what you want. But truth be told, I'm more confident than ever that we're meant to be together." He smiled at her. "Like I said, we've already lost two years and I'm not planning to repeat that mistake. I hope you aren't, either. We're not getting any younger, you know, and if we're going to have kids…"

That really seemed to upset her, because her eyes went wide with shock. At least, he hoped it was shock and not horror.

"Joy," he said, staying calm and clearheaded. "We were pretty involved physically a few minutes ago. I can't believe you'd allow a man to kiss you and touch you the way I just did if you didn't have strong feelings for him."

She backed away. "Josh will be here tomorrow, and all I ask is that you leave us alone."

He shrugged. "I'm not making any promises. You'd feel the same if some other gal was stepping in and trying to steal me away."

"I'm not a prize to be won at the carnival. You're so sure of yourself! I should marry Josh just to spite you."

That was an empty threat if he'd ever heard one. "You won't."

She made an exasperated sound and marched down the porch steps, almost tripping in her haste.

"Joy," he said, following her. "I don't want you to leave when you're this upset."

"I have to go!"

"I love you. If you want, I'll be furious and jealous and I'll corner Josh Howell and demand that he get outta town."

She shook her head vigorously. "Don't you dare!"

"I'm serious. I'm not willing to lose you to Josh."

"You've already lost me. I came here to tell you I'm not renewing my teaching contract."

Rather than argue with her, he sighed heavily. "Kiss me goodbye."

That seemed to fluster her more than anything else he'd said. "No!"

"Joy, my parents never went to sleep without settling an argument. That's the advice they always gave newly married couples. I don't want us to get in the habit of parting angry, either."

Aghast, she glared at him. "But we're not a couple!"

"But I believe we *should* be a couple. Because I love you and I know you love me."

She seemed about to burst into tears. "No, I don't. I refuse to love anyone as stubborn...and—"

"Pigheaded," he supplied.

Climbing into the car, she insisted one final time, "I don't love you!" She slammed the door shut and started the engine. A moment later, she tore out of the yard, kicking up a trail of dust.

"Oh, yes, you do," Lonny whispered. "You do love me, Joy Fuller. And I'm going to prove it."

Chapter 18

After the confrontation with Lonny, Joy barely slept that night. The man's arrogance was unbelievable. How dare he insist she was in love with him!

It'd seemed only right that she tell Lonny about her decision. Going to him had been a mistake, though, one that made her question her own sanity. He'd been condescending, and treated her as if she was too feeble-minded to form her own opinions. He'd practically laughed at her! Mortified, Joy wanted to bury her face in her hands.

She'd thought…well, she'd hoped they could part as friends. That was what she'd wanted to tell him. Instead, she'd ended their conversation feeling angry and more certain than ever. To be fair, she had to admit there was definitely a physical attraction between them. But that was his fault, not hers. Well, it wasn't really a question of *fault*. The man could kiss like no one she'd ever known. So of course she'd kissed him back; any red-blooded woman would.

She got out of bed, yawning, unable to stop thinking about last night. Just remembering the way he'd pulled her into his lap and then proceeded to seduce her, had her cheeks burning with embarrassment. As she readied for school, she chose her pink pantsuit. Today was the biggest event of the year in Red Springs. Her eyes already burned from lack of sleep and it was going to be a long, long day. First, the carnival, then the high school dance. On top of all that, Josh would show up sometime around four—when everything was getting started. If she could make it through today without losing her mind or breaking into tears, it would be a miracle.

The last day of school was more of a formality than an occasion to teach. The students were restless and anxious to escape. It was a bittersweet experience for Joy to see her students move on to the next grade. Each one was special to her. Most of the third-graders would be back in this classroom next year as fourth-grade students, and there'd be a group of new, younger kids, as well.

At noon, the bell rang and her pupils dashed out the door, shouting with excitement and glee.

Smiling, Joy walked onto the playground to wave goodbye, thinking this might be her last opportunity. The contract sat at home unsigned. Even now, she wasn't sure what to do. She'd made her decision and then Lonny had kissed her and all at once her certainty had evaporated.

The school buses had already lined up, their diesel engines running. The children formed straggling rows and boarded the buses with far more noise than usual. Most would return with their families for the carnival in a few hours.

As Joy grinned and waved and called out goodbyes, she reflected that her afternoon would be busy, getting everything done before Josh arrived. She'd made a reservation for him at the one and only local motel, the Rest Easy Inn. When she saw Josh, she told herself, she'd know her own feelings, know what was right for her. Joy couldn't help wondering what this weekend would hold for them both. She wished… Her thoughts came to a dead halt. What *did* she wish?

If Josh had contacted her a few months earlier, everything would be different, and yet the only real change in her life was Lonny.

"Goodbye, Ms. Fuller," Cricket said, coming up to Joy and throwing both arms around her waist.

"I'll see you later, won't I?" Joy asked, crouching beside the little girl.

"Oh, yes," Cricket said. "I'm going to ride the Ferris wheel with my daddy, and he said he'd buy me a snow cone and popcorn and cotton candy, too."

"I'll roll you an extra-big cotton candy," Joy promised.

An unfamiliar vehicle pulled into the parking lot. Wary of strangers, Joy narrowed her eyes suspiciously. Then the car door opened and a man stepped out.

"Josh," Joy whispered. He was early—and every bit as handsome as she remembered.

He gazed around as though he wasn't sure where to

go. Staring at him, Joy was again struck by his good looks. She'd been afraid he couldn't possibly live up to her memories—or her expectations. Wrong. He was even *more* attractive now. More everything. He exuded success and ambition.

Joy began walking toward him. "Josh!" She raised her arm high above her head.

As soon as Josh saw her, he smiled broadly and strode toward her. Then they were standing face-to-face and after a moment of smiling at each other, they hugged.

"Hey, let me take a look at you," Josh said, holding her at arm's length. "You've changed," he said, his bright blue eyes meeting hers. "You're more beautiful than ever."

His words embarrassed her a little and she laughed. "I was just thinking the same about you."

"Ms. Fuller, Ms. Fuller," Cricket said. She'd trailed after Joy and now stood there, her eyes as round as pie tins.

"Yes, Cricket?" Joy said, turning away from Josh to focus her attention on the child. "What is it?"

"Who's this man?" Cricket asked with uncharacteristic rudeness.

"This is my friend, Mr. Howell."

Cricket frowned.

"Mr. Howell drove to Red Springs to visit me," Joy elaborated.

"Is he your *boy*friend?" she asked.

Before Joy could answer, Josh did. "Yes, I'm Ms. Fuller's boyfriend." He slipped his arm around Joy's waist and brought her close to his side.

The girl's lower lip shot out. "I'm telling my uncle Lonny." Having made that announcement, Cricket stomped off the playground and boarded the school bus, the last child to do so.

"And just who is Cricket's uncle Lonny?" Josh asked, quirking his eyebrow at her.

"A local rancher," Joy said, not inclined to explain if she didn't have to.

"Really?" Josh didn't sound too concerned, which pleased Joy. She didn't want him to worry. And there was no reason for him to be jealous—was there?

"Did you tell me about 'Uncle' Lonny?" he asked.

"I'm sure I did," Joy said in casual tones. "He owns a ranch about twenty minutes outside town."

"He's not the one you had those near-collisions with, is he?"

"Yes," she cried, surprised Josh had remembered. "That's Lonny. We dated for a while when I first moved to Red Springs—I know I mentioned that in my emails—but we broke up and I haven't had much to do with him since." Because it was bound to happen at some point this evening, she added, "You'll meet him later." She dreaded the prospect, but there was no help for it. Her only hope was that Lonny would ignore both her and Josh, unlikely though that seemed.

"Is your rancher friend still being unreasonable about last month's accident?" Josh asked.

"Actually, he's been pretty decent about it lately. He said I should just forget the whole thing."

"And you have?"

She nodded, more than eager to get off the subject of Lonny. Taking Josh's hand, she smiled up at him.

"Let me finish a few things at school and then maybe we could go to lunch."

"Sure. In the meantime, I'll check into the motel."

"Okay." Releasing his hand, she nodded again. She hadn't expected Josh this soon and she still had loose ends to tie up in her classroom. All the arrangements were in place for tonight. When Letty had learned Josh would be coming, she'd volunteered to take the second half of Joy's shift so she'd have a chance to be with her visitor. From her past experience with the cotton candy machine, Joy knew she'd need time to clean up before the dance, too.

"There's a nice Mexican restaurant on Main Street," she suggested. "I could meet you there in an hour."

"Perfect."

Hands on his hips, Josh looked over at the school. "This is rather a quaint building, isn't it?"

Joy had thought the same thing when she'd first seen the stone schoolhouse, built fifty years earlier, but she'd grown used to it. The school felt comfortable to her, and it evoked an enjoyable nostalgia.

"I love it," she said fondly. "They just don't build schools like this anymore." While the budget called for a new schoolhouse two years from now, Joy would miss this one. Although, of course, it didn't matter because she wouldn't be here.

Josh nodded sympathetically. "I'll see you in an hour, then."

Joy felt light and carefree as she returned to her classroom. She intended to go into this new relationship with Josh wholeheartedly, see where it led. Deep down, though, Joy suspected neither of them was ready for marriage. Still, she wanted to make it work. The spoiler, so to speak, was Lonny Ellison. He arrogantly claimed she was in love with him and…he might not be wrong. Or not completely. But that didn't mean a long-term relationship between them would succeed.

By the time Joy hurried into the restaurant, she was later than she'd planned. She'd left several duties unfinished, which meant she'd have to go back to school in the morning. Because it was almost one-thirty, only a handful of people were in the restaurant.

Josh was seated in a booth, reading the menu, when she slid breathlessly into the bench across from him. She really didn't have time to linger over lunch. She had a hundred things to do before the carnival opened at five.

"Sorry I'm late," she said, glancing around for Miguel so they could order.

Josh reached for her hand. He'd changed out of his business suit and was dressed in slacks and a shirt, with the top two buttons left undone. He looked no less attractive in casual clothes—maybe more so.

"You didn't have any problem finding your way around, did you?" she asked, using a chip to scoop up some salsa. Miguel seemed to be busy in the kitchen.

"You're joking, aren't you?" He laughed as he said it. "There's only one road through town."

There were more, but apparently he hadn't felt any need to investigate the side streets.

"The other end of town is blocked off for the carnival," she reminded him. The motel and restaurant were located at this end of Red Springs.

"Have you decided what you'd like to eat?" she asked.

"I have."

As if he suddenly realized Joy had arrived, Miguel appeared to take their order. "I'll have the luncheon special. I can have the chili relleno baked, right?" Josh asked.

"We cook them the regular way," Miguel said with a heavy accent.

"Baked or fried?" Josh pressed.

Miguel looked to Joy to supply the answer.

"I believe they fry them, Josh," she said.

Josh frowned. "In that case, I'll have the enchilada plate."

Miguel gratefully wrote that down and turned to Joy, who nodded. He went back to the kitchen.

"Aren't you going to order?" Josh asked.

"I already did. I always have the same thing and Miguel knows how I like my tostada salad."

Josh clasped both her hands. "You look fabulous," he said, studying her. "Really fabulous."

She smiled at his words.

"I thought you'd come running home three months after you accepted this job," Josh admitted.

That wasn't exactly a flattering comment, but she let it slide.

"It's hard to believe you actually live here, so far from civilization," he added, glancing around as if he couldn't quite picture her in this setting.

"I remember thinking that when I first got to Red Springs. But it grew on me. I love it now."

"Don't you miss all the great restaurants in Seattle?"

"Well, yes, but…"

"This place is hardly Mexican," Josh murmured under his breath.

"The Mexican Fiesta isn't as fancy as the big chains in Seattle, but I like their food," she said, struggling not to sound defensive. She remembered her first visit to Red Springs. She'd wanted to live in a small community, but it had taken a while to adjust to the lack of amenities. The first time she'd eaten the town's version of Mexican food, she'd had to make an effort not to compare it to her favorite Seattle restaurant.

"We used to have Mexican almost every week," Josh said.

Joy didn't think it had been that often.

He wrinkled his forehead. "If I recall correctly, you used to order chicken enchiladas."

That was definitely some other girl he'd dated. Joy had never really liked enchiladas. He'd probably seen a dozen different women in the last two years, culminating in his now-ended relationship with Lori.

"You'd better tell me how everything's going to work this afternoon," he said. "I hear this town's going to be rocking."

Joy detected a hint of condescension but ignored it. "Everyone within a fifty-mile radius shows up. Ranching's a hard way to make a living these days," she said, remembering her many conversations with Letty. "There are only a few occasions during the year when the community has cause for celebration, and the end of school is one."

"My mother never celebrated my getting out of school for the summer," he joked. "If anything, she was crying in her martini. No more tennis dates for her when Julie and I were underfoot all day."

"A lot of these kids help around the ranch," she explained. "Families are important here. Tradition, too."

Josh's parents had split up and both had remarried by the time he started junior high. Fractured households seemed natural to him, and a community like this, with its emphasis on strong families, would seem an anomaly in his world.

"Everyone's thrilled about the carnival rides," Joy said. "This is the first year we're doing that." The children's excitement at such a modest pleasure wasn't something Josh would understand or appreciate, so Joy didn't bother to explain it further.

For the next few minutes until their lunches arrived, they chatted about Red Springs and her role in the community. Miguel delivered their orders with his usual fanfare, and Joy sensed that Josh was restraining a sarcastic smile. Her tostada salad was exactly the way she liked it, but she noticed that he just stared at his enchiladas.

"A high school dance," he repeated when she reminded him that he'd agreed to chaperone with her. Clearly he was amused.

"Come on, it'll be fun."

"I'm sure it will." His eyes twinkled as he took the first bite of his enchiladas.

"Tell me about your job," she said, wanting to turn the subject away from herself.

Josh had always been easy to talk to, and she was soon immersed in their conversation. He liked working for the investment firm, where he seemed to be advancing quickly. He'd purchased a home in Kirkland, outside Seattle. This she knew from the emails they'd exchanged. He described in some detail what it meant to be a home owner.

As he spoke, Joy realized that, despite her earlier decision, she couldn't imagine living in Seattle again. Josh was proud of his home and she was happy for him, yet she knew that living in Red Springs had changed her. His kind of neighborhood, with its expensive homes and anonymity, was no longer what she wanted. Neither was his social life—company functions and cocktail parties at which barbed remarks passed for wit.

"What if you have to move?" she asked. His company was well-known; with his ambition and energy Josh might be asked to relocate to a different city.

"I like living in Seattle. However, if the firm asked me to change offices, and it came with a big promotion, I'd definitely consider it," he said.

Joy nodded.

"What about you?"

"Me? You mean, would I move if the opportunity arose?"

He seemed intensely interested in her answer. With his elbows propped on the table and his fork dangling over his food, he awaited her response.

"From Red Springs?" She swallowed. "I don't know.... I've settled in nicely and I feel like I'm part of the community." She'd be viewed as a newcomer for the next sixty years, but that didn't bother her.

"If a once-in-a-lifetime opportunity came up, how would you feel?"

"That would depend on the opportunity," she said, sidestepping the question.

The restaurant door opened and sunlight shot into the darkened room. Joy didn't pay much attention until Lonny strolled directly to her table.

"Hello, Joy," he said.

She nearly dropped her fork. Fortunately, she hadn't taken a sip of her water or she could've been in serious danger of choking.

"Lonny." His name was more breath than sound.

"Would you introduce me to your friend?" he asked, staring down at Josh.

"Uh…"

Josh slid out of the booth and stood. "Josh Howell," he said, extending his hand. "And you are?"

Lonny grinned as the two men exchanged handshakes. "Lonny Ellison. I'm the man who's in love with Joy."

Chapter 19

Lonny nearly burst out laughing at the look on Joy's face.

"And how does Joy feel about you?" Josh asked coolly, before she managed to speak.

"She loves me, too, only she's not ready to admit it."

"Lonny!" Her fork fell to the table with a loud clang.

Lonny sent a glance at Josh and winked. "See what I mean?" The other man seemed to be somewhat taken aback but not angry, which boded well.

"What are you *doing* here?" Joy asked when it became apparent that he had no intention of leaving.

"Actually, Betty Sanders sent me to look for you," he told her. "She needs you for something, and Myrtle Jameson said she saw you come in here. There's a carnival that has to be set up, you know."

"I can see word spreads quickly in this town,"

Josh said, "if people are keeping track of your where-abouts."

Joy grabbed her purse and scrambled out of the booth. "I'll be right back."

As soon as she vacated the seat, Lonny replaced her. He was a bit hungry himself and selected a tortilla chip, dipping it in the salsa. "Take your time," he said nonchalantly. "I'll keep your friend company."

"I…I—" She was sputtering again. "I'll be back in five minutes," she promised Josh, and then returned to the table and kissed his cheek.

That, Lonny thought, was completely unnecessary; it was more as if she had a point to prove. He looked away before she could see how deeply that small display of affection for another man had affected him.

"Nice to meet you, Josh," Lonny said when Joy was gone, "but I can't stay long. My sister's got me helping, too. My hired hand and I are assembling the beanbag toss. You'd think two grown men could put this silly contraption together, wouldn't you? The problem is, the instructions are in Chinese." He left the booth a moment later and started to walk out of the restaurant.

"Do you need help with that?" Josh called after him.

"Thanks, but I think we've got it. A couple of others could use a hand, though."

Josh nodded. "I'll settle up here and be out soon."

"Thanks," Lonny said. Despite the fact that Josh was here to reconnect with the woman *he* loved, Lonny decided he rather liked him. He seemed to be a decent guy.

When he stepped outside, Lonny saw Joy trotting

down the sidewalk, toward the restaurant. She ignored him and kept moving.

"Did you find her?" Tom asked, when Lonny got back to the carnival site. The beanbag toss apparatus was up but balanced precariously, leaning to one side. They had to find a way to stabilize it.

"Cricket and I finished with the Go Fish booth," Chase announced triumphantly, carrying the little girl on his shoulders and joining Lonny and Tom.

Cricket smiled down at them from her perch. "We did a good job, too."

"Cricket," Letty cried, rushing toward them, hands on her hips. "Chase, put her down right this minute."

Lonny was grateful to see his sister. "I saw Joy," he said, striving to sound unconcerned.

Letty lifted her brows in question.

"She was with Josh Howell," Lonny added.

"He *said* he was her boyfriend," Cricket muttered indignantly. "He isn't, is he?" The question was directed at her uncle.

"No way," Lonny assured the little girl.

"Then how come he said that?"

The kid had a point. "He just doesn't know it yet," Lonny explained, not meeting Letty's eyes.

"Ms. Fuller will tell him, won't she?"

"She will soon enough," Lonny said.

"However," Letty cut in, "Ms. Fuller is the one making the decisions, not your uncle Lonny."

Cricket waited for Lonny to agree or disagree. Lonny shrugged. His sister wasn't wrong, but the situation was more complicated than that.

Letty was frowning. "Listen, we don't have time

to stand around discussing Joy's love life. The carnival's about to start."

"All right, all right." Lonny picked up the beanbag toss instructions again. He studied the drawing, turned it around and took another look. Ah, that made more sense....

By five o'clock, the streets of Red Springs were filled to capacity. This was the one time of year when the town got a taste of big-city living, complete with traffic jams. Parking slots were at a premium. Many streets were closed off and teeming with kids and adults alike, all enjoying themselves.

Chase and Lonny took a shift together, grilling hamburgers and serving them as quickly as they were cooked. While he was flipping burgers, Lonny caught a glimpse of Joy out of the corner of his eye. She was strolling through the grounds with Josh, sharing a bag of popcorn and sipping lemonade. He pretended not to notice but his gut tightened, and almost immediately the doubts began chasing each other, around and around. Maybe Josh would convince her, after all. Just as fast, a sense of well-being returned. Joy had as much pride as he did, but she wasn't stupid. She loved him. Lonny believed that...and yet there were a lot of factors he hadn't considered before. Such as the fact that Josh was so likable and that Joy had family and friends in Seattle. Josh could offer her a privileged life. All the reasons marriage to Josh might seem appealing presented themselves to his fevered mind.

Lonny's gut remained in knots until he saw Tom and Michelle stroll past, holding hands. His mood instantly lightened. This was probably Tom's first real date. Tom kept his emotions in check about most things, but he hadn't been able to squelch his enthusiasm for the carnival and the high school dance that was to follow. The kid had his chores finished before the sun was even up. He was ready to leave for town by ten that morning. Lonny had to assign him some extra work to keep him busy and distracted from his nervousness about Michelle. By two o'clock, though, he was dressed and waiting.

Apparently Michelle had informed him it wasn't necessary to wear a suit to the dance, so Tom had given it back to Lonny. The kid's eyes had lit up like Christmas morning when Lonny assured him he didn't need it anymore. He told Tom to keep the suit because he might be able to use it someday. Tom had purchased a new shirt and jeans for the dance and he'd even had his hair cut and he'd polished his black boots to a shine they'd likely never seen before.

Michelle had been good for Tom. She'd talked to him about college, reinforcing Lonny's suggestions, and encouraged him to apply for scholarships. Together Tom and Lonny had worked on completing the online application forms. Lonny felt pleased that Tom was looking beyond his past and toward the future.

In the same way Michelle had helped Tom, Joy had been good for Lonny. While it was true that they'd argued frequently, Joy had taught Lonny some important things about himself. Not the least of which was that he wanted marriage and a family. That was a new aspiration for him.

The moment he and Chase finished their shift, he

planned to seek her out. He couldn't stand by and do nothing while Josh escorted her about town.

Caught up in his own anxiety, he automatically followed Chase and Cricket to the long line of kids waiting for cotton candy. But after a few minutes he realized his sister was the one stirring up the sugary pink confection.

When Letty saw Lonny, she motioned for him to come to the front of the line.

"Don't do it," she said, looking at him sternly. Her mouth was pinched and she resembled their mother more than he'd thought possible.

"Do what?" he asked, playing innocent.

"Don't play games with me, big brother. I know you." All the while she was speaking, Letty rotated the paper cone along the outside of the circular barrel as it produced the cotton candy. "*Stay away from Joy.*" Smiling, she took two tickets from the waiting youngster and handed her the fluffy pink bouquet.

"But—"

"Chase, don't you *dare* let him go near Joy while she's with Josh."

Chase frowned. "I'm not his babysitter."

"Stay with him. You can do that, can't you?"

Chase obviously wasn't happy about it. "I suppose."

"Good."

"Here, sweetie," she said, giving Cricket a tube of cotton candy. She turned to Lonny again. "Stay out of trouble, okay?"

Feeling like a kid who'd just been reprimanded, Lonny mumbled, "I took your advice earlier. I suppose

I can again." He hoped Letty recognized how difficult this was going to be.

His sister narrowed her eyes. "Listen to me, Lonny," she insisted. "You've got to let Joy make up her own mind."

"But…"

"If you push her, you'll lose her. Understand?"

Lonny sighed. What choice did he have?

Chase took Cricket to all the kids' rides and Lonny felt like a third wheel walking around with them. Every now and then, he unexpectedly caught a glimpse of Joy and Josh. Once he saw them deep in conversation, their heads close together as they shared a bag of popcorn. Josh fed Joy a kernel and she smiled up at him as she accepted it.

Lonny's stomach convulsed at the sight. It came to him then that Josh might actually have the upper hand. He'd been so certain earlier, convinced to the core that Joy Fuller loved *him*. Now he wasn't as sure.

Confronted with Joy and Josh looking so comfortable, so intimate, was a rude awakening. Letty seemed to think doing nothing was the best response. It was killing him, but so far he'd managed. Barely.

"You okay?" Chase asked at one point.

"No," Lonny admitted from between clenched teeth. It began to seem that every time he turned a corner, there was Joy with her college boyfriend. When he saw them holding hands, he involuntarily started toward her. Chase grabbed his elbow, stopping him.

"Remember what Letty said," his friend muttered.

"How would *you* feel?" Lonny snapped, glaring at him.

"If I saw Letty holding hands with another man, you mean?" Chase asked. He shook his head. "Same way you're feeling now."

"That's what I thought."

"Josh will be on his way back to Seattle in a day, maybe two, and that'll be the end of it."

With all his heart, Lonny wanted to believe Joy would stay. "But what if she decides to go with him?" he asked. The possibility seemed very real at the moment.

"If she does, then it was meant to be."

Chase sounded so casual about it. So offhand. Apparently the love Lonny had for Joy didn't figure into this. Not according to his friend, anyway. Lonny didn't know how he was supposed to keep his mouth shut and pretend Chase was right. Like hell she'd leave with Josh What's-His-Name! He'd fight for Joy, make her understand how deep his feelings ran. He wasn't a man who gave his heart easily. He wasn't going to stand idly by and watch Josh walk off with her. Not in this lifetime. Not ever.

"You can't force her to marry you," Chase said, his hold tightening on Lonny's elbow.

"Sure I can," Lonny argued, for argument's sake.

Chase's reaction was to laugh.

"All right, all right," Lonny reluctantly agreed. He had to let this play out the way it would. The decision was up to her, and Lonny tried to believe that her good sense—and true feelings—would prevail.

"The dance is in an hour," Chase reminded him.

"Thank God for that." At least there he wouldn't be exposed to the sight of Joy and Josh holding hands and whispering to each other. He'd be able to concentrate on the kids and forget that his life was on the verge of imploding.

The dance was held in the high school gymnasium. Lonny got there early to avoid the risk of seeing Joy with Josh again. There was a limit to how much he could take.

The high school kids had done an admirable job of decorating the basketball court. The student body obviously had enough funds to hire a real band—well, a live band, anyway. They were tuning up, and discordant sounds spilled out the open doors. Groaning, Lonny had to resist plugging his ears. He only hoped Tom appreciated his sacrifice. Actually, he should be the one thanking Tom for an excuse to leave that blasted carnival. No telling how long those festivities would last.

Couples were slowly drifting in. While the guys were dressed in jeans and Western shirts, the girls all seemed to be wearing fancy dresses and strappy high-heeled shoes. If there'd been a dance like this while he was in school, Lonny didn't remember it. As he sat at the back of the gymnasium, guarding the punch bowl, he saw Tom and Michelle arrive.

Charley Larson's daughter was lovely. She wore a corsage on her wrist, and Lonny knew Tom had worried plenty about that white rose. But all his anguish and fretting seemed worth it now. They exuded such innocent happiness, Lonny found himself smiling.

Then, just when he'd started to relax, he saw Joy. He froze with a cup of punch halfway to his mouth. Sure enough, Josh tagged along behind her, one hand on her waist. Lonny felt as if someone had stuck a knife in his back. This dance was supposed to be his escape. Instead, it was fast becoming the scene of his emotional downfall. He didn't know how he'd manage to stand by and do nothing when Josh took Joy in his arms. Joy, the woman Lonny loved and hoped to marry.

The music began in earnest then. The lead singer stepped up to the microphone and announced the first dance.

Lonny set aside his punch and marched across the room.

When Joy saw him she scowled fiercely. "What are *you* doing here?" she demanded. She seemed to be asking that a lot today.

"I'm a chaperone. And you?"

"We're chaperoning, as well," Josh answered on her behalf.

Couples surged onto the dance floor all around them. "I believe this dance is mine," Lonny said and held out his hand to Joy.

She met his gaze without flinching, but didn't respond. She glanced at Josh, as if to ask his permission.

"Would you mind if I danced this number with Joy?" Lonny kept his voice as free of emotion as possible.

"Go ahead."

Lonny half expected Joy to argue with him and was pleasantly surprised when she simply followed him onto the floor. Since this was the first such event Lonny had chaperoned, he didn't know if the adults were allowed to dance. That, however, didn't concern him. If they wanted to fire him, they could. He didn't care. All that mattered was having Joy in his arms again.

He took her hand and she moved reluctantly into his arms. To his relief, this was a slow dance. Closing his eyes, Lonny brought her against him and noticed how stiff she was.

"I don't know what you think you're doing," she whispered heatedly.

He pretended not to hear. Despite her reluctance, he drew her closer and held her hand in his.

"I'm talking to you," she said. "Could you answer me?"

Lonny ignored her question. A minute or two later, he felt her relax slightly. After that, it didn't take long for her to sigh and begin to move with him.

This was what he wanted, what he *needed*. Her body flowed naturally in motion with his. The fear started to leave him and he tightened his arm around her waist. This was perfect. They even breathed in unison.

Although it was agony not to kiss her when the music stopped, Lonny dropped his arms and stepped back.

"Thank you."

Joy stared at him, her eyes wide and confused.

He held her gaze for a long moment, unable to look away. It was on the tip of his tongue to tell her how much he loved her.

But Joy turned abruptly and walked back to Josh, who stood waiting on the sidelines.

Chapter 20

Joy wanted to argue with Lonny. He'd purposely gone out of his way to embarrass her, first in the restaurant and now on the dance floor. Understandably, Josh had asked plenty of questions this afternoon. Joy had explained her complicated relationship with Lonny as well as she could. He'd listened, but hadn't pressured her. He'd responded as a friend would, and for that she was grateful. Joy had seen Lonny watching them at the carnival. Every time she looked up, he seemed to be there, his eyes following her like a hawk tracking its prey.

Then, to confuse the situation even more, Lonny had to insist on dancing with her. That was when the *real* trouble started. She'd expected him to argue with her, which would've been fine. Joy was more than ready to give him an earful. All afternoon she'd felt his disapproving gaze. And then, when they'd danced...

Even while her mind whirled with an angry torrent of accusations, her body seemed to melt in his arms. Somehow, without her being aware of it, her eyes had closed and her head was pressed against his shoulder. He hadn't uttered a single word. All Lonny had done was hold her, dance with her. When the music stopped, he'd simply released her.

She moved slowly to the edge of the floor.

"I believe the next dance is mine," Josh said as he came forward to claim Joy.

"Yes, of—of course," she stammered. Absorbed in her thoughts, she hadn't noticed Josh approaching her. The music began again.

"That would be..." She couldn't think of the right word. *Nice,* she mused, as Josh took her hand and led her onto the floor. The music was much faster this time, and the dance floor quickly became crowded.

Josh was an accomplished dancer. His movements were flamboyant, energetic but controlled—as good as anything she'd ever seen on TV. The teenagers gathered around him were clapping in time with the music. More and more people came to watch his performance, and it occurred to Joy that he wasn't dancing with *her,* the way Lonny had. They were just occupying the same space. She tried gamely to keep up with him. Joy was impressed with his dancing, all the while disliking the fact that the two of them were the center of attention.

Joy had gone to a number of dances with Josh during their college days, but she couldn't remember his being this smooth or agile. Apparently, it was a recently acquired skill.

The music stopped, and the crowd broke into spontaneous applause. Joy couldn't get off the floor fast enough. Josh followed her, but at a slower pace.

"Where did you learn to dance like that?" Joy asked, and realized there was a lot about him she no longer knew. Josh had changed; the thing was, Joy had, too.

"Lori and I went dancing a lot."

"You're great at it," Joy said sincerely. This was the first real dance she'd attended in two years and frankly, she could do with a refresher course. Beside Josh, she'd looked pretty lame, she thought ruefully. But there just weren't that many opportunities to dance in Red Springs. Most places served beer in jugs, played only country-western music and had floors covered with sawdust.

Josh's smile didn't quite reach his eyes. "I miss it, you know."

Joy suspected it was more than the dancing Josh missed, but she kept her opinion to herself.

When she glanced up, she saw that Lonny was watching her again.

Because she had a job to do, she walked along the perimeter of the dance floor, her eyes focused on the dancing couples. Josh strolled beside her. She noticed Tom, Lonny's hired hand, and Michelle Larson dancing together. Tom appeared awkward and uneasy, concentrating heavily on each movement. He was rigid and held Michelle an arm's length away from him. His lips moved as he silently counted the steps. Michelle, bless her, tried her best to follow his lead. They were a sweet-looking couple.

A moment later, Joy saw that she wasn't the only one watching Tom and Michelle dance. Kenny Brighton stood at the outer edge of the dance floor, eyeing the couple, his fists flexing at his sides.

Joy felt it was her duty to waylay trouble before it happened. Trying not to be obvious, she moved toward the other boy, pulling Josh with her, holding his hand.

"Good evening, Kenny," she said. "May I introduce you to my friend Josh Howell?"

Kenny didn't appreciate the interruption in his brooding. He acknowledged her with the faintest of nods, but his gaze didn't waver from Tom and Michelle.

"Kenny's family helped bring the carnival rides to Red Springs," Joy said brightly to Josh, as though this was a feat worthy of mention. "Isn't that right, Kenny?" she added when he didn't respond.

"If you say so," he muttered.

"Is there a problem between you and Tom?" she asked, deciding it was best to confront the issue head-on. Subtlety was getting them nowhere.

For the first time Kenny tore his eyes away from the dancing couple. "Michelle was supposed to be *my* date."

"You mean to say Tom kidnapped her?" she asked, trying to make light of the situation. Her attempt fell decidedly flat.

Kenny wasn't amused. "Something like that. I asked her first and she had some weak excuse for why she couldn't go with me. Next thing I hear, she's coming to the dance with Ellison's ranch hand." He practically spat the last two words.

"That's a woman's prerogative, isn't it?" Joy said, desperately hoping to keep the peace. This was the last official event of the school year, and she didn't want to see it ruined.

Kenny didn't appear to agree with her. "I'm twice the man that hired hand will ever be."

"Kenny, listen, we don't want any trouble here," she said, turning to Josh for help.

Josh nodded. "Why don't you find someone else to dance with," he suggested.

Kenny turned to Josh long enough to cast him a look of disdain. "I don't want to," he said sullenly. Joy could smell alcohol on his breath, strictly forbidden but furtively indulged in by the older boys.

She was afraid of what Kenny might do next, afraid he'd welcome an opportunity to fight Tom again. In his current frame of mind, Kenny might even see Josh as a convenient target, ridiculous though that was.

"Come on," Josh said, urging her away from Kenny. "I don't think you can do any good here."

Joy was reluctant to leave. As she moved past Kenny, she noticed Lonny keeping a close eye on the boy, too. He darted a look in her direction and she nodded, glancing at Kenny. Lonny's faint smile assured her he had matters well in hand.

Joy was astonished at how effectively they were able to communicate with just eye contact. This was a difficult situation with the potential to blow up into a major fracas. At the same time, she had every confidence that Lonny would know how to handle it. Sighing with relief, she patrolled the dance floor, smiling at students she recognized. She exchanged greetings with the other chaperones, and when she introduced Josh, she noted several surprised looks. Lonny wasn't the only one who seemed to think she was linked to him romantically.

"Would you like to dance again?" Josh asked when they'd made their way completely around the dance floor. They stood near the punch bowl, while Lonny was on the side of the room closest to Kenny. She kept her eyes trained on the boy in case a problem erupted. Not that there was much *she'd* be able to do…

"Joy?" Josh prodded.

"I'm not sure I should," she said.

Although she'd been out on the floor twice, making a spectacle of herself at least once, she was present at this event in an official capacity. She could sense trouble simmering and needed to take her chaperoning duties seriously. Still, she felt bad about abandoning Josh.

"I have to be aware of what's happening and I can't do that if I'm dancing," she murmured, standing on her tiptoes and stretching to look for Kenny. He was gone.

"Don't worry," Josh said. "I understand."

She thanked him with a smile. "Feel free to ask one of the other chaperones to dance." Josh really had been a good sport about all of this. "Do you see Kenny anyplace?"

Josh scanned the crowd. "No, I can't say I do."

Joy glanced around, looking for Tom and Michelle. Her suspicions were instantly aroused. Without explaining, she dashed across the now-empty dance floor toward Lonny.

Lonny must have known immediately that something was wrong, because he met her halfway and reached for her hands.

"Kenny's missing," she gasped out, "and so is Tom."

Lonny released a harsh breath. "I saw Kenny leave but I thought Tom was with Michelle."

"He isn't. I just saw Michelle come out of the restroom."

Lonny didn't wait for her to say any more. He hurried off the dance floor and out of the building. Not knowing what else to do, Joy followed. She left Josh talking to a couple of other teachers—both women.

The first thing she saw when she got outside was that a group of kids, mostly boys, had clustered in a ragged circle. Joy couldn't see what was taking place but she heard an ugly din, interspersed by girls' screams. She nudged her way through the crowd, behind Lonny.

As soon as he broke through the crowd gathered to watch, Lonny burst into the middle.

Joy saw that two boys were holding Tom down while Kenny Brighton took a swing at him. Tom kicked and bucked against the youths restraining him. Michelle stood to one side with her hands covering her face, moaning, unable to watch.

"If there's going to be a fight, it'll be a fair one," Lonny roared.

Outrage filled Joy. From the murmurs she heard around her, she wasn't the only person who objected to what was going on. She was about to interrupt Lonny and insist the fight be stopped altogether. But before she could say anything, Lonny rushed forward and tore the other boys off Tom. He flung them aside as if they were no more than flies.

Tom stood up, smudged with dirt and clutching his stomach. One eye was black, and the corner of his mouth was bleeding. Michelle ran forward, letting out a distressed cry as she saw Tom. Joy went over to the girl and placed one arm around her shoulders.

"What's your problem?" Lonny demanded, addressing Kenny.

"He stole my girlfriend," the larger boy shouted, his face twisted with rage. He raised his fists again as if eager to return to the pounding he'd been giving Tom.

"I'm not his girlfriend," Michelle shouted back.

"You were until he showed up," Kenny challenged, motioning toward Tom.

"You want to fight Tom?" Lonny asked.

Kenny nodded. "Let me at him, and I'll show you how much I want to fight."

"Tom?" Lonny asked.

Tom wiped the blood from his mouth and nodded, too.

"Fine. Then step back, everyone, and give them plenty of room."

Joy couldn't believe what she was hearing. Lonny was actually condoning the fight! "No," she cried. Not only was she against physical violence, which in her view was never an appropriate response, but she could tell that even one-on-one, this wouldn't be a "fair" fight. She felt she needed to point out the obvious discrepancies in their sizes. "Lonny, no! Kenny outweighs Tom by thirty or forty pounds."

Lonny ignored her protest.

"Stay back, gentlemen," Lonny told the two boys who'd been holding Tom down.

It seemed the entire gymnasium had emptied onto the field by this point. Joy remained at Michelle's side, still horrified that Lonny was allowing the two boys to continue fighting.

"I've got to break this up!" she said urgently.

"No," Michelle said, stopping her. "I hate it, but this is how things are settled here. Tom doesn't have any choice except to fight Kenny."

"He could get hurt." Joy knew Michelle didn't want to see Tom hurt any more than she did.

"Mr. Ellison won't let that happen," Michelle told her.

Although she'd been part of the community for two years, Joy didn't understand why quarrels like this had to be handled by such primitive means. Besides, Lonny seemed to be setting Tom up for defeat. Kenny was bigger and stronger, and poor Tom didn't stand a chance.

Kenny came out swinging, eager to take Tom down with one swift blow. To Joy's surprise, Tom nimbly ducked, and Kenny's powerful swing met nothing but air. The larger boy stumbled forward, and that was when Tom thrust his fist up and struck, hitting Kenny squarely in the jaw.

Kenny whirled back, a look of shock on his face.

"You ready to call it quits?" Tom asked him.

"Not on your life, you little weasel." Kenny swung again, with the same result.

This time, Tom drove a fist into Kenny's stomach, and the other boy doubled over.

"I'm not as easy to hit without someone holding me down, am I?" Tom said scornfully.

Joy loosened her grip on Michelle's shoulders, suspecting the fight was almost over. The girl took a deep shuddering breath.

Twice more Kenny Brighton went after Tom. Both times Tom was too quick for him. Whenever Kenny took a swing, Tom retaliated with a solid punch, until Kenny lowered his arms and shook his head.

"You finished?" Lonny asked, stepping forward.

Kenny nodded.

"Is this the end of it?" Lonny stood between them.

Tom nodded and Kenny did, too, reluctantly.

"Then shake hands."

Tom came forward with his hand extended and Kenny met him halfway.

"I don't have to like you," Kenny bit out.

"Same here," Tom said.

They stared at each other, then warily backed away.

Michelle immediately rushed to Tom's side and slipped her arm around his waist. "Are you all right?"

"I'm fine," he said smiling. "Are we going to dance or are we not?"

"Dance," she replied, and her eyes sparkled with delight. "Oh, Tom, I would never have guessed you could hold your own against Kenny."

They returned to the gym and in a few minutes, the crowd had dwindled. Kenny's friends gathered around him, but he brusquely pushed them aside and stalked to the parking lot.

"Is it over?" Joy asked Lonny, still a little nervous.

"There's nothing to worry about now," he assured her.

"I don't understand why they had to fight." Nothing like this would've been allowed anywhere else; she was convinced of that. Certainly not at a school in Seattle.

"You didn't see any of the other chaperones stopping the fight, did you?"

Joy had to agree she hadn't.

"This way it was fair and there were witnesses. Kenny learned a valuable lesson tonight, and my guess is it's one he won't soon forget."

Joy wasn't nearly as convinced of that as Lonny seemed to be.

"He'll go home and lick his wounds," Lonny continued. "Basically, Kenny's a good kid. It embarrassed him to lose, especially in front of his friends—and the girl he likes."

"What was the lesson he supposedly learned?" Joy asked, not quite restraining her sarcasm.

Lonny looked at her in puzzlement. "Kenny learned that being bigger and stronger isn't necessarily an advantage," he said as though that should be obvious.

"Yes, but—"

"He was humiliated in front of his classmates because they saw that it took two of his friends to hold Tom down in order for Kenny to get in a hit. No one wants to be known as a dirty fighter."

"But…"

"He won't make the same mistake twice. Kenny might not like Tom, but now, at least, he respects him."

Joy just shook her head. "I don't understand fighting and I never will."

"You're new here," he said with a shrug, as if that explained everything.

"In other words, I don't belong in Red Springs."

Lonny smiled. "I wouldn't say that, but I would definitely say you belong with me."

Joy walked slowly back to the dance, where she found Josh in the middle of the floor, once again the center of attention.

Chapter 21

As part of the carnival cleanup committee, Lonny got to town early the next morning. Tom accompanied him, but Lonny was under no delusion—the attraction wasn't sweeping the streets. Tom had come with the express purpose of finding Michelle Larson. Lonny was just as eager for a glimpse of Joy.

It was clear to him that Joy and Josh were completely incompatible, and he hoped she'd finally recognized it. After two years in Red Springs, Joy had become a country girl. Life in the big city was no longer right for her. According to what Letty had told him, Josh would be leaving Red Springs in a day or two. Soon, in other words, but not soon enough for Lonny.

Broom in hand, he walked down Main Street, sweeping up trash as he went. The carnival people had already packed their equipment, preparing to move on to the next town.

Red Springs was taking its time waking up after a late night. Uncle Dave's, the local café, didn't hang out the "open" sign until after seven-thirty. Their biscuits and gravy, with a cup of strong coffee, was the best breakfast in town. Whenever he had the chance, Lonny sat at the counter and ordered a double portion of the house special. Those biscuits would carry him all the way to evening.

He was busy dumping trash into a large plastic bag when he noticed Josh Howell leaving the restaurant, holding a cup of takeout coffee.

"How's it going?" Josh said, approaching Lonny. He surveyed the street, where the majority of the festivities had taken place.

"Okay, I guess." Lonny stopped sweeping and leaned against the broom. He liked the other man, but if it came to stepping aside so Josh could walk off with Joy, well, that was another matter.

"You said you love Joy," Josh murmured.

"I do."

Josh nodded soberly. "She's in love with you, too." He looked down at his feet and then up again. "The entire time we were together, she was watching you. She couldn't take her eyes off you."

It demanded severe discipline on Lonny's part not to leap into the air and click his cowboy boots in jubilation.

"I'm not sure Joy realizes it yet," Josh added.

Lonny shook his head. "She knows, all right—only she isn't happy about it."

Josh grinned as if he agreed. "I'll be heading back to Seattle later this morning. Earlier than I intended, but I can see the lay of the land. It's obvious that Joy and I don't have a future together." He met Lonny's eyes. "Good luck."

Lonny extended his arm and they exchanged hand-shakes.

"Are you planning to marry her?" Josh surprised him by asking next.

Lonny had thought of little else all week. "I am, just as soon as she'll have me." He didn't know how long it would take Joy to listen to reason. But with a deci-sion this important, he could be a patient man—even if patience didn't come naturally.

Josh left soon afterward and Lonny, Tom and the others spent the better part of two hours finishing their task. He was near-starved by that time, so he stopped off at Uncle Dave's for a huge order of biscuits and gravy. Tom joined him.

When they'd cleaned their plates, Tom made an ex-cuse to visit the feed store. That was fine with Lonny. He had personal business to attend to himself, and he was eager to do it. He just hoped Josh had already left town.

But when Lonny pulled up in front of Joy's place, he discovered, to his disappointment, that her PT Cruiser wasn't parked out front. That wasn't a good sign.

He hadn't expected to feel nervous, but he did— probably because he'd never asked a woman to marry him before. To show the seriousness of his intentions, he realized he should present her with a ring—except that he didn't have one. His mother's diamond was in the safety deposit box at the bank. Although it had minimal financial worth, its sentimental value was incalculable.

Pulling away from the curb, Lonny glanced at his watch and saw that he only had a few minutes to catch Walt Abler before the bank closed at noon, which it did on Saturdays. In his rush, Lonny forgot about the new stop sign at Grove and Logan and shot past it. A flash of red caught his attention just before a little green PT Cruiser barreled into his line of vision. Lonny slammed on the brakes, but it was too late. He would've broadsided the Cruiser if not for the quick thinking of the other driver, who steered left to avoid a collision. Unfortunately, the green car's bumper scraped against the stop sign post.

Lonny's heart was in his throat, and he held the steering wheel in a death grip, reflecting on what a narrow escape he'd had.

"What do you think you're doing?" Joy Fuller shrieked as she climbed out of her vehicle and slammed the door shut hard enough to jam it for good.

Lonny had known it was Joy the minute he saw the green car. He got out of the driver's seat and rushed over to her side.

"Are you okay?" he demanded.

"Yes, no thanks to you."

"I'm sorry. I don't know what I was thinking. I forgot the stop sign was there." His excuse was weak, but it was the truth. The irony of the situation would have made him laugh if he didn't feel so shaken.

Apparently Joy hadn't even heard him. "Look what

you've done to my car!" She sounded close to tears as she examined the damage to her bumper.

The dent was barely noticeable as far as Lonny could see. He walked over and ran his hand along her bumper and then stepped back.

"This is a new car," she cried.

"I thought you got it last year."

"I did. But it's still new to me and now you've, you've—"

"Have it fixed. I'll pay for it."

"You're darn right you will." She raised her hand to her forehead.

Fearing she might have hit her head, Lonny took her by the shoulders and turned her to face him. "Are you okay?" he asked again.

She nodded.

"You didn't hit your head?"

"I…I don't think so."

"Maybe you should sit down for a minute to be sure."

The fact that she was willing to comply was worry enough. Sitting on the curb, Joy drew in several deep breaths. Lonny welcomed the opportunity to calm his own heart, which was beating at an accelerated pace.

"Where were you going in such an all-fired hurry?" she asked after a moment. She bolted suddenly to her feet.

"The bank. But what does it matter where I was going?" he asked, standing, too.

"You can't drive like that in town! You're an accident waiting to happen."

"I…I—" He didn't know what to say. The accident

had been his fault. Twice in the past she'd caused the same kind of mishap and he'd been the one demanding answers to almost identical questions.

"You should have your driver's license suspended for being so irresponsible." Arms akimbo, she faced him, eyes flashing.

"Now, Joy…"

"I should contact the Department of Motor Vehicles."

"Joy." He was doing his level best to remain calm. "Getting upset like this isn't good."

"Don't tell me what I can and can't do!"

"Okay, fine, do whatever you want."

"I will," she snapped and started to stomp away.

He didn't want her to leave, not like this. "I love you, you know."

She paused, her back to him. Finally, she turned around, a thoughtful frown on her face. "You're sure about that?"

He nodded. "Very sure. Fact is, I was on my way to pick up an engagement ring."

Her frown darkened. "You said you were going to the bank."

"I was. My mother's diamond wedding ring is in the vault there. I intended to give you that. You can change the setting if you wish."

Joy seemed stunned into speechlessness.

"Letty wanted Mom's pearls and insisted I keep the ring in case I ever got married. She was thinking my wife-to-be would like that diamond." He was rambling, but he couldn't seem to stop himself. "It's not a big stone. It's just a plain, ordinary diamond, but

Mom loved it." He glanced at his watch again. "I'll have to wait until Monday now, and then you can see for yourself."

"A diamond ring?" From the look on her face, Lonny wondered if Joy had understood a single word he'd said.

"Now probably isn't the time or place to ask you to marry me." Letty had been telling him all along that he had a terrible sense of timing.

"No…no, I disagree," Joy said. "Continue, please."

Since she seemed prepared to listen, Lonny figured he should take this opportunity. He cleared his throat and removed his hat. "Will you?"

She blinked and craned her neck toward him. "Will I *what?*"

"Marry me." He thought it was obvious.

"That's it?" She threw her arms in the air. "*Will you?*"

He didn't see the problem. "Yes."

"This is the most important question of a woman's life, Lonny Ellison."

"It's important to a man, too," he said.

"I want a little more than *will you.*"

Annoyed with her tone, he glared at her. "Do you want me to add *please?* Is that it?"

"That would be an improvement."

"All right. *Please.*"

She motioned as if asking him to come closer. "And?"

"You mean you want *more?*" Lonny had never expected a marriage proposal to be this difficult. He wished now that he'd talked to his brother-in-law first. Chase would've advised him on the proper protocol.

"Of course." Joy didn't sound too patient. "For one thing, *why* do you want to marry me?"

That was a question he was beginning to ask himself. "I already told you—I love you."

"Okay. That's a good start."

"Start?" he repeated. "What else is there?"

"Quite a bit, as it happens."

Lonny shook his head. "Are you interested or not? Because this is getting ridiculous."

Joy folded her arms and cocked her head to one side, as if considering the question. "I might be, if the person doing the asking put a little more of his heart into it."

Lonny looked up at the sky and prayed for tolerance. "Joy Fuller, the luckiest day of my life was the day you ran me off the road last month, because that's when I discovered exactly how much I love you." He grinned. "Hey, this is our third accident—er, incident—together. And you know what they say. Third time's the charm."

She narrowed her eyes, apparently not all that charmed.

"Listen," he said hastily. "This might be news, but I'm not in the habit of kissing unwilling females. You were the first."

"And the last," she inserted.

"The absolute last," he agreed. "I kissed you because you made me so crazy I didn't know how else to react. I understand now that it wasn't anger I was feeling. It was attraction so strong it simply knocked me off my feet."

"Well, you infuriated *me*."

Lonny grinned again. "This isn't the best way to go about reconciling," he said.

She conceded with a curt nod.

Lonny stepped closer and reached for her hands, holding them in his. "I don't know that much about love. I've been a bachelor so long, I'd sort of assumed I'd always be one. Since meeting you, I've found I don't want to be alone anymore."

Her eyes went liquid with tenderness. "Really?"

"I don't need you to cook and clean and all that other stuff. I don't care about that. I've been doing those things for myself, anyway." He didn't like housework and Tom didn't, either, but between the two of them they managed.

"Then why do you want me?"

"I'd like you to sit on the porch with me in the evenings, the way my parents used to do. I like telling you my ideas and listening to what you think. I want us to be partners. If Chase and I go ahead with our guest-ranch idea, you'd be a real help because you know kids."

"*Are* you going to pursue that?"

"I haven't talked to him yet," he admitted, "but whether we do or not, I still want you as my wife."

She nodded slowly.

"Speaking of kids," he said, "I'd like a few and I hope you would, too." He should probably clarify his feelings on the matter right now. "I've seen you with the children at school, and Cricket thinks the world of you. Letty, too. As far as I'm concerned, you couldn't have any better character witnesses. They love you and I'm just falling in line behind them."

Joy gave him a quavery smile. "I want children, too."

"I was thinking a couple of kids. Maybe three."

She nodded, and the look on her face tightened his gut with a mixture of love and longing. Intent on making this proposal as perfect as possible, Lonny raised her hand to his lips. "Joy Fuller, will you marry me?"

"Yes," she whispered and tears rolled down her cheeks.

"Soon?" he asked, then added, "Please."

She smiled at that and nodded.

His heart full, Lonny put his arms around her and brought his mouth down on hers. He wanted this to be a gentle kiss, one that spoke of their love and commitment. Yet the moment her mouth met his, he thought he might explode. He wanted her with him, in his home and his bed, right then and there. Waiting even a day seemed too long.

Joy must have felt the same way, because she became fully involved in the kiss. She held nothing back, nothing at all.

By the time Lonny broke it off, they were both breathless. A car had stopped at the intersection— obeying the stop sign—and honked approvingly. Fortunately, traffic was unusually sparse for a Saturday.

"Wow," Lonny whispered, leaning his forehead against hers. "If we get a license first thing Monday morning, we can be married by the end of the week."

"Lonny, Lonny, Lonny." Her eyes were warm with

love as she straightened, shaking her head. "I only intend to get married once in my life, and I'm going to do it properly."

"Don't tell me you want a big wedding." He should've known she'd make a production of this.

"Yes, I want a wedding." She said this as if it should be a foregone conclusion. "Not necessarily *big,* but a real wedding."

This was getting complicated. "Will I have to wear one of those fancy suits with a ruffled shirt?"

She laughed, but he wasn't joking. "That's negotiable."

"How long's the planning going to take?"

"A few weeks."

He groaned, hating the thought. "Weeks. You've got to be kidding."

Her look told him she wasn't. Then she smiled again, and it was one of the most beautiful smiles he'd ever seen. It was full of love—and desire. When she kissed him, his knees went weak.

"I promise," she whispered, "that however long the planning takes, it'll be worth the wait."

With the next kiss, Lonny's doubts vanished.

* * * * *

THE WORLD IS BETTER WITH

Romance

Harlequin has everything from contemporary, passionate and heartwarming to suspenseful and inspirational stories.

Whatever your mood,
we have a romance just for you!

Connect with us to find your next great read,
special offers and more.

Love the Harlequin book you just read?

Your opinion matters.

Review this book on your favorite
book site, review site, blog or your own
social media properties and share
your opinion with other readers!

Be sure to connect with us at:
Harlequin.com/Newsletters
Facebook.com/HarlequinBooks
Twitter.com/HarlequinBooks

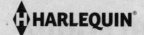

HARLEQUIN®

A *Romance* FOR EVERY MOOD™

JUST CAN'T GET ENOUGH?

Join our social communities
and talk to us online.

You will have access to the latest
news on upcoming titles and special
promotions, but most importantly,
you can talk to other fans about your
favorite Harlequin reads.

Harlequin.com/Community

Facebook.com/HarlequinBooks

Twitter.com/HarlequinBooks

Pinterest.com/HarlequinBooks

HARLEQUIN®

A *Romance* FOR EVERY MOOD™

**Stay up-to-date on all your
romance-reading news with the
Harlequin Shopping Guide,
featuring bestselling authors, exciting new
miniseries, books to watch and more!**

The newest issue will be delivered right to you
with our compliments! There are 4 each year.

Signing up is easy.

EMAIL

ShoppingGuide@Harlequin.ca

WRITE TO US

HARLEQUIN BOOKS
Attention: Customer Service Department
P.O. Box 9057, Buffalo, NY 14269-9057

OR PHONE

1-800-873-8635 in the United States
1-888-343-9777 in Canada

Please allow 4-6 weeks for delivery of the first issue by mail.